VIRAGO
MODERN CLASSICS
485

Jacqueline Susann

Jacqueline Susann was born in 1918, the daughter of a portrait painter. An indifferent student, she was nevertheless praised for her writing at school. She left her hometown of Philadelphia in her teens and moved to New York, where she acted extensively and won the Best Dressed Woman in Television award no fewer than four times. It was, however, the success of her three blockbuster novels – *Valley of the Dolls*, *The Love Machine* and *Once Is Not Enough* – that transformed her into the Pucci-clad superstar we remember today. The only writer ever to have three novels in a row hit number one on the *New York Times* bestseller list, Susann wrote her books on a hot-pink IBM Selectric typewriter, providing the model for the woman's blockbuster and the writers who came after her, including Danielle Steel and Jackie Collins. Jacqueline Susann was married to producer Irving Mansfield, had one son, and died in 1974.

Also by Jacqueline Susann

Every Night, Josephine!
The Love Machine
Once Is Not Enough
Dolores
Yargo

VALLEY
OF THE DOLLS

Jacqueline Susann

virago

VIRAGO

First published in the United States of America in 1966
Republished in the United States of America by Grove Press
A Grove/Atlantic Book
This paperback edition published in Great Britain in 2003
by Virago Press

19 21 23 25 24 22 20 18

A CIP catalogue record for this book
is available from the British Library.

ISBN 978-0-349-00832-5

Typeset in Goudy by M Rules
Printed and bound in Great Britain by
Clays Ltd, St Ives plc

Papers used by Virago are from well-managed forests
and other responsible sources.

MIX
Paper from
responsible sources
FSC
www.fsc.org   FSC® C104740

Virago Press
An imprint of
Little, Brown Book Group
Carmelite House
50 Victoria Embankment
London EC4Y 0DZ

A Hachette UK Company
www.hachette.co.uk

www.virago.co.uk

To Josephine

who sat at my feet, positive I was writing a sequel*

*but most of all to Irving

You've got to climb to the top of Mount Everest
to reach the Valley of the Dolls.
It's a brutal climb to reach that peak,
which so few have seen.
You never knew what was really up there,
but the last thing you expected to find
was the Valley of the Dolls.
You stand there, waiting for
the rush of exhilaration
you thought you'd feel – but
it doesn't come.
You're too far away to hear the applause
and take your bows.
And there's no place left to climb.
You're alone, and
the feeling of loneliness is overpowering.
The air is so thin you can scarcely breathe.
You've made it – and the world says
you're a hero.
But it was more fun at the bottom
when you started,
with nothing more than hope and
the dream of fulfillment.
All you saw was the top of that mountain –
there was no one to tell you
about the Valley of the Dolls.
But it's different
when you reach the summit.
The elements have left you battered,
deafened, sightless – and too weary
to enjoy your victory.

Anne Welles had never meant to start the climb.
Yet, unwittingly, she took her first step
the day she looked around
and said to herself,
'This is not enough –
I want something more.'
And when she met Lyon Burke
it was too late to turn back.

ANNE

The temperature hit ninety degrees the day she arrived. New York was steaming – an angry concrete animal caught unawares in an unseasonable hot spell. But she didn't mind the heat or the littered midway called Times Square. She thought New York was the most exciting city in the world.

The girl at the employment agency smiled and said, 'Aaah, you're a cinch. Even with no experience. All the good secretaries are away in those big-paying defense jobs. But honest, honey, if I had your looks I'd head straight for John Powers or Conover.'

'Who are they?' Anne asked.

'They run the top modeling agencies in town. That's what I'd love to do, only I'm too short and not skinny enough. But you're just what they're looking for.'

'I think I'd rather work in an office,' Anne said.

'Okay, but I think you're crazy.' She handed Anne several slips of paper. 'Here, they're all good leads, but go to Henry Bellamy first. He's a big theatrical attorney. His secretary just married John Walsh.' When Anne failed to react, the girl said, 'Now don't tell me you never heard of John Walsh! He's won three Oscars and I just read he's gonna get Garbo out of retirement and direct her comeback picture.'

Anne's smile assured the girl she would never forget John Walsh.

'Now you get the idea of the setup and the kind of people you'll meet,' the girl went on. 'Bellamy and Bellows – a real great office.

1

They handle all kinds of big clients. And Myrna, the girl who married John Walsh, she couldn't touch you in the looks department. You'll grab a live one right away.'

'A live what?'

'Guy . . . maybe even a husband.' The girl looked back at Anne's application. 'Say, where did you say you're from? It is in America, isn't it?'

Anne smiled. 'Lawrenceville. It's at the start of the Cape, about an hour from Boston by train. And if I had wanted a husband I could have stayed right there. In Lawrenceville everyone gets married as soon as they get out of school. I'd like to work for a while first.'

'And you *left* such a place? Here *everyone* is looking for a husband. Including me! Maybe you could send me to this Lawrenceville with a letter of introduction.'

'You mean you'd marry just anyone?' Anne was curious.

'Not *anyone*. Just anyone who'd give me a nice beaver coat, a part-time maid, and let me sleep till noon each day. The fellows I know not only expect me to keep my job, but at the same time I should look like Carole Landis in a negligee while I whip up a few gourmet dishes.' When Anne laughed the girl said, 'All right, you'll see. Wait till you get involved with some of the Romeos in this town. I bet you rush for the fastest train back to Lawrenceville. And on the way, don't forget to stop by and take me with you.'

She would *never* go back to Lawrenceville! She hadn't just left Lawrenceville – she had escaped. Escaped from marriage to some solid Lawrenceville boy, from the solid, orderly life of Lawrenceville. The same orderly life her mother had lived. And her mother's mother. In the same orderly kind of a house. A house that a good New England family had lived in generation after generation, its inhabitants smothered with orderly, unused emotions, emotions stifled beneath the creaky iron armor called 'manners.'

('Anne, a lady never laughs out loud.' 'Anne, a lady *never* sheds tears in public.' 'But this isn't public, I'm crying to you, Mama, here in the kitchen.' 'But a lady sheds tears in privacy. You're not a child, Anne, you're twelve, and Aunt Amy is here in the kitchen. Now go to your room.')

And somehow Lawrenceville had pursued her to Radcliffe. Oh, there were girls who laughed and shed tears and gossiped and enjoyed the 'highs' and 'lows' of life. But they never invited her into their world. It was as if she wore a large sign that said, *Stay Away. Cold, Reserved New England Type*. More and more she retreated into books, and even there she found a pattern repeated: it seemed that virtually every writer she encountered had fled the city of his birth. Hemingway alternated between Europe, Cuba and Bimini. Poor bewildered, talented Fitzgerald had also lived abroad. And even the red, lumpy-looking Sinclair Lewis had found romance and excitement in Europe.

She would escape from Lawrenceville! It was as simple as that. She made the decision in her senior year at college and announced it to her mother and Aunt Amy during her Easter vacation.

'Mama . . . Aunt Amy . . . when I finish college I'm going to New York.'

'That's a dreadful place for a vacation.'

'I intend to live there.'

'Have you discussed this with Willie Henderson?'

'No. Why should I?'

'Well, you've kept company since you both were sixteen. Everybody naturally assumes . . .'

'That's just it. In Lawrenceville *everything* is assumed.'

'Anne, you are raising your voice,' her mother said calmly. 'Willie Henderson is a fine boy. I went to school with his daddy and his mother.'

'But I don't love him, Mama.'

'No man can be loved.' This from Aunt Amy.

'Didn't you love Daddy, Mama?' It wasn't a question. It was almost an accusation.

'Of course I loved him.' Her mother's voice bristled. 'But what Aunt Amy means is . . . well . . . men are different. They don't think or react like women. Now take your father. He was an extremely dif-ficult man to understand. He was impulsive, and he enjoyed his drink. If he had been married to anyone but me he might have had a bad end.'

'I never saw Daddy drink,' Anne said defensively.

'Of course not. There was Prohibition, and I never kept a drop in the house. I broke him of the habit before it could take hold. Oh, he had a lot of wild ways in the beginning – his grandmother was French, you know.'

'Latins are always a little crazy,' Aunt Amy agreed.

'There was nothing crazy about Daddy!' Suddenly Anne wished she had known him better. It seemed so long ago . . . the day he had reeled forward, right here in the kitchen. She had been twelve. He never said a word, just slumped quietly to the floor and quietly died, before the doctor even reached the house.

'You're right, Anne. There was nothing crazy about your father. He was a man, but he was a good man. Don't forget, Amy, his mother was a Bannister. Ellie Bannister went all through school with our mama.'

'But Mama, didn't you ever *really* love Daddy? I mean, when a man you love takes you in his arms and kisses you, it should be wonderful, shouldn't it? Wasn't it ever wonderful with Daddy?'

'Anne! How dare you ask your mother such a thing!' said Aunt Amy.

'Unfortunately, kissing isn't all a man expects after marriage,' her mother said stiffly. Then, cautiously, 'Have you ever kissed Willie Henderson?'

Anne grimaced. 'Yes . . . a few times.'

'And did you enjoy it?' her mother asked.

'I hated it.' His lips had been soft – almost slimy – and his breath had smelled sour.

'Did you ever kiss any other boy?'

Anne shrugged. 'Oh, a few years back, when Willie and I first started dating, at parties we'd play Spin the Bottle. I guess I got around to kissing most of the boys in town, and as I recall, each kiss was as repulsive as another.' She smiled. 'Mother, I don't think we have one decent kisser in all of Lawrenceville.'

Her mother's good humor returned. 'You're a lady, Anne. That's why you don't like kissing. No lady does.'

'Oh Mama, I don't know what I like or what I am. That's why I want to go to New York.'

Her mother shrugged. 'Anne, you have five thousand dollars. Your father left that specifically for you to use as you wished. When I go, there will be a good deal more. We're not rich, not like the Hendersons, but we're comfortable and our family stands for something in Lawrenceville. I want to feel that you'll come back and settle in this house. My mother was born here. Of course Willie Henderson may want to add a wing – there's plenty of ground – but at least it will be our house.'

'I don't *love* Willie Henderson, Mama!'

'There is no such thing as love, the way you talk about it. You'll only find that kind of love in cheap movies and novels. Love is companionship, having friends in common, the same interests. Sex is the connotation you're placing on love, and let me tell you, young lady, that if and when it does exist, it dies very quickly after marriage – or as soon as the girl learns what it's all about. But go to your New York. I won't stand in your way. I'm sure Willie will wait. But mark my words, Anne, after a few weeks you'll come running home – you'll be glad to leave that dirty city.'

It *had* been dirty – and hot and crowded – the day she arrived. Sailors and soldiers joggled along Broadway with a reckless holiday spirit in their eager stares, and a convulsive, end-of-the-war excitement. But mingled with the dirt, humidity and strangeness, Anne had felt excitement, and an awareness of living. The littered and cracked pavements of New York made the trees and clear air of New England seem cold and lifeless. The unshaven man who had removed the 'Room for Let' sign from the window, after accepting a week's rent in advance, looked like Mr. Kingston, the mailman back home, but his smile had been warmer. 'It's not much of a room,' he'd admitted, 'but the ceiling is high and it kind of stirs the air. And I'm always around to fix anything you want.' She felt he liked her, and she liked him. There was an acceptance at face value in New York, as if everyone had just been born, with no past heritage to acknowledge or hide.

And now, as she stood before the imposing glass doors engraved *Bellamy and Bellows*, she hoped she'd find the same kind of acceptance from Henry Bellamy.

Henry Bellamy couldn't believe his eyes. She couldn't be for real. In her way, maybe she was one of the most beautiful girls he had ever seen, and he was accustomed to beautiful girls. And instead of wearing the outrageous pompadour and platform shoes that had come into style, this one just let her hair hang loose, natural, and it was that light blonde color that looked real. But it was her eyes that really rattled him. They were really blue, sky blue – but glacial.

'Why do you want this job, Miss Welles?' For some reason he felt nervous. Dammit, he was curious. She was dressed in plain dark linen,

5

and there wasn't a sign of jewelry except the small, neat wristwatch, but there was something about her that made one certain she didn't need a job.

'I want to live in New York, Mr. Bellamy.'

Just that. A straight answer. Why did it make him feel like he was snooping? He was entitled to ask questions. And if he made it too easy, she might not take the job. That was crazy, too. She was sitting here, wasn't she? She hadn't just dropped by for tea. Then why did he feel as if *he* were the applicant, striving to make a favorable impression on *her*?

He glanced at the form the agency had sent along. 'Twenty years old and a B.A. in English, eh? Radcliffe. But no office experience. Now tell me, what good is this fancy background going to do around here? Can it help me handle a bitch like Helen Lawson or get a drunken bum like Bob Wolfe to turn in a weekly radio script on time? Or convince some fag singer to leave the Johnson Harris office and let me handle his affairs?'

'Am I supposed to do all that?' she asked.

'No, I am. But you have to help.'

'But I thought you were an attorney.'

He saw her collect her gloves. He turned on one of his relaxed smiles. 'I'm a theatrical attorney. There's a difference. I draw up contracts for my clients. Contracts that have no loopholes, except in *their* favor. I also handle their taxes, help them invest their money, get them out of any and all trouble, arbitrate their marital problems, keep their wives and mistresses apart, act as godfather to their children and wet nurse to them, especially when they're doing a new show.'

'But I thought actors and writers had managers and agents.'

'They do.' He noticed the gloves were back in her lap. 'But the "jumbos," the kind I handle, they also need me to advise them. For instance, an agent naturally pushes them toward the job that pays the most. He's interested in his ten per cent. But I figure which job will do them the most good. In short, a theatrical attorney has to be a combination of agent, mother and God. And you, if you get the job, have to be their patron saint.'

Anne smiled. 'Why don't theatrical attorneys replace all agents?'

'They probably would, if there were enough dedicated schmucks like me.' He caught himself quickly. 'Excuse the language. When I get going, I don't realize what pops out.'

6

'What language? Schmuck?' She repeated it curiously.

It sounded so outrageous coming from her that he laughed out loud. 'It's a Jewish word, and the literal translation *would* make you blush. But it's become slang – for dope . . . Oh, don't let the fancy tag of Bellamy fool you, or even my freak Episcopalian face. I was born Birnbaum. When I was a kid I worked summers as entertainment director on cruises – wrote the ship's column. And they didn't like their fancy columns headed 'Boating by Birnbaum,' so one guy suggested Bellamy. I met a lot of important people on those cruises. A singer who was working the tour became my first client. A lot of people got to know me as Bellamy and I stuck with it. But I never let anyone forget that under Bellamy there's always Birnbaum.' He smiled. 'Now you have the whole picture. Think you can handle it?'

This time her smile was real. 'I'd like to try. I type fairly well, but I don't know much about shorthand.'

He waved his hand. 'I got two broads out there who could win shorthand contests. I want someone who is more than a secretary.'

Her smile vanished. 'I don't think I understand.'

Dammit! He hadn't meant anything like that. He ground his cigarette in the tray and lit another one. Jesus, she sat straight. Unconsciously he straightened in his chair.

'Look, Miss Welles, being more than a secretary means not sticking to the usual nine-to-five routine. There may be days when you won't have to come in until noon. If I've made you work at night I wouldn't expect you to come in. But on the other hand, if there was some crisis and even if you had worked until four in the morning, I'd expect you in before the office opened, because you would *want* to be there. In other words, you make your own schedule. But you'd also have to be available some evenings.'

He paused a second but she did not react, so he hurried on. 'Say I was having dinner at "21" with a prospective client. If I go for the right dinner and make with the right words, it's a pretty good bet he'll sign with me. But I may have to have six or seven drinks with him and listen to his gripes about his present management. Naturally I'll swear on my life not to do any of these things. I'll promise him everything – the moon with his name on it. Now I can't give him all the things I promise. No one could. But I will want to make an honest effort to avoid the mistakes of his present management and keep what promises

7

I can. Only the next morning I won't remember a goddam word. That's where you come in. You won't have a hangover, because during this thrilling evening you will have sipped *one* sherry and you will remember everything I have said. The following day you will present me with a list of all the promises and I can study them when my head is clear.'

She smiled. 'I'd be sort of a human Dictaphone?'

'Exactly. Think you could handle it?'

'Well, I have an excellent memory and I hate sherry.'

This time they laughed together.

'Okay, Anne. Want to start tomorrow?'

She nodded. 'Will I also work for Mr. Bellows?'

He gazed into space and said quietly, 'There is no Mr. Bellows. Oh, there's George, his nephew, but George is not the Bellows in Bellamy and Bellows. That was George's uncle, Jim Bellows. I bought Jim out before he went to war. I tried to talk him out of it, but no, he went to Washington and got carried away with that Navy uniform and a commission.' He sighed. 'War is for the young. Jim Bellows was fifty-three. Too old for war . . . but too young to die.'

'Was he killed in Europe or the Pacific?'

'He died of a heart attack in a submarine, the damn fool!' But the gruffness in his voice only punctuated the affection he felt for the dead man. Then, with an abrupt change of mood, he flashed one of his warm smiles. 'Okay, Anne, I guess we've exchanged enough of our life stories. I can start you at seventy-five a week – how does that set with you?'

It was more than she had expected. Her room cost eighteen, food about fifteen. She told him she could manage quite well.

October, 1945

September had been a good month. She had found a job she liked, a girlfriend named Neely and a gentle, eager escort named Allen Cooper.

October brought Lyon Burke.

She had been welcomed with instant acceptance by the receptionist and two secretaries. She lunched with them each day at the corner drugstore. Lyon Burke was their favorite topic, and Miss

8

Steinberg, the senior secretary, was the expert. She had been with Henry Bellamy ten years. She had *known* Lyon Burke.

Lyon had been with the office two years when war was declared, and had left to enlist the day after Pearl Harbor. Jim Bellows had often suggested that his nephew join the firm. Henry had nothing against George Bellows, but he had always refused. 'Business and relatives don't mix,' he had insisted. But with Lyon gone, Henry was left with little choice.

There was nothing wrong with George. He was a capable lawyer, but he lacked the chemistry of Lyon Burke – at least in Miss Steinberg's eyes. Lyon's activities in the war had been avidly followed by all of the staff, and when he had received his captain's bars, Henry had taken off half the day to celebrate. The last letter had come from London in August. Lyon was alive, Lyon sent regards – but Lyon said nothing about returning.

At first Henry had watched the mail each day. When September passed without word he moodily reconciled himself to Lyon's permanent withdrawal from the firm. But Miss Steinberg refused to give up. And Miss Steinberg was right. The wire came in October.

It was direct and to the point:

DEAR HENRY: WELL IT'S OVER AND I'M STILL IN ONE PIECE. VISITED SOME RELATIVES IN LONDON AND STOPPED OFF AT BRIGHTON FOR SOME SEA AND REST. AM IN WASHINGTON WAITING FOR MY OFFICIAL RELEASE. AS SOON AS THEY LET ME TRADE THEIR UNIFORM FOR MY OLD BLUE SUIT I SHALL RETURN. BEST. LYON.

Henry Bellamy's face lit up when he read the wire. He jumped from his chair. 'Lyon's coming back! Goddam, I knew he would!'

For the next ten days the office was in a turmoil of interior decorators, excitement and speculative gossip.

'I can't wait.' The receptionist sighed. 'He sounds just like my type.'

Miss Steinberg's smile was loaded with secret knowledge. 'He's everybody's type, honey. If his looks don't polish you off, the English accent does the rest.'

'He's English?' Anne was surprised.

'Born here,' Miss Steinberg explained. 'His mother was Nell Lyon. That was way before your time. Mine too. But she was a big English musical comedy star. She came here in a show and married an American lawyer, Tom Burke. She retired and Lyon was born here, so that makes him an American citizen. But his mother held on to her British citizenship, and when Lyon's father died – I think Lyon was about five – she took him back to London. She went back on the stage and he went to school there. When she died he came back and went to law school here.'

'I know I'll fall madly in love with him,' the younger secretary said.

Miss Steinberg shrugged. 'Every girl in the office had a crush on him. But I can't wait to see his reaction when he meets you, Anne.'

'Me?' Anne looked startled.

'Yes, you. You both have the same quality. A standoffishness. Only Lyon keeps blinding you with that smile and it fools you at first. You think he's friendly. But you can never get really close to him. No one could. Not even Mr. Bellamy. Deep down Mr. B.'s a little in awe of Lyon, and not just because of his looks or manner. Lyon delivers. You watch, Lyon Burke will own this town one day. I've seen Mr. B. pull some pretty brilliant deals, but he has to fight every inch of the way because everyone knows he's smart and they're prepared for him. Lyon just walks in with the English charm and the movie-star looks, and wham! he comes off with everything he wants. But after a while you realize you don't know what he's really like – and what he thinks of you, or of anyone. What I mean is, he seems to like everyone equally. So you get the feeling that maybe deep down he doesn't really care about anyone or anything – except his work. For that, he'll do anything. But whatever you think about him, you still wind up adoring him.'

The second wire arrived ten days later, on a Friday morning:

DEAR HENRY: HAVE BLUE SUIT. ARRIVE IN NEW YORK TOMORROW NIGHT. WILL COME DIRECTLY TO YOUR FLAT. SEE IF YOU CAN BOOK HOTEL RESERVATION. EXPECT TO START MONDAY. BEST. LYON.

Henry Bellamy took off at noon to celebrate. Anne was just finishing the mail when George Bellows stopped at her desk.

'Why don't we go somewhere and celebrate, too?' he asked casually.

She couldn't hide her astonishment. Her association with George Bellows had been confined to an official 'good morning' and an occasional nod.

'I'm asking you to lunch,' he explained.

'I'm very sorry, but I promised to join the girls at the drugstore.'

He helped her into her coat. 'Too bad,' he said. 'This may be our last day on earth.' He smiled ruefully and drifted back to his office.

At lunch she listened to the endless chatter about Lyon Burke with half a mind, wondering idly why she had turned down George's invitation. Fear of complications? From one lunch? How silly. Loyalty to Allen Cooper? Well . . . Allen *was* the only man she knew in New York, and he was very kind. Perhaps that did rate him a kind of loyalty.

She recalled the day he had burst into the office, determined to clinch some kind of deal – insurance, Anne later found out. Henry had been unusually cold and had gotten rid of him quickly. So quickly, in fact, that Anne's sympathies were aroused. As she led him out she had whispered, 'Better luck next stop.' He had seemed almost startled at the warmth in her voice.

Two hours later her phone rang. 'This is Allen Cooper. You remember me – the dynamic salesman? Well, I want you to know that my session with Henry was a wild success compared to my other stops. At least at Bellamy's I met you.'

'You mean you haven't made a sale?' She felt genuinely sorry.

'Nope. Struck out everywhere. Guess this just isn't my day . . . unless you want to give it a happy ending by having a drink with me.'

'I don't . . .'

'Drink? Me either. So let's make it dinner then.'

That's how it began – and continued. He was pleasant and had a nice sense of humor. She thought of him as a friend rather than a date. Very often she didn't bother to change her clothes after work. He never seemed to notice what she wore. And he always seemed eagerly grateful for her company. They went to little unknown restaurants and she always selected the least expensive item on the menu. She wanted to offer to pay her end, but she was afraid it might make him feel more of a failure.

Allen was hopelessly miscast as a salesman. He was too nice and mild-mannered for his profession. He asked questions about Lawrenceville, her days at school, even the events at the office. He made her feel like the most interesting, fascinating girl in the world.

She continued to see him because he made no demands upon her.

Sometimes in a movie he held her hand. He made no attempt to kiss her good night. Her feeling was one of relief mixed with a curious sense of inadequacy. It was almost embarrassing not to be able to arouse any passion in poor Allen, but she was content to let matters rest. The thought of kissing him brought on the same distaste she had experienced when she had kissed Willie Henderson back in Lawrenceville, and this made her wonder again about her own capacity for love. Perhaps she wasn't normal – or maybe her mother was right, maybe passion and romance did exist only in fiction.

Later that afternoon George Bellows stopped at her desk again. 'I've come to make another pitch,' he said. 'How about the sixteenth of January? You can't be dated up that far ahead.'

'But that's almost three months away.'

'Oh, I'll be glad to take anything that opens before then. But Helen Lawson just called, screaming for Henry, and it reminded me that her show opens on the sixteenth.'

'That's right, *Hit the Sky* goes into rehearsal next week.'

'Well, will you or won't you go with me?'

'I'd love it, George. I think Helen Lawson is wonderful. She used to break-in all her shows in Boston. When I was a little girl my father took me to see her in *Madame Pompadour*.'

'Okay, it's a date. Oh, and Anne, once this show goes into rehearsal, Helen is liable to come crashing in here a good deal. If you two ever get around to the small-talk department, don't come up with that 'I-loved-you-when-I-was-a-little-girl' routine. She might stab you.'

'But I *was* a little girl. And ridiculous as it sounds, that was only ten years ago. But even then Helen Lawson was a mature woman. She was at least thirty-five.'

'Around here we act like she's twenty-eight.'

'George, you can't be serious! Why, Helen Lawson is ageless. She's a great star. It's her personality and talent that make her so attractive. I'm sure she's too intelligent to think she looks like a girl.'

George shrugged. 'Tell you what. I'll phone you twenty years from now and ask you how you feel. Looking twenty-eight seems to be an infectious disease that most women catch the moment they hit forty. To play it safe, just don't bring up the subject of age around Helen. And please mark your calendar. January sixteenth. In the meantime, have a nice weekend and take it easy. It'll be plenty hectic around here on Monday – when the conquering hero comes marching home.'

The receptionist was wearing a tight new plaid. The junior secretary's pompadour was two inches higher. Even Miss Steinberg had broken out with last spring's navy suit. Anne sat in her cubbyhole outside Henry's office and tried to concentrate on the mail. But like the others, her attention was riveted on the door.

He arrived at eleven o'clock. With all the office gossip and speculation, she was still unprepared for anyone as striking as Lyon Burke.

Henry Bellamy was a tall man, but Lyon Burke towered over him by a good three inches. His hair was Indian black and his skin seemed burned into a permanent tan. Henry bristled with unconcealed pride as he led Lyon around and performed introductions. The receptionist colored visibly when she shook his hand, the junior secretary simpered and Miss Steinberg went absolutely kittenish in her excitement.

For the first time Anne was grateful for her rigid New England reserve. She knew she presented a calm she did not feel as Lyon Burke took her hand.

'Henry hasn't stopped talking about you. Now that we meet, it's quite easy to understand.' The English accent was definitely an asset. Anne managed a gracious answer and was grateful when Henry Bellamy steered Lyon toward the newly decorated office.

'Anne, you come in with us,' Henry ordered.

'It's overwhelming,' Lyon said. 'Makes one a bit apprehensive of the work expected in return.' He eased into a chair and smiled lazily. Anne suddenly understood what Miss Steinberg meant. Lyon Burke did smile at everyone, and that easy smile was impenetrable.

Henry beamed paternally. 'Just be the same lazy bum you were before you left and I'll redecorate for you every year. Now, let's get down to cases. Anne, Lyon needs an apartment. He's staying with me until he gets set,' Henry explained. 'Would you believe it? We couldn't get him a hotel room.'

She believed it. But she wondered why it should concern her.

'I want you to find him a place,' Henry said.

'You want *me* to find Mr. Burke an apartment?'

'Sure, you can do it,' Henry said. 'That's part of being more than a secretary.'

This time Lyon laughed heartily. 'She's a beauty Henry. She's everything you said. But she isn't Houdini.' He winked at Anne. 'Henry's led a very sheltered life. He hasn't looked for a flat in New York lately.'

Henry shook his head. 'Listen, this girl arrived here two months ago and she didn't know Seventh Avenue from Broadway. She not only found an apartment the first day, but landed this job and has me eating out of her hand.'

'Well, mine isn't really an apartment. It's very small . . .'

His direct gaze was unsettling. 'My dear Anne, after some of those bombed-out places I slept in during the war, anything with a ceiling looks like the Ritz.'

'Anne will come up with something,' Henry insisted. 'Try for the East Side. Living room, bedroom, bath and kitchen, furnished, around a hundred and fifty a month. Go to one-seventy-five if you have to. Start in right away, this afternoon. Take tomorrow off, take as long as you need . . . but don't come back until you have the apartment.'

'Henry, we may never see this girl again,' Lyon warned.

'My money's on Anne. She'll come up with something.'

Her room was on the second floor of the brownstone. Today the two flights suddenly seemed insurmountable. She stood at the landing, holding the battered *New York Times*. She had spent the afternoon visiting every apartment listed, and they had all been taken. Her feet ached. She had dressed that morning for the office, not for apartment hunting. Tomorrow she'd get an early start – in flat heels.

Before she tackled the stairs she knocked at Neely's door. There was no answer. She plodded up the shaky stairs and let herself into her room. She was grateful to hear the steam hissing through the ancient radiator.

Regardless of Lyon Burke's 'I'll-take-anything' attitude, she couldn't quite visualize him in a room like this. Not that it was a bad room. It was clean and conveniently located. Of course, compared to her spacious bedroom in Lawrenceville it was an awful room! The lumpy studio bed looked as if it might not last another year. Sometimes she wondered how many people had slept on it – hundreds, perhaps. But she didn't know them, and perhaps it was just this anonymity that made it *her* bed. As long as she paid her rent, everything in this room belonged to her. The small, battered night table, crisscrossed with scratches and old cigarette burns; the bureau with the three drawers that had to be left slightly open because they stuck if they were closed and if you pulled too hard the knobs came off; and the pregnant easy chair, its lowered belly bulging with springs that just longed to burst through.

It could be made attractive, but there was never enough money left at the end of the week. (She was determined not to touch the five thousand she had in the bank.) She was still paying off her Bloomingdale bill for the good black dress and the good black evening coat.

She heard the familiar knock and called, 'I'm in,' without looking up.

Neely entered and flopped on the chair, which groaned and came perilously close to disemboweling itself. 'What's with the ads in the *Times*? Thinking of moving?'

When Anne explained her new assignment, Neely laughed out loud. 'You mean he doesn't want a terrace thrown in, along with about four walk-in closets?' Then, dismissing the incident as impossible and thereby closed, she turned to the Important Matter. 'Anne, did you get a chance to talk about *it* today?'

'It' was a favor Neely had been hammering at for two weeks.

'Neely, how could I? Today of all days . . . with Lyon Burke coming back.'

'But we've got to get into *Hit the Sky*. For some crazy reason Helen Lawson seems to like our act. We've been called back to audition three times and she was there at all our auditions. Now just one word from Henry Bellamy would cinch it.'

'We' meant Neely and her two partners. Neely's formal name was Ethel Agnes O'Neill ('Isn't that a pistol?' she had exclaimed), but the nickname of Neely had stuck since childhood, and since she was one third of a dance team called The Gaucheros, there was no need to do anything about the unwieldy names.

Anne's acquaintance with Neely had begun with a casual nod in the hall and had rapidly moved into a warm friendship. Neely looked like a gurgling, exuberant teenager. She had a snub nose, large brown eyes, freckles and curly brown hair. And in fact, Neely *was* a teenager, a teenager who had toured in vaudeville since she was seven.

15

It was hard to think of Neely as a performer. But one night she had dragged Anne along on a club date at a midtown hotel. And there, a strange transformation had taken place. The freckles vanished under a thick coat of greasepaint, and the childish figure matured with the help of a sleazy sequined dress. It was a passable, pedestrian kind of an act. Two men in frayed sombrero hats and tight pants, gyrating with the inevitable foot stamping and finger clicking designed to pass for Spanish dancing. Anne had seen similar acts in vaudeville back home. But she had never seen anyone like Neely. She wasn't sure whether Neely was exceptionally good or outrageously bad. She never actually became a part of The Gaucheros. She danced in time with them, spun with them, and bowed with them, but it wasn't a trio. You watched only Neely.

But without the costume and makeup, sitting on the sagging chair, Neely was just an eager seventeen-year-old girl. The first real friend Anne had ever known.

'I wish I could help you, Neely, but I can't go to Mr. Bellamy with a personal matter. Our relationship is strictly business.'

'So what? Everybody in town knows he was Helen Lawson's lover way back and that she still listens to everything he says.'

'He was *what?*'

'Her lover. Her guy. Don't tell me you didn't know.'

'Neely, where did you hear a silly thing like that?'

'Silly! Geez, you mean nobody told you about it? It was a long time ago, and she's had three husbands since then, but they were the hottest item around for years. Why do you think I've been on your neck about talking to Bellamy? Can you mention it to him tomorrow?'

'I'll be apartment hunting tomorrow. And Neely, I've told you – it just isn't right, bringing your personal life into the office.'

Neely sighed. 'Those fancy manners are gonna stand in your way, Anne. You gotta go in a direct line for the thing you want. Come right out and ask for it.'

'And what happens if you get turned down?'

Neely shrugged. 'So what? You're no worse off than if you haven't asked. At least this way you give yourself a fifty-fifty chance.'

Anne smiled at Neely's logic. Neely had no education, but she had the inborn intelligence of a mongrel puppy, plus the added sparkle that causes one puppy to stand out in a litter. This puppy was clumsy, frank and eager, with a streak of unexpected worldliness running through her innocence.

Neely had spent the first seven years of her life in foster homes. Then her sister, who was ten years older, met Charlie, one of The Gaucheros, and married him. They turned the act into a trio, and she immediately rescued Neely from the monotony of a foster home and formal schooling and introduced her to the life of a traveling third-rate vaudeville troupe. That was the end of school, but there was always someone on the bill who took a hand in helping Neely with her reading and arithmetic. She learned geography through train windows and picked up history from the European acts who played on the bill. And there was always a friendly doorman who sent in the alarm when an investigator from the Board of Education came around to check.

When Neely was fourteen her sister retired to have a baby, and Neely, who knew the act backwards, replaced her. And now, after all the small-time years, The Gaucheros had a chance at a Broadway show.

'Maybe I can bring it up with George Bellows,' Anne said thoughtfully as she freshened her makeup. 'He invited me to the opening of *Hit the Sky*.'

'That's the long way around,' Neely said, 'but it's better than nothing.' She watched Anne change into a tweed suit. 'Oh, seeing Allen tonight?'

Anne nodded.

'I figured. With Mr. Bellamy it's the black dress. Gosh, doesn't he ever get tired of that same black dress?'

'Mr. Bellamy never even notices me when I go out with him. It's business.'

'Hah!' Neely snorted. 'Boy, it sure sounds jazzy working in that office. Show business is a drag in comparison. You got George for an opening coming up, Mr. Bellamy for those fancy dinners at "21," you even found Allen in the office. And now Lyon Burke! Geez, Anne, you got four guys and I haven't even got one!'

Anne laughed. 'Mr. Bellamy is not a date, the opening isn't until January, and to Lyon Burke I am nothing more than a renting agent. And Allen . . . well . . . Allen and I just date.'

'That's still four times the action I got. I've never had a real date.

The only men I know are my brother-in-law and his partner Dickie. And Dickie's a fag. My big social life is going over to Walgreen's Drugstore and talking to the other out-of-work actors.'

'Haven't you met any actors who could take you out?'

'Ha! You don't know actors if you ask a question like that. Take you out? They won't even lift your tab for a five-cent Coke. It's not that actors are born cheap, but they're out of jobs so much they got to be. And most of them have jobs at night – they're busboys, elevator operators, desk clerks, anything that'll leave them free to job hunt during the day and see the managers.'

'Do you expect to go on the road soon?' Anne suddenly realized how much she would miss Neely.

'I hope not. My sister says the baby's just beginning to know his father. That's why Charlie's knocking himself out taking all these club dates. But Dickie's beginning to holler. We can make more money on tour. They want us for a nightclub route in Buffalo, Toronto and Montreal. That's why we've got to land this spot in *Hit the Sky*. Helen Lawson shows are always hits. We'd be able to stay in New York for a whole season, maybe more. Then maybe I'd be able to meet a decent guy and get married.'

'Is that why you want to be in the show? To meet someone and get married?'

'Sure, because then I'd be somebody. I'd be *Mrs*. Somebody. I'd live in one place. I'd have friends. People on the block would know who I was.'

'But what about love? It isn't that easy to find someone you really love.'

Neely wrinkled her nose. 'Look – if someone loved me, I'd love him. Geez, Anne, if you'd only go to Mr. Bellamy . . .'

Anne smiled. 'All right, Neely, I will. The first chance I get. Who knows, you might become the next Pavlova.'

'What's that?'

'She was a great dancer.'

Neely laughed. 'That's for the birds. The star bit. Oh, I think I *could* be a star. Not with *this* act. But something funny happens inside of me when I get before an audience. I dance fairly well, but I feel if they applauded loud enough, I could fly. I don't have a really good voice, but I feel if they liked me, I could do opera. It's a feeling I get when I'm out there . . . like they're all taking me in their arms or something. I talked to Dick and Charlie about it, but they think I'm crazy. They don't feel a thing.'

'Neely, maybe you should study, go to acting classes. Maybe you can make it to the top.'

Neely shook her head. 'The odds are too tough. I've met too many old-timers on the circuit who told me how they *almost* made it.'

'But you're talking about people who weren't quite good enough,' Anne said.

'Listen, no one sticks in show business because it's got good hours or steady dough. Every kid who goes into it thinks she can make it. But for every Mary Martin, Ethel Merman or Helen Lawson there're thousands of bit players who *almost* made it starving in fifth-rate road companies.'

Anne was silent. She couldn't argue with Neely's logic. She gave her makeup a final pat. 'All right, Neely, I'll do what I can with Mr. Bellamy. But who knows, maybe you'll get the job anyway. They must like your act if they've called you back three times.'

Neely laughed out loud. 'That's what I don't get. *Why* have they called us back? How could Helen Lawson like our cockemamie act? Unless every other dance team in town has smallpox or something. Listen, if I thought our act was good, I wouldn't be nagging at you. I can't understand why Helen Lawson seems interested – unless she's got a letch for Charlie. She's supposed to have eyes for anything in pants, and even though Charlie's not too bright, he is good looking.'

'But what would Charlie do if she did like him? After all, there's your sister.'

'Oh, he'd lay Helen Lawson if he had to,' Neely said without emotion. 'He'd figure he was doing it for my sister in a way. After all, he wouldn't really enjoy banging Helen. She's not exactly a great beauty.'

'Neely, you mean you'd stand still and let that happen? Your sister would never forgive you.'

'Anne, you not only talk like a virgin but you think like a priest. Look, I'm a virgin, but I do know that sex and love are two different things for a man. Charlie used to live in the cheapest room on the road and send my sister three quarters of his pay check so she and the baby could live nice. But that didn't mean that once in a while he wouldn't take a flier with a nice-looking girl on the bill. He just needed sex . . .

It had nothing to do with his love for Kitty and the baby. I've hung on to my virginity because I know men put a high value on it, and I want some man to love me the way Charlie loves Kitty. But it's different with a man. You don't expect *him* to be a virgin.'

The buzzer sounded in Anne's room. That meant Allen was at the front door. She pressed the button to signal she was on the way down and grabbed her coat and bag. 'Come on, Neely, I've got to go. Allen may be holding a cab.'

'Wait – got any more of those terrific chocolate marshmallow cookies left?' Neely began poking around in the small closet.

'Take the whole box,' Anne said, holding the door open.

'Oh, marvelous!' Neely followed her, cradling the box. 'I've got a library copy of *Gone with the Wind*, a quart of milk and all these cookies. Wow! What an orgy!'

They went to a little French restaurant. Allen listened attentively as she told him about her new assignment. When she finished, he gulped down the remainder of his coffee and called for the check.

'Anne, I think the time has come.'

'Time for what?'

'Time for the moment of truth. Time for you to leave Henry Bellamy in a blaze of glory.'

'But I don't *want* to leave Mr. Bellamy.'

'You will.' His smile was strange. Confident. His entire manner had changed. 'I assume getting Lyon Burke an apartment would be a great achievement.'

'You mean you know of one?'

He nodded, smiling mysteriously as though at a private joke. Outside, he signaled a cab and gave a Sutton Place address.

'Allen, where are we going?'

'To see Lyon Burke's new apartment.'

'At this time of night? Whose apartment is this, anyway?'

'You'll see,' he said. 'Just be patient.' The rest of the ride was silent.

The cab stopped in front of a fashionable building near the East River. The doorman sprang to attention. 'Good evening, Mr. Cooper.' The elevator man nodded and automatically stopped at the tenth floor. Allen nonchalantly slipped a key into the door of the apartment. He switched on the lights, revealing a skillfully decorated living room. He pressed another button and soft music drifted through the room. It was a perfect apartment. An apartment made to order for Lyon Burke.

'Allen, whose apartment is this?'

'Mine. Come see the rest of the place. The bedroom is quite large . . . good closet space.' He pulled open sliding doors. 'Bathroom here, kitchen out there. Small, but it has a window.'

She followed him around without speaking. It was inconceivable. Mild little Allen living here?

'Now I'll show you the one sour note.' He walked into the living room and drew the floor-length drapes, exposing a neighboring apartment and a window that looked almost near enough to touch.

'That's the sad story,' he said. 'This dream house has everything but a view. Although I've got to admit there's a fat guy across the way who fascinates me. He lives alone, and in two years I've never seen him touch a drop of food. He lives on beer – breakfast, lunch and dinner. Look!' As if on cue, a stout man in his undershirt lumbered into the kitchen and opened a bottle of beer.

Allen drew the drapes. 'I used to worry about him in the beginning. I was sure he'd wind up with a vitamin deficiency or something. But he seems to be thriving on it.' He led her to the couch. 'Well, does it fit the bill for Mr. Burke?'

'I think it's wonderful, even with the fat man. But Allen, why would you ever give up such a marvelous apartment?'

'I've found a better one. I can move in tomorrow. But I want you to see it first. It's important that you like it too.'

Good Lord! He was going to ask her to marry him! Nice, sweet little Allen? She didn't want to hurt him. Maybe she could pretend not to understand.

She forced an impersonal airiness into her voice. 'Allen, just because I've been assigned to find an apartment for Lyon Burke doesn't mean I'm an expert. This was just done to expedite things at the office, because Lyon Burke can't take the time off. If you found this apartment on your own, you certainly don't need any advice from me . . .' She knew she was talking too fast.

'You say he can pay one fifty,' Allen said. 'But he could go to one seventy-five. Tell you what – we'll give it to him for one fifty. That should make a real hero out of you. He can take over my lease. That's what I pay, unfurnished, but I'll throw in the furniture as a bonus.'

She was suddenly concerned. 'But you'll need it in your new place,' she protested. 'Besides, it must have cost a lot . . .'

'It doesn't matter,' he said gaily. 'Can Lyon Burke move in here right away?'

'Well, I guess—'

'Sure he can,' Allen said. 'Come on, I'll show you my new place.' He hustled her out and down in the elevator, ignoring her protestations about the late hour.

On the street again, the attentive doorman charged over. 'Taxi, Mr. Cooper?'

'No, Joe, we're just going down the street.'

He led her down the block and into another building, one that seemed to be hanging over the river.

The new apartment was like a movie set. The living room was covered with forty feet of thick white carpet. The bar area was inlaid with Italian marble. There was a long staircase that obviously led to some upstairs rooms. But the breathtaking feature was the view.

Glass doors opened on to an immense terrace that overlooked the river. He led her out. The cold wind blew the dampness in her face, but the beauty of the scene was overpowering. Bright lacework bridge lights looped the river, and tiny diamonds trickled across the spans. She stared, transfixed, not noticing Allen at all.

'Shall we drink to the new apartment?' he asked.

She came out of her reverie to accept an offered Coke.

'Allen, whose apartment is this?' she said quietly.

'Mine, if I want it.'

'But who does it belong to now?'

'A man named Gino. But he says it's too big for him. He lives at the Waldorf – likes it better that way.'

'But Allen, you can't afford anything like this!'

'You'd be surprised at what I can afford.' He was wearing that strange smile again.

She started back inside. 'Allen, I think I had better go. I'm very tired . . . and very mixed up.'

'Anne . . .' He caught her arm. 'I'm rich, Anne – very, very rich.'

She stared at him silently. And suddenly she knew he was telling the truth.

'I love you, Anne. In the beginning I just couldn't believe you were going with me all this time and didn't know.'

'Know what?'

'Who I am.'

'Who are you?'

'Oh, I'm still Allen Cooper. That's the only thing you do know about me. My name. Only to you it doesn't seem to ring any bells. You accepted me as an unsuccessful little insurance salesman.' He grinned. 'You don't know what it's done to me these past few weeks, hiding you out at inexpensive restaurants, watching you order the least expensive thing on the menu, knowing you were worried about my sales. Anne, no one has ever really cared about *me* before. At first I thought it was a gag, that you knew and were conning me. Oh, it's been tried before. That's why I asked so many questions – where you came from, all about Lawrenceville. Then I had a detective make a check.'

He saw her eyes narrow and grabbed her hands. 'Anne, don't be angry. You were too perfect to be true. Gino couldn't believe it. But when the reports came in, when it all turned out to be on the level – the family home, the widowed mother, the aunt and your good New England background – you're class, Anne, real class. Jesus, when I found out I wanted to send off rockets. I'd been so sure nothing like this could ever happen to me – that someone I worshipped could like me for myself! Can't you see what that means to me?' He danced her around the room. 'You care! You really care! Not for what I have, but for me!'

She broke away from him and caught her breath. 'Allen, how would I know who you were – or about any of this – unless you told me?'

'I don't know how you *couldn't* know. I was always in the columns. I figured one of your girlfriends would tell you. Or certainly Henry Bellamy.'

'I don't read the columns, and I have no girl friends except Neely. She only reads *Variety*. And I never discuss my personal affairs with Mr. Bellamy – or anyone else at the office.'

'Well, now you can give them a big piece of news. About us!' He took her in his arms and kissed her.

She stood there limply – then abruptly broke the embrace. God, it had happened again! At his kiss, a surge of revulsion had swept through her.

He looked at her tenderly. 'My sweet little Anne. I know you must be confused.'

She walked to the mirror and repaired her lipstick. Her hand was trembling. Something was wrong with her. Why should she feel this cold distaste at a man's kiss? Many girls enjoyed kissing men they didn't love. It was supposed to be normal. And she liked Allen, he wasn't a stranger. So it wasn't just Willie Henderson or the boys in Lawrenceville. The trouble must lie within herself.

He stood behind her. 'I love you, Anne. I realize this has come very fast. It's enough to confuse anyone. But I want to marry you. And I want you to meet Gino – my father.'

He handed her a key. 'Give this to Lyon Burke tomorrow. Tell him to get in touch with me at my office. I'll have the lease switched immediately. And Anne, if this apartment is too overdone for you, you can throw everything out. Redo it. Gino spent a fortune on it, but somehow I guess it doesn't look like you. Or if you like, we can buy a town house – anything you want.'

'Allen . . . I . . .'

'We've talked enough for one night. I love you. And you're going to marry me. Just hold that in mind for now.'

She was deep in her own thoughts as they drove home. She knew the truth now. She was frigid. That awful word the girls at school used to whisper about. Some girls were born that way – they never reached a climax or felt any real passion. And she was one of them. God, she couldn't even enjoy a kiss! Maybe she was lucky she had found someone like Allen. He was kind, he might be able to help her. She might as well marry him. Her mother had been right. That great feeling – it didn't happen to a 'lady' who felt revulsion at a kiss. But at least she had escaped Willie Henderson and Lawrenceville. Some people never even had half a dream come true.

He held the cab when they reached her brownstone. 'Try to dream of me, Anne.' He leaned over and kissed her lightly on the cheek. 'Good night.'

She watched the cab disappear, then she ran inside and banged on Neely's door. Neely appeared, her head bent over *Gone with the Wind*.

Without putting the book down, she motioned Anne in and continued to read.

'Neely, put that book away for a minute. This is important.'

'I wouldn't leave Rhett Butler right now for anything in the world!'

'Neely, have you ever heard of Allen Cooper?'

'Hey, what is this, a gag?'

'I've never been more serious. Who is Allen Cooper? Does the name mean anything to you?'

Neely yawned and closed the book, carefully turning the corner of the page to hold Rhett in place. 'All right, if you want to play games. Allen Cooper is a very nice boy who dates you three or four nights a week. From what I've seen of him from my window I'd say he wasn't exactly Cary Grant, but he's reliable. Now. Can I go back to Rhett? He's lots more interesting, and Scarlett doesn't seem to appreciate him at all.'

'Then you've never heard of Allen Cooper?'

'No. Should I? Has he been in pictures or something? I know about Gary Cooper and Jackie Cooper, but Allen Cooper . . .' She shrugged.

'All right, go back to Rhett Butler.' Anne started for the door.

'You're acting funny tonight,' Neely muttered. 'Hey, you didn't have a drink or something, did you?'

'No. See you tomorrow.'

Neely nodded absently. She was already back with Rhett and Scarlett.

In the darkness, Anne lay awake sorting the facts. Allen was not a poor little insurance agent – Allen was rich. But why should she have heard about him? Was there something else she should know? How could she find out more about him? George Bellows! Of course. If there was anything to know about Allen or anyone, George Bellows would know.

George Bellows looked up in surprise when she entered his office. 'Hey, aren't you supposed to be out apartment hunting?'

'May I talk to you, George? It's personal.'

He crossed the room and closed the door. 'Any time. Sit down. And make it as personal as you like. Here, how about some coffee?' He poured her a cup from a thermos. 'All right now, let's have it. Something bothering you?'

She studied the coffee. 'George, do you know Allen Cooper?'

'Who doesn't?' He looked at her carefully. 'Hey . . . don't tell me you've gotten involved with him!'

'I know him. I understand he's quite rich.'

'Rich!' He chuckled unpleasantly. 'Baby, they'd have to invent a new word for his kind of money. Of course, his father, Gino, started the empire. They own half the real estate in this town. They're rumored to be partners with those millionaire Greek shipping tycoons. *Time* magazine did a piece on Gino a few years ago. Maybe I can dig up a back copy in the library for you. They said his wealth couldn't even be estimated. They ran Allen's picture, too. Sole heir to the entire empire. You can imagine what an ad this was for the pair of them. Ever since, they've needed elephant guns to keep the girls away. So if you've met Allen, I give you one piece of advice – don't take him seriously. He's a louse.'

'He seems very nice,' she insisted.

George laughed. 'Oh, he's smoother than glass – but I think he's as tough as his father underneath. He's put over some pretty shrewd deals on his own. Managed to stay out of the Army by buying some plant that made parachutes, I believe.'

She stood up. 'Thanks, George.'

'Any time, honey. I can give you a rundown on every wolf in town – with your looks you're bound to meet them all.'

Henry Bellamy's face sagged with disappointment when he saw her. 'Now don't tell me you've given up already! Look, Anne, I know it's tough. I called a few renting agents myself today. But you've got to keep trying.'

'I have the apartment for Mr. Burke.'

'No! Good God, you are sensational!' He buzzed Lyon's office and called him in.

'I have the key,' she said. 'Mr. Burke can look at it this afternoon.'

'What's wrong with this morning?' Lyon said as he walked in. 'Can't give them a chance to change their minds. Anne, you are a wonder! What's the address?'

He scribbled it down. 'Great location. Can I afford it?'

'It's a hundred and fifty a month.'

He shook his head. 'You're a wizard. But why the key? Is the tenant away?'

'No. He's probably at his office.'

'What's the name?'

'Allen Cooper,' she said quietly.

Lyon merely wrote down the name, but Henry looked at her curiously. 'How did you find this apartment, Anne? Through an ad?'

'No. Allen Cooper is a friend of mine.'

Henry's expression relaxed. 'If he's a friend of yours, he can't be the Allen Cooper I know.'

'I met him in this office, Mr. Bellamy.'

'Here?' Henry seemed puzzled. 'By God you did!' He rose with such violence that his chair banged against the wall. 'Anne! You and Allen Cooper! No . . .' He shook his head in disbelief.

'I thought he was just an insurance salesman when I met him,' she said.

'The sonofabitch was here trying to get a chorus girl off his back. One of our minor clients. Wanted me to pay her off and throw a scare into her. I threw him out pretty quick.' He shot Anne an angry scowl. 'But obviously not quick enough!'

'Henry!' Lyon's voice was sharp. 'Anne is certainly capable of choosing her own friends.' Then, with a quick smile at the older man, he added, 'You're not being very fair. You send Anne out on an impossible assignment, and when she delivers, instead of shouting her praises you fire accusations and pry into her personal life.'

'Allen Cooper . . .' Henry repeated the name in disbelief. 'Lyon, if you knew this Allen Cooper—'

Lyon smiled. 'I don't want to know him. I just want his apartment.'

'Have you ever heard of him?' Henry asked.

Lyon looked thoughtful. 'Seems I have. He's frightfully rich, I believe. But one shouldn't hold that against him.'

'But Anne's no match against a guy like that. She doesn't play in their league. She's got to get killed,' Henry insisted.

She stood there quietly, slightly annoyed that they were talking about her as if she weren't there.

'Okay!' Henry turned and retrieved his chair. 'It's none of my business. Just as long as I go on record how I feel. From now on it's your ball game.'

'And I'm sure she knows the rules,' Lyon said. He turned to her and smiled. 'I'd like very much to look at the apartment. Mind if Anne goes with me, Henry?'

Henry waved his hand in dismissal and returned to his work. Anne heard him sigh heavily as they left the office.

She fastened her attention on the taxi window as they drove crosstown. It was one of those last wonderful days in October, when the air is balmy and the faded sun tries to pretend it's spring.

'Don't be angry,' Lyon said quietly. 'Henry only blew off because he's fond of you, in the nicest possible way. He doesn't want you to get hurt.'

'I'm not angry – just confused.'

'Since everyone seems to be offering unsolicited advice, let me add some of my own. Never judge anyone by another's opinions. We all have different sides that we show to different people.'

She smiled. 'You mean that even Hitler could be soft and playful with Eva Braun.'

'Something like that. And King Henry didn't kill *all* of his wives. If I recall correctly, the last one actually henpecked him.'

'But Allen is really very nice,' she insisted.

'I'm sure he is. And if this is his building, it's quite impressive.'

The cab had stopped. A different doorman was on duty. 'We've come to see Mr. Cooper's apartment,' Anne said.

He nodded. 'Mr. Cooper told me about it. Tenth floor.'

She handed Lyon the key. 'I'll wait in the lobby.'

'What? No guided tour? Come, my girl, I expect you to point out all the advantages of the flat. Where the linens are stored, how to work the stove, where the fuse box is hidden . . .'

She felt herself blushing. 'I was there only once, to look at the apartment for you.'

'Then you still know more about it than I,' he said easily.

He liked everything about the apartment. He even insisted he liked the view of the fat man across the way. 'Makes it rather neighborly. I shall call Allen Cooper this afternoon and thank him. But first I must express my gratitude to you. I suggest we both have a very expensive lunch on Henry.'

They went to the Barberry Room. She liked the soft blue darkness, the tiny artificial stars twinkling in the ceiling and the generous arm-chairs. She accepted a sherry. In the last twenty-four hours too many things had happened so fast. She felt unnerved and strangely off balance.

Lyon didn't pressure her into conversation. He talked on easily about the marvels of the new apartment, the luxury of civilian food, his new appreciation of civilian life. Gradually she felt herself unwinding. She liked his clipped accent, the soothing atmosphere of the room. She liked watching his face . . . his changes of expression . . . his quick smile.

'You'll have to bear with Henry's meddling in your life,' he said as he leaned across to light her cigarette. 'But it's only because he wants the best for you. He's placed you on a bit of a pedestal.'

'You're the one he's put on a pedestal,' she said. 'One about seventy feet high. You're the future of Bellamy and Bellows.'

'He felt that way four years ago,' Lyon said. 'People change in four years.'

'Mr. Bellamy hasn't changed his opinion of you.'

He took her hand. 'Anne, can't we cut this "mister" business? I'm Lyon. "Mister" Bellamy is Henry.'

She smiled. 'All right . . . Lyon. You must know how anxiously Henry's been waiting for you to come back.' She stopped suddenly. This was none of her business. She had never intruded into anyone's personal life before. But she felt an urgency to protect Henry. She suddenly understood Henry's stand against Allen – it was part of being a friend. She also saw the logic behind Neely's argument with new charity. You couldn't be a real friend and remain politely impersonal. She *would* speak to Henry about Neely and *Hit the Sky*. She felt a new freedom, as if she had shed another shackle that bound her to Lawrenceville.

'I'm aware of Henry's hopes and plans,' Lyon answered. 'And perhaps I won't let him down. But God! It's a bastard business at best, neither lawyer nor agent.'

'But everyone said you were a – a dynamo. You have to love something to give it such energy.'

'I loved a good fight . . . the challenge . . . even the wheeling and dealing.'

She was confused. Everything he said contradicted the reputation that had preceded him.

He took her silence as concern for Henry. 'Now don't fret. I probably just have a touch of battle fatigue.'

'But you *are* glad to be back with Henry?'

'I am back, am I not?'

She looked puzzled. 'You say it as if there was really something else you'd rather do.'

'Does anyone actually have the luxury of doing exactly what he wants to do?'

'I'm doing what *I* want to do.'

He flashed his smile. 'I'm flattered.'

'I mean working for Henry. Living in New York. But what *do* you want to do, Lyon?'

He stretched his long legs under the table. 'Be dreadfully rich, for one thing. Sit in some lovely spot in Jamaica, have several beautiful girls who look exactly like you to look after me and knock out a best-selling novel about the war.'

'You want to write?'

'Of course.' He shrugged. 'Doesn't everyone who comes out of the Army feel positive he has the *only* true war novel in him?'

'Then why not write it?'

'For one thing, working for Henry is a full-time proposition. And that charming flat I'm inheriting does not come rent free. I'm afraid literature's loss will be Henry Bellamy's gain.'

She realized Lyon Burke could not be categorized and neatly filed away. He had feelings, but he would always mask them with a smile or a contradictory statement.

'It's odd, but you don't strike me as a quitter,' she said boldly.

His eyes narrowed. 'I beg your pardon?'

'Giving up without even trying. I mean – if you want to write, if you honestly feel you have something to say, then do it. Everyone should at least *try* to do the thing he wants to do. Later in life situations and responsibilities force people to compromise. But to compromise now . . . it's like quitting before you start.'

He leaned across and cupped her chin in his hand. Their eyes met, and he looked at her intently. 'Henry certainly doesn't know you. You can't be the girl he's been talking about. So far the only thing he's been right about is your incredible beauty. By God, you're a fighter, you are.'

She sat back in her chair. 'This isn't really me today.' She felt drained. 'I'm kind of off balance. Things have happened too quickly. And when nothing has ever happened to you for twenty years, I guess you do act strange. I mean . . . all this about Allen Cooper. I didn't even know who he really was until last night.'

'Don't let Henry's opinion bother you. He's not exactly eager to break in someone new. He'll fight off your suitors with hand grenades if necessary.'

'Allen is just a friend . . .'

'That's excellent news.' This time he looked at her without smiling.

She felt flustered. To cover her embarrassment she said, 'What I said before, about people trying to do the thing they really wanted to do. I meant that. I did it when I came to New York. No one should give up a dream without giving it a chance to come true.'

'I have no dreams, Anne. I never had. This idea of writing just came to me after the war. Before the war I was dedicated to success, and making a pile of money. But now I'm not even sure I want that any more. In fact I'm not sure there's anything I particularly want.' Then, with one of his quick changes of mood, he smiled. 'Yes, there's one thing I do want. I want to be aware of the minutes and the seconds, and to make each one count.'

'I can understand that,' she said. 'It's a natural feeling for anyone who's been in the war.'

'Oh? I was beginning to wonder if any females over here recalled there was a war.'

'Oh, I'm sure everyone felt the war.'

'I can't agree. When you're over there, in it, you don't think there's anything else in life. You can't believe that somewhere people are sleeping in comfortable beds or sitting in a restaurant like this. It's different in Europe. Everywhere you walk you see a bombed-out building – you live with the constant reminder. But when I came back here all of the death and bloodshed seemed so remote. It seemed that it couldn't have actually happened – that it was some hellish nightmare. There was New York, the Paramount Building was still standing, its clock running just as it always had. The pavements had the same cracks, the same pigeons or their relatives were messing up the Plaza, the same lines were standing outside of the Copa, waiting to see the same stars.

'Last night I was out with a beautiful creature who spent hours telling me about the hardships she had endured during the war. No nylons, plastic lipstick containers, no bobby pins . . . it was awful. I think the shortage of nylons affected her the most. She was a model, and her legs were important to her. She said she was terribly glad we finally discovered the atom bomb – she had been down to her last six pair when it hit.'

'I suppose if you're in it, nothing matters but getting out alive,' she said quietly.

'You don't chance thinking even that far ahead,' he answered. 'You think from day to day. If you allow yourself to think of the future – any personal future – you lose your nerve. And suddenly you recall all the senseless time-wasting things you've done . . . the wasted minutes you'll never recover. And you realize that time is the most precious thing. Because time is life. It's the only thing you can never get back. You can lose a girl and perhaps win her back – or find another. But a second – this second – when it goes, it's irrevocably gone.' His voice was soft, remembering, and she noticed the fine lines around the corners of his eyes.

'There was this corporal . . . we were spending the night in what was left of a barn. Neither of us was sleepy. The corporal kept sifting some of the earth through his hand. He kept saying, 'This is great earth.' Seems he had a farm in Pennsylvania. He began telling me the trouble he had with his peach trees, and about his plans for enlarging the farm when he returned. He wanted it to be a good farm for his children when they grew up. But the soil bothered him. It wasn't rich enough. That's all he talked about. Soon I found myself worrying about his miserable soil – even offering suggestions. I think I fell asleep dreaming of fertilizers and acres and acres of peach trees. The next day was a bad one. We ran into land mines . . . snipers . . . the weather was foul. That night I made the reports on the missing men. I checked the dogtags. One of them was the corporal. I sat and stared at the dogtag . . . Last night it had been a man – a man who wasted his last night on earth worrying about fertilizer and soil. And now his blood would fertilize some foreign soil.'

He looked at her and suddenly smiled. 'And here I am, wasting your time talking about it.'

'No, please go on.'

He looked at her strangely. 'I've said a great many things today . . . things that probably should have stayed locked away in my mind.' He

32

signaled for the check. 'But I've taken up enough of your time. Make the rest of the afternoon count. Buy a new dress, have your hair done – or do any of the wonderful things a beautiful girl should do.'

'This girl is going back to the office.'

'Nothing of the kind. *I'm* giving *this* order. Henry expected you to be gone several days. The least you deserve is a half-day holiday. And a two-week salary bonus. I'll see to that.'

'But I couldn't think of—'

'Nonsense. I expected to hand a renting agent a full month's rent under the table. Let's call this my first official act at Bellamy and Bellows. You get a two-week salary bonus and the afternoon off.'

She took the afternoon off, but she didn't do any of the things he suggested. She walked up Fifth Avenue. She looked at the new winter styles. She sat in the square at the Plaza. And she thought about Lyon Burke. He dwarfed anyone she had ever known. She had been overwhelmed by the smiling, inscrutable Lyon, but the Lyon who talked about the war – he seemed accessible, capable of caring. He had cared about the corporal. Who was Lyon Burke, really?

She left the square and walked down Fifth Avenue. It was getting late. She had to go home and change. Allen was picking her up. *Allen!* She couldn't marry Allen! That would be refuting everything she had said. That was really giving up! It was too early to compromise with even part of a dream.

She would tell him at dinner. But it had to be brought up gently, with tact. She couldn't just open with, 'Hello Allen I'm not going to marry you.' But during dinner, she'd work into it and break it easily – but firmly. It was as simple as that.

But it wasn't. No quiet little French restaurant now. Allen no longer needed to hide his identity. They went to '21.' Waiters bowed to him and everyone called him by name. He seemed to know most of the people in the room.

'By the way, Anne, do you like country living?' he asked suddenly. 'We have this house in Greenwich . . .'

This was the opening. 'No, I had enough of that in Lawrenceville. As a matter of fact, Allen, there's something I want to say . . . something you've got to understand . . .'

He looked at his watch and suddenly signaled for the check.

'Allen!'

'Go on, I'm listening.' He was signing the check.

'It's about what you said last night. And now about country living. Allen, I like you very much but—'

'Oh, I'm glad you reminded me. I sent the lease over to Lyon Burke. Talked to him this afternoon. He sounds like a nice guy. English, isn't he?'

'He was raised in England. Allen, listen to me.'

He stood up. 'You can tell me in the cab.'

'Please sit down. I'd rather tell you here.'

He smiled and held her coat. 'It's dark in the cab – more romantic. Besides, we're late.'

She stood up helplessly. 'Where are we going?'

'Morocco.' He tipped his way out of the room with a series of surreptitious handshakes. In the cab, he settled back and smiled. 'My father is at Morocco. I told him we would stop by. Now, what did you want to tell me?'

'Allen, I'm very flattered about the way you feel. I'm also very grateful about the apartment for Lyon Burke. It's saved me a lot of trouble and pavement pounding. I think you're one of the nicest people I've ever met, but—' she saw the neon sign of El Morocco and her words rushed out – 'but about marriage . . . what you said last night . . . I'm sorry, Allen, I—'

'Good evening, Mr. Cooper!' The doorman at El Morocco sang the greeting as he swung open the door of the cab. 'Your father is inside.'

'Thanks, Pete.' Another bill exchanged hands. Allen led her into the club. She had failed to make her point – or had Allen consciously made it a point *not* to understand?

Gino Cooper was sitting with a group of men at a large round table near the bar. He waved at Allen, signaling he'd join them. The waiter led Allen to a table against the wall. It was ten-thirty, still early for El Morocco. Although this was Anne's first visit to the famous club, she had seen pictures, in newspapers and magazines, of various celebrities sitting against the famous zebra stripes. She looked around. There were plenty of zebra stripes, but otherwise it was just a large room with a fairly good orchestra playing some show tunes.

Gino joined their table immediately. Without waiting for any introduction, he grabbed Anne's hand and pumped it violently.

'So this is her, huh?' He whistled softly. 'Kid, you were right. This one was worth waiting for. She's got real class. I can tell without her even opening her mouth.' He snapped his fingers; a captain seemed to materialize from the atmosphere. 'Bring some champagne,' he ordered without taking his eyes away from Anne.

'Anne doesn't drink,' Allen began.

'Tonight she'll drink,' Gino said heartily. 'Tonight's an occasion.'

Anne smiled. Gino's warmth was infectious. He was swarthy, heavyset and floridly handsome. His black hair was streaked with gray, but his immense vitality and enthusiasm were almost boyish.

When the champagne was poured, he toasted her. 'To the new lady in our family.' With one gulp he drained half his glass. He wiped his mouth on the back of his hand and said, 'Are you Catholic?'

'No, I—' Anne began.

'Well, you gotta convert when you marry Allen. I'll make an appointment with Father Kelly at the Paulist Center. He can rush it through with private instruction.'

'Mr. Cooper—' It had been almost a physical effort to find her voice.

Allen quickly interrupted. 'We haven't discussed religion, Dad. And there's no reason for Anne to convert.'

Gino considered this. 'Well, no . . . not if she's dead set against it. Long as she marries in the Church and promises to raise the kids Catholic—'

'Mr. Cooper, I'm not going to marry Allen!' There! She had said it, loud and clear.

His eyes narrowed. 'Why? You *that* anti-Catholic?'

'I'm not anti-anything.'

'Then what's the hitch?'

'I'm not in love with Allen.'

At first Gino's stare was blank. Then he turned to Allen in bewilderment. 'What in hell did she say?'

'She said she wasn't in love with me,' Allen answered.

'Say, is this a gag or something? I thought you said you were gonna marry her.'

'I did. And I will. But first I have to make her love me.'

'You both crazy or something?' Gino demanded.

Allen smiled pleasantly. 'I told you, Dad – up until last night,

Anne thought I was just a struggling little insurance agent. She has to readjust her thinking.'

'What's to readjust?' Gino asked. 'Since when did money become a handicap?'

'We never discussed love, Dad. I don't think Anne allowed herself to take me seriously. She spent too much time worrying I'd lose my job.'

Gino looked at Anne curiously. 'You really went with him all these weeks and ate at those hash houses he told me about?'

Anne smiled faintly. She was beginning to feel conspicuous. Gino's voice carried, and Anne was sure half the room was enjoying their conversation.

Gino hit his thigh and laughed aloud. 'This is a good one!' He poured himself more champagne. A waiter leaped to assist him. Gino motioned him away. 'I used to open these bottles with my teeth. Now six flunkies feel they gotta help me pour it.' He turned to Anne. 'I like you! Welcome to the family.'

'But I'm not going to marry Allen.'

He waved his hand in dismissal. 'Listen – if you lived through six weeks of bad eats and accepted him as a punk, you'll love him now. Drink your champagne. Start cultivating rich tastes, you can afford it. Hi, Ronnie.' A thin young man had appeared from nowhere and was standing silently at their table.

'This is Ronnie Wolfe,' Gino told her. 'Sit down, Ronnie.' Gino snapped his fingers and called into space, 'Bring Mr. Wolfe his usual.' And from space a waiter appeared and placed a pot of coffee before the stranger.

'Now, don't tell me you never heard of Ronnie – everybody reads his column,' Gino said proudly.

'Anne's new in New York,' Allen said quickly. 'She only knows about the *Times*.'

'Good paper,' Ronnie said crisply. He pulled out a worn little black leather book. His dark eyes darted from Allen to Gino. 'All right, let's have her name – and who's staked the claim? Father or son?'

'Both of us this time,' Gino said. 'This little girl is gonna be related to me soon. Anne Welles. Spell the name right, Ronnie – she's gonna marry Allen.'

Ronnie whistled. He looked at Anne with curious respect. 'Big

36

story, all right. New model in town lassos big prize. Or actress? Now don't tell me – see if I can guess. Texas?'

'I'm from Massachusetts and I work in an office,' Anne said coldly.

Ronnie's eyes twinkled. 'Next thing I expect you'll even tell me you can type.'

'I hardly think that's news for your column. And I also think you should know that Allen and I—'

'Now Anne,' Gino said quickly. 'Ronnie's a friend.'

'No, let her go on.' Ronnie was looking at her with something close to respect.

'Aw, have some more champagne,' Gino said, refilling her glass.

She picked up her glass and sipped it in an effort to control her anger. She wanted to insist she was not marrying Allen, but she knew Gino had deliberately stopped her and probably would again. It would be embarrassing to him to be contradicted in public. The moment Ronnie Wolfe left she would tell Gino not to make any more statements. She had told them both – father and son – that she was not going to marry Allen. Did money give people a blind spot? Rob them of their hearing?

'Who do you work for?' Ronnie asked.

'Henry Bellamy,' Allen said. 'But that's temporary.'

'Allen!' She turned to him angrily, but Ronnie interrupted.

'Look, Miss Welles – questions are my job.' He smiled in a frank and friendly way. 'I like you. It's refreshing to run into a girl who didn't come to New York to be an actress or a model.' He looked at her closely. 'Great cheekbones. You could make a fortune if you wanted. If Powers or Longworth ever saw you, you might even get richer than your boyfriend.' He winked at Gino.

'If she wanted to work we'd buy her a modeling agency,' Gino bellowed. 'But she's gonna settle down and raise babies.'

'Mr. Cooper—' Anne's face was burning.

Allen broke in. 'Dad, let's take first things first.'

Ronnie laughed. 'Here comes your friend, Gino. Does she know the news?'

They looked up as a tall, stunning girl approached the table. Without rising, Gino moved over and patted the seat. 'This is Adele Martin. Sit down, baby, and say hello to Anne Welles, my son's fiancée.'

37

Adele's penciled brows shot into a higher arch. Without acknowledging Anne, she looked from Allen to Ronnie for verification.

Ronnie nodded, his eyes bright with amusement at Adele's consternation. But the girl's recovery was quick. She snuggled beside Gino and offered Anne a weak smile. 'How'd you swing it, honey? I've been trying to drag this baboon to the altar for seven months. Give me the magic word and we can make it a double ceremony.' She looked up at Gino adoringly.

'You're a career girl, Adele,' Ronnie said, winking at Gino.

Adele stared at him murderously. 'Listen, Ronnie, it takes a certain amount of talent to be a showgirl. Don't knock it.'

Ronnie smiled and tucked his notebook away. 'I think you're the best showgirl in town, Adele.'

'You can say that again,' she said, somewhat mollified. 'I've turned down two movie offers to stay with my baby here.' She leaned over and kissed Gino's cheek.

Ronnie rose and jerked his head in farewell. Anne watched him join another table as another waiter swiftly appeared with a fresh pot of coffee. Ronnie sipped the coffee slowly and took out his black book, his eager eyes constantly darting to the door to scan each new arrival.

Allen followed her glance. 'Ronnie's a nice guy. No legmen . . . gets all his own items.'

Adele sneered. 'He's a busybody.'

'You're just mad because he printed we're engaged to be engaged,' Gino said.

'Well, it's a hell of a line. Made me look like a fool.' Then she smiled. 'How about it, baby? You can't let your son beat you to the altar.'

'I been to the altar,' Gino said. 'After Rosanna died, that was the end of my married life. A guy can only have one wife. Romances? Plenty. But one wife.'

'Who made that rule?' Adele demanded.

Gino poured the girl some champagne. Anne sensed that they had covered this ground many times. 'Adele, forget it.' His voice was cold. 'Even if I did remarry, it couldn't be you. You been divorced.'

Then, as Adele sulked, he said, 'Oh by the way, I told Irving to bring two coats to your place tomorrow. Take your pick.'

Adele's expression changed instantly. 'Both mink?'

'What else? Maybe muskrat?'

'Oh, Gino . . .' She snuggled close to him. 'Sometimes you get me so mad, but I have to forgive you. I love you so.'

Gino looked down at Anne's silk coat lying crushed on the seat. 'Hey, Allen. Okay with you if I send one over to Anne as an engagement present?' Then, without waiting for an answer, he turned to Anne. 'What color do you like?'

'Color?' Anne had always thought mink was brown.

'He means ranch or wild, honey,' Adele explained. 'I think wild mink would go great with your hair.'

'I'm afraid I couldn't accept it,' Anne said quietly.

'Why not?' Gino snapped.

'Perhaps Anne would like her coat to come from me – after we're married,' Allen said quickly.

Gino laughed. 'You mean when you get your mink you want it to be legal?'

'What's illegal about taking a mink coat?' Adele asked. 'I think it's illegal to turn one down.'

Anne felt uncomfortable. The champagne made her feel warm. The club was packed; the dance floor had shrunk as waiters frantically placed dime-sized tables on the floor for important new arrivals. People were mashed against the velvet rope and there wasn't an inch of space on the side of the room where they were sitting – yet curiously enough there were some empty tables on the other side. Allen explained that that was 'Siberia.' If you sat on that side of the room no one respected you. Squares and out-of-towners sat there. They didn't know the difference. But a 'regular' would die of embarrassment if he had to sit there.

There was a constant swirl of people, a continuous flow of introductions. At some point another columnist joined them briefly and someone took their picture. Gino ordered more champagne. Girls who looked like exact replicas of Adele stopped by the table and congratulated Allen and tossed sympathetic winks at Adele. Some greeted Allen with familiarity – a hug and a kiss, explosive declarations of eternal devotion or 'Did Anne realize how lucky she was,' stares of envy, and of curiosity.

She sat quietly, her outward calm denying her mounting panic. She had to straighten this out with Allen on the way home. Then he could call Ronnie Wolfe and the other columnist. She had to make him understand.

She tapped his arm quietly. 'It's one o'clock, Allen. I should be getting home.'

Gino looked amazed. 'Home? That's a dirty word. The party's just getting going.'

'I have to work tomorrow, Mr. Cooper.'

Gino smiled expansively. 'Little lady, you don't ever have to do anything again except be good to my boy.'

'But I have a job—'

'So quit it,' Gino said, pouring champagne all around.

'Quit my job?'

'Why not?' This time it was Adele Martin who asked the question. 'If Gino asked me to marry him, I'd give up my career in a second.'

'What career?' Gino laughed. 'Standing around as a backdrop two hours every night?' He turned to Anne. 'Miss America here has to show up for work. She belongs to some kind of an actors' union. But you got no contract.'

'I like my job and I wouldn't walk out on anyone,' Anne replied.

Gino shrugged. 'Okay, I go along with that. You've got class. A guy should get notice. Tell him tomorrow, give him a chance to find someone else.' He signaled for the check. 'Guess we could all stand one early night for a change.'

Anne slipped into her coat. She'd straighten this out when she got Allen alone in the cab going home . . .

But there was no cab. A long black chauffeured car was waiting. Gino motioned them inside. 'Get in,' he said. 'We'll drop Tillie the Toiler first.'

When they reached her brownstone, Gino and Adele waited in the car and Allen walked her to the door.

'Allen,' she whispered, 'I've got to talk to you.'

He leaned over and kissed her lightly. 'Anne, I know tonight has been wild, but it won't be like this again. You had to meet Gino. That's over and done with. Tomorrow we'll go out alone.'

'I like Gino. But Allen, you've got to tell him!'

'Tell him what?'

'Allen, I'm not marrying you! I never said I would.'

He stroked her hair lightly. 'I don't blame you for panicking.

Tonight would scare anyone. But tomorrow everything will be different.' He took her face in his hands. 'And believe it or not, you *are* going to marry me.'

'No, Allen.'

'Anne . . . are you in love with someone else?'

'No, but—'

'That's enough for me. Just give me a chance.'

'Hey!' Gino bellowed out of the window. 'Cut the gab and kiss her good night!'

Allen leaned over and kissed her lightly. 'I'll pick you up at seven-thirty tomorrow night.' He turned and ran down the steps.

She stood there shivering as the car rolled away. Well, she had tried. If Ronnie Wolfe printed it, he'd have to retract it. She ran up the stairs to her room. There was a white envelope pasted on her door. The childlike printing said: *Wake me no matter what time you come in. Urgent! Neely*.

She looked at her watch. It was two o'clock. But the 'urgent' was underlined. She made her way slowly down the stairs and tapped lightly, half hoping Neely wouldn't hear her. She heard the bed creak, saw the sliver of light appear under the door. The door opened and Neely rubbed her eyes.

'Geez, what time is it?'

'It's late, but your note said urgent.'

'Yeah. Come on in.'

'Can it wait until tomorrow? I'm awfully tired too, Neely.'

'I'm wide awake now. And freezing!' Neely balanced from one bare foot to the other on the cold floor. Anne followed her into the room as she bounced back into bed and under the covers. She bunched up her knees and grinned. 'Well, guess what!'

'Neely – either tell me or let me go to sleep.'

'We got the show!'

'Fine. Now Neely, if you don't mind, I've got to—'

'That's it? Fine? And good night? The biggest thing that ever happened to me? We land *Hit the Sky* and you dismiss it?'

'*I am* thrilled for you,' Anne said, trying to force some enthusiasm into her voice. 'It's just that this has been a terrible evening.'

Neely looked instantly concerned. 'What happened? Did Allen try to get fresh or something?'

41

'No. He asked me to marry him.'

'What's terrible about that?'

'I don't want to marry him.'

'Then tell him.'

'I did, but he won't listen.'

Neely shrugged. 'Tell him again tomorrow.'

'But it will be in a column.'

Neely looked at her strangely. 'Anne, you're acting funny again. Why on earth would any columnist print that you are marrying some jerky little insurance guy?'

'Because that jerky little insurance guy is a millionaire.'

When Neely finally understood, she was ecstatic. 'Anne!' She leaped out of bed and danced around the room. 'Anne! You've made it!'

'But Neely – I don't *love* Allen!'

'With all that money it will be easy to learn,' Neely insisted.

'But I don't want to get married, or give up my job. I'm on my own for the first time, and I'm not ready to give it up. I've only had two months of freedom—'

'Freedom! You call this freedom?' Neely shrieked. 'Living in a hall bedroom, getting up at seven and rushing to the office, eating lunch at the drugstore, maybe tagging along to '21' once in a while with Bellamy and some client and freezing in that black silk coat? You want to stay free for this kind of gloriousness? Tomorrow is November first. Wait until January and February. Boy, it's gorgeous in New York in February! Nothing but black slush. And that one little stinking radiator in your room is gonna seem like a matchstick. What are you giving up? Just tell me!'

'My identity, maybe my future, my whole life. Giving up before it begins. Neely, nothing ever happened to anyone in my family. They married, had children, and that was it. I want things to happen to me. I want to feel things, to—'

'But it's happened!' Neely hollered. 'Only you hit the jackpot right away. Are you angry because you didn't have to slave away for years, wear six-dollar shoes and bargain-basement clothes? Anne, if you blow this it won't happen again. Do you think when you're bored playing secretary another millionaire will suddenly appear on the scene and say, "Okay, Anne, time to get married"? Ha!'

'I'm not especially looking for someone rich. That's not important.'

Neely sneered. 'You've never been poor.'

'Neely . . . let me put it this way. You're thrilled because you've landed *Hit the Sky*. Suppose after a few weeks of rehearsal someone like Allen came into your life and asked you to marry him and chuck the show before it even opened. Would you?'

'Would I? But so fast it'd make your head spin. Look, let's say I have real talent. And let's say someday I get a chance to prove it. If I work real hard for years, what will I wind up with? Money, position and respect. That's it. That's all there is. And it could take me years of hard work to get that. Allen is handing you the works on a silver platter.'

Anne couldn't believe her ears. Neely with the scrubbed face, looking younger than her seventeen years, pinning everything down so cynically. She started for the door. She was too tired to argue. 'Good night, Neely. We'll talk about it tomorrow.'

'Talk, nothing. You marry him! Maybe I'll come live with you if *Hit the Sky* bombs.'

November, 1945

When the alarm went off, Anne woke with her usual sense of well-being. But as she stretched and came into full consciousness she felt a sudden stab of apprehension. Something was wrong . . .

Allen! Last night! Ronnie Wolfe! Then her apprehension changed to anger. She had done her best. How many ways were there to say no?

She dressed quickly. She'd phone Allen the moment she reached the office. She would settle it once and for all.

There were several men standing in the hall outside the office when she arrived. They parted to let her through. Suddenly one shouted, 'Hey, it's her!' Cameras flashed, questions were shouted. Through the confusion she heard Allen's name. She pushed past them, but they followed her into the office, calling her name. It was like one of her childhood nightmares, where she was pursued and no one tried to help. There was the receptionist – smiling! And the secretary and Miss Steinberg – they were smiling too! Finally she stood trembling behind her desk, surrounded and alone. 'When did you meet Allen Cooper, Miss Welles?' Cameras flashed and blinded her. 'Hey, Annie, look this way, will you . . . that's a good girl . . . smile, Annie . . .' Flash . . . flash . . . 'Will it be a church wedding, Miss Welles?' 'Hey, Annie! How does it feel to be Cinderella?'

She wanted to scream. She dodged around them and fled into Henry Bellamy's office. Lyon Burke caught her as she stumbled in. She started to speak but the door burst open. They had *followed* her! And Henry was smiling . . . greeting them. Lyon was smiling, too.

Henry put his arm around her paternally. 'Now Anne, you've got to get used to this. It's not every day a girl gets engaged to a million-aire.' He felt her trembling and tightened his grip. 'Come on, just relax and make a statement. After all, these boys have to earn a living.'

She faced the reporters. 'What do you want?'

'They want a follow-up story on this.' Henry reached over to his desk and held up a morning tabloid. She stared at the large picture on the front page. There she was, smiling . . . and Allen . . . and the zebra-striped walls. There were big black headlines: BROADWAY'S NEWEST CINDERELLA – ALLEN COOPER TO WED SECRETARY.

Henry put his arm around her again. 'All right, fellows. Take one more. You can title it "Henry Bellamy congratulates his new million-aire secretary."'

More flashes. Someone told her to smile . . . someone asked for another shot . . . someone climbed on a chair and shot down at her . . . several voices asked her to look this way, their voices seeming to come from a distance. It was as if the sea was roaring in her ears, and through it all she saw Lyon Burke watching with a slight smile.

Then Henry was shaking hands, playing the jovial host as he led them out of the office. As the door closed she heard him saying, 'Yeah, they met here in the office . . .'

She stared numbly at the closed door. The sudden silence seemed more unreal than the confusion. Lyon walked over and handed her a lit cigarette. She inhaled deeply and coughed.

'Take it easy,' Lyon said pleasantly.

She collapsed into a chair and looked up at him. 'What shall I do?'

'You're doing fine. You'll get used to it. In time you may even get to like it.'

'I'm not going to marry Allen Cooper.'

'Don't let this throw you. Everyone panics at front-page publicity.'

Henry bustled back into the office. 'Well!' He looked at her with genuine pride. 'Now why did you let me make such a fool of myself yesterday? If I had known the guy was serious I'd never have said those things.'

'Anne has a rare talent,' Lyon said. 'She lets others do the talking.'

She felt her throat close up. (A lady doesn't cry in public.) This was insane. Lyon with that cold smile . . . Henry acting like a proud father.

'I'll call the agency right away,' Henry said. 'You must have a pretty crowded schedule, Anne. Don't worry about things at the office. We'll manage. I'll find someone.'

She felt light-headed. A funny weakness, beginning somewhere under her stomach, seemed to separate her head from her body. Everyone was pulling away from her. Henry was actually thumbing through the phone book for the employment agency!

'You expect me to quit my job?' Her voice was strained.

Henry took her by the shoulders, smiling warmly. 'Honey, I don't think all this has penetrated yet. Wait till you start with the wedding list, the invitations, the fittings, interviews . . . You're going to need a secretary of your own.'

'Henry, I've got to talk to you.'

'I'll leave,' Lyon said. 'Henry rates a private good-by.' He nodded at Anne, and winked. 'Good luck. You deserve the best.'

She watched the door close and turned to Henry. 'I can't believe it. Neither of you seems to care.'

Henry looked bewildered. 'Care? Of course we care. We're delighted for you.'

'But – just like that, you expect me to walk out, never see me again . . . and it doesn't matter. You just replace me with a new girl and life goes on.'

'It matters,' Henry said quietly. 'It matters like hell. Do you think anyone can follow you? Do you think I like the idea of breaking in someone else? But what kind of a friend would I be if I let it matter? And what kind of a friend are you? So you expect to walk out of here and never see me again? Oh no! I'm not letting you off that easily. I expect to be invited to the wedding . . . to be godfather of your first child. Hell, I'll be godfather to all of them. And I'll even learn to love Allen. Actually, I really have nothing against him. He's just so goddam rich, and I was afraid you might get hurt. But now it's different, now I love his money!'

She felt her throat thicken again. 'Lyon didn't care either.'

'Lyon?' Henry looked puzzled. 'Why should Lyon care? Miss Steinberg takes care of his mail and—' He stopped suddenly. His expression changed. 'Oh no . . .' It was almost a groan. 'Not you, Anne. One lousy lunch and you get hooked?'

She looked away. 'It isn't that . . . but we talked . . . I thought we were friends . . .'

He sank down on the leather couch. 'C'mere.' She sat down and he took both her hands. 'Look, Anne, if I had a son I'd want him to be just like Lyon. But if I had a daughter, I'd tell her to stay the hell away from him!'

'That doesn't make much sense . . .'

'Honey . . . without meaning it, some guys are bad news to women. Allen used to be, but you've taken him out of circulation.'

'Bad news in what way?' she asked.

He shrugged. 'Things come too easily to them. With Allen, they came because of his money. With Lyon, it happens because he's so goddam beautiful. And in a way I can understand. Why should these guys settle for one woman when they can have them all, just for the taking? But Anne, you landed Allen, a thing the whole town would have bet couldn't happen. And instead of sending up Roman candles, you're sitting around moping.'

'Henry, I don't love Allen. I dated him for about six weeks in the most casual way. I didn't even know who he was. I mean, I thought he just sold insurance. Then, suddenly, two nights ago, all this began.'

Henry's eyes narrowed. 'He's like a stranger to you, huh?'

'That's right.'

'But one lunch with Lyon, and suddenly you're soul mates?'

'That isn't true. I'm talking about Allen now. I don't love him. Lyon has nothing to do with it.'

'You're a liar.'

'Henry, I swear it. Allen never meant a thing to me.'

'So how come you dated him all these weeks? He was fine until Lyon came along.'

46

'That's not true. I dated him because I didn't know anyone else. And I felt sorry for him. He seemed so innocuous. There was never any talk of romance between us. Why, he never even tried to kiss me good night. Then, two nights ago . . .' She stopped and fought for composure. Her voice was quiet when she went on. 'Henry, I told Allen I didn't love him. I told his father the same thing.'

'You told them that?' He sounded incredulous.

'Yes. Both of them.'

And what did they say?'

'That's what's so unbelievable. I've never known people like them. They seem to ignore anything they don't want to hear. Allen keeps saying he loves me – and that I'll learn to love him.'

'That can happen,' Henry said quietly. 'Sometimes it's the best kind of love. Being loved.'

'No! I want more than that.'

'Sure – like staying here!' Henry snapped. 'Want me to draw the picture for you? You give Allen the air. Sure, why not? Millionaires with marriage proposals are a dime a dozen. In a little while this will blow over. Allen will start dating someone else. Then you figure Lyon will ask you out. That's what you want, isn't it? Oh, it'll be great . . . in the beginning. For maybe a month. Then one day I'll come in and see your eyes are all red. You'll give me a story about a headache, only the red eyes will continue, so I'll talk with Lyon. He'll shrug and say, "Henry, sure I dated the girl. I like her a lot. But she doesn't own me. Have a talk with her, will you? Get her off my back."'

'It sounds like you've had experience,' she said bitterly. 'Do you always make this speech to your secretaries?'

'No – not to my secretaries. But then we've never had one who looked like you. But yes, I have made the speech before, dozens of times. To girls with more know-how than you. Unfortunately, I had to make the speech *after* the damage was done, when they were carrying a torch bigger than China. But at least they didn't go around giving up millionaires first.'

'You make him sound like quite a heel,' she said.

'What heel? He's a guy, free and single. And any girl who appeals to him is the right girl – for the moment. And there are a hell of a lot of moments and a hell of a lot of right girls around this town.'

'I can't believe every man feels that way.'

47

'Lyon Burke isn't "every man." Just like New York isn't "every town." Sure, maybe there will come a time when Lyon gets his fill and will settle for one girl. But that will only come after a lot of living – and even then he'll never *really* settle for just that girl.'

The phone jangled. Automatically Anne started to get it. He waved her aside. 'Sit down, heiress. Remember, you don't work here any more.' He walked to the desk. 'Hello . . . sure, put her on. Hi, Jennifer. Yeah, it's all set . . . What? Yeah, how about that? Matter of fact, she's sitting right here. Sure she's thrilled. You should see her – she's wearing out my rug dancing for joy.' He turned to Anne. 'Jennifer North sends you her congratulations.' He returned to the phone. 'Yeah, you bet she's lucky. Listen, baby, the contracts should be ready today. Soon as I okay them, I'll send them around for you to sign . . . Fine, honey . . . check with you around five.' He hung up. 'Now there's a smart girl. Jennifer North.'

'Who is she?'

Henry groaned. 'Oh, come on! Don't you ever read the papers? She just unloaded a prince. She's been on the front pages almost every day. She burst into town from nowhere, like a cyclone – actually she's from California, about your age – and wham! along comes this prince. The real thing, with money, too. He courts her, the whole works – mink coat, diamond ring. The AP, UP, all the press covers it. A mayor in Jersey officiates. Every celebrity in town goes to the reception. Four days later, front pages – she wants an annulment.'

'But you aren't a divorce lawyer.'

'No. She's got a good lawyer working on that, but he recommended me as a business manager. And she sure needs one. For a smart girl, she did one very stupid thing. Seems she signed a little thing like a premarital agreement. If she wants out, she doesn't get a dime. And she wants out. Won't say why – just wants to unload him. So she's got to work.'

'Is she talented?'

Henry smiled. 'She doesn't need talent. If she wants it she's a cinch for pictures. You've never seen such a kisser. And her figure . . . I'd say Jennifer North is about the most beautiful girl in the world.' He paused. 'Actually, that's not true. You're more beautiful, Anne. The longer a guy looks at you, the more beautiful you become. But Jennifer – her beauty hits you right in the eye. The first glance carries a thousand volts. She's got it made. As soon as we get that annulment and she opens in *Hit the Sky,* I'm a cinch to land her a big movie deal.'

'Does she sing?' Anne asked.

'I told you – she does nothing.'

'But if she's in *Hit the Sky* . . .'

'I've set her in a small bit – sort of a glorified showgirl – with feature billing. Helen okayed it. That's one thing I taught Helen way back. Carry the show talentwise, but surround yourself with pretty scenery. But why am I talking about Helen, or Jennifer? It's you I'm concerned about. I've got my lumps coming up with them later.'

'Henry, I want to keep my job with you . . .'

'Translated, "Henry, I want to have a go at Lyon Burke,"' he snapped.

'I won't even look at him if that's what's worrying you.'

Henry shook his head. 'You're begging for a broken heart and I'm not going to be a part of it. Now get out of here – you're fired! Go marry Allen Cooper and be happy.'

She stood up. 'All right. I'll get out. But I won't marry Allen Cooper. I'll get another job.' She started for the door.

'Go ahead. If you louse up your life, at least I won't have to sit and watch.'

'You're not really a friend, Henry.'

'I'm the best friend you'll ever have.'

'Then let me stay,' she pleaded. 'Henry, you don't understand. I don't want to marry Allen. But if I leave here and get another job, it might be a job I don't like. And Allen would be pressuring me, and all the publicity that would follow if I took another job . . . and Allen's father with the questions. You don't know what happens when Gino and Allen start in. It's like you're carried along, with no will of your own. Henry, please – help me. I don't want to marry Allen Cooper!'

'Anne, he's got millions – billions, maybe.'

'I ran away from Willie Henderson in Lawrenceville, Henry. Maybe he didn't have as many millions as Allen, but he had money. And I've known Willie all my life, and his family. Can't you see it doesn't mean anything to me? I don't care about money.'

He was silent for a moment. 'Okay,' he said finally. 'You can stay . . . on one condition. You stay engaged to Allen.'

'Henry! Are you out of your mind? Haven't you been listening to me? I don't *want* to marry Allen.'

'I didn't say marry. I said engaged! That way you'll be safe.'

'Safe?'

'Yes. At least I won't worry about you getting involved with Lyon. One thing about Lyon – he doesn't go after another guy's girl.'

She smiled faintly. 'At least you give him some code of honor.'

'What honor? He doesn't need that kind of trouble. There's too much free stuff thrown at him.'

'And what about me? If I stay engaged, what do I do with Allen?'

'Stall him. You can do it. If you were smart enough to land him, you're smart enough to stall him.'

'But that's dishonest. I don't want to marry Allen, but I still like him as a person. It wouldn't be fair.'

'You'll be more fair in the long run. First of all, you'll be fair to me. I'll have enough to worry about with the show starting without worrying about you. And you'll be fair to Allen . . . yes, you will. Because at least he'll have a chance to make a decent pitch. But most of all you'll be fair to yourself because right now you can't see any further than Lyon Burke.' He raised a hand to silence her objection. 'No matter what you think, you're stuck on him. But hang around, start reading the Broadway columns and see how fast he changes girls. The glow will wear off from that wonderful luncheon. And you'll have saved your virginity and a lot of heartache.' He smiled as she colored. 'Look, Anne, you're pretty rare – we've got to take care of you.'

She thought about it a moment, then shook her head. 'I couldn't do it, Henry. It would be living a lie.'

'Anne . . .' His voice was gentle. 'In time you'll learn everything doesn't have to be black or white. You can be honest with Allen. Tell him New York is still new, that you want to be on your own for a little while, not rush right into marriage. When will you be twenty-one?'

'In May.'

'Fine. Tell him you want to wait until then.'

'And then what?'

'By May another atom bomb could fall. Allen could meet another girl. Lyon Burke could turn into a fag. Who knows, anything can happen. You might even fall in love with Allen. But you can change your mind in May. Remember, you're never stuck until you're at the altar. And even then you can make a run for it before the final words are said.'

'You make it sound so easy.'

'When you're climbing Mount Everest, nothing is easy. You just take one step at a time, never look back and always keep your eyes glued to the top.'

She spotted the reporters and cameramen standing in front of her brownstone when she came home. She held her head down and dashed up the steps, brushing through them into the safety of the building. Neely was standing in the hall waiting.

'Anne, oh golly – I almost fainted when my sister called me this morning. Here' – she proudly extended a flat package – 'it's my engagement present to you.'

It was a large scrapbook filled with the newspaper stories and pictures of Anne. 'I worked on it all day,' Neely said proudly. 'I filled six pages and this is only the beginning. Wait until the marriage and all . . . Golly, you're gonna be famous!'

That night Allen arrived with the limousine. 'We're having dinner alone,' he said, 'but Gino will join us for coffee. I know I promised we'd be alone, but he insists on taking us to Tony Polar's opening at La Ronde.'

'Tony Polar?'

He smiled. 'Anne – don't tell me you're not one of his fans?'

'I've never even heard of him.'

Allen laughed. 'He's the biggest singing sensation since Sinatra.' He leaned across and spoke to the chauffeur. 'Leon, drive through the park till I tell you to stop.' Then he rolled up the window. 'You're probably starving, but I have a special reason for the drive.'

He took her hand. She pulled it away. 'Allen, I've got to talk to you.'

'Not just yet – shut your eyes.' He snapped open a small velvet box. 'Now you can look. I hope it fits.'

Even in the darkness of the car, with only the intermittent streetlights to give it life, the diamond was overwhelming.

She shrank away. 'I can't take that!'

'Don't you like it?'

'Like it! It's the most fantastic thing I've ever seen!'

'Ten karats,' he said easily. 'But in a square cut it's not at all ostentatious.'

'Of course not.' She laughed nervously. 'Every secretary has one.'

'Which reminds me – have you handed in your notice to Henry Bellamy?'

'No, and I don't intend to. Allen, you've simply got to listen to me. We're not engaged—'

He slipped the ring on her finger. 'It just fits.'

She looked at him intently. 'Allen . . . can't you understand what I'm trying to tell you?'

'Yes. That you're not in love with me.'

'Then why do you go on like this?'

'Because there's nothing in the world you can't get if you want it badly enough. And I've never really wanted anything – until I met you. I'm determined to have you, Anne. Just give me a chance. That's all I ask. You've seen me for the past weeks as some timid jerk. One month with the real me and you'll either love me or hate me. I'll take the chance.'

He rolled down the window. 'Okay, Leon. Take us to the Stork Club now.'

She was silent. Did he really think things would change? Rich or poor, his chemistry was the same. Allen was Allen, in a cheap French restaurant or at El Morocco.

She felt the world closing in on her. It was easy for Henry Bellamy to sit behind a desk and deal with facts and offer ultimatums. He wasn't dealing with people. He couldn't see the expression in Allen's eyes.

Her depression lasted through the ride, and she could find little to say as they were ushered through the echelons of captains to the Stork Club's Cub Room ('It's the only room') and presented with a gift-wrapped box ('It's perfume – Sherman sends it to all his favorites') and champagne ('We'd better drink it or we might hurt Sherman's feelings').

Gino arrived at ten, greeting friends at various tables in a loud voice that brought a slight frown to Allen's face. At last Gino joined their table and tore into the champagne.

'Dad, you shouldn't table-hop here,' Allen said quietly. 'You know they don't like it.'

'Who cares?' Gino said loudly. 'Listen kid, this here's your hangout. You can have it. I don't go for the snob treatment. When someone's willing to take my money, I want to act the way I feel comfortable . . . not to some crazy set of rules. What you do is your own business.'

Allen seemed relieved when they left the Stork and went to La Ronde.

Judging from the voracious welcome Gino got from all the captains, La Ronde was one of his favorite haunts. He hugged several of them and called them *paisan* as they escorted him to a choice ringside table. It was eleven o'clock and the club was already filled. Gino ordered champagne and a bottle of Scotch. 'Adele likes Scotch,' he said. 'She'll be here after her show. She says champagne is too fattening.'

Anne watched the people crowding to the tables, arguing for better locations, palming bills discreetly into the captain's hand. Photographers hired by the club to service the newspapers came over and took pictures of Anne and Allen and returned to the door to await more celebrities.

Adele arrived at eleven-thirty wearing full stage makeup.

'Whaddaya wearing that crap for?' Gino demanded. 'You know I hate it.'

'Gee, sweetie, I powdered it down and took off my false lashes. I didn't want to miss anything and it takes so long to get this off and put on a new face.' She looked around the room while she spoke. 'God, this is the biggest opening of the season. Everyone is here.' She waved gustily at a columnist.

'A couple of years ago it was Sinatra,' Allen said. 'Now the women are killing themselves over Tony Polar. I don't get it.'

'Don't knock it,' Gino said with a grin. 'They're both our *paisans*.'

'Hey, look . . .' Adele pointed. 'There's Helen Lawson at the door. Look at her mink, it's practically turning red. I bet it's ten years old. And with all her money. I hear she's the tightest – Hey, that must be Jennifer North!'

'*Maron!*' Gino pounded the table. 'Now that's what I call a build! Hey, Adele – beside her, you look like a boy.'

Anne's attention had also been drawn to Jennifer North, who was now surrounded by photographers. The girl was undeniably beautiful. She was tall, with a spectacular figure. Her white dress, shimmering with crystal beads, was cut low enough to prove the authenticity of her remarkable cleavage. Her long hair was almost white in its blondeness. But it was her face that held Anne's attention, a face so naturally beautiful that it came as a startling contrast to the theatrical beauty of her hair and figure. It was a perfect face with a fine square jaw, high cheekbones and intelligent brow. The eyes seemed warm and friendly, and the short, straight nose belonged to a beautiful child, as did the even white teeth and little-girl dimples. It was an innocent face, a face that looked at everything with breathless excitement and trusting enthusiasm, seemingly unaware of the commotion the body was causing. A face that glowed with genuine interest in each person who demanded attention, rewarding each with a warm smile. The body and its accoutrements continued to pose and undulate for the staring crowd and flashing cameras, but the face ignored the furor and greeted people with the intimacy of meeting a few new friends at a gathering.

Somehow the captains managed to lead her to a ringside table directly across the room. Anne did not see Henry Bellamy until the party was seated.

'Say, your boss really picks his dates,' Allen said. 'Helen Lawson and Jennifer North. That's some parlay.'

'No, there's another guy,' Adele said. 'See, he's just sitting down. That must be Jennifer's date. Hey, he's gorgeous!'

'That's Lyon Burke,' Anne said quietly.

'Oh, so that's Burke,' Allen said.

Anne nodded as she watched Lyon help Jennifer adjust her fur on the back of the chair. Jennifer rewarded this courtesy with a blinding smile.

Allen whistled. 'I wonder if that Golden Venus is going to be bouncing around in my old bed tonight.'

'She's Mr. Bellamy's client,' Anne said coldly. 'I imagine Lyon Burke is just acting as escort.'

'Sure. And he's making Henry pay him overtime for such a rough assignment.'

'Well, Henry struck it rich with Helen Lawson,' Gino said. 'That old bag pays better dividends than A.T.&T. She's got a lotta mileage on her, but I'll still pay a broker fifty bucks for a pair of seats to see her. She's got a great set of pipes.'

54

Allen pointed out the continuing flow of arriving celebrities, giving a complete rundown on their personal lives. Anne managed a show of interest, but her attention kept returning to Henry's table. What could a girl like Jennifer be saying that was so amusing? And what was Lyon saying to her? It was obvious he wasn't telling her about the bombed-out barn and the corporal. She saw him throw back his head and laugh. He hadn't laughed like that at the Barberry Room. No, she had been the dreary girl from the office who had urged him to write, had gotten him all involved so he remembered the ugly things in his past. She turned away as he lit a cigarette and handed it to Jennifer.

The lights suddenly dimmed. Waiters dashed to take last-minute orders. Gradually all activity stopped, the audience grew expectantly silent, the room went dark and the orchestra played a song identified with Tony Polar. The spotlight centered on the stage and then Tony walked on, to a boisterous ovation. He bowed and accepted the applause with pleasant modesty. He was tall and good-looking, with a boyishness that made him seem vulnerable and appealing. A girl would trust him. A woman would want to protect him.

Although he appeared shy, he sang well and handled the audience with an easy assurance. After his first set of songs, he loosened his tie to show he was really working hard, took a hand mike and walked around the room, spotting various celebrities, singing to them, clowning with the newspapermen, selecting a few matrons and favoring them with portions of a love lyric, smiling shyly as they gushed openly, oblivious to the presence of their embarrassed husbands.

When he passed Jennifer, their eyes met. He missed a lyric and moved along quickly. Then, as if not believing what he had seen, he slowly retraced his steps and finished the song with his eyes riveted on her. The audience, transformed into a body of eavesdroppers, watched eagerly. When he finished his song, he bowed, returned to the center of the room and went through the rest of the performance without looking at her again.

The audience refused to let him off. He took bow after bow. The lights came up but the applause continued, accompanied by stamping and demands of 'More! More!' The orchestra, uncertain, played a few bars of his theme as if waiting for some definite order. The applause grew more insistent. He stood there, smiling in boyish gratitude. He pointed to his throat, gesturing fatigue. The applause grew even louder. Then, shrugging good-naturedly, he held a hurried conference with his accompanist and returned to the center of the floor.

When the music began, he turned and sang directly to Jennifer. It was a current love ballad, and like many popular songs, the words could take on a highly personal meaning. It seemed to have been written just so Tony Polar could confess to Jennifer and the eight hundred people in the room that he had suddenly found love.

He finished the song, bowed to the audience, turned back and looked at Jennifer intently for an embarrassingly long moment, and then walked off. There was more insistent applause, but the lights came up and the orchestra went into a loud set of dance music.

Allen asked Anne to dance. As she rose, she noticed Lyon leading Jennifer to the floor. He saw her and waved.

'Anne! And this must be Allen, my landlord.' His smile was quick and warm. Introductions were exchanged as they all swayed to the music. Several times Anne was jostled by couples who pressed closer to stare at Jennifer.

Jennifer smiled warmly at Anne. 'Isn't it murder? Every time I move, at least a hundred beads pop off this dress.'

Anne searched for an answer, but she could only manage a frozen smile. They parted, and Allen danced her off to another part of the small floor.

The crowd quickly thinned out, leaving only the few stragglers who remained to drink out their minimum. Anne noticed that Jennifer's table had been one of the first to be deserted. She wondered where they had gone. Some place with a larger dance floor, perhaps. Her head ached and she wanted desperately to leave, but Gino showed no inclination to end the evening.

'Let's go to Morocco for a nightcap,' he said when the waiter brought the check.

Anne secretly blessed Adele, who announced it was too late – she had a matinee the following day.

A few days later Anne was back in the columns. Ronnie Wolfe had an item about the engagement ring. She arrived at the office to find Miss Steinberg and the girls waiting in quivering excitement.

'Let's see it!' the receptionist demanded. 'When did you get it?'

'Is it really over ten karats?' Miss Steinberg asked.

Anne reluctantly held out her hand as they gasped over the ring. She had been wearing it turned the other way and it had escaped detection. It was too valuable to leave in her furnished room, and she had been promising herself to return it to Allen as soon as she could – but now it was an item.

She was sorting the mail when Lyon Burke came in. He stopped at her desk, picked up her hand, whistled and dropped it. 'Heavy, isn't it?' Then he added, 'He seems like quite a decent chap, Anne.'

'He's very nice,' she said lamely. 'And Jennifer North seemed very nice too.'

A curious expression crossed his face. 'Jennifer North is one of the nicest girls I have ever known,' he said quietly. '*Really* nice.' Then he walked into his office.

She sat back miserably. Had she sounded insincere? Jennifer *was* nice. She had meant it. Perhaps it had come out wrong because she was flustered.

She ducked lunch with the girls and spent the hour wandering along Fifth Avenue. Staring vacantly into the window of a novelty shop, she thought of Neely. She had bought Neely a rabbit's foot yesterday – rehearsals for *Hit the Sky* started this morning. She envied Neely, so vibrant and uncomplicated. Nothing bad could ever happen to someone like Neely.

There was a newspaper propped up on her desk when she returned. One of the girls had probably put it there. Probably some other item about the ring. She was about to drop it into the waste basket when she saw the office memo clipped to the corner. *Memo from Lyon Burke* was printed on it, and in his hand was scribbled, *Perhaps of interest to Anne Welles. Story on page two.*

It was a beautiful picture of Jennifer – and Tony Polar! The black caption blazed: BROADWAY'S NEWEST ROMANCE. The story was written tongue in cheek. 'It was a lightning bolt that struck me,' Tony was quoted as having said. Jennifer's prose was less explosive, but she blushingly admitted the attraction was mutual. They had been introduced after the show by a mutual friend, Lyon Burke.

'Lyon just brought her in and handed her over,' Tony had gone on. 'He said to me, "Tony, I told you I had an opening night present for you."'

57

Anne closed the paper and sat back, suddenly weak with an inexplicable happiness. 'Lyon handed her over . . .' The line kept running through her mind.

'Anne . . .'

She came out of her reverie. Neely was standing in front of her desk.

'Anne, I know it's awful my coming here. But I couldn't go home. I had to see you.' Neely's face was splotched with tears.

'Why aren't you at rehearsal?' Anne asked.

Neely suddenly broke into uncontrolled sobs.

Anne shot a worried look toward the closed door to Henry's office. 'Neely, sit down.' She pushed Neely into her chair. 'Stay there . . . try to control yourself. I'll get my coat. We'll go home.'

'I don't wanna go home,' Neely said stubbornly. 'I couldn't face that room. I was so happy when I left it this morning. I wrote "The Gaucheros make Broadway!" on the mirror in lipstick. I couldn't face it now.'

'But Neely, you can't sit here and – have a breakdown.'

'Who says I can't? I didn't go to Radcliffe. If I feel like having a breakdown, I'll have it wherever I want. And right now I happen to be here.' The tears spilled down her face and onto her dress. '*Ooooh!*' She sobbed louder. 'Look . . . my new dress, and it's all spotted with my crying. It's ruined, isn't it?'

'Button your coat. It will clean.' She watched Neely obediently button her coat. Secretly, she couldn't feel sorry about the dress. It was awful. ('Neely, people don't wear purple taffeta to work,' she had said when Neely brought the dress home. 'You don't,' Neely had argued, 'but I want to stand out at rehearsal.')

Anne sat down. 'All right, Neely, if you insist on staying here. Try to tell me about it quietly. Why aren't you at rehearsal?'

'Anne, I'm not in the show.'

'You mean they're not using The Gaucheros?'

'Oh, Anne, it was awful! They are – and they aren't . . .'

'Well, start from the beginning. What happened?'

'I got there this morning, five minutes early even. I was all caked up and I had your rabbit's foot in my bag. Then some skinny fag with a crew cut came in, carrying a book of the script. Dick and Charlie arrived next—'

'Neely, get to the point!'

'There is no point. I'm telling you how it happened. Then the showgirls arrived. I began to feel real crummy. Even in my new dress. You should see the getups on some of those showgirls. Six of them had real mink coats, and the rest had beaver or silver fox. Not one cloth coat! And everyone knew everyone else, except us. And when Jennifer North arrived, you'da thought Rita Hayworth was making an entrance. The assistant director rushed to her with cooing noises like how glad he was she was joining them. She was ten minutes late and he was making like it was a thrill that she managed to come. I felt lousy, like we just didn't fit. We looked like vaudeville and cheap clubs. Charlie hadn't shaved close enough and Dick seemed more faggy than ever, and my taffeta dress suddenly looked like it cost ten ninety-eight. For about fifteen minutes everyone kept greeting everyone and talking about the last show they did together. Even the chorus kids knew each other. Then the director got there. I think he's a fag, too.'

'Neely . . .' Anne tried to cover her exasperation. 'Please, just tell me what happened.'

'I am! I'm not leaving out a thing. Then Helen Lawson walked in like the Queen of England. The director introduced her. He said, "Cast, your star. Miss Lawson." I felt like maybe we should all stand up and sing *The Star-Spangled Banner* or something. The director walked around with her and introduced her to the people she didn't know. Then she met us . . .' Neely stopped. Her eyes brimmed with fresh tears.

'Then what?' Anne was insistent.

'She nodded at Dick and Charlie but looked right over me like I wasn't even there. She's ice water, Anne. Then she said, real tough like, to Dick and Charlie, "Oh yeah. You're The Gaucheros. We're gonna do a dance together. You fellas better eat a lot of spinach, because you're gonna have to toss me around."'

'*Her?*'

'That's right. *Her.* I stood up and said, "Hi, Miss Lawson. You know there's three Gaucheros. I'm one of them. I'm Neely . . ." And without even looking at me, she turned to the director and said, "I thought that had all been settled." Then she turned and walked away. Then maybe a few minutes later the director called Charlie off into a corner and they had a little talk. It looked like the director was telling

Charlie off good, and Charlie was trying to explain something. Then Charlie comes back and says, "Look, Neely, they didn't pick us to really do our dance. They picked us because they want us to do a comedy number burlesquing our dance. It's a dream sequence, and we're supposed to toss Helen Lawson around."'

'But what about you?' Anne demanded. 'You have a contract.'

Neely shook her head. 'Charlie always signs our contracts. This one just says "The Gaucheros." It's for five hundred a week. He and Dick were to get two hundred each and I was to get one hundred. Now Charlie says I'll get the hundred anyway, even if I don't work. But I don't trust him. If he'd toss me out this easy, how can I believe he'll pay me? Besides, what am I supposed to do? Just sit in that lousy room and mope? I don't know anyone – my whole life has been the act.'

'It *is* awful,' Anne agreed. 'But I can see Charlie's dilemma. If they just sprang this on him, he can't afford to walk out on all that money. Maybe to keep busy you could find another job.'

'Doing what?'

'Well . . . let's go home and talk about it. We'll figure out something. I can send you to the employment office I went to and—'

'I can't type. I got no college degree. I can't do anything – and besides, I wanna be in the show!' Neely started to sob violently again.

'Please, Neely,' Anne begged. She knew Miss Steinberg and the girls were staring, but her worst fear materialized when Lyon Burke opened his door. She smiled at him weakly as he came over and stared at the shrieking Neely.

'This is Neely. She's a little upset.'

'I'd say that was a classic understatement.'

Neely looked up. 'Geez, I'm sorry. When I cry, I cry loud.' She looked at him, wide eyed. 'You're not Henry Bellamy, are you?'

'No, I'm Lyon Burke.'

Neely smiled through her tears. 'Geez, now I see what Anne means.'

'Neely's had a big disappointment today,' Anne said quickly.

'Disappointment! I'm ready to die.' Neely went on to prove it with a fresh outpouring of sobs.

'Well, it must be quite uncomfortable dying out here in a straight-backed chair,' Lyon said. 'Why don't we transfer this wake into my office?'

60

Sprawled comfortably in Lyon's leather chair, Neely repeated the entire story, punctuated with fresh howls.

When she had finished, Anne looked at Lyon and said, 'It *is* a shocking thing to have happen. This show meant so much to her.'

Lyon nodded sympathetically. 'But I can't believe Helen would do such a thing.'

'She's a killer,' Neely shouted.

Lyon shook his head. 'Oh, I'm not defending her. She's rough – but this is just not like Helen. She'd have someone else do her axing – unless she was taken by surprise.'

'It happened just like I said. I'm not making it up,' Neely insisted.

Lyon lit a cigarette and seemed thoughtful for a moment. Then he said, 'Would you accept being in the show even if you weren't part of The Gaucheros?'

'Those bums! After the way they dumped me, I'd do anything not to have to work with them again. But what could I do in the show?'

'A musical is quite elastic,' Lyon said. 'Now it's up to us to stretch it a bit.' He picked up the phone and dialed. They both listened as he asked for Gilbert Case, the producer of the show. Lyon was affable as he exchanged greetings, discussed the coming football schedule. Then, almost as an afterthought, he added, 'By the way, Gil, you've signed an act called The Gaucheros . . . Yes, I know Helen wants to clown a dance with them. But you did know there were *three* Gaucheros . . . yes . . . of course it's not your business . . .' He held his hand over the receiver while Gil Case ranted on and whispered to Neely, 'Your brother-in-law is really a louse – he sold you out before he signed the contract.'

Neely leaped up. 'You mean that slob let me come to rehearsal and make a fool of myself! Why I'll—'

Lyon motioned her to be quiet. But Neely's eyes were blazing with anger. 'I'm gonna go over there and kill him,' she muttered.

'Look, Gil,' Lyon said in an easy voice, 'I know it's not really your concern. Technically you're in the clear. If the boys promised you they'd take care of their partner, quite naturally you believed them.'

Anne saw him staring at Neely. She knew he was stalling for time. He put his hand over the phone again and whispered, 'Neely, how old are you? Truth!'

'Nineteen—'

'She's seventeen,' Anne hissed.

'I have to say I'm nineteen to work in some states,' Neely argued.

Lyon's face broke into a victorious smile. 'Look, Gil,' he said cheerfully. 'We certainly don't want any trouble. We have Helen Lawson in the show, plus the choreographer and Jennifer North. It's to our advantage to have everything run smoothly. The last thing any of us wants is a lawsuit. Yes, I said lawsuit. Gil, this little partner The Gaucheros brushed off is only seventeen. And these chaps have been trotting her across the country for some time, lying about her age. Now if she wanted to sue them it could get messy. I imagine the contract is just for The Gaucheros . . . nothing about an agreement to dissolve the current act. Gil, I *know* they told you it would be all right – but the fact is, it *isn't* all right. How do I know she'll sue? Because she's sitting right here.' He winked at Neely and leisurely lit a fresh cigarette.

'Now Gil, of course I know it's rough to start looking for a new dance team. But I think we can solve things right on the phone. The Gaucheros have a standard Equity contract for five hundred, right? You can drop them any time during the first five days without paying them a dime, right? Then just give them the facts of life and issue them a new contract for four hundred, then issue another contract to their little partner for one hundred. Put her in the chorus, let her understudy, do bits – anything, just so long as she's in the show. It doesn't cost you an extra penny and everyone's happy . . . Of course. Yes, I'll tell her to report back to rehearsal tomorrow . . . Delighted . . . The Copa? When, tonight? Love to join you. All right, see you there.'

He hung up and smiled at Neely. 'Young lady, you are in the show.'

She crossed the room and threw her arms around him in a spontaneous burst of gratitude. 'Oh, Mr. Burke . . . golly, you're terrific!' Then she rushed back to Anne and hugged her. 'Oh, Anne, I love you! I'll never forget this. You're the only friend I have. Even my brother-in-law turned against me. And my sister – that louse musta known about it! Charlie wouldn't dare pull this whammy without letting her know. Oh, Anne, if I ever make it – or get anywhere – or if you ever need anything, I'll repay you. I swear, I'll—'

Anne gently released herself from the frenzied embrace. 'I'm glad for you, Neely. Really I am.'

The phone buzzed. Lyon picked it up. 'It's Gil Case again,' he whispered, one hand over the mouthpiece. Anne felt a lurch of apprehension until Lyon laughed.

'I don't know, Gil.' He turned to Neely. 'By the way – what *is* your name?'

The childish eyes opened wide. 'It's Neely.'

'Neely,' Lyon repeated into the phone. 'Yes, N-e-e-l-y.' He looked back to Neely for confirmation. She nodded vaguely. Then he asked, 'Neely what?'

She stared at him. 'Oh gosh . . . I don't know. I mean, I've never had to bother with a name because I've been one of The Gaucheros. I can't use Ethel Agnes O'Neill.'

Lyon placed his hand over the phone. 'Shall I tell him to wait until tomorrow, until you come up with something?'

'And give him a chance to change his mind? Not on your life! Anne, what shall I call myself? Can I use your name? Neely Welles?'

Anne smiled. 'You can think of something more exciting.'

Neely looked at Lyon wildly. 'Mr. Burke?'

He shook his head. 'Neely Burke has no magic.'

Neely stood still for a moment. Suddenly her eyes flashed. 'Neely O'Hara!'

'What?' Lyon and Anne choked on the word together.

'Neely O'Hara. It's perfect. I'm Irish, and Scarlett is my favorite person—'

'She's just read *Gone with the Wind*,' Anne explained.

'Neely, I'm sure we could come up with something more euphonious,' Lyon suggested.

'More what?'

'Yes, Gil, I'm still with you,' Lyon said. 'We're just having a small board meeting on a name.'

'I want to be Neely O'Hara,' Neely insisted stubbornly.

'It's Neely O'Hara,' Lyon said with a grin. 'Yes, O'Hara. That's right. And have the contract at rehearsal tomorrow – she's the nervous type. And Gil, make it a white contract – standard Equity, not chorus. Let's start the girl off right.' He hung up. 'And now, Miss Neely O'Hara, you'd better go over to Actors Equity and join immediately. There's a rather stiff initiation fee – might be well over a hundred dollars. If you need an advance . . .'

'I've got seven hundred dollars saved,' Neely said proudly.

'Fine. And if you're really determined to stay with the name, I'll be glad to put through the necessary forms to make it legal.'

'You mean so no one can steal it?'

He smiled. 'Well – let's say it will make things easier. Your checking account, Social Security . . .'

'Checking account? Geez, when would I ever need a checking account?'

The phone buzzed again. 'Oh, Geez,' Neely muttered. 'I bet he's changed his mind.'

Lyon picked it up. 'Hello? Oh, hi . . .' His voice changed. 'Yes, I saw the story in the paper. I told you all along I was just playing Cupid . . . Come now . . .' He laughed. 'You make me feel seven feet tall. Look, Diane angel, there are some people in the office and I'm keeping them waiting. We can talk about it tonight. Would you like to see the show at the Copa? Gil Case invited us along . . . Fine, I'll pick you up around eight . . . Good girl. 'By.' He turned back to Neely and Anne with a slight smile that begged forgiveness for the interruption.

Anne stood up. 'We've already taken up too much of your time. Thank you very much, Lyon.'

'Not at all. I owed you a whopper of a favor . . . in fact, I owe you the very bed I sleep in. At least this helped even the score.'

When they were in the outer office, Neely did a pirouette and hugged Anne ecstatically. 'Anne, I'm so happy I could shout at the top of my lungs!'

'I'm very happy for you, Neely.'

Neely stared at her. 'Hey, what's the matter? You look upset. Are you mad because I busted in like I did? I'm sorry. But Lyon wasn't mad and Mr. Bellamy didn't even know I was here. See, it all worked just fine. Please, Anne, say you're not mad or it will ruin my whole day.'

'I'm not mad – just a little tired. Honestly, Neely.' Anne sat down at her desk.

Neely looked puzzled. 'Yeah, I guess we both have been through a lot of excitement.' She leaned over and hugged Anne. 'Oh, Anne, some day I'll make this all up to you . . . somehow. I swear I will!'

She watched Neely skip out of the office. Mechanically, she inserted a fresh piece of paper in the typewriter. The carbon smudged her engagement ring. She polished it carefully, then began to type.

*

Anne found herself living with *Hit the Sky*. In the beginning her exposure was limited to Neely's detailed descriptions of the daily rehearsals. Neely was in the chorus, and for three days she showed Anne every step. Then came the startling announcement: Neely had a 'part' – three lines in a crowd scene. But the crowning achievement was the understudy role.

'Can you stand it?' Neely asked. '*Me* – understudying Terry King! Terry has the second lead, and usually with Helen they have the dreariest ingenue they can find. But Terry King is sexy and beautiful. Imagine me ever trying to look sexy and beautiful!'

'Then why did they choose you?'

'Guess they were stuck. I'm the only one in the chorus who can sing. And besides, they usually don't hire real understudies until the show comes in. I'm just a standby job for the tour.'

'Do you sing well, Neely?'

'Huh? Oh, I sing like I dance. Though I must say I get the steps a lot quicker than most of those chorus girls.' She did a high kick and narrowly missed a lamp. 'Now all I need is a boyfriend and I'll be set.'

'Is there anyone attractive in the show?'

'Are you kidding? A musical is like a sexual desert – unless you're a fag. Dickie is having a ball with all those chorus boys – it's like smorgasbord. The leading man is straight – handsome, too – but he has a wife who looks like his mother, and she sits around and watches him every second. The guy who plays opposite Terry King is bald without his rug. The only normal man is the old lech who plays Helen's father. He's sixty-five if he's a day, but he's always trying to grab a feel. But one of the girls in the chorus has a boyfriend who's got a friend named Mel Harris. He's a press agent, and she's going to arrange for me to double-date with them. I hope something comes out of it . . . It'd be awful not to have a date on my own opening night. Are you still going to the New York opening with George Bellows?'

'Of course not. I'm . . . well . . . I'm engaged to Allen.'

'Then lemme buy you a pair of seats for the opening. It'll be my present to you.'

'Don't you get seats free?'

'Are you kidding? No one does, not even Helen Lawson. But she gets to buy four house seats every night, and someone told me when a show is a hit she sells them to a scalper and makes a fortune.'

'But Neely, I couldn't let you buy my seats . . . Allen will get them. And Neely, if the Mel thing doesn't work out, we'll take you out after your opening.'

Neely had her date with Mel Harris the following week. He was divine, she insisted. He had taken her to Toots Shor's and told her all about himself. He was twenty-six, had been graduated from New York University, was a press agent but one day hoped to be a producer. He lived in a small midtown hotel and went to Brooklyn every Friday night to have dinner with his family.

'You see, Jewish men are very family conscious,' Neely explained.

'Do you really like him?' Anne asked.

'I love him!'

'Neely, you've only had one date. How can you be in love?'

'Look who's talking. All you had was one lunch with Lyon Burke.'

'Neely! There's nothing between Lyon Burke and me. I don't even think about him. In fact, I'm getting quite fond of Allen.'

'Well, I *know* I love Mel. He's beautiful. Not beautiful like Lyon, but great.'

'What *does* he look like?'

Neely shrugged. 'Maybe a little like Georgie Jessel, but to me he's gorgeous. And he didn't try to get fresh, either. Even when I lied and said I was twenty. I was afraid seventeen would scare him off.'

Neely cocked her head toward the open door. They were sitting in Anne's room, and the telephone was downstairs in front of Neely's room. It was both a convenience and a hazard. She was constantly forced to take messages for everyone in the house.

'This time it's for me,' she shrieked as she heard the tinny ring.

Five minutes later she bounded back, breathlessly triumphant. 'It was him! He's taking me to the Martinique tonight. He handles some singer there.'

'He must do very well,' Anne said.

'No, he only makes a hundred a week. He works for Irving Steiner and Irving handles about twelve big accounts. But soon he's going out on his own, though he's trying to get connected with radio. You know, Jewish men make marvelous husbands.'

'So I've heard. But how do they feel about Irish girls?'

Neely knit her brows. 'Look, I can always tell him I'm part Jewish. That I took the O'Hara as a stage name.'

'Neely, you'd never get away with it.'

'If I had to, I would. I'm going to marry him. You watch.' She hugged herself and danced across the room, singing softly.

'That's a pretty song. What is it?'

'From the show. Hey Anne, why don't you take that mink coat Allen's father offered you and sell me your black coat? I need a black coat.'

'Neely, sing that song again.'

'Why?'

'Just sing it.'

'It's Terry King's number. But I think Helen Lawson is planning to take it. She's already taken one of Terry's songs. Poor Terry only has two left, this and another. One's a real torcher – Helen can't take that from her. Helen's character can't sing that number in the show. It'd be against the plot.'

'Sing the song, Neely – the one you were singing.'

'If I do, will you sell me your black coat when you get the mink?'

'I'll *give* it to you . . . if I ever take the mink. Sing the song.'

Neely sighed, and like a child forced to recite, stood in the center of the room and sang the ballad. Anne could hardly believe it. Neely had an extraordinary voice, crystal clear. Her low notes were strong and melodious, and her higher range had power and beauty.

'Neely! You can really sing!'

'Oh, anyone can sing,' Neely said, laughing.

'Not like that. I couldn't carry a tune if my life was at stake.'

'If you grew up in vaudeville you could. I can dance, juggle, even do some sleight of hand. You stand around in the wings, you pick it up.'

'But Neely, you sing *well*. Really well.'

Neely shrugged. 'That and a nickel will get me a cup of coffee.'

Anne became personally involved with *Hit the Sky* at the end of the second week of rehearsals. Henry called in late one afternoon just as she was about to leave the office.

'Anne, thank God you're still there. Look, honey, you can save my life. I'm stuck at N.B.C. The Ed Holson show airs tonight at nine and the last twenty minutes has to be rewritten. Ed is a ballbreaker – the writers are ready to quit and he's thrown out the producer. I can't leave. And Helen Lawson expects me to drop by with a portfolio of her new stocks. It's on my desk.'

'Shall I send it by messenger?'

'No, *take* it to her. But don't say I'm at N.B.C. Tell her I'm locked in a board-of-directors meeting on that real-estate deal she's interested in and that I couldn't get away. As long as she thinks I'm out making a buck for *her*, she won't mind. Give it to her personally, and for God's sake be convincing with the message.'

'I'll do my best,' Anne promised.

'Take it to the Booth Theatre, backstage entrance. They should be breaking any minute. Tell her I'll go over everything in detail with her tomorrow.'

She was sorry Henry had caught her. If only she had left earlier. She wasn't good at things like this. Meeting Helen Lawson face to face was not her idea of a casual everyday encounter.

She was nervous when she reached the theatre and timidly opened the black, rusted stage door. Even the old doorman who sat near the radiator reading the racing form looked formidable.

He looked up. 'Well? Whaddaya want?'

She wondered about all those movies where the gay chorus girls called a paternal stage doorman 'Dad.' This one was staring at her as if she were in a police lineup.

She explained, pointing to the portfolio as added proof. He jerked his head, said, 'In there,' and went back to his paper.

'In there' she bumped into a frantic man holding a script. 'What the hell are *you* doing here?' he whispered angrily.

She went through the entire explanation again, secretly cursing Henry.

'Well, they're still rehearsing,' he grumbled. 'You can't stand here in the wings. Go through that door and sit in the audience till we break.'

She groped her way into the dark, empty theatre. Gil Case was sitting on the aisle of the third row, his hat tilted to shade his eyes from the glaring work light on the stage. The chorus girls were sitting in a tired little group against the back wall of the bare stage. Some were whispering quietly among themselves, a few were massaging their calves, one was knitting. Neely was sitting erect, her eyes fastened on Helen Lawson. Helen stood in the center of the stage, singing a love song with a tall, handsome man.

68

She was belting out the lyrics in her famous style. Her smile was bright and merry, and even in the love song she exuded her familiar hale and hearty attitude. Her eyes flashed with grinning humor when the lyrics went into comedy, and her face went serious when the song moved into the inevitable lover's lament. Her figure was beginning to show signs of middle age – the thickness through the waist, the slight spread in the hips. Recalling Helen's appearance in the past, Anne felt as if she were gazing at the cruel distortion of a monument. Age settled with more grace on ordinary people, but for celebrities – women stars in particular – age became a hatchet that vandalized a work of art. Helen's figure had always been her biggest asset. Playing broad comedy in a high-styled wardrobe had been a Helen Lawson trademark. Her face, although never classically beautiful, had been attractive and viva-cious with her shock of long black hair.

Helen had not had a Broadway opening for five years. Her last show had enjoyed a two-year run, then a year on tour. She had met her last husband on that tour. There had been a whirlwind courtship in Omaha, Nebraska, then a huge wedding, with Helen telling the press that she intended to settle on his ranch as soon as the show ended its run. There she would play her greatest role, her final role – that of a wife. The big, smiling husband, Red Ingram, also assured the press that Helen's place was on his ranch. 'I never saw this little girl in any of her shows,' he told the world. 'Just as well – I mighta nipped her career long ago. She's for me.'

Helen had settled down – for two years. Then her image once again flashed across the AP and the UP wires as she told the world that 'it's been pure hell on the ranch' and that Broadway was her real home. Henry had quickly gone through the arrangements for a Reno divorce, composers and librettists rushed to Helen with their newest scores, and now Helen was back where she belonged – rehearsing for *Hit the Sky*.

She couldn't be the love interest, Anne decided. Not with that padding of flesh on her jawline. It was practically a double chin. Yet she was singing a love song, her eyes still flashed merrily, the old vivacity was still intact, the long shock of curly black hair was still shoulder length . . . From the lyrics of the song Anne realized Helen was playing a widow, searching for a new love. Well, it probably would work – but why hadn't Helen taken off about fifteen pounds before she tackled the show? Or didn't she realize the change the years had brought? Maybe it happened so gradually you never noticed. I haven't seen her in eight years, Anne thought, so it comes as a shock to me. Maybe Helen still looks the same in her own eyes.

These were the thoughts that rambled through her mind as she watched Helen do the number. At the same time she was conscious that Helen's magnetism did not rely on her face or figure. There was something that compelled you to watch her, and soon you forgot the wide waistline, the sagging jaw-line, and felt only her tremendous warmth and rakish good humor.

When she finished the number, Gilbert Case called out, 'Wonderful, Helen! Just great!'

She walked to the edge of the stage, looked down at him and said, 'It's a piece of shit!'

His expression never changed. 'You'll get to love it, dear girl. You always feel this way about boy-girl ballads in the beginning.'

'Are you kidding? I loved the one I did with Hugh Miller in *Nice Lady*. I loved it the second I heard it. And Hugh was tone deaf – I had to carry the slob. At least Bob keeps on key.' She tossed her head to acknowledge the handsome, wooden man at her side. 'So don't tell me I'll get to like it. It stinks! It doesn't say anything. And I hate combining comedy with torch. The tune's okay, but you'd better tell Lou to come up with a better set of lyrics.'

She turned and walked off the stage. The assistant director shouted an eleven o'clock call for the following day and that the names of those with costume fittings were posted on the call board and for God's sake to get to Brooks in time. There was a general buzzing all around and no one seemed at all concerned with Helen's attack on the song – including Gilbert Case. He rose slowly from his seat, lit a cigarette and walked to the back of the theatre.

When the stage had cleared, Anne gingerly made her way back. The young man with the script pointed toward the door of Helen's dressing room.

Anne tapped, and the famous raucous voice yelled, 'Come in!'

Helen looked up in surprise. 'Who in hell are you?'

'I'm Anne Welles and I—'

'Look, I'm tired and busy. What do you want?'

'I came with this portfolio.' Anne placed it on the makeup table. 'Mr. Bellamy sent it.'

'Oh. Well, where in hell is Henry?'

'He's tied up with some real-estate board meeting. But he said he'll talk to you tomorrow and explain anything you don't understand.'

'Okay, okay.' Helen turned back to the mirror and waved her hand in dismissal. Anne started for the door and Helen shouted, 'Hey, wait a minute. Aren't you the girl I read about? The one who got Allen Cooper and the ring and all?'

'I'm Anne Welles.'

Helen grinned. 'Well, hey . . . glad to meet you. Sit down. I didn't mean to be nasty, but you should see some of the characters who slip by the stage doorman and get in to see me. All of them with something to sell. Hey, lemme see the ring!' She grabbed Anne's hand and whistled in appreciation. 'Wow, that's a beaut! I got one twice that size, but I bought it for myself.' She stood up and slid into her mink coat. 'I bought this myself, too. No man ever really gave me anything.' She said it plaintively. Then she shrugged. 'Well, there's always tomorrow. Maybe I'll meet a right guy who'll shower me with presents and rescue me from this rat race.'

She grinned at Anne's surprise. 'Yeah, that's what I said. You think it's fun going through these four stinking weeks of rehearsal, and then the hell that goes on during the out-of-town tryout? And if you come in with a hit, so what? Big deal – you still wind up with the *News* and *Mirror* after the show.' She started for the door. 'Where are you going? I have a car, I can drop you.'

'Oh, I can walk,' Anne said quickly. 'I live right near.'

'So do I, but that's one thing I get in my contract – the producer pays for the car and chauffeur to pick me up and call for me. During rehearsals and after performances of the New York run. Unless I get lucky and have a date,' she added with a grin.

It was drizzling when they came out of the stage door, so Anne accepted Helen's lift. 'Drop me first,' Helen called to the chauffeur, 'then take Miss Welles wherever she wants to go.'

When they stopped before Helen's apartment building, she took Anne's hand in an impulsive gesture and said, 'Come up and have a drink with me, Anne. I hate to drink alone. It's only six. You can call your fella from my place. He can pick you up there.'

Anne wanted to go home – it had been a long day – but there was an urgency about the loneliness in Helen's voice. She followed Helen into the building.

Inside the apartment, Helen's mood changed as she looked around proudly. 'Like it, Anne? I paid a fortune to the faggot who did it. That's a real Vlaminck over there . . . and that's a Renoir.'

It was a warm, attractive apartment. Anne stared at the bleak snow scene by Vlaminck with deep admiration. This was a side of Helen she never would have imagined . . .

'I don't know my ass from my elbow about art,' Helen went on. 'But I like to have the best of everything around me. At this point in my life I can afford it. So I told Henry to pick me some good pictures that would go well with the apartment and be good investments. The Renoir's not bad, but that snow scene – *ugh*! But Henry says a Vlaminck will triple in value. Come on in the den. That's my favorite room . . . the bar's in there.'

The walls of the den were a pictorial cavalcade of Helen's theatrical life. Glossy photographs were neatly framed and mounted with assembly-line precision. There were pictures of Helen in short skirts and the frizzy hair of the twenties, autographing a baseball bat for Babe Ruth. A smiling Helen with a mayor of New York . . . Helen with a famous senator . . . Helen with a well-known songwriter . . . Helen receiving the Best Broadway Star award . . . Helen sailing to Europe with her second husband . . . Helen in affectionate poses with other theatrical luminaries. There were also plaques, framed scrolls, commendations, all proclaiming Helen's greatness.

There was also a bookcase filled with leather-bound volumes – Dickens, Shakespeare, Balzac, De Maupassant, Thackeray, Proust, Nietzsche. Anne surmised that Henry had also been assigned to furnish the bookcases.

Helen noticed her looking at the books. 'All the right classic junk, huh? I tell you that Henry knows everything. But you'll never convince me people actually read that shit. I tried a few pages once . . . Christ!'

'Some of them *are* tough going,' Anne agreed. 'Especially Nietzsche.'

Helen's eyes widened. 'You *read* those books? Know something? I never read a book in my life.'

'Now you're teasing me,' Anne insisted.

'Nope. When I work in a show, I work hard. After the show, if I'm lucky I have a date. If not, I come home from the show alone. And by the time I take a bath and read the trade papers and the columns, I'm ready to pop off. I sleep till noon, read the afternoon papers, go through my mail, get on the horn with my friends . . . by that time I'm ready for dinner. I never go out for dinner when I'm doing a show and I never have a drink till after the show. But after the show I like to hoot. Oh, yeah . . . I almost read a book during my last marriage. That's when I *knew* it was going sour. How do you like your champagne – on the rocks?'

'I'll take a Coke, if you don't mind,' Anne said.

'Oh, come on, take some of my bubbly water. It's the only thing I drink, and if you don't help me with it, I'll wind up killing the bottle myself tonight. And let me tell you, the grape adds bloat.' She patted her waistline knowingly. 'I'm still trying to get rid of the weight I gained on the ranch.' She handed Anne a glass. 'Christ! You ever lived on a ranch?'

'No. I come from New England.'

'I thought I was gonna live on that ranch for life. C'mere . . .' She dragged Anne into the bedroom. 'See that bed? It's eight feet wide. That was the bed I had custom made when I married Frank. He was the only man I ever loved. I had that fucking thing shipped all the way to Omaha when I married Red, and I had it shipped back here again. I bet I paid more for shipping that bed around than it cost to begin with. That's Frank.' She pointed to a photograph on her night table.

'He's very attractive,' Anne mumbled.

'He's dead.' Tears came to Helen's eyes. 'He got killed in an auto accident two years after we were divorced. It was that bitch he married that drove him to it.' Helen's sigh went through her entire body.

Anne glanced at the clock on the night table. It was six-thirty. 'Do you mind if I use your phone?'

'Come on in the den and use it there. You'll be more comfortable.'

Helen poured some more champagne while Anne called Allen.

'Where are you?' he asked. 'I've called you three times and got Neely every time. She was getting pretty tired of me, especially since she's dressing for a date with her big love. Which reminds me, I'm with Gino. He wants to know if you mind his horning in on our dinner date tonight.'

73

'I'd love it, Allen. You know that.'

'Fine. We'll pick you up in half an hour.'

'Okay, but I'm not at home. I'm at Helen Lawson's.'

There was a fractional pause, then Allen said, 'You can tell me about *that* at dinner. Want me to call for you there?'

He wrote down the address. 'She's at Helen Lawson's,' she heard him tell Gino. 'What? You're kidding!' This was also to Gino. Then he returned to her. 'Anne, believe it or not, Gino says to bring Helen Lawson along for dinner.'

'Oh . . . do they know one another?' Anne asked.

'No, but what difference does that make?'

'Allen, I couldn't—'

'Ask her!'

Anne hesitated. You just didn't ask a woman of Helen's stature to come along on a blind date. And with Gino, of all people! Allen noticed the pause. 'Anne, are you still on?'

She turned to Helen. 'Allen would like to know if you would care to join us. His father is coming along.'

'As his father's date?'

'Well . . . there'd be just the four of us.'

'Sure!' Helen shouted. 'I've seen him at El Morocco. He's kinda sexy looking.'

'She'd like to very much,' Anne said coolly into the receiver. Then she hung up. 'They'll call for us in half an hour.'

'Half an hour? How can you go home and get dressed up in that time?'

'I won't. I'll go this way.'

'But you're wearing a polo coat. And a tweed suit.'

'Allen's taken me out like this before. He won't mind.'

Helen's face puckered into a pout, causing her to look like a bloated baby. 'Aw gee, Annie, I wanted to get all gussied up. Now I can't. I'd look like a Christmas tree with you dressed like that. And I wanna make a good impression on Gino. He's a live one.'

This couldn't be happening. Helen Lawson acting like a high school girl over a date with Gino. And this sudden attack of coyness did not fit Helen's personality, which drew its strength from a certain roughneck dignity. She found herself hoping this baby pout was a rare side of Helen's nature.

'Call them back and tell them to make it a little later,' Helen suggested. 'That way you'll be able to run home and change.'

Anne shook her head. 'I'm too tired. I've been working all day.'

'What the hell do you think *I've* been doing?' Helen's tone was that of a child who has been left out of a game. 'I was up at nine this morning. I worked for three hours on a dance routine with those slobs The Gaucheros. I fell on my ass at least six times. I went through that stinking song a hundred times. And I'm still raring to go. And I'm a little older than you. I'm . . . thirty-four.'

'I haven't got that kind of energy,' Anne said, managing to cover her surprise. Thirty-four! George Bellows had been right.

'How old are you, Anne?'

'Twenty.'

'Stop with the bullshit! I read that in the papers. How old are you really?' The expression in Anne's eyes made Helen change her tone. She broke into a little-girl smile. 'Hey, are you one of those broads who faints at four-letter words? My old lady gets so mad when I use them. Tell you what, I'm gonna try and stop. Any time tonight I use bad language, you just give me one of those icy looks of yours.'

Anne smiled. There was something appealing in Helen's swift changes of mood. She was guileless in her honesty and so vulnerable in spite of her position.

'Are you really only twenty, Anne?' Then she added quickly, 'It's just so fantastic that you made it so fast, catching someone like Allen Cooper. I'll wear a black dress and just a little jewelry.' She started for the bedroom to change, talking all the while. 'Hey, c'mon in with me. I may have the biggest voice on Broadway, but I can't make it from there.'

Helen kept up a running stream of conversation while she dressed. Most of it concerned her husbands and how badly they had treated her. 'All I ever wanted was love,' she kept repeating mournfully. 'Frank loved me – he was an artist. God, if he could only see me with a real Renoir. Not that Frank painted like that. He was an illustrator, but on the side he used to paint what he called serious. His dream was the day he could afford to give up illustrating and paint like he wanted to.'

'Oh, were you just beginning then?'

'Hell, no! I was starring in *Sadie's Place* when we got married. It was my third starring show. I was making three thousand a week and he was only making a hundred bucks, so you can see I really married for love.'

'Then why couldn't he paint as he liked?'

'*I* should support *him*? Are you kidding? If I did, how would I know if a man was marrying me for love and not my loot? I put it to him square on the line. I had a big apartment then, and I like to live good. I said, "Frankie, you can move in. I'll pay the rent. I've been paying it anyway. I'll also pay for the maid, my clothes, the bar and the food. But when we go out, you pick up the tabs." He used to complain that two nights on the town took up his whole week's salary. With the free rent and all. God, I loved him. I even tried to have a baby with him, and that woulda meant blowing a whole season. So you can see how much I loved him. But I just never got knocked up. Here, zip me. How do I look?'

Helen looked good. Anne thought she had a little too much jewelry on, but after all, she *was* Helen Lawson. She could get away with it.

The buzzer sounded. Helen reached for a flaming red silk coat, trimmed with sequins. She looked at Anne. 'Too flashy?'

'Why not wear the mink you wore this afternoon?' Anne asked.

'How conservative could I be? A black dress and a brown coat. Look, I believe if you got 'em, wear 'em. I'm not one of those blue-book fancy broads.'

The buzzer sounded again. 'All right, all right!' Helen yelled. She hesitated for a second, picked up the mink coat and smiled. 'You win, angel. I know you got taste.'

The meeting between Gino and Helen went off like a Roman candle. They decided on El Morocco, a place they both adored. They ordered the same food, howled incessantly over each other's jokes, consumed endless champagne. Columnists stopped by the table to pay their respects to Helen; the orchestra played and replayed the scores from Helen's past hits. Anne quickly caught the mood of hilarity and even found herself laughing at some of Helen's off-color jokes. It was impossible not to like Helen.

Gino roared in approval. 'I love this girl!' he shouted, slapping her on the back. 'She says what she means. No phoniness with her. Tell you what, Helen. We'll make up a big party to celebrate your opening night.'

Helen's entire personality changed. Her smile was shy, and in a small, girlish voice she said, 'Oh, Gino, that's wonderful! I'd love to have you as my date at the opening.'

Gino was taken off guard. Anne knew he had meant Adele to be along. He naturally assumed Helen would have her own escort.

'When is the exact date?' Gino asked slowly.

'January sixteenth. We leave for New Haven in two weeks. Then we do three weeks in Philadelphia.'

'We'll come to New Haven,' Gino said quickly. 'Anne, Allen and I—'

'No!' Helen wailed. 'New Haven's a mess. We only have three performances there to iron things out before Philadelphia.'

'We'll make allowances,' Gino said easily.

'It isn't that,' Helen pouted, her face contorting into the unflattering babyish pucker. 'But we open on Friday night and have a matinee the next day and often a rehearsal the morning before, to stick in new things. If you come, I'll want to stay up late and hoot. And I can't hoot the night before a matinee.'

'January is too far off for me to plan anything,' Gino said firmly. 'With my business, I could be out of the country by then. New Haven is possible – unless you don't want us to come.'

Helen moved closer to Gino, put her arm through his and winked coyly. 'Aw no . . . I'm not letting you off the hook. I'll settle for New Haven. And if you're in town, you'll come opening night in New York too.'

'You mean see it twice?'

'Listen, you sonofabitch, people come to see my shows five times,' Helen said good-naturedly. 'Come on, Annie,' she said. 'Let's go to the little girls' room and fix our faces.'

The attendant in the powder room threw her arms around Helen. 'She was my first dresser,' Helen told Anne.

'You shoulda seen her,' the woman said affectionately. 'She was all legs and as friendly as a puppy.'

'I still got good legs,' Helen said. 'But I gotta knock off a few pounds. Ah, that'll happen on the road.' Helen sat down and powdered her face. When the attendant turned to assist a new arrival, Helen said, 'Anne, I like Gino.'

She said it quietly, and the lack of expression on her face seemed to intensify the feeling behind the words. Helen played with her hair and kept her eyes on her own image. 'I mean really like him, Anne. Do you think he likes me?'

'I'm sure he does,' Anne said, trying to keep her voice light.

Helen turned to her urgently. 'I need a fella. Honest, Anne, that's all I want – someone to love.'

Anne's heart went out to the battered, pathetic face, the eyes pleading for reassurance. She thought of all the violent stories she had heard about Helen Lawson, stories undoubtedly spread by the legions of lesser people, jealous of her success or shocked by her coarseness. But it was hard to see how anyone could honestly dislike this woman whose ribald personality was a mask for a sensitive nature and a desperate longing for affection.

'Gee I like you, Annie. We'll be buddy-buddy. And we'll double-date a lot. I don't get a chance to have many girl friends. Hey, Amelia' – Helen's voice boomed out to the attendant – 'gimme a pencil and a piece of paper.'

The attendant brought a pad. 'Miss Lawson . . . while you're at it, will you write your autograph for my niece?'

'I wrote three of them for you last week,' Helen grumbled as she scribbled her name. 'Whaddaya do, sell 'em?' She handed the attendant the paper, then scribbled a number and handed it to Anne. 'This is my phone number. Don't lose it, it's unlisted. And for Chrissake don't give it to anyone – except Gino. Tattoo it on him if you can. Here, write down your number.'

'You can always reach me at Henry Bellamy's office.'

'Yeah, yeah, I know – but in case I want you at home.'

Anne wrote down the number of the hall telephone on West Fifty-second Street. 'But I'm at the office from nine-thirty to five,' she repeated. 'And I'm usually out with Allen every night.'

'Okay.' Helen stuffed the paper into her purse. 'We better be getting back. They'll think we fell in.'

It was close to three when the black car drove up to Anne's rooming house. They had dropped Helen first. Gino was almost asleep and Allen seemed tired, but Anne felt keyed up after the exciting evening. There was a light showing under Neely's door, so she tapped lightly.

'I've been waiting for you,' Neely said. 'Have I had an evening! I told Mel the truth, that I was only seventeen. And he doesn't care. He

78

says I've seen more of life than most girls of twenty. I also told him I was a virgin.' Then she added, 'Where've you been so late?'

Anne told Neely about her evening with Helen Lawson, starting with the meeting at rehearsal. When she finished, Neely shook her head in disbelief. 'You act like you had a great time. Next thing, you're gonna tell me you *like* Helen Lawson.'

'I do. I like her very much, Neely. All those stories about her – they're told by people who don't even know her. Once you know her, really know her, you have to like her. Confess – now that you're over the idea that she tossed you out of the show the first day – and now that you've worked with her – don't you really like her?'

'Oh sure, she's adorable.'

'I mean it.'

'Are you *sick?*' Neely reached out and touched Anne's head. 'She's a horrible woman. No one likes her.'

'That's not true. Anyone who talks against her just doesn't really know her.'

'Look. The only people who adore her are those in the audience, and that's because they're separated from her by an orchestra and a stage. And they don't like her, they like the part she plays. Listen, one thing people overlook – Helen is not only a big musical comedy star, she's also a terrific actress. Because she plays those warm, heart-of-gold gals and makes you believe it. But Helen really – when she's not acting – she's cold. She's a machine.'

'Neely, you don't know what she's really like.'

'Oh boy! You kill me, Anne. You go out with Allen for a whole month and know *nothing* about him. But wham! One night with Helen Lawson and you're an authority. You're ready to buck all the people who've worked with her and know her and hate and despise her. She's rough, tough, unfeeling, coarse and rotten. Maybe she had her company manners on with you tonight, or maybe she wants something from you. But let me tell you, if you get in her way, she'll step on you as if you were a worm.'

'That's how you see her. You've heard the legend so long you won't even try to see her as she really is. I don't doubt she can be tough when she's working. That's her job. She has to fight for what she wants. But divorce her from her work and you'll find a sensitive, lonely woman, longing for a real friend. And for someone to love.'

'Love!' Neely screeched. 'Anne, the *real* Helen Lawson is the monster I see at rehearsals. And it has nothing to do with being a star. She was born that way. You don't get that way. Why, if I was ever a star, I'd be so darned grateful that an audience loved me . . . that people would pay just to see *me* . . . that writers would write for *me*. *Wow!* I'd go around kissing the world. Listen, even Mel, who only met her once at a benefit, calls her Jack the Ripper.'

'I won't argue any more,' Anne said wearily. 'But I don't want you to knock Helen in front of me, Neely. I like her.'

'*Geeeez* . . .'

The phone jangled outside the door.

'Now what nut would call anyone at this hour?' Neely asked. 'Must be a wrong number.'

'I'll get it.' Anne went to the phone.

'Hi, girl . . .' Helen's happy voice rang over the phone.

'Helen! Is anything wrong?'

'*Helen!*' Neely shouted through the open door. 'Gosh, you're not kidding. You *are* chummy!'

'I just wanted to call and say good night,' Helen said cheerfully. 'I've gotten undressed, washed my panties and stockings, creamed my face, set my hair, and now I'm in bed.'

Anne thought of Helen luxuriating in the eight-foot bed and involuntarily shivered as she stood in the unheated hallway. Then, in spite of Neely hovering at her elbow, her curiosity got the best of her. 'Helen, did you say *you* washed your stockings and pants?'

'Aw, you must be kidding,' Neely whispered.

'Sure I do,' Helen answered. 'Honest. It's a habit my old lady taught me, and even though I have a personal maid, I do this every night before I go to bed. I guess that's the Irish in me, the O'Leary side.'

'Is that your real name?'

Neely couldn't stand it. 'I'll be right back. I'm gonna put my bathrobe on if we're gonna chat. It's freezing out here.' She ran into the room.

'No – my real name is Laughlin,' Helen answered. 'That's Scotch. I'm Scotch, French and Irish. But I changed the Laughlin to Lawson. I figured it would look better in lights.'

'You sound as if you always knew it was going to be in lights.'

'You bet your ass. I was singing at lodge benefits when I was ten. At sixteen I started singing lessons. After two years I started auditioning. I got into a Broadway show with a small part and one song and copped all the notices. Everyone seemed surprised but me. If I didn't think I was a hell of a singer I wouldn'ta auditioned for the part.'

'Then you never had any trouble, never had to job hunt?'

'She made it right away.' Neely was back, wrapped in a warm bathrobe, nibbling at a Fig Newton. 'That's why she's mean to people like me – she doesn't know what it is to struggle.'

'No, I made it easy,' Helen went on. 'I admit it's not that easy for everyone. But if you've got it, you make it. Period! It might take some a little longer, but no one who really has it gets lost in the shuffle. I can't stand all this hard-luck shit I hear . . . all the talent that never gets a chance. It takes more than just a set of pipes to make it. Hell, lots of girls can sing. I've heard plenty of band singers who make seventy-five a week who sound better than me. But they haven't got it.'

Anne shifted her weight and shivered. She had left her coat in Neely's room. 'Helen, I've got to get in bed. The heat's turned off and I'm freezing.'

'I'll wait.'

'But I can't . . . I mean . . . the phone . . .'

'Isn't the wire long enough?'

'The phone is in the hall.'

'*Whaaat?*'

'It's in the hall. I live in a rooming house. I don't have my own phone.'

'You must be kidding! You mean you wear a rock on your finger worth fifty G's and you don't have a phone? Where in hell do you live, anyway?'

'On West Fifty-second Street – right near Leon and Eddie's.'

'But that's a *crummy* neighborhood!' Helen screamed. Then her voice changed. 'But what the hell, you're getting married soon. But how can you live without a private phone in your room?'

'I never really need it.'

'Well, for Chrissake!' Anne heard a yawn and the sound of news-paper rustling. 'Oh, I see I've made two columns,' Helen said sleepily. 'All right, angel, go to sleep. Drop by at rehearsal tomorrow after you've finished work.'

'Well, I finish pretty late. And then I rush home and dress to see Allen.'

'Yeah, you better. Dress, I mean. You're real good-looking, Anne, but that polo coat and tweed suit department has gotta go. Remember, the most important thing in the world is to have a man who loves you. Dress up for him. I'll call you at the office tomorrow.' The phone clicked.

Anne walked back to Neely's room. She picked up her coat and bag. Neely followed her to the door. 'I don't get it, Anne.' She stood there shaking her head. 'I don't get it. If I hadn't heard it with my own ears I wouldn'ta believed it.' Then her expression changed. 'But I still say she's gotta have an angle.'

'No, she hasn't. She had fun tonight . . . She's so lonely really. And she liked Gino.'

'Then *that's* it!' Neely screamed. 'She's just using you to get Gino.'

'That's not true. She was warm and friendly even before I arranged the date. She had me up to her apartment—'

Neely grinned. 'Maybe the old war horse is turning queer in her old age.'

'Neely!'

'It happens. Listen, some of those big stars – especially broads like Helen who like sex – they get so fed up with the cold shoulder from men that they turn to women for their kicks. There was this faded movie star who played at a nightclub with us, and—'

'Neely, Helen is absolutely normal!'

Neely yawned. 'Okay, I won't fight you on that. She's got too big a reputation for being man crazy. She'll lay anything in pants. She's always been known for that. That's how she lost her first husband. He came home and found her doing it with a gangster she had gone with way back.'

'Neely, that's untrue. She loved her first husband.'

'Anne, I sit and gab with the girls all day. Everyone knows Helen sang in a speakeasy that was owned by Tony Lagetta. She was mad for him. But he was Italian and Catholic and had a wife and seven kids. He'd lay her, sure – but that's all. When she made it in her first show, Henry Bellamy stepped in and made her drop Tony. She was getting too famous, and if the wife sued it could hurt Helen's image. She had a long affair with Henry, but she still slept with Tony on the sneak.

Everyone knew but Henry. He just kept managing her and making her a star and a millionaire. Then Tony found someone else, and Helen got so mad she married the first guy who came along – the artist. By this time there were no more speakeasies and Tony ran some fancy joint – a French-Italian restaurant – and Helen used to bring this artist she married in and neck with him to get Tony jealous. I guess it worked, because one day the artist comes home and he finds Helen and Tony having this little reunion . . . He left her and he was never the same. He got married again – but he was a drunk.'

'And where did you get all this folklore?'

'The Tony part I knew ages ago. Geez, when anyone mentioned Helen's name they used to say 'Tony's girl,' but the Henry Bellamy part and the husband part I got from the kids in the show. Everyone knows—'

'Everyone knows,' Anne interrupted impatiently, 'like you know – through hearsay. And like everyone, you'll spread the same story to everyone you meet. And it will grow. But were *you* there? Did *you* ever see Helen and Tony together? I've *talked* to Helen. I *know* how she felt about her husband. Look, Neely, Helen has a few rough edges, sure. I think she made it so fast she never had time to catch up with her talent. It took her to the top, but at heart she's still a little girl from New Rochelle. And she pretends to be tough so she won't get hurt.'

'All right, I give up,' Neely said. 'She's adorable, she's sweet, and since it looks like you two are gonna be inseparable and you're the only one who understands her, why not tell her what a big talent your *second*-best friend has. Maybe she'll toss me a few bits in the show.'

Anne smiled. 'Neely, no one could replace you.'

'Sure. I can just see it. The three of us all getting together and having little girlish chats.'

'Why not? Neely, tomorrow walk over to Helen at rehearsal. Tell her you're my close friend.'

'Oh, sure.'

'Why not?'

'Because no one just walks over and chats with Helen.'

'Try it, you might be surprised.'

'Sure. Maybe I'll ask her to compare notes on washing stockings. Does she use Lux or Ivory? Or if she gets her kicks that way, I'll be glad to send her a few of my slips that need washing.'

83

'Good night, Neely.'

'Good night. But Anne, I mean it. If this glorious friendship does continue and you do get the chance, slip in a word for me. Try it . . . please?'

'Now this is what I call an unusual foursome,' George Bellows said as he placed the morning paper on Anne's desk. She stared at the picture that had been snapped the night before at Morocco. Helen looked grotesque; Gino was grinning; Allen was partially out of the picture. Her own likeness was more than flattering.

She managed a smile. 'Who is Nick Longworth?' she asked as she studied the messages on her desk.

'One of the top modeling agencies in town. Why – did Longworth make you an offer?'

'I don't know. I just came in and found these messages to call him.'

'That's what you should be doing. You're a born model. But you probably would have wound up the same way. Kismet.' He looked at her ring.

Her phone rang. George waved and wandered back to his office.

It was Allen. 'Have you recovered from last night?'

'It was really fun, wasn't it?' she asked cheerfully.

He was silent.

'Allen?'

'I can't believe I'm hearing right.'

'I like Helen Lawson,' she said defensively.

'What do you like about her? Her charming jokes? Her ladylike manner? Look, Gino can be pretty tough to take, but I'm stuck with Gino. He's my father. But Helen—'

'I like your father.'

'You don't have to be polite, Anne. I always say, you can't pick your relatives – but you can pick your friends.'

'Allen, that's a terrible thing to say.'

'Why? I'm just being honest. If I met Gino and he wasn't related to me, I'd find him loud and obnoxious. I might admire his business ability, just as I admire Helen's talent on the stage. But socially I can do without either of them. Once we're married, we're going to find a whole new set of people, the right people. I'll explain it better tonight.'

Her head had begun to throb with a hammering headache. 'Allen,

I've had very little sleep. I think I'll have to beg off tonight. I want to go home after work and fall into bed.'

'That's another thing we've got to discuss. How long do you intend to hang on to that job? Right up till the day we get married?'

'I want to work, Allen – and I *don't* want to get married. I've told you that.'

He forced a light laugh. 'You *are* tired. All right, I'll give you a night off. But Anne . . . I know I promised not to rush you, but start thinking about marriage. Just think . . . that's all I ask.'

The day dragged on. The Longworth Agency called again. She told them she was not interested in becoming a Longworth model. Yes, she would call them if she ever changed her mind.

Henry came in after lunch. She brought the mail into his office, but he tossed it aside. 'Sit down.' He lit a cigarette. 'Well, we got good reviews on the Ed Holson show, but the sonofabitch is murder.'

'The show or Ed Holson?' She leaned her head against the leather chair and massaged her temples.

'Holson. What do you do when you have a lush for a client? A goddam genius, but a lush!' He shook his head. 'Got stoned right after the show, in front of the sponsor. Naturally, I had to pretend it had never happened before. Twenty thousand a week and he gets drunk with the sponsor. And I was lucky – he was on one of his polite drunks. When he gets on a rude drunk he starts calling people Jew bastards.'

'Why do you handle him?'

'Figure out what twenty-five per cent of twenty thousand a week comes to, and you'll have your answer. He also happens to be a real talent. I pick friends that I like, clients for their talent.'

Her headache had spread. It was banging at the backs of her eyes. 'I guess it is hard to have integrity in everything,' she said wearily.

'This has nothing to do with personal integrity. This is business integrity. You pick the best, and you can't let your feelings count. The minute you start thinking with your heart instead of your head you'll get clobbered.'

The private phone on his desk began to ring. 'Hello. Oh, hello, honey, how's everything going? Yeah, sure I saw it. You looked good, baby. Sure, she's sitting right here.' He handed the phone to Anne. She stared at him questioningly. 'It's Helen,' he said.

'Hi!' Helen yelled cheerfully. 'How's the working girl?'

'A little tired.'

'Me too. I had to be at rehearsal at ten. I just took a five-minute break. Listen – there's a new show opening at the Copa tonight. I called Gino and suggested the four of us go and he was all for it. We'll catch the second show. That'll give us both time to take a little nap first.'

'Does Allen know?'

'How should I know?' Helen paused, and the little-girl voice came on. 'Don't you wanna go to the Copa, Annie?'

'Well . . . yes, I guess it would be fun. Especially if I get a little rest first.'

'Sure. And get dressed real fancy – everyone will be there.'

'You mean a long dress?'

'Nah, just a short gussy one. And please, a fur jacket. That camel-hair job has to go!'

'I have a black coat . . .' Anne looked up suddenly. Lyon Burke had entered the office.

'Fine. Oh, and when you get home you'll find a little present from me.'

'A present? But why?'

'It's a happy-happy. Well, I gotta go back and make a buck.' The phone clicked.

'Anne is Helen Lawson's new pal,' Henry said to Lyon.

Lyon sat down and stretched his legs. 'Anne's from sturdy New England stock. She'll survive.'

Anne smiled faintly. 'I'm almost getting tired of saying this, but I happen to genuinely like Helen Lawson.'

'Good,' Henry said briskly. 'Helen needs a real friend. Deep down I think she's very lonely.'

Lyon laughed. 'Helen has a new friend every season.'

'She's never had a real one,' Henry insisted. 'Most women try to use Helen, even make fun of her on the side. She went up too fast to learn the little niceties. Half the broads in town start with no knowledge of taste or manners. But they learn – in chorus dressing rooms, from other girls – they learn what books to read, or say they've read, how to dress. And by the time they make it they've smoothed out the rough edges. Helen spent a couple of years singing in a speakeasy. She learned nothing. Then in her first show she shot up like a skyrocket. And people accept anything from someone who's a hit. Helen was suddenly too big for anyone to tell her how to dress, how to talk. They laughed good-naturedly at her gutter language and made her feel it was colorful. Stick with her, Anne, she needs someone like you.'

Henry's phone buzzed. The receptionist announced the call. Henry nodded and handed it to Anne. 'Allen.'

'I can take it outside,' she said quickly.

Henry waved his hand. 'Relax, you're with friends.'

She took the telephone, conscious that Lyon was watching her.

'You were too tired to have a quiet dinner with me!' Allen's voice crackled over the wire. 'Now I hear we're all going to the Copa.'

'Helen and Gino arranged it,' she said lamely.

'I get it. I'm easy to brush, but you can't say no to Helen. What are you, celebrity happy?'

'Allen, I'm in Mr. Bellamy's office. If you like, we'll cancel tonight.'

'No . . . wait a minute. I didn't mean to sound off. We'll go.'

Henry's private phone began to ring.

'I'll talk to you later, Allen.'

'Anne, I'm sorry. I realize you work for Henry and she's his client. But after tonight, let's lose her. If you have to see her, then go shopping together, have lunch together – but keep her out of my life.'

Henry was holding the phone. It had to be Helen.

'Allen, I'll see you tonight.' She hung up. Henry handed her the other phone. 'Looks like we'll have to get her a private secretary,' Henry said with a wink at Lyon.

'Hey, what's your address?' Helen sang out. 'I got to have it so the happy-happy can be delivered.'

Anne told her.

'Oh shit, there's no pencil here. Wait—'

'Helen,' Anne said quickly. 'Ask Neely O'Hara.'

'Who?'

'Neely O'Hara. She's in your show. We live in the same building. She'll write it down for you.'

'What does she do? In the chorus?'

'Yes. Originally she was part of The Gaucheros.'

There was a slight pause. 'Oh, that one.'

'She's a very close friend of mine, Helen. She's only seventeen.

She's just dancing in the show, but she can sing, too. She's really very talented.'

'Okay,' Helen said brightly. 'I'll get it from her. You say she sings, huh? Maybe I can swing something for her. She had a rough deal. Honest, I had nothing to do with it. But never mind . . . maybe I can do something now. I got an idea.'

Anne returned to her desk and lost herself in her work. Her head was still throbbing when the day finally dragged to an end. When she got home, she ran up the stairs, thinking only of a nap. Neely's door was wide open. She dashed out and followed Anne up the stairs.

'I'm really tired, Neely. We'll talk later.'

'I won't stay. I just want to see the expression on your face when you see Helen's present. It's in your room. I called the super from rehearsal and had him unlock your door.'

Anne looked around her room. She saw no package, nothing new anywhere.

'There!' Neely pointed to the rickety night table. Anne stared stupidly at a shiny black telephone.

'She's paying for the installation and for the first two months' bill. She said after that you'll probably be married to Allen.'

'But I can't let her do this.'

'Listen, she's already done it. I don't know, Anne . . . maybe you *have* put some kind of a hex on her. She sure was nice to me after you told her I was your friend.' Then, as Anne smiled, Neely snapped, 'But it doesn't change things. I still think she's a beast!'

The Copa was a repetition of the previous evening. All the attention gyrated around Helen. Her shrill laughter; the cheerful, raucous voice calling out to everyone she knew; Gino urging her on, replenishing her champagne. Warmed by Helen's personal attention, exhilarated by a second glass of champagne, Anne became a participating member in the good-natured camaraderie. Allen remained aloof and taciturn.

'We'll drop Annie first,' Helen announced when they finally settled in the limousine.

'Yes, I am the nearest,' Anne said quickly, avoiding Allen's demanding eyes. When the car stopped in front of her brownstone, she leaped out without waiting for the chauffeur to help with the door. 'Stay where you are,' she told Allen. 'It's freezing out.' She waved and ran quickly up the steps, aware that Allen's jaw was clamped sullenly, his displeasure obvious even in the gray darkness.

Twenty minutes later her new phone jangled with its first cry of life.

'I had to initiate it,' Helen said cheerfully. 'Did I wake you?'

'No . . . I'm in bed, though.' She felt positively luxurious. Even in Lawrenceville, a phone by the bed was unheard of.

'It was fun, huh?'

'I had a wonderful time. One of the best evenings of my life.'

'Yeah . . .' Helen paused. Then her voice changed. 'Annie, I'm not getting anywhere with Gino.'

'He had a wonderful time,' Anne said truthfully.

'But he didn't even try to kiss me good night,' Helen whined. 'We dropped Sonny Boy off after you. I was positive he'd ask to come up for a nightcap. I snuggled against him and said I had a bottle of Dom Perignon on ice. But when he reached my place he just slapped me on the back and said, "Good night, sport." '

'Well . . .' Anne groped for the right words. 'That shows he has respect for you.'

'Who wants respect? I want to get laid!'

Anne's gasp was audible, but Helen went right on. 'Look, angel, when you've been around as long as I have, you'll know that's the only way a guy shows you he's hung on you.'

'You can't mean that, Helen. In fact it's just the opposite.'

'Opposite my ass! How else can he show it?'

'By taking you out, spending time with you – having fun together.'

'Are you kidding? In my book, if a guy digs you he wants to jump in the feathers with you. Even that bastard Red Ingram, my last husband – why, he leaped on me the first night we met. After we got married he slowed up a little, to maybe three, four times a week. Then it got to once a month, then nothing. That's when I put detectives on him and found he was cheating on me.'

'But Helen, I've had tons of dates with Allen and he's never . . . tried to get fresh.'

'Stop the shit!'

For a moment the silence was heavy. Then Helen broke it with her little-girl voice. 'Now don't be mad, Annie-pie. I believe you. But Jesus, don't you want to? I mean, how do you know you'll like marriage with the guy? He may be lousy in the kip. You're going to have a trial run first, aren't you?'

'I certainly am not.'

This time Helen was momentarily silenced. Then in a hard voice strangely tinged with admiration, she said, 'Then it's just his loot that interests you.'

'I went with Allen for six weeks when I thought he was just a poor little insurance agent.'

A slight pause. 'Well, what the hell – you one of those frigid dames?'

'I don't think so.'

'Whaddaya mean *think*! Next thing you'll be telling me you're a virgin. Anne? You still on? Oh, Jesus, I bet you are a virgin at that.'

'You make it sound like a disease.'

'No, but even at twenty most girls aren't . . . I mean, hell, if you dig a guy, you *want* him to jump on you. You can't wait.'

'Is that the way you feel about Gino?'

'Sure – and I'm not even in love with him yet. But I could be.'

'Well, give it a little time,' Anne said wearily.

'I'll try tomorrow night. There's an opening at La Martinique.'

'Do you have a date with him?'

'Not yet. I'll call him at the office tomorrow and make one.'

'Helen . . . why not wait?'

'For what?'

'Give him a chance to call you.'

'But suppose I wait and he doesn't call.'

'But you wouldn't want to go out with him if you were forcing it, would you?'

She could hear Helen yawn. 'Why not? Sometimes you get to be a habit with a guy whether he started out wanting you or not.'

Anne felt Gino could not put off Adele three nights in a row. But most of all, she did not want Helen to be humiliated. 'Helen, do me a favor. Don't call Gino tomorrow. Give him a chance to call you.'

'Suppose he doesn't?'

'He might not. He might not call for several days – even a week.'

'A week! Aw no, I'm not waiting *that* long!'

'You might not have to. But try it . . . don't call tomorrow. Maybe Gino isn't up to three nights in a row.'

'All right.' Helen sighed. 'But I still think my way is best. I'll give him a day to call me. Only I wanted to go to the opening of La Martinique.'

'Isn't there someone else who can take you?'

'Oh, I can always scare up someone. My designer will take me, or Bobby Eaves, my accompanist. But they're both fags. That's the trouble – no real men these days. Plenty of fags, but no men. I hate to go to an opening with a faggot. It's like wearing a sign: "This is all I could get."'

'I would think you could have your pick of men.'

'That's what every girl thinks when she first hits New York. It used to be like that, in the good old days when they had Prohibition. I guess they knew what they were doing making booze legal, but it sure was a great time. The speakeasies were great – places like the Park Avenue Club, The Ha-Ha. There's no night life any more. I liked the days when you dressed, when Eddy Duchin played in the Casino-in-the-Park, when Society Charlies sat at ringsides of speaks, when you went to Harlem for breakfast . . . In those days Tony thought nothing of handing out fifty-dollar tips. Today, if a guy gives you a quarter to go to the can he thinks he's a big spender. God, how I loved that Tony! Now there was a man!'

'I thought you said Frankie was the only man you ever loved.'

'He was. Tony was exciting – a great guy in the kip – but he was a shit at heart. Frankie was good and kind and . . .' Suddenly Helen began to sob. 'Oh Annie, I did love Frankie . . . honest . . . he was the only man I ever loved. And now he's gone.'

'But Helen, at least you had the real thing once,' Anne stammered.

'I guess so . . .' Helen seemed appeased. 'I guess I was lucky having one guy I really loved. Some women never have that.'

'Didn't you love Henry?'

'What do you mean?'

'Well, you were in love with Henry Bellamy, weren't you?' But somehow Anne sensed she had said the wrong thing.

'Did he tell you that?' Helen's voice was cold.

Anne was shaken by the incredible change of tone. In an instant the warm intimacy of their friendship had vanished.

'No, I just assumed it from the warm way he spoke about you,' Anne said evenly. Her head was spinning with confusion and fatigue.

'Hey, wait a minute! Jesus, you're touchy. Sure, I knew Henry way back. But why can't people forget it? We went to bed together, but it meant nothing. To me, anyway. I never dug him that way. But I was young and Henry was important for my career and there was no one else I could be seen with and – oh, hell, that's ancient history. I sometimes forget there was ever anything like that between us. But he's still my business manager, so for Christ's sake don't you ever tell him this.'

'Now Helen, why should I? I like Henry. I wouldn't want to hurt him.'

Helen yawned. 'Funny, about a year ago we went out. I was depressed, so Henry came home with me. And we decided to try it for old times sake. Nothing! I couldn't pretend, and Henry couldn't get it up. Well, after all, Henry's getting on – he's in his fifties. I guess it's not easy to put starch in his lob.'

Anne muffled an involuntary exclamation. Then she said, 'But Gino's in his fifties . . .'

'He's Italian, and those wops got real fire in them all the time. There's nothing like a wop in the kip. That Gino! I can't wait! Listen, I'm gonna call him now and say good night to him . . . make him dream of me.'

'Helen! You can't! It's four in the morning. You'll wake him.'

'Nope, because outta the blue just now, I thought of him. Know what that means? It means he's thinking of me. Whenever you think of someone out of the blue like that it means the other person is thinking of you.'

'This was not out of the blue,' Anne said sternly. Helen's warmth had restored her confidence in their friendship. 'We've been talking about Gino on and off for almost an hour. You just can't call him now, Helen.'

'All right,' Helen promised. 'I'll listen to you. I'll wait till he calls me.'

'That's right.'

'Okay, angel,' Helen said sleepily. 'Talk to you tomorrow. Sleep well . . .'

Three days passed and Gino didn't call. Helen impressed this on Anne several times a day. She called at the office, she called when Anne was dressing to meet Allen, she called at two in the morning.

Neely was also pressing her for advice. She was going to Brooklyn to have dinner with Mel's family. She dragged out her entire wardrobe; Anne had to help with the decision. Naturally she knew the purple taffeta was the right thing. She just wanted to be sure. A violent argument ensued when Anne insisted on a tan wool. 'Geez, that's two years old.' They argued about it endlessly. Neely finally gave in and went off in the tan wool, much against her better judgment.

The office was filled with the activity of the Ed Holson radio show. But Anne was exhilarated with all the excitement around her. She was busy with her work; Henry needed her; Helen and Neely needed her; she was climbing Mount Everest and the air was invigorating and wonderful. Even if every second verged on crisis, this was part of living – not just watching from the sidelines.

On the fourth day of Gino's silence, Helen demanded action. 'Listen, I don't care how busy he is,' she shouted on the phone. 'If a guy digs you, he can at least get on the horn to say hello.'

'Well . . . maybe I was wrong. I mean . . . maybe he doesn't care,' Anne said carefully. Allen had tickets for the theatre. It was late and she wanted to get home and change.

'He dug me, I can feel it,' Helen said stubbornly. 'I'm gonna call him now.'

'Helen, please . . .'

'Listen. Your advice is for the birds. I been winding up with nothing listening to you.'

'But you said if he cared, he'd call . . .' Anne said patiently.

'I let it go too long. If I'da called, by now I'd be a habit with him. Christ! That's the story of my life. I always get kicked in the ass . . .' She began to sob. 'Honest, Anne – the minute I'm nice to a guy he dumps me. I been hurt more than any girl alive. I've got nothin'. I just work, work, work – make money for everybody – and I'm so alone. I thought Gino liked me. You said so too that night at Morocco. Why hasn't he called, Annie?'

Anne's heart rushed out to the woman. She felt a sense of responsibility – she had introduced them. It wasn't right for Gino not to call even once. It wouldn't hurt him to see her once in a while. He should be flattered.

'Helen, give it one more day . . . please.'

That night after the theatre Anne suggested going to El Morocco.

Gino was at his usual table. He waved at them effusively and insisted they join him. Adele was glowing in the new mink, her arm possessively linked through Gino's. Anne suddenly wondered what she had hoped to accomplish. She had forgotten how beautiful Adele was. Ronnie Wolfe joined them. Adele mentioned a new nightclub that was opening the following evening; Gino enthusiastically formed a party, inviting Anne and Allen along.

It had been a mistake coming to Morocco. Why had she come? Had she hoped, in some crazy way, that seeing her might remind Gino of Helen? She watched his hand caress Adele's shoulder and thought of Helen, with her bloated face and figure. She ached with compassion for the middle-aged star.

'C'mon, Anne, dance with me.'

It was Gino, hauling his robust form from behind the table. 'I never yet danced with my son's intended.' He winked at Ronnie Wolfe. 'Can't pass up a chance like this.'

After they had circled the floor and Gino had nodded to everyone he knew, he said quietly, 'Listen, Anne, you gotta do me a favor. Get that Lawson dame off my back.'

'I don't understand . . .' She forced herself to sound innocent.

'She called me tonight. Wants to know when we're going on the town again. You know what – she had the nerve to ask if I was sick because I hadn't called.'

'But *why* haven't you called? I thought you liked her.'

'Sure. She's a good Joe. I liked taking her out. She was a lot of laughs. I'd take her out again – if that was all she wanted.'

Anne's voice was cool. 'I think you're reading something into it that doesn't exist.'

'Anne . . .' He lowered his voice. 'I wasn't gonna tell you this, but you got to know so's you'll understand. After we dropped you and Allen that night, that old bat practically touched my – my privates . . . and begged me to come up for a nightcap. I pretended not to understand. Boy, I ran for my life!' He shuddered at the memory.

'I think she's . . . attractive,' Anne said lamely.

'That's because she's old enough to be your mother and you got respect for older people and respect for her talent. But listen, Anne, to a man she's not attractive. Oh sure, when she's on a stage and belts out a song, no one can touch her. But when it comes to romance . . .'

He glanced over to the table at Adele. 'I'm only interested in the body in my arms.'

Anne took a deep breath. She couldn't stand the thought of seeing Helen humiliated by such total rejection. With a little time – and with the play going out of town – Helen would probably forget him. But at the moment, Helen's pride was at stake.

'I'm surprised at you, Gino,' she said quietly. 'A man like you . . . a man who has created an empire. You mean you can fall in love with a girl just because she has a pretty face? Why, Helen Lawson is a living legend. She's someone you should be proud to be seen with. Someone of stature.'

'Look, honey, you got this all wrong. Who said anything about love? Do you think I'm in love with that featherbrained broad over there? I was in love once – with Allen's mother. She was a lady. But when a man my age thinks about love, then he's in for trouble. Who needs love now? I just want a girl who's pretty, who has a good body. She doesn't have to have brains or be a legend. She just has to look good and satisfy me. And I pay my part of the tab with a few furs and trinkets to keep her happy.' He shrugged. 'What do I want with Helen Lawson? She's like a bull in heat. Now Anne, do me a favor – call her off my back or I'll have to insult her.'

'But you will go to New Haven for her opening?'

'New Haven?'

'Gino . . . you suggested it. You promised!'

'New Haven. Jesus, that's hours on a train. I musta been drunk. Look – she wasn't too hot for us coming there anyway. Tell her I'll come to Philadelphia.'

'Will you?'

'No, but that's a long time off. I'll think of something by then.'

'No, Gino. She's a friend of mine. I won't be part of a deception like that.'

'All right, then I'll tell her. I'll tell her she's an old cow and to leave me alone.'

'If you do that I'll never forgive you.' Anne's voice was quiet, but her eyes were dark with anger.

Gino looked at her. He smiled. 'Anne, Anne. What do you want from me? I don't want to hurt her. But I can't be a loverboy with her, either.'

'You can go to Philadelphia for the opening.'

'And then what? It'll only encourage her.'

'I wouldn't take myself that seriously,' Anne said coldly. 'You're a very attractive man, but I hardly think Helen will wither from your neglect. It's just that I introduced you, and when someone makes a promise I think it should be kept. Once her show opens on Broadway you'll have to stand on line at the stage door to see her.'

'Okay, okay. God forbid I should cause a situation with a coming member of my family. I'll make a deal with you. I'll go to Philly – there's a late train I can take back the same night – but only if you promise to get her off my back until then. Is that a deal?'

'All right, Gino, it's a deal.'

Helen had been even more difficult. Anne invented a story about Gino being involved with some new business deal. He was too busy to see her, but he would come to Philadelphia for the opening.

'Whaddaya mean *he's* in the middle of a business deal?' Helen had shrieked. 'What the hell do you think *I'm* doing, peeling potatoes?'

'But you *wanted* him to come to Philadelphia rather than New Haven.'

'Yeah, but this jazz about a business deal. Listen, no matter how busy I am, if I like someone I can find time to see him.'

'Well, then forget Gino,' Anne said wearily. 'He's not worth all this trouble.'

'But I need a guy – and I don't have anyone, Annie.' Her voice was small. 'So I've just gotta get Gino.'

'Helen, maybe Gino doesn't really want a steady girl . . .'

'Sure he does. I got all the dirt on him. He goes with a showgirl, a big broad named Adele something.'

'You know that?'

'Sure, I read the columns. But look, he took me out while he was going with her, didn't he? So he's not that hot for her. I heard he's been keeping her for about six months, but you notice he hasn't asked her to quit her show to spend full time with him. So I figure he's ready for a change. And it's gonna be me! We had a ball both nights we were together. I could tell he digs me. I think maybe because of who I am he's a little afraid – the legend and all that shit. I'm gonna call him now!'

'*Helen!*'

'Well for Chrissake! So he'll say no and I won't see him tonight. Just sitting and not calling isn't gonna bring him to me.'

'Helen, he's coming to Philadelphia.'

'How can I be sure?'

'Because Allen and I are also going. I promise you he'll be there.'

'Okay.' Helen was cheerful again. 'Maybe it's for the best. The next ten days will be kinda hectic. And there'll be a big party after the opening in Philly. Gino and I will make a fast appearance and then sneak off to my suite and have a ball. Boy, Annie, once I get him in the feathers . . .'

The week before 'Getaway Day,' as Neely tagged the New Haven opening, was one never-ending crisis. The office was filled with hysterical meetings on the Ed Holson show as writers came and went. Helen called several times a day, sometimes just to chat, but mostly to complain about Gino. He'd been at El Morocco with Adele Martin three nights in a row – her designer had seen them. What was with his business deal?

'But Helen . . . he doesn't have to meet her until after eleven. Perhaps it was just for a quick drink.'

'I'd meet him for a quick drink.'

'I'm sure he thinks too much of you to make you wait around like that . . .'

Then, in the middle of the chaos, Allen took a sudden stand. With Helen temporarily out of the picture, they had returned to their easy relationship. They were at the Stork Club; she was idly stirring a wooden stick in champagne and making a pretense of sipping it.

Suddenly he said, 'Anne. How long does this go on?'

'What do you mean?'

'When are we going to get married?'

'Married?' She repeated the word tonelessly.

'Well, it *has* been the general idea.'

'But Allen . . . I thought you understood. I mean . . .'

'I said I'd wait. And I've waited. It's been a month.'

'Allen, I don't want to get married.'

When he spoke his eyes were strange. 'I'd like to know something. To settle it in my own mind. Is it marriage you dislike – or me?'

'You know I don't dislike you. I think you're very nice.'

'Oh, God . . .' It was a groan.

'I can't say I love you if I don't,' she said miserably.

'Tell me something. Have you ever loved anyone?'

'No, but—'

'Do you think you're capable of loving someone?'

'Of course!'

'But it isn't me.'

She swizzled the champagne again and stared at the bubbles. She couldn't bear to see his eyes.

'Anne, I think you're afraid of sex.'

This time she looked at him. 'I suppose you're going to tell me that I'm unawakened . . . that you will change all that.'

'Exactly.'

She sipped the champagne to avoid his eyes.

'I suppose you've been told this before,' he said.

'No, I've heard it in some very bad movies.'

'Dialogue is often trite because it's real. And it's easier to sneer at the truth.'

'The truth?'

'That you're afraid of life – and living.'

'Is that what you think? Just because I'm not rushing into marriage with you?' There was a hint of a smile in her eyes.

'Do you think it's natural to reach twenty and still be a virgin?'

'Virginity isn't an affliction.'

'Not in Lawrenceville, maybe. But then you said you don't want to be like the people in Lawrenceville. So let me give you a few facts. Most girls of twenty aren't virgins. In fact, most of them have gone to bed with guys they weren't even crazy about. Their curiosity and natural sex drive led them to try it. I don't think you've ever even had a decent necking session with a guy. How can you know you don't like something if you haven't tried it? Don't you ever have any urges or feelings about anything? Isn't there anyone you ever unbend with? Have you ever thrown your arms around anyone? Man, woman or child? Anne, I've got to break through to you. I love you. I can't allow you to shrivel away into another New England old maid.' He grabbed her hands. 'Look – forget me for a minute. Isn't there someone you care about? Sometimes I want to shake you, to see if I can't rattle some feeling into that perfect face of yours. Didn't last Thursday mean anything to you?'

'Thursday?' Her mind raced back.

'It was Thanksgiving, Anne. We celebrated it at "21." Jesus, doesn't anything reach you? I was hoping you'd invite me home to Lawrenceville for Thanksgiving. I wanted to meet your mother and your aunt.'

'Someone had to be in the office on Friday, and Miss Steinberg went to Pittsburgh to see her family.'

'What about you? You're an only child. Aren't you close with your mother? What does she think about us? Do you realize you never mention her?'

She played with the swizzle stick again. In the beginning she had written every week. But her mother's replies had been forced and dutiful, so after a few letters she had stopped writing. Her mother really wasn't interested in New York, Neely or Henry Bellamy.

'I phoned my mother after the newspapers carried our engagement.'

'What did she say?'

('Well, Anne, you probably know what you're doing. Everyone in Lawrenceville read about it in the Boston papers. I suppose one New York man is the same as any other. No one knows anything about their families. I don't suppose he's related to the Coopers in Plymouth?')

Anne smiled faintly. 'She said I knew my own mind. As usual, she was wrong.'

'When will I meet her?'

'I don't know, Allen.'

'Do you want to work for Henry Bellamy the rest of your life? Is that the height of your ambition?'

'No . . .'

'What *do* you want, Anne?'

'I don't know. I only know what I *don't* want to do! I don't want to go back to Lawrenceville. I'd rather die.' She shuddered. 'I don't want to get married – until I fall in love. And I *do* want to fall in love. Allen, I want that desperately. And I want children. I want a daughter. I want to love her . . . be close to her . . .'

He beamed at her. 'Good girl. This is the most you've opened up since I've known you. You may not love me, but you want everything I want. We'll have that little girl – now, no objections.' He put his fingers to her lips as she tried to speak. 'And that little girl will go to the best schools and make a debut. With your looks and background, I'll get us to the people we should know. I'll get a social press agent, and we'll play up your family background. You watch – we'll really move. Newport, Palm Beach – no more Miami for me, no more Copa.'

'But I don't *love* you, Allen . . .'

'You don't love anyone. But I saw a spark in your eyes when you said you wanted to be in love . . . wanted to have a child. It's there, buried, just waiting to get out. You're the kind who will be a wild woman in bed once you've tried it—'

'Allen!'

He smiled. 'Now don't knock anything you haven't tried. I don't like to brag, but I've been around. I'll arouse you. I'll have you begging for more—'

'I won't sit and listen to this!'

'All right. I won't say another word. I won't press you about marriage . . . until Christmas. We'll set a date then.'

'No, Allen . . .'

'I always get what I want, Anne – and I want you. I want you to love me. And you will! Now – not another word until Christmas.'

That had happened on Tuesday.

On Wednesday the cast of *Hit the Sky* left for New Haven to prepare for the Friday night opening.

On Thursday Henry Bellamy said, 'Oh by the way, Anne, we're taking the one o'clock train tomorrow for New Haven. I've booked a room for you at the Taft Hotel.'

'Me?'

'Don't you want to go? Lyon and I have to make the opening, and I took it for granted you'd want to be there. After all, Helen is your buddy, and you're also friendly with the little O'Hara kid who's in the show.'

'I'd love it! I've never been to an opening.'

'Well, fasten your seat belt, because there's nothing like a New Haven opening.'

December, 1945

They met at Grand Central Station. It was a cold, brisk day. Henry looked puffy and tired under his clean shave. Lyon Burke greeted her with a warm, quick smile.

They settled in the parlor car; both men opened attaché cases and hunched over contracts and legal papers. The train ride was merely an extension of their usual working day.

Anne tried to concentrate on her magazine. The bright sunlight that flashed through the window disclosed the wintry bareness of the countryside. It made her think of Lawrenceville. In New York you forgot how cold and bleak winter could be. The neon lights, the moving crowds, the taxi-filled streets stampeded the snow into slush and the slush into gray water that quickly disappeared and you forgot about the bare, desolate ground of the outside world. The loneliness of winter. The long evenings sitting in the large, clean kitchen with Mother and Aunt Amy. Or the occasional trips to the movies, or the bowling alley, or to play bridge. O God, she prayed, thank You for giving me the strength to run. Never make me go back – never!

When they pulled into the dark station at New Haven, both attaché cases snapped closed and the men stood to stretch their legs. Henry's face took on a look of tired apprehension.

'Well, here we go – into the line of fire,' he said.

Lyon took Anne's arm. 'Come, my girl, you're going to enjoy your first opening in New Haven. We won't let Henry spoil it for you.'

'I've been to New Haven fifty times,' Henry said mournfully, 'and I always forget how much I hate it until I get here. New Haven is always a trouble city. Except with a Helen Lawson show – then it's total disaster!'

The Taft Hotel looked gloomy and forbidding. 'Wash up and meet us in the bar,' Henry told her. 'And if I were you I wouldn't call Helen. She's a killer in New Haven. She's probably still at the theatre. I'll go on over and check in with her. It's right next door.'

Anne unpacked her bag quickly. The room was small and depressing. But nothing could dampen her exuberance. She felt like a girl on her first trip alone, and she was filled with a sense of expectancy – as if at any moment something very wonderful could happen.

She went to the small window and looked down on the street. The early winter darkness was closing in on the city, and street lamps began to show in the grayness. Across from the hotel a neon sign on a small restaurant flickered uncertainly. She turned quickly at the shrill ring of the phone.

It was Neely. 'I just got back from rehearsal. Mr. Bellamy was at the theatre to see Helen. He told me you were here! I'm so thrilled!'

'So am I. How's it going?'

'Awful!' Neely gasped in her breathless way. 'Last night we had a dress rehearsal that lasted till four in the morning. Helen is trying to cut another number from Terry King. Terry ran out of the theatre in a fit, and her agent arrived this afternoon for a showdown with Gil Case. Terry says Helen can't cut the song. And the dance with The Gaucheros is awful. I bet it gets cut and Charlie and Dick get the sack,' Neely added cheerfully.

'It sounds awful. Is Helen back yet?'

'No, she's still at the theatre locked in her dressing room with Henry Bellamy. I don't see how they'll work it all out.'

'You mean the show won't open tonight!'

'Oh, they'll get the curtain up somehow,' Neely said happily. 'But it'll be a doozy. Hey Anne, Mel is here.'

'He probably took the same train we did.'

'No, he came up last night.' After a pause Neely said, 'Anne . . . I . . . we did it.'

'Did what?'

'You know.'

'Neely . . . you mean . . . ?'

'Uh huh. It hurt a lot and I didn't come. But Mel made me come the other way.'

'What are you talking about?'

'He went down on me.'

'*Neely!*'

'Now Anne, stop acting so prissy. Just because you're not hot for Allen doesn't mean I'm a tramp. I happen to be in love with Mel.'

'And that makes it right.'

'You're darn right it does! We both want each other. Nowadays people don't get married just to do it. Mel respects me and loves me just as much today as he did yesterday. Even more, because now he *really* loves me. And I love him. Besides, we can't get married yet. He helps support his folks. But if the show's a hit and I can count on my hundred a week, then we'll get married.'

'But Neely . . . what you did . . .' Anne choked with embarrassment.

'You mean let him go down on me? Listen, Mel says anything two people do together when they're in love is normal. And besides, it feels sensational! Oh, Geez, I can hardly wait until tonight. And

Anne . . . when he touches my breast I can feel it down there. I bet coming the other way won't be half as great—'

'Neely, for God's sake!'

'Wait till it happens to you. You'll see. See you after the show. Watch for me. I have three lines in the second scene.'

Lyon was waiting at a table in the bar. 'Henry's still at the theatre.' He grimaced in sympathy. 'I ordered a ginger ale for you. Right?'

She looked at the glass with a smile. 'Maybe I should learn to sip at a Scotch. I feel even the waiters stare at me with disapproval.'

'Then stare right back. Never let anyone shame you into doing anything you don't choose to do. Keep your identity.'

'I don't think I have an identity yet.'

'Everyone has an identity. One of their own, and one for show. I rather think you enjoy playing the passive Girl Friday role for show while you look for the real you.'

'I recall that you said I was a fighter . . .'

'I think you are – but for others.'

She sipped at her ginger ale. He offered her a cigarette. 'Have I said the wrong thing?'

'No, I think you've hit on a very big truth.' Then she looked up brightly. 'But I did fight for one thing. I—'

'Yes, you came to New York. But tell me, Anne, is that going to be the one glorious achievement in your life?'

'What about you?' Her eyes suddenly flashed in anger. 'The war is over. Life goes on. Are you going to fight again?'

'I'm fighting right now,' he said quietly.

'I never seem to say anything light and airy when I'm with you,' she said wryly. 'But I didn't start it this time. And I think I will have a Scotch.'

He signaled the captain and got two drinks. She raised the glass in a toast. 'Perhaps if I down this I can say something that will make you laugh.'

'I'll be delighted to laugh. And you needn't drink the Scotch.'

She gulped down half the drink. Then she said weakly, 'It tastes awful and I still can't think of anything funny to say.'

He took the glass from her. 'Why is it important to make me laugh?'

'I saw you that night at La Ronde – with Jennifer North. You were laughing a great deal. I thought about it . . .' She reached for the drink. What was she saying? She took another swallow.

'Go ahead, finish the drink. It was a good idea at that. At least you're fighting for yourself now.'

'And what are you fighting for, Lyon?'

'You.'

Their eyes met. 'You don't have to fight,' she said quietly.

He took her hand quickly. Allen's diamond cut into her finger with almost a personal rage of its own. But she made no sign that she felt its sharp edge. Lyon's eyes were close . . .

'Well, I can see you two have had a few.' Henry Bellamy was striding cheerfully toward them. He motioned the waiter for a drink.

Anne withdrew her hand hastily. The ring had actually cut into her flesh. Henry sat down and sighed.

'Go back to your handholding,' he said nonchalantly. 'Don't let me stop you. Hell, you're both young, enjoy it. I mean it – when you're young you think you'll always be young. Then one day you suddenly wake up and you're over fifty. And the names in the obituary columns are no longer anonymous old people. They're your contemporaries and friends.' The drink arrived. He drained it without stopping for breath.

'Come on, Henry,' Lyon said, laughing. 'Nothing can be that bad.' He reached under the table and recaptured Anne's hand with a warm intimacy.

'It's worse,' Henry insisted. 'In fact, this one promises to be the daddy of them all. Either Helen's getting tougher or I'm getting older.'

'Helen's always a barracuda until the show opens in New York,' Lyon said easily.

Henry pulled out a notebook and stared at a scribbled list. 'Want to hear a few beefs? And these are just for openers. Bad light on rhythm number; second scene evening dress stinks; orchestra too loud on ballad; Terry King's ballad holds up show and she sings it like a dirge; dream sequence chorus number too long; all my songs end with black-out – want to take my bows in one; want ballad with guy made into solo for me – he's tone-deaf; Terry King plays part too tough, throws show off balance.' He shook his head and signaled for another drink.

'God, I hate this bar,' he said, looking around and waving affably to a few agents and producers who had arrived for the opening. 'I hate every sonofabitch who comes up here hoping to see a flop.' He smiled at someone across the room. 'And Gil Case draws them all. They love to see a "gentleman" producer flop. He's crammed that Harvard background down their throats so much . . .' He sighed again. 'This is the most miserable bar in the world, and I've spent some of the most miserable nights of my life in it.'

Anne and Lyon exchanged an intimate smile. She looked around. It was the most beautiful room in the world. If I could just hold this moment, she told herself. No matter what happens to me the rest of my life, this will be the happiest moment I will ever know.

They had a quick dinner in the old-fashioned hotel dining room. Henry and Lyon knew almost everyone in the room. None of the cast was present. They were busily grabbing a sandwich in their rooms and resetting limp hair. Through the chatter and excitement she watched Lyon constantly. Occasionally their eyes would meet and hold for a quick, personal moment. She could hardly believe this was happening to her . . . happening exactly as she had hoped it would . . . feeling as she had dreamed she would . . .

Henry signaled for the check. 'Anne, I can see you're all nerves before an opening. You haven't touched your food. Well, you can eat later. Gil Case is having a big spread after the show.'

The theatre was sold out. With the flood of theatrical people on hand, the audience took on the excitement of a New York opening. Anne sat between Lyon and Henry in the third row. The lights went down and the orchestra burst into the overture. Lyon reached for her hand. She returned the pressure, dizzy with happiness.

The show opened with a bright musical number. The costumes were clean, colorful and new; the chorus girls, who had been limp and unattractive just a few hours back, looked beautiful in their peach-colored makeup. Within minutes, the air became charged with the electricity of a hit – an intangible current that passed between the audience and the performers.

When Jennifer North walked on, spotlighted apart from the other girls, an audible gasp rolled through the entire house. She walked slowly, undulating to the music, in a gold-beaded dress that seemed molded to her incredible body.

'Jesus,' Henry hissed under his breath. He leaned across Anne.

105

'Lyon, we can't miss. Weiss is here from Twentieth, and Meyers is here from Paramount. She's a cinch for a five-year deal.'

'It will have to be a good one,' Lyon answered. 'She's hung on Tony Polar. She won't leave him unless the contract is too big to pass up.'

'Tony'll never marry her. Leave this to me.'

'There's your little friend,' Lyon said quickly. Anne looked just as Neely disappeared across the stage, accompanied by two chorus boys.

When Helen made her entrance, all action suspended as the audience stampeded a reception that bordered on hysteria. Helen stood quietly, half smiling, and accepted the acclaim. Everyone was on that stage because of her; the theatre was filled because of her; every musician in the pit was there because of her; the book had been written just for her. Protected by footlights, Helen received love on a mass scale. If Gino were here, he'd be screaming and applauding like the others. After the show he would beg Anne to 'get her off my back,' but for this moment she was everyone's love.

It was Helen's show from start to finish. Each song brought on a new and stronger frenzy of applause. They were no longer an audience, they were a cult, united in the worship of Helen Lawson. The raucous laugh, which made Anne wince in public, seemed wholesome and vibrant across the footlights. Neely sparkled in her tiny bit. Jennifer North reappeared in a new revealing gown, and the audience thundered its approval. Terry King received appreciative applause for her two songs, delivered in a voice sweeter and more appealing than Helen's. But Helen was compelling; her authority was an art in itself.

'I think Terry is good,' Anne whispered to Lyon. 'But she's no competition for Helen. She's just an average performer.'

'Unfortunately, her looks are above average,' Lyon answered.

At intermission everyone crowded into the small lobby. Gilbert Case motioned to Henry, and they followed him into the bar next door.

'Gil, it's Helen's biggest show,' Henry said, as they all sipped at the weak bar Scotch.

'That's how I see it, dear boy,' Gil said with a hearty smile. 'A little cutting here and there and it comes in exactly as it is. I won't need Boston; we'll be able to do it with just four weeks in Philadelphia.'

'Easy. If the cutting is in the right spots.'

They looked at each other silently. Then Case quickly forced a hint of a smile. 'Come now, Henry, you know I'm in a bind. I can't fire Terry King. She's got a run-of-the-play contract.'

'How did she get that?' Lyon asked.

He shrugged. 'An excellent question. Do you think any decent ingenue will sign for a Helen Lawson show without it? Look at the track record. Betty Mobile – fired in Boston. Notices too good. Sherry Haines – part written out in Philly. Notices too good. Need I go on? You can't get an ingenue for a Helen Lawson show without a run-of-the-play contract. Not unless you're willing to settle for a pig.'

'Helen won't let her open in New York, I can tell you that,' Henry said quietly.

'Henry, I beg of you – talk to her,' Gil pleaded. 'If I fired Terry, how could I justify it to my backers? I've got two more shows lined up for this season. I need those backers. If I fire Terry, I have to pay her four hundred a week until June first, and I have to pay the same salary to the girl who replaces her. With Helen's salary, plus her percentage . . . well, I just can't take on anything like that.'

'It'll wind up costing you even more if you keep Terry, plus a lot of aggravation. If Terry King stays, Helen will gripe about the numbers and the orchestrations. You'll have to book three weeks in Boston. Figure on trucking and traveling, you stand to lose eight thousand a week. Then Helen will suddenly become dissatisfied with all her costumes. She'll also want you to get outside lyricists. I can see an extra twenty-five thousand right there. But get rid of Terry and Helen will start loving everything about the show, including you, and you'll come in after Philly. It's as simple as that.'

Gil shuddered. 'Well, there's always the other way . . .'

Henry nodded silently.

Gil sighed. 'I'll give it a try. But I'm getting too old for these executions.'

Henry left a few bills on the bar and they returned to the theatre.

The second act mounted in excitement. Helen belted out two show-stoppers in a row and was forced back for three encores. The show was an electrifying hit; the audience refused to let her leave the stage. They were still applauding when the curtain rang down for the final time.

Henry's program was marked with curlicues and notations on cuts and changes. His forehead was crinkled as they stood in the crowded lobby.

'You'd think the show was a flop, from your expression,' Anne said gaily.

'No, honey, I just know the battles ahead.' Then he smiled. 'It's her biggest hit so far. She's topped herself.' He stamped out his cigarette. 'Well, let's fight our way backstage.'

The entrance to Helen's dressing room looked like a mob scene. The hall was crowded with well-wishers who waited patiently in line to give the star a hurried kiss and a congratulatory compliment. Helen stood at the door, the heavy makeup appearing grotesque up close. She smiled and accepted the accolades with a false heartiness. She saw Henry, Anne and Lyon as they tried to get through the crowd. 'Hi!' she yelled gaily. 'Get inside.' She nodded toward the entrance of her dressing room. As Anne passed, Helen whispered, 'As soon as I get rid of these crumbs we'll go to Gil's party.' Then she turned brightly to the next person waiting in line, flashed her merry smile and continued with her boisterous greetings.

The party was going strong when they arrived, but at Helen's entrance all activity stopped and everyone turned toward the door. There was a split second of silence that exploded into a frenzied ovation. Helen acknowledged it with a smile and a good-natured wave that commanded the party to return to the festivities at hand. The show's press agent leaped forward to guide her to the local press and some of the important backers. Lyon led Anne to a quiet corner and brought her a ginger ale and a plate of listless, dry chicken sandwiches.

'There's hot food across the room,' he said as he settled beside her. 'I'll have a go at it after the crowd clears a bit.'

'I'm not really hungry,' Anne insisted as she nibbled at one of the tasteless sandwiches. Her eyes roved around the room. 'I don't see Neely.'

'I'm afraid only the principals are invited to this party. The chorus and showgirls have their own shindig.'

'Why, that's awful!'

'Not really. They take up a collection among themselves, get much better sandwiches at the delicatessen, hole up in someone's room and have a perfectly marvelous time knocking the higher-ups.'

Another hush suddenly enveloped the room. Anne's eyes automatically swung to the door. Jim Taylor, a leading columnist in New

Haven, had just entered with Jennifer North. Each time she saw Jennifer the girl's incredible beauty came as a fresh surprise. She watched the backers swarm over for an introduction, and once again she was doubly surprised at Jennifer's warmth, her easy interest in everyone she met.

Helen ambled over and pulled up a chair. 'You two are smart, sneaking off in a corner like this. God, how I hate these parties. But it's Gilbert's way of paying off the backers. Gives them one night to mingle with Showbiz.' She punctuated the last word with a grin.

Gil Case joined them. 'There's wonderful chicken à la king over there. Chinese food, too.'

'Gil, why do you always serve such shit at these parties?' Helen asked.

'It's good food. The hotel recommended it.'

'I'm sure they also recommended roast beef – but that's too expensive.'

'Now Helen,' Gil said pleasantly, 'this is your night. Enjoy it.' He disappeared into the milling crowd.

'Hey, Gil!' Helen shrieked. 'We got a little talking to do.' She leaped from her chair and followed him.

'He hasn't a chance,' said Lyon, smiling.

'Do you think she'll keep at it – about Terry King, I mean?' Anne asked.

'She won't relent – not an inch.'

'Maybe I should talk to Helen,' Anne said thoughtfully. 'Terry King is good. She deserves a chance. And she's no competition to Helen. I'm sure I could convince her—'

'Anne, don't try. You'll have your head snapped off.'

'No, Lyon, we're friends. That's the trouble. No one treats Helen like a human being. She's easy to talk to. I know she'd listen to me.'

He took her hand and looked into her eyes. 'I believe you mean it. Anne . . . wonderful Anne . . . how did anyone as lovely as you get into such a rat race? You only *think* you know Helen. Underneath the greasepaint there's cast iron.'

'You're wrong, Lyon. I do know Helen. I talk to her at night, late, for hours – when the mask is off – and she speaks from the heart. She's a wonderful woman. The toughness is all put on. No one takes the trouble to dig beneath it.'

He shook his head. 'I'll go along that this sweet side exists – but it isn't Helen. It's perhaps one of the small sides of Helen, one that is rarely shown and one that is capable of dissolving at a moment's notice. But the toughness – that is always there.'

'Oh, Lyon . . .'

Suddenly there was a surge to the door. A bellhop entered, his arms burdened with advance copies of the morning papers. Helen grabbed a set and scanned the notices quickly. Gil Case read them aloud.

The show was an unqualified hit. The critics praised the music, raved about the book and riotously acclaimed Helen. She was a living legend, the greatest musical comedy star alive, an accomplished actress, and on and on. Terry King also received a few nice mentions and Jennifer North was rewarded with superlatives on her physical attributes.

Everyone congratulated everyone. Backers walked around with silly smiles, shaking hands and crowding Helen with praise.

'This is a marvelous spot for us to make an exit,' Lyon suggested.

They had just reached the door when Henry blocked the way. 'Going somewhere?' he asked nonchalantly.

'Thought we'd go across to the diner and get some decent food,' Lyon answered.

'Oh no, my boy – you don't leave me alone with this.'

'With what?' Lyon asked innocently. 'The show's home.'

'Sure. Only Helen insists on an immediate meeting with Gilbert.'

'When?'

'In ten minutes, in Gil's suite. And I need you, if for nothing more than just moral support.'

Anne covered her disappointment with a smile. 'Go on, Lyon. It is late. I'm not really hungry.'

'Not on your life,' he said as he tucked her arm in his. 'You know the *real* Helen. Perhaps you can dig her up for us tonight. We'll need all the help we can get.'

The atmosphere in Gil Case's suite offered a violent contrast to the festivities of the party. Helen sat on a couch, sipping at a glass of champagne, sulking with the unflattering childish pout. The stage makeup had caked and run, emphasizing the wrinkles and forming unattractive little cracks on her face.

'This is complete madness!' Gil Case threw his arms to the ceiling in despair. 'Here we are, all sitting around as if we're at a wake, and we've got the biggest hit of the season going for us.'

'You bet your ass it's a hit!' Helen snarled. 'Every show I do is a hit. It's gonna make you a rich man, Gil. You'll get a big picture sale and I'll sit back and watch Betty Grable or Rita Hayworth do my part. Okay, that's the game. But I don't have to sit back and watch a little whore like Terry King get a Hollywood ticket through my efforts.'

'Helen, she barely got a mention.'

'Oh yeah? One paper said she was a cinch for pictures. She's also got the best song in the show.'

Henry spoke up. 'Helen, we've gone over that. There's no way that song can be rewritten for your role. The boys sat up two nights trying to lick it. It's an ingenue's song.'

'And they also said Jennifer North was a cinch for pictures,' Gil added.

'Jennifer North doesn't sing!'

'Helen – Terry King can't hurt you,' Henry pleaded.

'You bet your ass she can't! Because she isn't gonna get the chance. This is *my* show, and I'm not Santa Claus. The only star that comes out of a Lawson show is Lawson.'

'But the girl is good,' Gil insisted. 'The two songs she does help the show. And what's good for the show is good for you. As you said, it's your show.'

'Well, if she's so fucking good, go star her in your next show. How much money would your backers come up with for her?'

Henry stood up. 'Helen, you're too big for this. The girl can't hurt you, and she deserves a chance. You had to start too. Remember your first show? Suppose Nancy Shaw had insisted you get the boot in New Haven. Where would you be today?'

'Where in hell is Nancy Shaw today?' Helen snapped. 'Listen, Henry, she was pushing forty when I came along. If she'd been smart she'd have gotten rid of me. But she was stuck-up – she was a beauty, and all those great beauties are stuck-up. She figured I was no competition in the looks department. Maybe I wasn't. But I managed to walk off with the show. Not that this could happen with Terry King. She's no Helen Lawson. When you get down to it, Nancy Shaw was no Helen Lawson either. But I learned from her mistake – no one uses me or my show to feather their own little nest.'

Gil shrugged. 'She's got a run-of-the-play contract.'

Helen's smile was nasty. 'I know all about run-of-the-play contracts.'

'But Helen, she received decent notices. I can't go to my backers and say I have to pay her off because she's no good.'

'I agree,' Helen said amiably.

'And it wouldn't do you any good in the business to have it known she was fired.'

'Right!' Helen agreed. 'That's the last thing we both want. At least we're settled on that.' Her eyes narrowed. 'Now go to it. Get rid of her the sensible way. You can do it. You've done it before.'

Gil Case seemed to shrink three inches in size. Then, with a heavy sigh, he said, 'All right. But I had better wait until after the Philadelphia opening.'

'Oh no you don't!' Helen bellowed. 'And let her get another set of notices? I want her out as of this weekend!'

Gil lost some of his patience. 'My dear girl, then what? Who replaces her Monday for the Philadelphia opening?'

'Send for Penny Maxwell. She auditioned for the part, and she's a quick study. Besides, I wanted her in the first place.'

'She's rehearsing for Max Seller's new show.'

'You're kidding! Christ! She sings sharp, and she's a pig!'

'Then it's settled,' Gil said. 'Terry opens in Philadelphia. She has to. Even if I get on the phone tomorrow morning with every agent in New York, there's no one who can get up in the part in time.'

'I know someone who could,' Anne said suddenly. Everyone turned and stared at her. 'I know it's none of my business,' she added nervously.

'Who do you know, angel?' Helen asked kindly.

'Neely O'Hara. She's Terry's understudy. She knows every song, and she really sings quite well.'

'Out of the question,' Gil said haughtily. 'I put her on as understudy only to cover us on the road. I intend to get a real understudy when we hit New York. She's too insignificant. Reminds me of Orphan Annie.'

Helen's eyes narrowed. 'And what should an ingenue look like? A fucked-out redhead with big tits?'

'Helen, it's a good part. I can't take a chance for the Philadelphia opening with an unknown kid.'

112

'She's been in vaudeville all her life,' Anne offered. 'She's used to audiences. Really, Mr. Case, Neely might be wonderful.'

He hesitated. 'Well . . . we could try her, I suppose. I'd have three weeks in Philly to find someone else if she doesn't work out.'

Helen stood up. 'Then everything is settled. We can all go to sleep.'

'Like little lambs,' Gil said angrily. 'Except I'm the one who has to handle Terry King.'

'I'll bet you did plenty of that before you signed her,' Helen snapped. She walked to the door. 'Call a rehearsal for everyone at eleven tomorrow – except me. Start the ball rolling then. I gotta get some sleep. We got a matinee yet.' She turned to Anne. 'Glad you came tonight, Annie-pie. I'll check in with you when I get in bed.'

Gil closed the door after Helen. 'You boys weren't any help,' he said accusingly.

'I tried.' Henry hunched his shoulders. 'But I knew it was useless.' He looked at Lyon and Anne. 'Go on, have your eggs. I'll stay with Gil and map out the slaughter.'

As they rang for the elevator Lyon said, 'Shall we try that little beanery across the street?'

'I'm not hungry.'

'Tired?'

'No, not a bit.' Her eyes were shining.

'I think I could stand some air. How about it, want to brave the winter in New Haven?'

They walked down the deserted street. 'What will they do about Terry King?' Anne asked.

'Force her to quit.' Lyon's breath smoked the darkness.

'But how?'

'Come to rehearsal tomorrow – if you have a strong stomach.'

She shivered. 'Well, at least Neely will get a chance.'

'You were wonderful. I'd like a friend like you.'

She looked at him suddenly. 'Lyon, what do you *think* I am? Do you suppose I'm walking with you on a cold December night just because I enjoy freezing?'

'I'm walking because I *am* a friend, Anne. I'm also a realist. New Haven will end, but you have a great clump of a diamond on your

113

finger and a nice guy that goes with it. You're much too nice for a quick out-of-town romance.'

'Is that all it would be?'

'Could it be any more?' He stopped and looked down at her.

'It can be anything you want, Lyon.'

Without a word, he spun her around and led her back to the hotel. They didn't speak until they entered his room. It was a duplicate of the colorless old-fashioned room that had been assigned to her. Lyon took her coat. For a moment he stared at her tenderly, then he held out his arms. She rushed to him, to his lips, cold from the night air but firm and demanding as they met her own. Her arms slid around him. She was surprised at the urgency with which she returned his kiss, as if she had always been waiting to kiss like this. She clung to him, her mind spinning deeper and deeper into the wonder of that kiss.

When she broke away she looked at him with tears in her eyes. 'Oh, Lyon, thank you for making me believe . . .'

'Believe?'

'I – I can't explain . . . just hold me.' She threw her arms around him. He kissed her again and she prayed it would never stop. Her whole body trembled with the pure joy of his touch.

Suddenly he broke away. He held her at arm's length. His voice was hoarse – but gentle. 'Anne, I want you very much, but you must make the decision.' He looked down at her ring. 'You can make this mean whatever you wish. But if it does turn out to be – just for New Haven – I would understand.'

'Lyon, I don't want it to be an out-of-town romance.'

'Sit down, Anne.' He led her gently to the edge of the bed. 'If I thought you did, I would never have brought it up. And if I wanted a girl just for the weekend, there's a large cast to choose from. I would-n't have to go after one who was taken. There's a strange hysteria connected with a New Haven opening. Tonight will pass and Monday will come . . . You'll be back in New York on Monday. It will be another world, and this whole weekend may seem unreal. I want you to know, if that happened . . . I would understand.'

'And what about you?' she asked. 'Could this be hysteria for you too?'

He laughed. 'O dear God! Anne, do you know how many New Havens, Philadelphias and Bostons I've been through? This is just another night – with one wonderful exception. You're here.'

She reached out and touched his face with her fingertips. 'I love you, Lyon.'

'I also won't hold you to that.'

'Don't you believe me?'

'I think you mean it, this moment. I don't think you're a girl who goes to bed with a man unless she believes it's love.'

'I've never said that to anyone. Lyon, I do love you.'

He stood up and lit a cigarette. When he turned around, his face was set. 'I'm going to send you back to your room.' He walked over and picked up her coat.

She sat on the bed. 'Lyon . . . I don't understand . . .'

'This can wait. See how you feel about it on Monday – in New York.'

'I'll still feel the same.'

'I can't take that chance.'

She got up slowly. 'You really want me to leave?' Her vision was growing misty.

'Good God, Anne, it's the last thing I want. But for your sake . . . I . . .'

'Lyon . . . I want to stay,' she said, almost humbly.

He looked at her curiously, as if measuring the meaning of her words. Then suddenly he flashed one of his quick smiles and tossed off his jacket. He crossed the room and held out his arms. 'Come here, you beautiful golden wench. I tried being noble, but you've ripped away my last shred of resistance.'

She felt her lips twitch as she tried to match his smile. He hugged her lightly and released her. Now what? He was taking off his tie. What was she supposed to do? She truly wanted to go to bed with him, but there must be a certain etiquette involved. She couldn't start pulling off her clothes like a burlesque queen. Oh, Lord, why hadn't she worn her new slip – and why hadn't she asked someone how one went about this? Now he was taking off his shirt. She had to do something – she couldn't just stand there . . .

He unbuckled his belt and nonchalantly pointed toward the bath-room. 'Want an undressing room?'

She nodded dumbly and rushed in. Safely behind the closed door, she undressed. Now what? She couldn't just stalk into the bedroom naked. She had dreamed of just such a moment, of giving herself to a man she loved. But *not* like this – not in a small hotel room in New Haven! In her daydreams she had envisioned a lush double bed, had pictured herself floating, in a white gossamer nightgown, into her husband's arms. The lights would be dim, and she'd glide ethereally under the sheets and into the tender arms of her lover. Her dream had never gone beyond that, had never progressed to the actual act of making love – she had only dreamed of the emotion and the romantic setting, and her lover had been a vague, faceless man. Now he had a face – and she had no gossamer gown. She was standing naked and shivering under a harsh bathroom light and she didn't know what to do.

'Hey there! It's awfully lonesome out here,' Lyon called.

She looked around frantically and grabbed a large bath towel. She draped it around her and timidly opened the door.

Lyon was in bed, with the sheet up to his waist. He squashed out the cigarette he was smoking and held out his arms. She turned to grope for the light switch in the bathroom.

'Leave it on,' he said. 'I want to see you . . . to believe it's really you in my arms.'

She approached the bed and he took her hands. The towel dropped to the floor. 'My lovely Anne,' he said softly. His admiration and the natural, easy way he appraised her body dissolved her embarrassment. He tossed aside the sheet and drew her into his arms. The strength of his body against her own suddenly seemed the most natural feeling in the world. Like the impossible and delirious new sensation of feeling his mouth on hers, kissing her deeply, searchingly. She felt herself responding to his embrace with an ardor she had never dreamed she possessed, her mouth demanding more and more. She couldn't kiss him deeply enough. His hands caressed her body, gently, then intimately. Yet her emotional excitement dominated all physical sensation. To have him in her arms . . . to be close, to feel free to kiss his eyelids, his brow, his lips . . . to know that he wanted her, that he cared . . .

And then it was happening. Oh God, this was the moment! She wanted to please him, but the pain caught her unaware and she cried out. He pulled away immediately and released her.

'Anne . . .' She could see the surprise in his eyes.

'Go on, Lyon,' she begged. 'It will be all right.'

He lay back with a groan. 'Holy God! It can't be . . .'

'But Lyon, it's all right. I love you.'

He leaned over and kissed her gently. Then he lay back with his arms behind his head, staring into the semidarkness.

She was very still. He reached out for a cigarette and offered her one. She refused, and watched him silently, miserably. He inhaled deeply and said, 'Anne, you must believe me. I never would have touched you if I had thought—'

She jumped out of bed, dashed to the bathroom and slammed the door. She buried her face in a towel to muffle her sobs.

He followed her instantly and pushed open the door. 'Don't cry, my darling. Everything is still intact – you're still a virgin.'

'I'm not crying because of that!'

'Then what is it?'

'You! You don't want me!'

'Oh, my dearest . . .' He took her in his arms. 'Of course I want you. I want you desperately. But I can't. You see, I never dreamed . . .'

A faint show of anger burned through her tears. 'What did you expect? I'm not a tramp!'

'Of course you're not. I just assumed that somewhere along the line – in college – or certainly with Allen . . .'

'Allen never touched me!'

'So it would seem.'

'Does it make so much difference to you? My being a virgin?'

'All the difference in the world.'

'I'm sorry.' She heard her own words with utter disbelief. The entire situation was insane. Here they were, standing naked in the bathroom under the ugly, unshaded little light, arguing about something that should be sacred. She grabbed a towel and covered herself. 'Please get out and let me dress. I never thought I'd have to apologize for being – inexperienced. I thought the man I loved would be . . . pleased . . .' Her voice broke and she turned her head to hide fresh tears of humiliation.

With a quick gesture he swept her up and carried her into the bedroom. 'He *is* pleased,' he whispered. 'Just overcome . . . and handling it all like a blundering idiot.'

He placed her gently on the bed and lay down beside her. 'I'll try to be gentle,' he said softly. 'And if you find you don't want to go through with it, just tell me.'

'I want to . . .' She buried her head in his neck. Her voice was muffled. 'I love you, Lyon. I want to make you happy.'

'But it must work both ways – and this may not be easy for you. The first time rarely is, I understand.'

'Don't you *know*? I mean, haven't you ever – had a virgin before?'

'Never,' he admitted with a smile. 'So you see, I'm just as nervous about this as you.'

'Just love me, Lyon, belong to me – that's all I ask.'

She clung to him. She didn't care about the hurt or discomfort – just to belong to this wonderful man was the greatest happiness she could ever know. When the pain came, she clenched her teeth and made no sound. And when she felt his body go tense, she felt only surprise that he had drawn away from her. But he had groaned in satisfaction . . . Then suddenly she understood, and her happiness doubled. At the height of his passion he had thought to protect her. She leaned over and took him in her arms. His back was moist with perspiration. All at once she knew – this was the ultimate in fulfillment, to please a man you loved. At that moment she felt she was the most important and powerful woman in the world. She was flooded with a new sense of pride in her sex.

Later, he held her in his arms with a new tenderness. 'It wasn't much fun for you tonight,' he said. 'But it will get better – I promise you.'

'Just promise to hold me close. Oh, Lyon, I love you so!'

'And I adore you. I could spend the rest of the night telling you how wonderful you are.' He stroked her hair. 'How beautiful you are . . . But I think we both should get some sleep. There's that eleven o'clock rehearsal tomorrow.'

'Rehearsal?'

'Well, that's what they call it. You come along and tell me what *you* call it.' He reached down and pulled up the sheet. 'Now. Let's both get some sleep.' He held her gently and shut his eyes.

'Lyon . . . I can't sleep here.'

'Why not?' He sounded drowsy already.

'I don't know . . . In case Helen or Neely call in the morning.'

'Forget about them. I want to find you in my arms when I wake up.'

She kissed his face, his brow and his eyes. Then she slid out of his arms. 'We'll have that, Lyon, many, many times. But not tonight.' She went into the bathroom and dressed quickly. It wasn't because of Helen or Neely – it was just too much, all at once. She wouldn't have slept a wink, lying there beside him. And in the morning . . . Well, things like this had to be taken in stages. Men were much more casual about it than women. But the most important thing in the world had happened. She knew the feeling of love – and she knew it was the whole reason for living.

She came out of the bathroom and walked over to the bed. She started to speak, then saw that he had fallen asleep. Smiling, she went to the desk, found a piece of hotel stationery and scribbled, *Good night, sleeping beauty. See you tomorrow. I love you.* She propped the note by the phone and quietly slipped out of the room.

In her own bed she lay awake, too excited to sleep. Her mind relived the entire evening, recalling every word he had said, every expression on his face. 'It will get better – I promise you.' Would it? Would she ever shudder and tremble and stiffen with the ecstasy he had felt? It didn't matter. All that mattered was Lyon, to hold him in her arms, to please him – to know that she could feel love, that this remarkable man wanted her body against his . . . She drifted off into a soft, dark sleep.

She was out of bed at nine. It was a clear, windy day. She looked out of the window, saw a man walking against the wind, holding his hat, a girl waiting for a bus. She felt sorry for them. She felt sorry for everyone in the world because they couldn't feel as she did. 'Oh, you poor people! You think this is just another cold day. Look up at me – I want to tell you how happy I am. The whole world belongs to me. In this very building there is a man – the most wonderful man in the world – and he belongs to me!' The watery neon sign on the diner seemed to blink at her. She winked back. It was a beautiful day! A beautiful diner! A beautiful town!

She took a hot bath, and when the water penetrated the soreness within her, it became a tangible memory of him. Her spirits soared.

She took pains with her hair. She changed her lipstick twice. And she alternated in watching the clock and staring at the telephone.

At ten-fifteen she began to feel uneasy. Did he mean to meet her at the theatre? But he had said, 'We'll go together.' Or had he said, 'Come along'?

When the phone rang she dashed across the room. It was Neely. 'You coulda at least come to say hello to me after the show,' she said.

'I thought you'd be at the party.'

'Me? I'm regarded as chorus. And now I got a rehearsal. Is that the end, calling a rehearsal before a matinee? Poor Mel – he's beat.'

'Where is he?'

'Downstairs in the coffee shop. I'm meeting him there.'

'I'll see you at rehearsal.'

'Why should you come? It'll just be a drag.'

'Neely . . . now don't say a word . . . but there's a chance you may replace Terry King. You know her numbers, don't you?'

'Know them?' Neely squealed. 'Backwards! I know all of Helen's songs, too. Anne, are you kidding me?'

'No, there's some plan. I sat in on the conference last night. But don't say a word, just sit tight.'

'Oh, golly! I can't believe it. Oh, Lordy, wait till I tell Mel! 'By. See you at the theatre!'

Ten-forty-five. Lyon hadn't called. Three times she had started for the phone to call him, but decided against it. She lit a cigarette and stood staring at the wintry sunlight from the window. The minutes ticked by . . . Somewhere a steeple bell chimed. Well, now what? Was she going to stand around in the room all day? Or go to the theatre alone? No, that wouldn't look right. If he was there and hadn't called her, it would look as if she were running after him. Ridiculous! This wasn't Lawrenceville, and Lyon wasn't just a date. There were no silly rules now. She marched resolutely to the phone and asked for his room.

His voice was muffled at first. Then he shot into action. 'Good God, darling! Is it really five of eleven? I thought I left a call for ten o'clock!'

'I don't see how you could, unless you woke up somewhere in the middle of the night.'

His laugh was sheepish. 'I'm just reading your note. Boy, I'm a real Sir Galahad! Come on down and keep me company while I shave.' She could almost hear him stretching over the phone. 'I'll order some coffee for us.'

The door was ajar and he yelled a cheerful 'Come in' to her light tap. He was standing in his shorts in the bathroom. He pulled her over and gave her a careful kiss, avoiding the lather on his face. Then he turned back to his shaving. His very casualness seemed to enhance the new intimacy between them, as if it were the most natural thing in the world for her to be there, watching him shave while he stood in his shorts. She sat on the rumpled bed, happier than she had ever been in her life. He washed the remaining lather off his face and came in. This time he leaned over and kissed her tenderly Then he began the business of putting on his shirt. He whistled as he knotted his tie. Her happiness was making her feel weak. She had never known anything like it.

She wondered whether Lyon felt the same intimacy. He couldn't. So, many girls had probably seen him stand in his shorts while he shaved . . . She quickly pushed the thought from her mind. No girl had felt what she was feeling, and that made the difference. Nothing was going to ruin the most wonderful day of her life!

The waiter knocked and wheeled in a table. Lyon scribbled his name on the check. He motioned her to sit down as he gulped his orange juice standing. Then he carried his coffee to the phone and asked for Henry Bellamy's room.

Henry was going to be late, too. Lyon laughed. 'All right, coward, let's synchronize our watches. I have eleven-thirty. Let's say we both walk in at eleven-forty.' He hung up and turned to Anne with a grin. 'Think you can face the execution?'

'I wouldn't miss it. What's going to happen?'

'Nothing much. Just a few strong men will gang up on a little girl and force her to quit.'

'You act like you've been through this before.'

'I have. It can be sloppy. Every now and then you run into a Terry King who turns out to be an embryonic Helen Lawson. You put the knife in her back but she doesn't bleed. That's when you lose.'

They met Henry in the elevator. If he was surprised to see her with Lyon, he showed no sign.

The entire cast, with the exception of Helen, was at the theatre. The chorus girls sat in slacks or huddled in their fur coats, their dark glasses concealing the lack of eye makeup. They sipped coffee from paper cups and looked disgruntled. Neely sat on the edge of a chair, tense, waiting to spring.

Anne sat in the fourth row with Henry and Lyon. Jennifer North entered in a rush, apologizing to everyone for oversleeping. The director turned from a huddle with the orchestra leader and nodded good-naturedly. 'Nothing's changed for you, princess. If you like you can go back to bed for a few hours.'

Jennifer smiled and came down into the darkened theatre. Henry motioned her to sit beside them. She recognized Anne and smiled warmly. 'Isn't it wonderful,' she said enthusiastically. 'We have a hit! I shouldn't say *we* – I do nothing. But it's such a great show, I'm thrilled to be in it.'

'You're very lovely in it,' Anne said sincerely.

'Thanks, but I don't think my name will bring any customers to the box office.'

'Don't sell yourself short,' Henry answered. 'Once this show hits New York you'll get plenty of newspaper space. I guarantee you a picture deal within six weeks of opening night.'

Jennifer dimpled. 'Oh, Henry . . . honestly, I'd adore it.' Then a slight frown came between her eyes. 'But only if it's a big contract. Not one of those starlet deals.'

'Starlets often turn into stars,' Henry said carefully.

The frown grew deeper. 'Starlets with talent. I have no talent, Henry. That's why I'd need a good contract. If they pay you enough, they have to use you. And they have to teach you – and train you.'

'Let me decide on that. If it's short money with a good studio and I say take it, you take it. With the smell of television in the air, they're not handing out those big contracts so easy.'

'Then perhaps I'm better off in New York. I've had offers from Powers and Longworth to model, and I could earn quite a bit with that, along with the show.'

Henry turned to her suddenly. 'Level with me, Jennifer. Do you want a picture deal? Or a career? I don't want to knock myself out if you don't really care. And what's with Tony Polar? How serious is it between you?'

Jennifer smiled. 'The newspapers blow it up. I adore Tony, but I don't think either of us wants to rush into marriage. Besides, I'm still legally married to Prince Mirallo.'

'The papers are practically signed for the annulment. Just remember the lines when you go before the judge – you're a nice Catholic girl and you wanted children and this bastard didn't want any.'

'Are you Catholic?' Lyon asked.

Jennifer shrugged. 'My mother was, but my father wasn't. They divorced. I was never even baptized. But no one will check, will they, Henry?'

'Just do as I say. You're a Catholic. You wanted to be married by a priest, but the Prince picked a civil ceremony. From then on you're halfway home. Then you talk about the children you wanted. Anne will be your witness.'

'I *what?*' Anne burst in.

'We have to have a witness. I meant to tell you. Don't worry, it will be a closed court. You just have to say that you're a friend of Jennifer's and that she confided to you before she married this prince how ecstatic she was about marrying the jerk, that she was even willing to go to Italy to live and that she wanted dozens of children. But be sure and remember the children part.'

'But I'd be lying under oath,' Anne argued.

'Cross your fingers,' Henry said. Then, turning his attention to the stage, he whispered, 'Hold your hats . . . here we go!'

Terry King was standing in the center of the stage staring at the director in complete disbelief.

'Cut the *ballad!*' she yelled. 'Are you mad? Did you read the reviews?'

'The show's running long, honey, and we have enough ballads.' The director's voice was casual.

'So what? Cut some other ballad. You know damn well mine is the best song in the show'

'Those are my orders,' he said wearily.

'Where's Gil Case?'

'He's not here. He's busy with the writers. Bill! Hey, Bill Towley!' A thin young juvenile appeared. 'Bill, the love scene you and Terry have is out. We're working on a new solo dance routine for you to go in its place for Philly. Instead of telling Terry how much you love her, you do a dance. It'll speed up the action.'

Bill nodded in delighted acceptance and disappeared.

'And what do I do while he does this dance, sit in my dressing room?' Terry shrieked. 'Do you realize if the love scene is cut and the ballad goes, it leaves me with two lines in the first act and a rhythm number in the second and that's all?'

'The rhythm number stays in,' the director answered. 'But we're putting the chorus behind you. They'll do a dance to the second chorus.'

'And what do I do?'

'Instead of singing the second chorus, you'll go to stage left. You'll stand there . . . then the light will go off you and you'll slip offstage while the chorus takes over.'

'That's what you think!' She grabbed her coat and rushed off the stage and out of the theatre. The director went on giving cuts and blends as if nothing had happened.

Ten minutes later Terry reappeared, armed with a small man who looked like a raccoon. The raccoon bristled down the aisle. 'Now what's this all about?' he demanded.

The director turned and looked down. 'What's what about?' he asked innocently.

'Listen, Leroy!' the raccoon hollered. 'Don't think your innocent girlish face is going to fool me. I know this routine. Helen's scared of Terry. Only this time Terry has a little luck going for her. She's got the biggest hit ballad of the show. You can't tell me the boys are going to let Helen cut their best song from the show.'

'Call them,' Leroy suggested.

'I have. They're in conference with Gil Case. Besides, you mean Case is willing to pay Terry four hundred bucks just to do two lines and half of a rhythm number?'

'If she wants to remain and do that, I suppose he'll have to.'

'Oh, so that's the bit. The Equity dodge. You'd love her to quit. Then you could put someone else in the part for chickenfeed. But if you fire Terry, you'll have to pay her till next June *plus* her replacement.'

'No one is firing Terry King.'

'You can't afford to. That's why you're trying to make her quit.'

The director sat on the edge of the stage and said, with exaggerated patience, 'No one is trying to make Terry quit. We're not thinking in personalities now. We're looking at the show as a whole. As an agent, you're only thinking of your client. I don't blame you, Al, that's your business. But my business is to think of the show. It runs too long. I'm cutting where Gil Case, the writers and all of us think it should be cut, regardless of who it affects.'

The raccoon stamped out a cigarette on the thick carpet of the theatre. 'Don't give me that bullshit! You're following orders Case got from Helen Lawson. He has no choice – he has to protect Old

124

Ironsides. And with that brassy voice of hers she needs protection from a good singer.'

'Let's not get personal about this,' Leroy snapped.

'Why? You and I both know she's dated and corny. If that old bag was trying to get started today she'd never get past the first audition—'

'I think we can cut this out!' Henry's voice shot out of the darkness.

The agent whirled around. 'I didn't see you, Mr. Bellamy. Hi. Say, look, it's nothing personal. I'm just fighting for my client – the same way you probably did for Miss Lawson twenty years ago.'

'I didn't fight for Helen by knocking a great star when she wasn't there to defend herself,' Henry thundered. 'Who in hell are you – a weasel with desk space on West Forty-sixth Street. How dare you stand there and insult one of the greatest living stars in the theatre?'

The little man cringed. 'Mr. Bellamy . . . what would you do if you were in my place?'

'It would depend on who my client was. If it was Helen Lawson, we would have handed in our notice and walked out with dignity. Because with a Helen Lawson – even a Helen Lawson who was just beginning – there would always be another show and a better part. But with your client, I'd take whatever crumbs were offered. I'd stay with two lines and half a chorus and milk the producer for the salary. So what if she's a joke to all the other producers at the Broadway opening? It's her funeral, not yours. Maybe you'll find someone else after you bury her. But you'd better make her stick in the show and grab your lousy ten per cent, because it's obvious you're scared. This may be the only show she'll ever get, and you're not about to pass up an easy buck.'

Terry King suddenly came to life. 'Listen, I can outsing Helen Lawson anywhere! And Al and I aren't afraid. This lousy show isn't the only one – and I'll be a bigger star than Helen Lawson. You bet I'll walk out! And with dignity! Right now!' She was practically screaming.

'Honey, wait . . .' Al pleaded. 'This is exactly what they want you to do!'

'And what do *you* want me to do?' she snarled. 'Open in Philadelphia and New York looking like a bit player? Just so you can collect your lousy ten per cent!'

'That has nothing to do with it. You know that. We can make double this money playing clubs. But we both agreed that a Broadway show would get us a picture deal.'

'Picture deal!' This was Henry. 'God, that kind of thinking went out with Ruby Keeler movies. Any agent who thinks all you have to do is get on Broadway and it means a picture deal is small time. Sure Broadway helps, but you've got to *do* something on Broadway. Unless your client wants a stock contract – I can get that for her without this show. But a real picture deal, no. Only a star gets that. And an agent builds a star by never allowing her to appear *anywhere* unless she looks like a star, whether it's on Broadway or in a saloon. But as I say, you obviously don't think your client has it, because you'll let her walk on looking like a bit player.'

Terry grabbed Al's arm. 'Come on, Al. Let's get out of here.'

'Wait a minute. We still have a contract, and you have a matinee to play,' Al reminded her.

'I won't walk on the stage with those cuts.'

'I'm afraid you'll have to,' Henry answered. 'You still have to hand in a two-week notice and play Philadelphia.'

'I won't be humiliated that way,' Terry insisted. 'I won't appear before the Philadelphia critics in a bit part.'

'What's all the fuss about?' Gil Case called as he walked down the aisle. 'Who's not going to appear?'

'Mr. Case!' Terry rushed to him, almost in tears. 'You've cut my part. I can't appear on the stage as a bit player.'

'I've told her she has to,' Henry said slowly. 'Even if she does hand in her notice right now.'

'Now wait a minute,' Gil said kindly. 'No one wants to hurt anyone more than necessary.' He looked at Terry sympathetically. 'My dear child, I hadn't realized how small the part was after the cuts. It *is* hardly more than a bit now . . .' He looked concerned.

'I can't play it.' Terry was insistent.

He suddenly smiled. 'You don't have to.'

'What about the matinee?' Henry asked.

Gil waved his hand. 'Forget it. We can put on the understudy. The part's such a small bit, it really doesn't matter.' He put his arm around Terry. 'Let's go back to my suite – you too, Al. Terry can write her formal notice, and I'll give her two months' salary as a bonus.' He paused to consider. 'I'll tell you what we'll do. I'll call my press agent and have him notify the New York papers, and you'll come out of this with tons of publicity. Dear girl . . . by next week every producer in town will be after you. It gives you stature to walk out on a Helen Lawson show.'

He led her up the aisle and out of the theatre with the raccoon shuffling behind.

The moment they were gone Henry walked to the stage and had a quick consultation with the director. He nodded and sprang into action. 'Neely O'Hara!' he called. Neely rushed up to him. 'Can you learn the one chorus of the rhythm number by two-thirty?'

'I know both choruses now.'

He smiled faintly. 'Okay, we do the one chorus and we put in the dance. Come on, kids, we got work to do. Neely, you go to wardrobe, see how Terry's costumes fit you. Now, chorus, let's take it from the top.'

Henry stood up. 'Let's go. I think we all need some fresh air.'

Outside, they stood in embarrassed silence. 'I think I'll take a nap,' Jennifer said. She walked away toward the hotel. Henry stood silently staring into space. Lyon pressed Anne's hand.

'I think it's revolting,' Anne said. Then, forcing a faint smile, she said, 'But I suppose that's show business.'

'It's not show business,' Henry snorted. 'It stinks. No matter how you slice it, it stinks. I want to vomit. I felt like Joe Louis in a ring with two crippled midgets. Jesus! Well, I'll call Helen and tell her the good news.' He walked slowly to the hotel.

Lyon led Anne across the street to the diner. He ordered eggs for both of them. 'Henry's wrong,' he insisted. 'We scratched the kitten and she didn't scratch back. And the agent is just an agent, not a Henry Bellamy. Henry's a champ, and twenty years ago he was a champ. And twenty years ago, if you'd scratched Helen Lawson, you'd have broken your fingers. Henry wasn't a louse – they just didn't have it.'

'But they cut the ballad out, and half the rhythm number. How could Terry fight back? What Henry said made sense.'

Lyon attacked his eggs. 'Do you honestly think that ballad will remain out? Once Terry's notice is signed and she's on a train back to New York, everything goes back as it was. If Terry had stuck, they'd have held off till the end of the out-of-town run. Helen would have made everyone miserable, but everything would have gone back opening night, and Terry would have won. It's like a game of poker. Terry had the winning hand, but Henry bluffed her out of the pot.'

Fifteen minutes later Henry joined them at the diner. He forced down a dry chicken sandwich, claiming his ulcers were acting up again. At one-thirty some of the chorus drifted over for a quick sandwich. They sat in little groups, gossiping about the new events. Neely was the big news of the day.

Anne decided against visiting Neely backstage before the matinee. Knowing Neely, she realized things must be chaotic. She stood with Lyon at the back of the packed house during the performance. Neely managed the part with professional ease. As far as Anne could see, she would neither hurt nor help the show. The part had been sliced to such proportions that it meant very little.

'Anne, I know you had something to do with it,' Neely gasped when Anne went back to congratulate her. 'Helen told me about it today. Oh, Anne, I love you so much. You're really like a sister. Oh . . . this is Mel.'

Anne turned toward the young man who had been standing in a corner trying to look inconspicuous. He darted forward, shook hands and receded back against the wall. He was tall, too thin, and his alert dark eyes were fixed on Neely with naked adoration. His warmth hit Anne right away, and she was suddenly very glad for Neely.

'Wasn't she sensational?' Mel said proudly.

'Just wonderful,' Anne said warmly.

'And next Monday in Philly I get the ballad back and the love scene,' Neely burbled. 'And Helen Lawson said she'll see to it I get a new set of costumes for New York. She thinks Terry's costumes are too sophisticated for me.'

Helen was enthusiastic about Neely. 'Wasn't your girl friend just great!' she shouted when Anne stopped by her room.

Anne was surprised. Neely had been adequate, but Helen's enthusiasm was way overboard. 'She made that whore look sick,' Helen continued. 'Neely's just what the part calls for – a nice, innocent kid. You watch, when she sings the torch song on Monday, it'll really hit home. An innocent-looking kid, torching, gets to them.'

Anne started for the door.

'Hey, where the hell you rushing to?' Helen demanded.

'Lyon Burke is waiting downstairs.'

Helen looked at her peculiarly. 'Listen, I saw you holding hands at that party last night. If you want to ball it up in New Haven, okay. But just remember, that hunk of ice on your finger is the real thing.'

'I'm giving it back.'

'*Whaaat?*' Helen shouted. 'Listen, Annie – for God's sake don't go taking a one-night stand seriously.' Anne turned away. Helen softened immediately. 'Look, angel . . . you're young. I know how it is, and Lyon is a real hunk of man. Have a ball, you only live once. But don't give up Allen for a quickie romance.'

Anne smiled weakly and started for the door.

'You going back to New York now?' Helen asked.

'I think so.'

'We're going to Philly tomorrow morning and rehearse. Put back the ballad, tighten a few things up. I think by Monday night we'll have a real slick show. And your girl friend will have herself a good part. I already told Gil Case not to look for anyone else for New York. I'm satisfied with Neely.'

'Good luck on Monday,' Anne said lamely.

'I'll see you then, when you come with Gino and Allen. Remember, we have a big date after the show.'

Allen! The opening! Gino!

'See you then,' Helen called gaily.

Lyon was waiting outside. 'Paid all your duty calls?'

She nodded. He slipped her arm under his. 'I've gotten us a pass,' he said. 'We can take the next train back. I was afraid we might have to stick around, but Henry is remaining. He'll go on to Philadelphia and we'll meet him there on Monday.'

She felt a sudden surge of exuberance at Lyon's easy assumption that she was quite naturally 'with him' from now on. But her spirits sank again at the thought of facing the inevitable with Allen. For the first time in her life she understood the value of a 'Dear John' letter. How simple it would be if she could just drop him a note and say: *Dear Allen, Enclosed find ten-karat diamond ring. I think you're awfully nice but I'm in love with someone else. It happened during our long separation of forty-eight hours.*

They had dinner on the train and without discussion went directly to Lyon's apartment. She felt a slight shudder when she entered. The apartment seemed almost familiar to her.

As if reading her thoughts, Lyon said, 'This really is your apartment. I've always thought of it that way.'

'You mean you actually thought of me . . . before . . .'

He took her in his arms. 'Anne, do you think I suddenly saw you for the first time in New Haven?'

'I don't know . . . it never occurred to me that you were ever aware of me.'

'Well, I can't seem to recall you leering at me, either,' he said.

'I think I loved you all along,' she said. 'I just wouldn't admit it. Not even to myself.'

'Think of all the wasted time . . .'

'It's your fault. After all, what is a girl supposed to do? She can't walk up to a man and say, "By the way, even though we've just met, I think you're the man I've been waiting for."'

'I think it's a marvelous idea. Believe me, the first girl who does that sort of thing will certainly make an impression. Especially if she looks like you. Now you settle down on the couch and I'll fix us a drink. I'm going to give you a light Scotch. It will help you relax.'

'Do I seem jittery?'

He handed her the drink. 'Not a bit. But you must be feeling some nerves. Everything is so new . . . I'm new . . . sex is new . . .' He sat beside her and stroked her hair gently.

She snuggled against him. 'I feel closer to you than I've ever felt to anyone in my life. I want to know everything about you . . . I don't want us to have any secrets. We're one, Lyon, part of one another. I belong to you.'

He moved away and sipped his drink thoughtfully. 'I wonder if I can measure up to that kind of love, Anne. I don't want to hurt you.'

'You couldn't hurt me, Lyon. You've given me so much already. If nothing more ever happened after today, I'd still be grateful for the two most wonderful days of my life.'

He smiled gently. Then he took her hand and patted the finger with the large ring. 'Aren't we forgetting something?'

'That's over. I'm returning the ring.'

'Anne . . . the way I feel about you . . . it's very real. I want you to know that. But I've given all I might ever be able to give you. I—'

'And it's enough! It's all I want – your love. I don't love Allen. I never have. I never really intended to marry him. It just happened so fast and I was carried along. But even if you hadn't happened, I could never have gone through with it.'

'I'd like to believe you, Anne. My conscience would be easier.'

'Your conscience? Lyon, don't you love me?'

He looked into space as if searching for an answer. He saw the quick tears spring to her eyes. 'Anne!' He grabbed her shoulders. 'Yes, yes, I do love you. I love you and want you. But your kind of love frightens me – and I wonder if my love will be enough for you.'

She closed her eyes in relief. 'Oh, Lyon, you scared me. Of course you can't love me like I love you. I don't expect it. No one could love anyone that much.' She looked at him closely. 'Just love me, that's all I ask. Love me as much as you can. And let me love you.'

She woke up in his arms the following day. She lay there, not moving, looking at his strong profile. He was beautiful in sleep. Sex had been painful again, but she had reveled in the satisfaction she had given him. And for the first time she felt she belonged to someone. All the things she had never even discussed with girls – things that seemed too personal to talk about, even with Neely, she had talked about openly and freely with Lyon. The rhythm system, all the precautions . . .

She eased herself out of his arms and went into the kitchen. She had coffee going and eggs in a pan before she looked at a clock. It was after noon.

He was awake when she placed the eggs on the table. He praised her cooking – the eggs were perfect, the coffee a work of art. After breakfast he settled down with the *Times* while she showered.

He looked up in surprise when she appeared, fully dressed, her coat on her arm.

'Walking out on me?' He pulled her down on the couch. 'You are the most fleeting romance I've ever had.' He kissed her neck, and she felt herself go limp. She forced herself to pull away.

'Lyon, I can't go to the office tomorrow in the same clothes. I need a change of stockings . . . underwear . . . I've got to get home.'

He looked at his watch. 'Fair enough. I'll pick you up at seven. We'll have dinner. And be prepared to go to the office from here.'

She kissed him gratefully. She had been momentarily frightened that he wouldn't ask her to return. She took the luxury of grabbing a cab; it was already three o'clock, and she had so much to do before seven.

The moment she walked into her room, the world closed in on her. There was a large vase of flowers on the bureau. The card was from Allen. *Hope you missed me like I missed you. Call me the second you get in. I love you. Allen.*

Until Friday, this room had known another life. Now she felt like a stranger. She had shed the room like she had shed Lawrenceville. She looked at the roses. It couldn't be put off; she was going to Philadelphia tomorrow with Lyon, and Allen expected to go – and Gino!

She dialed Allen, but stopped halfway and hung up. Maybe she could send a wire. But she had to return the ring. It hung lifelessly and heavily on one side of her finger.

She dialed again. He answered on the second ring. 'Well, how was New Haven and your girl friend, Old Ironsides?'

'The show is a hit.'

'I know. Gino ran into some people at Morocco last night who had been to New Haven.'

'How was Morocco?'

'I wasn't there. Remember me? I'm an engaged man. I sat home both nights with a good book, waiting for my girl to get back.'

'Allen . . . Allen, I've got something to tell you.' She rushed on, knowing it had to come in a burst or she'd lose her nerve. 'Allen, I'm not your girl and I'm not engaged to you and I want to give back the ring.'

There was a long silence. Then he said, 'Anne, I'll be right over.'

'No, Allen . . . I'll meet you somewhere . . . I'll give you back the ring.'

'I don't want the ring. I want to talk to you.'

'But there's nothing to talk about.'

'There isn't? Good God, Anne, for three months I've been in love with you. Now you want to wash the whole thing up with a phone call. What happened? Did someone talk against me in New Haven? Look, I've done a lot of crazy things in the past. Sometimes I wasn't a very nice guy – but that was before I met you. You can't

132

hold anything I did then against me now. Nothing meant anything until you came along. Someone's scared you off me and I'm going to see you and find out. I won't give up just like this. I have a right to present my side.'

'Allen, no one spoke against you in New Haven. And talking to me won't change things.'

'I'll be right over.'

'Allen, don't come!' She shrieked it. 'I'm in love!'

This time the silence was even longer. Finally she said hesitantly, 'Allen? Do you understand?'

'Who is he?'

'Lyon Burke.'

His laugh was unpleasant. 'You mean the homeless cockney who's in my old apartment? Well . . . glad to have provided you with a decent honeymoon cottage.'

'Allen, it just *happened*.'

'Sure, just like that. And it just happened you fell out of love with me.'

'I never told you I loved you. Remember that. You were the one who insisted on being engaged.'

'Okay, Anne. Good luck.'

'How do I get the ring back to you?'

'I'm not worried about it. Why are you?'

'But I want you to have it back.'

'You mean Lyon Burke gets offended seeing it on your finger. Or has he already replaced it? From what I've heard about him, the only ring you'll get is one through your nose.'

'Allen, let's not part this way.'

'What do you want? Shall I send you a singing telegram? Boy, this is really the prize. The first time in my life I treat a girl on the level and I get it in the end! But I'll see you around. With Lyon Burke it will be a long, long walk to the altar.'

'Please, Allen . . . may I see you at lunch tomorrow and return the ring?'

'No, my little iceberg, keep it.'

'What?'

'Keep it! You bitch . . . I don't need the ring. I can buy a lot of them. But you're going to need it. It's very hockable. Or better yet, wear it! Let it cut into your finger every time some guy screws you like you've screwed me. I have a hunch Lyon Burke will be the first!' The receiver slammed in her ear.

She dialed him back immediately. 'Allen, I know you're furious at me – and the things you've said, you've said in anger. I want us to remain friends.'

'I like men for friends,' he said coldly.

'All right, but I can't keep the ring.'

'If that's what you called about, forget it!'

'Allen, wait!' She knew he was going to hang up. 'I want to remind you about Gino. He promised to go to Philadelphia tomorrow.'

'You mean that's still on with us?' There was a sudden tinge of hope in his voice.

'Well, not with *us*. I can't go with you now. But there's no reason for Gino not to go. Helen is expecting him.'

'Oh, no! You must be kidding!' His laugh was almost a groan.

'Why? Helen's reserved a room for him. He operates independently of you. I see no reason for Helen to be disappointed because of us.'

'You don't? Well, now I've heard everything. Do you think Gino wanted to go? Do you think it's a thrill for him to wrestle with Old Ironsides?'

'Stop calling Helen that! She's darned attractive, and your father should be thrilled that she wants to be with him. She's a big star and—'

'And a big brassy bore! My father can have any girl in town. This is a man's world – women only own it when they're very young. You'll find that out some fine day. And your Helen Lawson may be the biggest star on Broadway, but she's still a bloated, loud-mouthed broad the moment she steps off stage. Sure, he was coming tomorrow . . . and don't think he didn't try and get out of it. But I forced him. Isn't that a laugh? I made him do it for you. And I spent all weekend trying to figure out how to keep him there overnight. He agreed to come but swore he was driving back right after the show. I finally said it would be like a wedding present to me if he'd give in to Helen, just for the night. Can you imagine that? A guy compromising his own father just to please his girl! All weekend I've been working on Gino. And all weekend you've been . . .' He stopped; his voice had almost broken. 'Well, at least one good thing has come out of it. Gino is spared. And now I'm tossing the ball to you – and to Lyon Burke. Let *his* father hump your girl friend!' The receiver clicked.

The Philadelphia opening of *Hit the Sky* was a much smoother and glossier version of the New Haven premiere. Anne was amazed at the changes that had been accomplished in such a short time. She sat beside Lyon, identifying with the cast rather than the audience. He held her hand, and she wondered if he had noticed the absence of the large diamond. It was resting in a plain manila envelope in her new safe-deposit box. It had seemed cruel leaving the large solitaire all alone in that cold tin box. It had seemed to glitter in outraged anger, as if it were protesting its uncalled-for rejection.

Lyon's whisper snapped her thoughts back to the stage. It was Neely's big moment. The ballad had been reinstated. Anne sat on the edge of her seat when Neely began to sing. It was a completely different interpretation. Terry King in her slinky red satin dress had seemed disenchanted and sultry. Neely in a blue dress with a Peter Pan collar was haunting, forlorn and alone. There was a vibrant wail to her voice. Now it was a torch song, very different and more plaintive. She received a tremendous ovation.

Several times during the show Anne glanced nervously at the three empty seats in the fourth row. Helen had reserved those seats. And she was supposed to be sitting there, between Allen and Gino. She had not broken the news to Helen. She felt it might hurt her performance.

The curtain came down at eleven-fifteen. There was no doubt of the show's success. Even Henry Bellamy's usual look of harassment had evaporated. He passed Lyon and Anne as they came backstage. 'The party will be at the Warwick.'

Lyon looked at his watch. 'You don't really care about going, do you?'

She hadn't thought about it. She had assumed Henry had reserved rooms for them at the hotel. They had come to the theatre directly from the train. She had an oversized handbag in which she had crammed a nightgown and a toothbrush. She suddenly realized Lyon was without his usual attaché case.

'If we make a fast dash backstage and congratulate Helen and Neely, we can catch the twelve-twenty-five back to New York.'

'Whatever you say, Lyon.'

'I think I'd rather have my drink in the club car with you. We both need one good night's sleep, and this party is bound to last way into the morning.'

They elbowed their way through the crowd cluttering the hallways of the dressing rooms. Anne went directly to Neely's room. She was standing outside the door, surrounded by a few newspapermen. Members of the cast stopped by, offering congratulations. Mel stood at her side, silent and beaming with pride.

Anne embraced her. 'Neely, you were wonderful!'

'Was I really? Honest? It'll be even better after I get used to it. And these were makeshift costumes. I'm getting a new set for New York.'

Lyon offered his congratulations. Neely looked startled. 'Where's Allen?'

'I'll tell you some other time,' Anne said quietly.

'Nothing's wrong, is it?' Neely insisted. 'Gosh, Helen was like a school girl because Gino was out front tonight. And you're supposed to be with Allen.'

Anne felt herself coloring. Neely's clear voice carried halfway down the hall.

'Allen isn't here,' Anne said through her teeth.

'That's obvious,' Neely said. 'Hey – the ring!' She grabbed Anne's hand. 'Where's the ring?'

'Neely, we'll talk about it another time. I've got to go down and congratulate Helen.'

'If Gino isn't here, you better get out of town fast.'

They pushed their way through the crowd into Helen's dressing room. Helen broke away from several people and came toward Anne with her arms outstretched. 'Hi!' she said merrily. Then her eyes went past Anne expectantly. When she saw Lyon she looked at Anne questioningly. 'Where is everybody?'

'They didn't come.'

'*What?*'

'It's a long story, Helen.'

'That sonofabitch! What happened?'

'I'll tell you later.'

'It had better be good. Come on inside while I change and tell me.'

'Helen . . . we're – Lyon and I – we're taking the twelve-twenty-five back to New York.'

'You're kidding!'

Anne shook her head mutely.

'You mean you're not coming to the party?'

'I have to be in the office tomorrow, Helen.'

'Balls! If I say I want you here, then that's it! It's the least Henry can do for me. He went back tonight, so you stay.' Then, turning to everyone in the room, she shouted, 'Hey, the party's at the Warwick. You'll have to scram now so I can change.'

There was the usual hum of good-bys mingled with more congratulations.

When they were alone, Helen turned to Anne and Lyon. 'Lyon, you wait in the hall. Anne can sit here while I change.'

He looked at his watch. 'We'd best be leaving, Anne, if we want to catch the last decent train.'

'Oh, swell! Henry doesn't even leave you as a replacement? Next thing I know he'll be sending me that owl-faced George Bellows. He's gonna hear from me! Who in hell is going to escort me to the party?'

'Why didn't Henry stay?' Anne asked.

'Because I told him Gino would be here,' Helen snarled. 'I wanna hear about that. What in hell happened?'

Lyon glanced at his watch again. 'I'll hail us a cab, Anne.' He smiled briefly at Helen and left the room.

'Boy, am I getting stood up all around tonight,' Helen said. She sat at the dressing table and began powdering down her makeup.

'Helen, the show was just great tonight,' Anne said. 'I'm sorry I have to leave now, but Lyon wants to make that train . . .'

'Then let him, for Chrissake. What's that got to do with you?'

Anne searched for an excuse. 'I have no hotel reservation.'

'So what? I have a suite with two beds. You can stay with me.'

'But I came with Lyon.' She looked longingly toward the door.

Helen's eyes widened. 'Oh, I get it. Still playing footsies with Lyon. Jesus, you're like all the rest. You, the one girl who had class, who I cared about – my buddy-buddy – running out on me. But go on. Hell, that's the story of my life. I give all of myself . . . I always trust people . . .' Tears began to roll down her face. 'I believed in you, Annie . . . my one friend. But you're like all the others, kicking me in the ass, walking out when I need you. Here I am, alone on my opening – no guy, and my only girl friend wants to take a powder . . .'

'Helen, *I am* your friend. Maybe there's a later train. Let me talk to Lyon . . .'

'Nah, anything after the twelve-twenty-five is a milk train.' Helen began to blot at her running mascara. 'But go on. I was crazy to expect you to be different.'

'Wait . . . let me talk to Lyon.' She dashed out of the room.

Lyon was holding a cab. She rushed to him. 'Lyon, we can't leave her alone. She feels so hurt.'

He stared at her. 'Anne, nothing can hurt Helen.'

'You don't understand her. She was crying. She feels so alone on her opening night.'

'Helen's tears come easily. And go quickly. Look, Anne, the Helen Lawsons of this world create their own loneliness.'

'But we can't do this to her.'

'We owe Helen nothing other than a business loyalty. Simple things like the crucifixion of Terry King. That she understands – and demands. But there is nothing in my contract that states I must escort her to parties.'

'But Lyon, she's my friend.'

'And you choose to remain?'

'I feel we should . . .'

He smiled. 'Okay. Good-by, friend,' he said lightly. Then he jumped into the cab.

At first she couldn't believe it. But the cab was gone. She didn't know whether to be angry or frightened. Had she let Lyon down? Or had he let her down? If she had gone with him, she certainly would have let Helen down. God knows she had let Allen down. She suddenly felt tears coming to her eyes. Everything seemed to be crumbling around her. She was hurting everyone – most of all herself.

The party at the Warwick was a repetition of the party in New Haven, except for Neely's appearance as a full-fledged principal. There were more people from New York, different newspapermen – and Helen, drinking heavily, was still every inch the hearty, good-natured star. There had been people in the dressing room when Anne had returned, and she had not been able to explain about Gino. So she sat through the festivities, watching, feeling outside of everything, worrying about Lyon – and feeling numb. At two in the morning, when

138

she saw Neely and Mel steal away, she felt a stab of envy. Lyon would be just arriving in New York now. She wondered if he was angry – or did he feel miserable, too?

They returned to Helen's suite at three in the morning, and Helen opened a split of champagne. She poured herself a large glass. 'Okay, now tell me – what happened to Gino?'

Anne searched for the right words. 'It's all my fault, I suppose,' she said carefully. 'You see, I broke up with Allen.'

'Why?'

'Well – Lyon and I . . . we were together . . .'

'So?' Helen asked. 'I knew you were balling Lyon in New Haven. What's that got to do with Allen?'

'I couldn't see Allen any more if I'm in love with Lyon.'

Helen's eyes narrowed. 'Are you kidding? You don't think just because he's banging you he's gonna marry you, do you?'

'Of course he will—'

'Has he mentioned marriage?'

'Helen, this all just happened three days ago.'

'So where is your big Romeo now? I notice he didn't stick with you.'

Anne didn't answer. Helen rushed on, driving her point home. 'Listen, a guy who is in love with you sticks with you. Allen stuck – and he probably feels awful. That's why Gino didn't come, I bet. He probably thinks I'm as cheap as you.'

'Helen!'

'You think you're classy, acting this way. You wear a guy's ring and leap in the feathers with that limey! And fuck me up with Gino. Sure, he thinks we're the same kind. He's afraid to see me now – afraid I'd hurt him like you hurt his son.'

'What I did with Allen has nothing to do with you and Gino.'

'Then why isn't he here? He dug me pretty good. I can tell. We had laughs together. If it wasn't for you throwing yourself at Lyon Burke, he'd be here with me now. I've lost a guy I love because you're a little tramp.'

Anne dashed across the room and grabbed her coat.

'Where do you think you're going?' Helen asked, refilling her glass.

'Any place just to get away from you!'

'Ha!' Helen sneered. 'Honey, you got no place to go but down. Do you think anyone cares about you? You and your prissy blue nose? At least I come out and call a spade a spade. But you played it the great lady. Sure, as long as you wore that diamond you were someone. I put up with you. I figured you must have something if Allen Cooper wanted you. It was your only claim to fame. You're nothing now – just another broad who's been balled by Lyon Burke.'

Anne stared at her. 'And I thought you were my friend—'

'Friend! What in hell have you got that I should be your friend! Who in hell are you? A stinking secretary and a big bore! And I lose a guy who digs me because of you, yet!' Helen stood up, her legs wobbling. 'I'm going to bed – sleep on the couch if you like.'

Anne's rage made her calm. 'Helen, you've just lost the only friend you ever had.'

Helen's face twisted. 'Things would be pretty rough if I had to rely on you for laughs and kicks.'

Anne went to the door. 'Good-by, Helen. And good luck.'

'No, sister, you're the one who needs the luck. All you got left is maybe a few more bangs from Lyon Burke before he gets bored with you. And he gets bored easily. I know – I had my innings with him six years ago.' She smiled at Anne's incredulous stare. 'That's right, me and Lyon. I was doing a new show and he had just joined Henry Bellamy. He was playing it smart – gave me the big romance treatment. He liked being seen with me. But at least I wasn't a jerk like you. I took it for what it was worth – enjoyed him in the kip and when it petered out that was it. And believe me, I had more to offer him than you, a two-bit secretary.'

Anne opened the door and rushed out, sick with disgust and anger. She reached the elevator and suddenly stopped. Her panic grew as she frantically searched through her bag. She had no money. She had rushed to meet Lyon so quickly that she hadn't bothered to cash a check. She made a final search and found eighty-five cents. It was after four – she couldn't call Neely. But she couldn't walk to New York, either.

She sat on a chair near the elevator in the hall. If she went to the lobby and sat – till nine maybe – then she could call Neely. Oh, God, she had ruined everything. She felt an overwhelming sense of loss. Helen was no longer her friend. But then it seemed Helen had never been her friend . . . Everyone had warned her. She had been warned about Lyon, too. Lyon and Helen. No – it couldn't be! But Helen wouldn't make up an outrageous lie like that. Oh, God! Why had Helen told her? She began to sob, muffling the sound in her hands.

She heard the elevator stop. She dabbed her eyes with her handkerchief and kept her head down. A girl got off and walked past, then stopped and turned around.

'It's Anne, isn't it?'

Anne dabbed frantically at her eyes again. It was Jennifer North.

'What's wrong?' Jennifer asked.

Anne looked at the radiant girl. 'Just about everything, I'm afraid.'

Jennifer smiled compassionately. 'I've had days like that. Come on, my room is right down there. Maybe we can talk about it.' She took Anne's hand and led her firmly down the hall.

Sitting on the bed, chain smoking, Anne found herself telling Jennifer the entire story.

At the end Jennifer grinned. 'Wow, have you had a weekend!'

'I'm sorry I put you through all this,' Anne said. 'And at such an hour.'

'That's all right, I never sleep anyway.' Jennifer smiled. 'That's my big problem. But one of your problems is solved, anyway. You stay here tonight.'

'No – I really want to get back to New York. If you would lend me the money, I'll mail you a check tomorrow.'

Jennifer reached into her bag and tossed over her wallet. 'Help yourself. But I think you're mad. I've got two beds. You can get a good night's sleep and go back tomorrow on a decent train.'

'I want to get back now.' Anne took a ten-dollar bill from the thick wallet. 'I'll mail you a check.'

Jennifer shook her head. 'No, wait till I get back to New York – then you can take me to lunch. I want to hear the end of this.'

'This *is* the end.'

Jennifer smiled. 'Sure, with Helen – and possibly Allen. But not with Lyon. Not the way you look when you mention his name.'

'But how can I go back to him now, after what Helen said?'

Jennifer looked incredulous. 'You mean that bothers you? You didn't think he was a *virgin*, did you?'

'No, but *Helen* . . . He seems to think so little of her as a woman.'

'Maybe he thought more of her six years ago. He was probably impressed with her. You know, working for Henry Bellamy, trying to be a success. I don't blame him if he did it with Helen – he probably had to. But I blame her for being such a rat as to throw it at you when she knows you care.'

'But she says he hits and runs . . .'

'Anne, I'm sure every man hits and runs with Helen. And she salves her pride by believing that the man acts that way with everyone. She'll even con herself into believing that Gino adored her. Anne, I'm sure Lyon is really stuck on you. Maybe not in love, but really stuck.'

'But I've ruined everything now. He walked out on me.'

'He probably feels you walked out on him. In a way you did, choosing Helen over him.'

'I didn't choose. I felt sorry for her. She was my friend.'

'Some friend!' Jennifer made a face. 'Look. Tomorrow when you see Lyon, be really nice. Let your eyes fill with tears. Tell him you just learned how stupid you were to feel anything resembling friendship for Helen. Play it sweet – sweet and wounded. And for heaven's sake, don't dare mention what Helen told you about him!' She followed Anne to the door. 'Remember, there's only one way to own a man – by making him want you. Not with words. Now sleep on it. In fact, I should chain you up here for a few days so you don't mess things up.'

'No. I want to go back.'

'Anne . . .' Jennifer followed her to the door. 'I like you. We'll be good friends. I want a real friend too. Trust me – do it my way if you want Lyon.'

Anne smiled weakly. 'I'll try, Jennifer, I'll try . . .'

The ride back to New York seemed endless. The sun was shining when she finally reached Penn Station. It was morning . . . people were pouring out of the Long Island section. She'd just have time to bathe, have breakfast and get to the office. Her eyes felt gritty in the cab and her legs were like lead as she climbed the stairs to her room.

She saw the telegram sticking out under her door. Lyon! It had to be! She tore it open.

AUNT AMY PASSED AWAY IN HER SLEEP LAST NIGHT. FUNERAL WILL TAKE PLACE WEDNESDAY. IT WOULD BE NICE IF YOU COULD ATTEND. LOVE. MOTHER.

*

She stared at the telegram. How like her mother. Not 'Please come,' or 'I need you,' but 'It would be nice . . .'

Well, she wouldn't go. Her mother didn't really care. Didn't really want her there. It would just 'look nice' for Lawrenceville. But she belonged here . . . she belonged to Lyon. She reached for the phone and impulsively dialed him. After four rings he answered. His voice sounded sleepy. She felt a twinge of anger. She had sat up all night on a cold train while he had been *sleeping . . .*

'Hello?' He was awake now, and irritated. She realized she was holding the receiver and not speaking.

'Hello . . . is someone on?' Lyon's voice clipped through the wires. She was frightened. He sounded angry.

'Is it Elizabeth?'

Elizabeth! She stared into the phone stupidly.

'Come now, this is a juvenile thing to do,' Lyon said coldly. 'Elizabeth, if you want to talk, say something or I'll hang up.'

He waited a moment, then put the receiver down with a click.

Elizabeth? Who was Elizabeth? She felt sick at the sudden realization that Lyon had a complete life she knew nothing about. She had really only known him four days. God, was it just four days! Of course there was an Elizabeth – probably many Elizabeths.

She called Western Union and wired her mother that she would come immediately. Then she checked the trains. The next train to Boston left at nine-thirty. She threw some things into a bag. It was eight-thirty – she would have time to get to the bank and cash a check. But the office wasn't open yet. She had to let Henry know she wouldn't be in. She dialed Western Union again.

DEAR HENRY. PERSONAL CIRCUMSTANCES CALL ME AWAY. WILL RETURN AND EXPLAIN ON FRIDAY. ANNE.

She left for Boston, never realizing her formal wire would be misinterpreted.

Henry had crushed the wire angrily. 'Goddamnit – she probably eloped with Allen Cooper.' He kept his suspicions to himself, but found himself being unusually short with Miss Steinberg and the rest of the office staff. On Friday, when he walked in and found her at her desk, he stared in delighted astonishment.

'You're back!' he shouted.

'I said I would be back on Friday.'

'I was positive you were married,' he said.

'Married?' She stared in amazement. George Bellows had come in. He seemed surprised to see her, too. 'Married?' she repeated. 'To whom?'

'I just thought . . .' Henry looked foolish. 'I was afraid you had eloped with Allen.'

'*Eloped?* My aunt died. I had to go to Boston. The office wasn't open, so I sent you a wire. Who said I eloped?'

Henry threw his arms around her. 'Never mind. You're back. And I'm so glad.'

It was at this moment that Lyon entered. He stopped abruptly when he saw her. Henry released her and turned in boyish relief. 'She's back, Lyon . . .'

'Yes, I see.' Lyon's voice was emotionless.

Anne dropped her eyes. 'I'm sorry if you all got the wrong impression.'

'Her aunt died,' Henry said jubilantly. Then, forcing a sober expression, he added, 'I'm sorry, Anne.' He turned to Lyon. 'She only went to Boston for the funeral.'

Lyon smiled and went to his office.

'Come on in,' Henry said insistently. 'Here, want some coffee? A Danish? A raise? Anything – I'm so happy – just name it.'

The buzzer on his desk sounded. He flipped a switch and Anne heard Lyon's clipped voice. 'Henry, could you please send Anne in with the management contract for Neely O'Hara?'

Henry winked and clicked off the intercom. He opened his file cabinet and shuffled through some papers. 'We're handling your little friend. She hasn't any agent. She has only a small kind of future – strictly on the stage – but we're taking her on because of you.' He handed Anne the papers and motioned her toward Lyon's door.

Lyon stood up when she entered. 'I suppose Henry told you we're taking Neely on. She insists – says it will make her feel like a star.'

Anne kept her eyes on the contract. 'Yes, Henry told me.'

He came over to her and took the papers. 'Has he also told you that I've been a lost soul for the past four days?'

She looked at him and he took her in his arms. 'Oh, Lyon, Lyon . . .' She clung to him.

'I'm sorry about your aunt. None of us knew why you had gone – Henry acted as if you were actually never coming back. I couldn't believe that. I refused to believe you had gone out of my life. I know I acted badly, Anne – I should have waited that night. Helen is your friend, and . . .'

'No, I was wrong. I'll never put anything before you again. Helen wasn't worth it. No one is worth it. Oh, Lyon, I love you so much.'

'I love you, Anne.'

'You do! Oh, Lyon, do you really?' She clung to him even harder.

He kissed the top of her head. 'Really, really,' he said lightly. But when she looked at him she knew he meant it. And once again she told herself she could never be as happy as she was this moment.

She spent the weekend at Lyon's apartment. She responded eagerly to his lovemaking. On the second night she fell back, shaking and weak. He held her gently and stroked her hair.

'Oh, Lyon – it happened.' She shivered a little.

'For the first time,' he said.

'I was beginning to worry about myself.'

'Not at all – it's very rare for a girl to actually feel anything or reach a climax in the beginning.'

She kissed his face eagerly. 'I function, Lyon – I'm a woman!'

That night she was aggressive in her lovemaking. She had never dreamed her physical passion could match her emotions, and she was glad and frightened at the same time. She not only loved Lyon because he was Lyon, she hungered for him physically. Her love seemed insatiable.

There was only one nagging thought that crept through the perfect weekend. On Monday she was to go to court and testify for Jennifer's annulment.

'I know you hate to do this, Anne,' Henry had said. 'But you're the only one I can trust. Jennifer's a stranger in New York. She doesn't know any girls. It'll be over and done with before you know it. Don't worry about it. Just be in the office at nine-thirty. We're due in court at ten-thirty. Jennifer is coming in from Philadelphia for the day. We'll rehearse the whole deal before we leave the office.'

She mentioned it several times during the weekend. And there were times she even thought about it when she was in Lyon's arms.

'Look, if it really bothers you, you don't have to do it,' Lyon said.

'I know it's silly, Lyon, but I'm scared. It *is* perjury, isn't it?'

'Technically, yes. But it's done every day. I mean, no one really cares. Not even the judge. But if this is against your principles, just tell Henry so. If necessary, he can get Miss Steinberg.'

'Why didn't he ask her in the first place?'

'He thought about it. Naturally she was our first thought. But how far could we go, even with a sympathetic judge? Would Jennifer North look like the kind of girl who made Miss Steinberg her chum and confidante?' He reached for the phone. 'But don't fret about it. I'll ring Henry now. You don't owe Henry or Jennifer North a bloody thing, so why should you—'

'Oh, Lord!' She sat up in bed. 'Lyon, don't call Henry.'

'Why not?'

'I owe Jennifer a great deal – ten dollars among other things. I completely forgot. She loaned me money for train fare from Philadelphia.' She had told him the Helen Lawson incident, carefully omitting Helen's reference to him. But she had forgotten to tell him how Jennifer had sympathized and bailed her out. 'I meant to send her the money. But when I got back to New York, there was the wire, and I just took off for Lawrenceville.'

'Well, you can relax. I'm sure Jennifer isn't worried about ten dollars. I'll give it back to her tomorrow.'

'Still, she was awfully nice to me that night. I guess the least I can do is testify for her.'

'Very well, if you think it will even the score.'

She looked at him. 'That's such a final expression, Lyon. As if it finishes you off with a person, like a paid bill. I remember when you used it with me. It was like closing a door in my face.'

'With you? When?'

'When I thanked you for Neely, for getting her the job. You said it evened the score for getting you this apartment.'

'Our apartment now,' he said.

She looked at him mistily 'Our apartment?'

'Why not? Unless you're attached to that room on West Fifty-second Street. I think we have ample closet space here. And I'm quite neat to live with.'

She threw her arms around him. 'Oh, Lyon! We haven't known

each other long, but I think I knew. I knew the moment we met that you were the only man I'd ever want to marry.'

He broke the embrace gently. 'I'm asking you to move in, Anne. That is all I *can* ask – for the present.'

She turned away from him, more embarrassed than hurt. Lyon took her by the shoulders and turned her gently to face him. 'Anne, I do love you.'

She tried to blink back the tears. But they choked through her words. 'When people love one another they get married.'

'In Lawrenceville perhaps – where things are settled at birth and futures are all in place.'

'Your future is very much in place. Henry believes in you . . .'

'I'm not sure I want to stay with Henry. I suddenly don't seem to be sure of anything – but I am sure I don't want Henry's kind of life.' He looked thoughtful. 'You see, I had decided after the war that I wasn't coming back to Henry, and to the old way of life. But I did come back, and Henry's enthusiasm got to me. I almost slipped into the old pattern. And then we had lunch in the Barberry Room. You gave me quite a jolt that day – started me thinking. Then the weekend in New Haven – and the Terry King business.' He shook his head. 'Then the smashing blow when you disappeared. I started to evaluate things carefully – and I made a decision. I'm going to have a go at writing that book.'

'That's wonderful, Lyon. But how would marriage change things?'

'Let's say I still have a few old-fashioned ideas. I do think a husband should support his wife. If I married you, I'd throw myself into the action at Henry's one hundred per cent. I'd make a lot of money, but we'd have a bad marriage.'

'Are you going to leave Henry?'

'Unfortunately, I can't. I have enough money saved to take a few months off, but it's too big a risk. I'll stay with Henry and write the book on the side. A few snatched hours at night . . . weekends . . . It's not the ideal way, but unfortunately at the moment it's the only way – there is no country home to retreat to. And I'm aware of the hazards ahead. Even if it's accepted, the advance for an unknown writer is small. It takes six or eight months to come out, and sometimes, even with a good book, an author makes very little money. The runaway best sellers are the rare exceptions. So I have two alternatives – remain

147

with Henry and work in my free time, or find a rich old woman to sub-sidize me.'

'I'm not old or rich, but I have some money, and I could go on working.'

He ran his hand through her hair, watching the heavy silk fall between his fingers. 'With your marvelous stipend from Henry and my savings, we still couldn't swing this apartment.'

'But I told you, I have money. I have five thousand that my father left me and I just inherited seven thousand from my aunt. That's twelve thousand, Lyon – it's more than enough.'

He whistled. 'Good Lord, I've found me an heiress.' He kissed her warmly. 'Anne, I'm truly touched. But it couldn't work. Right now I'm not sure if I *can* write. I'm not sure the book will even be good. At this very moment there must be half a million ex-GI's sitting at typewrit-ers and hammering out their personal versions of Normandy, Okinawa or the London Blitz. And each of us – we really have something to say. It's just a matter of who says it first – and who says it best.'

'I'm sure you can write,' she insisted. 'I just know it.'

'Then you know more than I. Which is delightful, devoted – and I love you for it.'

'Lyon . . . after the book is finished, will you marry me?'

'I shall be delighted to – if the book turns out to be a good one.'

She was silent for a moment. 'But you said yourself . . . even a good book doesn't always make money.'

'I didn't say money was the barometer. If the book was good, even if it didn't make a dime, I'd continue to write. I'd work even harder, because then I'd know it was more than a dream. And we'd make out somehow. But if it turns out to be unacceptable to any publisher, then I would go at my job with Henry on the double. I'd haul out the old Lyon Burke and make up for the wasted years – and I'm not sure that you would care very much for me.'

'What was the old Lyon Burke like?'

He thought for a moment. 'No wasted moments. Yes, I guess that would be appropriate. I never made a move without a premeditated reason. Not even this—' His hand stroked her breast.

The memory of Helen's shrill voice filled her ears. Then it was true – the old Lyon would have had an affair with Helen. He had practically admitted it.

148

He took her in his arms. 'But that Lyon Burke was killed in action, or perhaps he died the night the boy talked about the peach trees. If so – perhaps he didn't spend his last night in vain.'

She put her arms around him. 'You could never go back. Not when you talk like this. If this book doesn't make it, then you'll work on another and another. You are what you are now, and nothing will ever change that again. If you want to stay with Henry and write, I'll wait. I'll wait forever, if it takes a dozen books. Just stay being you.'

'I don't know whether me is that great to be. But it is better than being Henry Bellamy. And that's where I was heading. In fact, I'd have been even bigger than Henry, because I wasn't as nice. Henry vacillates, takes time out to care. I have a one-track mind. I'd have been a king-sized Henry – a large success and a personal failure.'

'Is that what you think of Henry?'

'Henry's struggled for thirty years to get where he is – the top, I guess you'd call it. It's a trite word. He calls it Mount Everest. And that's where he is, financially and professionally. But what about his personal life? If one were to write up Henry's *Who's Who*, there would be several paragraphs devoted to his theatrical and business achievements. To his personal life, one line – unmarried, no living relatives. In short, no life aside from the business. Alone on the summit of Mount Everest.'

'But you're only proving my point, Lyon. Henry kept waiting to get married. You're doing the same thing.'

'No. Because a marriage is meaningless on Mount Everest. There are men like Henry who marry and have children and families, but their personal life is the same. After all, let's suppose Henry had gotten married. To a nice girl – out of the business. The children would be married now, attending to their children. The wife would be spending the winter in Florida. She'd have given up nagging at Henry for his erratic hours, and by now she would be accustomed to living without his companionship – a thing she never had. She would have settled for the nice things that came out of Henry's dedication – the large apartment or town house, the furs, the style of living. There are many Henrys who are married and who wind up on top alone. They have to be alone, because they've alienated everyone along the way. In this rat race you whore, lie, cheat and use every trick you can employ to get up there where Henry is. This business demands it. And that's what I'm ranting against. Not Henry personally, but what everyone turns into if he sticks in it long enough.'

They were both quiet for a few moments. Lyon spoke first. 'Sorry I sounded off like this.'

'No, I'm glad. I understand you better. I'm just worried about one thing.'

He looked at her warmly. 'What?'

'When *are* you going to marry me?'

He laughed out loud. She wondered if he knew how wonderful he looked when he did that. She had never known anyone who laughed like that – who threw his head back and let go. His laugh had a wonderful ring to it.

'I'll tell you what – you shall be the first to read the completed manuscript, and then *you* can tell *me*.'

She snuggled against him. 'I'd better go to sleep,' she whispered. 'I've got a lot to do tomorrow.'

'Oh yes, the annulment business.'

'Mmm . . . and Lyon . . . have you an extra key to your apartment?'

He held her tight. 'I'll have one made. Then you *are* moving in?'

'No, but I'm moving in a typewriter and plenty of blank paper first thing tomorrow. A bright shiny new typewriter. It'll be my pre-wedding gift to you.'

'I'll accept it . . . on one condition. You move in with it.'

'No. I'll come and stay like this whenever you want me. I'll spend weekends with you and type up your pages. But I won't live with you. I'll live *for* you . . . and wait.'

He kissed her brow. 'As a lawyer I should tell you that you're getting the short end of the deal. But as your lover, I promise I shall try very hard not to let you down.'

The court appearance was brief. Any fears Anne might have had were immediately dismissed as she watched the cut-and-dried procedure. Henry handed some papers to the judge. The judge made a pretense of reading them, a few questions were exchanged, Jennifer testified with her rehearsed speech, Anne chanted her lines. In less than ten minutes Jennifer had her annulment.

Henry took both girls to lunch. He ate quickly. 'I have work waiting,' he explained, 'but you two girls can sit and rehash all the events. Anne, take the rest of the afternoon off.'

The moment Henry left, Jennifer turned to Anne and asked, 'Now tell me, how did it work out with you and Lyon?'

Jennifer listened while Anne told her everything that had happened. It surprised Anne how quickly and easily she confided in Jennifer. There was something about Jennifer that invited trust.

Jennifer shook her head. 'He sounds rough. You'll never be able to control him.'

'But I don't want to control Lyon . . .'

'I don't mean that way. A man must feel he runs things, but as long as you control yourself, you control him. Get him to put a ring on your finger, then be the slave girl if you wish.'

Anne looked at her ringless hand. 'That's not important. I have the biggest ring you ever saw lying in a safe-deposit box.'

Jennifer stared at her with new respect. 'You mean you managed to get rid of Allen and *keep* the ring?'

'He didn't want it back.'

Jennifer shook her head. 'You must really do something special in bed. I thought I had all the answers.'

'I never went to bed with Allen.'

For a moment Jennifer was speechless. Then she grinned. 'That's what was special. You were a challenge to Allen.'

'Well, I'm afraid I'm no challenge to Lyon.'

'Still, I'll keep my fingers crossed. At least you did one thing right – you refused to move in with him. I'm doing the same thing with Tony Polar. He wants me to quit the show and travel with him. No marriage talk, either. But I'm no camp follower. By the way, how large is your apartment?'

'One room. I live in a boarding house – same place as Neely.'

'I have no place to live when the show comes in,' Jennifer said. 'It would be nice if we could find a place to share.'

'Sounds wonderful, but I don't think I can really afford even half of an apartment.'

'Say!' Jennifer's eyes sparkled. 'I've got a great idea. You say Neely has a room. What if the three of us took a place together? Then we could afford it.'

'I'd love it,' Anne said.

'We come back to town in three weeks. Maybe you could swing something by then.'

'I'll look, but things are pretty tight. I found Lyon's apartment right away, but Allen did that for me.'

Jennifer's blue eyes suddenly narrowed. 'Anne, what are you planning to do about the ring?'

Anne shrugged. 'Leave it in the vault, I guess. I certainly have no desire to wear it.'

'Just leave it there? When it could be working for you?'

'How?'

'Sell it. Invest the money.'

'But it's not really mine.'

'You offered it back and he refused. It's yours. And you earned it. Any time you put up with a man's company when you can't stand him you should have something to show for it. Sell it.'

Anne thought of Lyon. Perhaps Jennifer was right. At the end of the year, if the book wasn't successful and she did have some real money . . . 'Maybe you're right. I could sell the ring and put the money in the bank and let the interest pile up.'

'You'll do nothing of the kind,' Jennifer said. 'Sell the ring and ask Henry Bellamy to invest your money in the market. You can double your money in a few years. There's always a bull market after a war.'

'But isn't that risky?'

'Not now. And not if Henry manages it for you. Henry told me the market is going to boom. I wish I had some money. I haven't a sou – just what's on my back and what I make in the show. But the minute I get my hands on some big money I'm letting Henry invest it.'

JENNIFER

Hit the Sky had three performances to go in Philadelphia. Henry's predictions had been correct. They were able to eliminate Boston and bring the show into New York earlier than planned. The cast was eager for the New York opening, confident they had a hit, but the tension was high. New York critics were unpredictable. Nothing could be taken for granted.

Jennifer was oblivious to this pre-opening hysteria. Philadelphia had been a most profitable engagement. She stood in the lobby of her hotel and flashed one of her most glorious smiles at the persistent Philadelphia lawyer who was pleading for one last nightcap.

'It's three o'clock,' she begged. 'And I must get some sleep.'

'You can sleep all day tomorrow. Come on, I know a wonderful after-hours club – it's right up the street.'

'It's cold. And I want to get some sleep, Robby, honestly. Besides, I don't drink, and if I have one more Coke I'll explode.'

'How can you be cold in that coat?' He looked meaningfully at the new beaver she was wearing.

She patted it affectionately. 'You were an angel to give it to me. It's really warmer than my mink. But I've got to get some sleep.'

'Let me come up with you,' he begged.

'You were with me last night, Robby.'

'Is there a rule about two nights?'

'Yes, when I'm working. Call me tomorrow.' Her smile was promising.

'What time?'

'Around six. We'll have dinner before the show.'

'And after . . . ?'

'And after.' She nodded. She blew him a kiss and stepped into the elevator.

There were some messages lying on the floor under her door. One was from a columnist. There were two requests to call Operator 24 in Cleveland. Well, it was too late to call her mother now. She looked at the time on the last Cleveland message – one-thirty. Even her mother wouldn't have the tenacity to wait this long for a return call. There was also a message from Anne. She had signed the lease for the apartment she had found and everything was fine. Anne was a wonderful girl. Jennifer envied her, the way she felt about Lyon. It must be great to be able to feel that way. But then if you did, you couldn't do the other. She stroked the beaver coat – one night with Robby. That's what a great body was for, to get things you wanted. She wondered what it would be like really to care, to love someone like Lyon Burke. Lyon would be easy to love . . . she had thought about it when they first met.

'We'll catch Tony Polar's opening tonight,' Henry had said. 'You must be seen around, to keep the publicity going. I've arranged for Lyon Burke to escort you. I'm taking Helen.' She had been unprepared for someone like Lyon. She had felt a surge of excitement in meeting a man she knew she wanted, a man she wanted for nothing beyond her own pleasure. She had intended to have him that night; then Tony Polar had materialized. It had been a tense moment of decision. The spotlight on Tony; Tony singing to her; everyone in the room staring; keeping her smile frozen in place; feeling the magnetism of Lyon Burke, yet aware of the public embrace Tony Polar was offering. As a man Tony could not compare with Lyon. They were the same age, she imagined – both around thirty. But one would always be a boy, while the other had long been a man. But Lyon Burke was only an agent; Tony was a star. That had made her decision . . . It was that simple.

She got undressed, dropping her clothes carelessly on the chair. Maybe she would let Robby stay tomorrow night. She could do with a new evening gown. She wrinkled her nose. He was so unattractive and he breathed so hard. But she needed some clothes, and men who looked like Robby were always generous. They had to be. Now Lyon Burke . . . But he was a luxury she couldn't afford. Some unknown mechanism seemed to click within her mind, automatically eliminating the impractical with the precision of an IBM machine, acting as a nerve block to her emotions when they might complicate her decisions.

It hadn't always been like this. In the beginning her emotions had fought back. But that was long ago. Now the decisions came automatically. She thought of Lyon Burke again. Too bad – the timing had been unfortunate that night. That night it had to be Lyon or Tony and there had been no contest.

Lyon had seemed to understand. She was suddenly struck by a new thought. 'We're alike!' Of course, that had to be the answer. She was a luxury he couldn't afford. But Anne – certainly Anne couldn't fit into his scheme of things. A new and foreign thought struck her. Perhaps she just hadn't appealed to Lyon. But that was ridiculous. She appealed to every man. She dropped her bra and pants to the floor and stood before the full-length mirror. She surveyed her body with clinical interest. It was perfect. She turned sideways and examined the profile of her breasts. They were as upright as ever. She folded her arms and methodically did twenty-five breast-tightening exercises. She opened the medicine cabinet and took out the large jar of cocoa butter. With almost surgical precision she massaged the butter into her breasts with gentle but firm upward strokes. Then, with equal care, she creamed the makeup off her face. Once this was accomplished, she opened another jar and put some cream under her eyes. She took a V-shaped plaster out of a box and pasted it between her eyes, on the bridge of her nose. She did twenty-five more breast exercises and slid into a nightgown.

She looked at the clock. Good Lord, it was almost four and she still wasn't sleepy. When did they turn the heat on in this hotel? It was freezing. She got under the covers and glanced through the morning papers. There were two pictures of her. One was a wire-service photo, showing her with Tony. Tony! He'd have asked her to marry him by now if it weren't for that sister of his. She frowned as she thought of Miriam. The 'frownie' plaster stabbed a warning. She relaxed her face instantly. What was she going to do about Miriam? They could never shake her. If it wasn't that Tony was so eager to go to bed with her, she'd never see him alone. Come to think of it, that was the only time they did get rid of Miriam.

The phone rang timidly, as if frightened to interrupt anyone at such an hour. She picked it up hopefully. Sometimes Tony stayed up till dawn, too. But it was the Cleveland operator. She sighed and accepted the reverse-charge call.

'Jen . . .' It was her mother's whining voice. 'I've been trying to get you all night.'

'I just got in, Mother. I thought it was too late to call you back.'

'How could I sleep? I'm so upset. There was a big story about you in the Cleveland papers. Said you didn't get a cent out of your annulment from the Prince.'

'That's right.'

'Jen, are you crazy? You know John is going to be retired next year. And we'll never be able to live on his pension. As it is, we can't make ends meet.'

'I sent you fifty dollars last week, Mother. And I'll send fifty more as soon as I get my pay check this week.'

'I know, but Gran's been sick. I had to take her to the doctor, and then we had a bad leak with the oil burner, and—'

'I'll see if I can dig up some more, Mother.' She thought of Robby again. 'But I only make a hundred and twenty-five in the show – less Social Security and income tax.'

'Jen, I didn't starve and do without to send you to school in Switzerland just so you'd wind up as a showgirl making that kind of money.'

'You never starved, Mother. It was money Daddy left me. And you only sent me to Switzerland for that year to break me up with Harry.'

'Because I was determined you weren't going to wind up as poor little Jeannette Johnson, marrying a garage mechanic!'

'Harry was not just a garage mechanic. He was studying to be an engineer and I loved him.'

'Well, he's still a mechanic, with black fingernails and three grimy kids. Harriet Irons was once one of the prettiest girls around; she's your age but looks forty now, married to him.'

'Mother, how can a girl of twenty-five look forty?'

'When a girl has no money and marries for love, she ages real fast.

Love doesn't last. Men only care about one thing. Remember your father!'

'Mother, this is long distance,' Jennifer said wearily. 'You didn't call me just to complain about Daddy. Besides, John's been a wonderful husband to you. I don't even remember Daddy, but I'm sure he couldn't have been as nice as John.'

'He was a louse, your father. Rich, handsome and a louse. But I loved him. Our family never had money, but we had a name. Don't forget – Gran is a Virginia Tremont. And I still think you should have taken Tremont as your stage name instead of that ridiculous North.'

'Didn't we agree that I was to take a strange name so no one could trace me? If I'm to pass as nineteen, I have to be Jennifer North. If I took Tremont, someone in Virginia would trace me. If I took Johnson, everyone in Cleveland would remember me.'

'With your publicity, they all remembered you. The whole town's been talking about you since you eloped. One paper sniped about your claiming to be only nineteen, but they were all so impressed with the Prince that it didn't matter. And I felt it didn't matter because you were safely married. Now you go and throw it all away without collecting a penny.'

'Mother, why do you think I ran? Just before we were to go to Italy, I found out he had no money.'

'What do you mean? I saw the pictures in the papers! The diamond necklace, the mink coat . . .'

'The necklace belongs in his family. He bought me the mink, but I think he got it free for the publicity we gave the furrier. He had a whole floor at the Waldorf, but a wine company was footing the bill. He was like a good-will ambassador for them. His title is legitimate – very royal – but he hasn't a dime. They lost everything when Mussolini took over. They have some horrible big castle outside of Naples. I could live there, scrounging among the international set, wearing the family jewels . . . living in genteel poverty. I was lucky I found out in time. He told me he was rich because he thought a beautiful American wife would be an asset over there. After we were married I learned the bitter facts. Then he started telling me of some rich Italian wine merchant I had to play up to – go all the way if the guy wanted me. Mother, he was a high-class pimp, when you get down to it. I was lucky to be able to keep the mink coat.'

'Well, what about this Tony Polar?' her mother asked.

'He's real cute.'

'Jen!'

'Mother, he *is* cute . . . and I like him. And he also happens to have a lot of money. Besides, my lawyer thinks I may get a movie contract.'

'Forget about pictures!'

'Why? I might make it.'

'It's too late. You're *not* nineteen. Look, you're lucky – you have a gorgeous face and the kind of body men go for . . . though your kind of figure doesn't last. What have you told this Tony Polar about your background?'

'An airtight story, based on some truth. That my father was wealthy and was killed in a bombing in England, that he left everything to his second wife—'

'That's true . . . what else?'

'That my father had left me a small inheritance, enough to see me through school in Switzerland. Since I'm supposed to be nineteen, I left out about staying in Europe for over five years.'

'What did you tell him about me?'

'I said you were dead.'

'What?'

'Mother, what should I tell him? That I have a mother and a step-father and a grandmother living in Cleveland who can't wait to move in with us?'

'But if you marry him, how do you explain me?'

'You'll be my aunt – my mother's dear sister whom I support.'

'All right. Are you watching your weight?'

'I'm very thin, Mother . . .'

'I know, but don't gain and lose. That's the worst thing for your breasts. Big breasts like yours are going to drop soon enough, and then they'll be an eyesore. Make them pay while you have them. Men are animals – they seem to like them. Maybe I wouldn't have lost your father if I hadn't been flat-chested. Then I could have had a decent life .. . .' She started to sob. 'Oh, Jen, I can't take it any more. I want to leave and be with you, baby!'

'Now Mother – you can't leave John or Gran.'

'Why can't I? Let John stay with Gran. He and that piddling job of his. Where else could he go? He could never even afford to buy a house.'

'Mother!' Jennifer clenched her teeth and held onto her patience. 'Mother, please. Let me marry Tony first, then I'll take care of you.'

'Has he mentioned marriage?'

'Not yet—'

'What are you waiting for? Jen, in five years you'll be thirty. I was twenty-nine when your father got tired of me. Jen, you haven't got much time.'

'It's not that simple, Mother. He has a sister. She manages him, writes all his checks. Their mother died when Tony was born. She's raised him and she loves him. And she hates me.'

'Jen, you've got to be tough. Get rid of her. Take her place. You can't let her move in with you if you marry him. It would ruin your life – and she'd never let me come. Baby, use your head. Be smart. If a woman has money, nothing can ever hurt her. I only want the best for you, baby . . .'

The radiators began to crackle; the sun was sneaking in under the blinds. Jennifer was still awake. Her mother's call had not particularly disturbed her. She was used to it. But she worried about not sleeping. The one way to hold your looks was plenty of rest. Even if you didn't sleep, lying in bed and resting was almost as good. She had read that somewhere. She lit another cigarette. But what kind of rest was it if you paced around and smoked an entire pack of cigarettes during the night? She walked to the bathroom and put some more cream under her eyes. No lines yet, but how long could this go on? She hadn't averaged more than three hours sleep a night since – since those last weeks in Spain. She sighed. Before that she had always been able to sleep. In fact, sleep used to be an escape. When problems became insurmountable, she would look forward to the night. Until those last weeks in Spain with Maria . . .

Maria . . . Maria had been the most beautiful girl in school, and Jennifer, along with the other polyglot first-termers, had idolized the glacial Spanish beauty. Maria was a senior, and she spoke to no one. And if she was aware of the hero worship she inspired in the other students, it failed to touch her; she made no friends. This hauteur only added to her glamour with the younger girls, and to the speculation and envy among her contemporaries. It looked as if Maria would graduate and leave Switzerland without allowing anyone to penetrate the imperial barrier. Until that day in the library . . .

Jennifer was in tears, reading a letter from her mother. The money had run out; she was to return home at the end of the term. Had she made any valuable contacts? Cleveland was still feeling the depression, although the war in Europe was opening new factories. Harry had married Harriet Irons and still worked in a gas station. It was the part about Harry that had brought on the tears . . .

'Come, nothing can be that bad.'

Jennifer looked up. It was Maria. The majestic Maria, talking to her! Maria sat down, Maria was sympathetic. She listened while Jennifer talked.

'I don't know what my mother expected,' Jennifer finished wearily. 'Maybe she thought the English teacher would be a lord with a manor . . .'

Maria laughed. 'Parents . . .' Her English was stilted but excellent. 'I am twenty-two. I will be expected to make a marriage with a man of my father's choice. It will be a matter of his land adjoining ours, or other mutual family interests. Since our civil war our country is devastated. It is the duty of the few remaining families in power to unite. I agree with these decisions, but unfortunately, as a woman, I am expected to sleep with this pig . . .'

'I was in love with Harry,' Jennifer said sadly. 'But he didn't suit my mother.'

'How old are you, Jeannette?' Jennifer had been Jeannette then.

'Nineteen.'

'Have you ever had a man?'

Jennifer blushed and stared at the floor. 'No, but Harry and I . . . we went pretty far. I mean – I let him touch me . . . and once I touched his . . .'

'I have gone to bed with a man,' Maria stated.

'All the way?'

'But of course. Last summer. I vacationed with an aunt in Sweden. I met a beautiful man. He had been in the Olympics. He was working as a swimming instructor. I knew the men my father was considering. It would be a fat German who escaped with all the art treasures, or one of the Carrillo family. None of the Carrillo boys have chins. So I decided to at least try it for the first time with a beautiful man.'

'I wish I had done it with Harry. Now he's married to another girl.'

'Be glad you didn't! It was awful! The man . . . he mouths your breasts . . . he pushes into you. It hurts. Then he perspires and breathes heavily like an animal. I bled – and I got pregnant.'

Jennifer couldn't believe this was happening. Maria, the unapproachable school goddess, confiding in her!

'Oren!' Maria spat out the name. 'He took care of things. A doctor . . . more pain . . . and good-by pregnancy. Then I got the fever and was very sick. I was taken to the hospital . . . the operation . . . I can never have children.'

'Oh, Maria, I'm so sorry.'

Maria smiled slyly. 'No, it is good! I will let my father make all the arrangements he wishes. Then I will tell the man. No man wants to marry a woman who cannot have children. I will never have to marry,' she said triumphantly.

'But what will your father say?'

'Oh, my aunt has taken care of the answer. She had to learn the truth. But I was her responsibility, so she must stand behind me. I shall say I was ill, that I had a tumor in my uterus and it had to be removed.'

'Was it?'

Maria nodded. 'Yes, my uterus was removed – peritonitis had set in. But it is wonderful. I am no longer bothered with the monthly period.'

Jennifer wanted to say she was sorry, but she couldn't offer sympathy to a girl who regarded the incident as a stroke of marvelous luck. 'Well, at least you've got everything settled,' she said. 'But I still have to return to Cleveland.'

'You do not have to return,' Maria said emphatically. 'You are too beautiful to spend your life waiting to be mauled by the first available man.'

'But what can I do?'

'In two weeks the term is ended. You come back to Spain with me for the summer. We will think of something.'

'Maria!' It was too wonderful. 'But I have no money – just a return ticket home.'

'You will be my guest – I have more money than I can use.'

The last two weeks in school had been a personal triumph for Jennifer. The news raced through school – Little Jeannette Johnson had been befriended by Maria. The girls stared in envy. Maria continued to keep her imperial distance, even with Jennifer, except to stop and chat briefly whenever they passed in the hall.

The moment they left school, Maria's attitude changed. She became warm and friendly. It began when they took the cab to Lausanne. 'We can't leave for Spain right away. My father's cable . . .' She handed it to Jennifer. It advised Maria to spend the summer in Switzerland. Spain was still feeling the devastation of the war. With one million dead and several hundred thousand injured, it was impossible to staff the house at present, so they had closed it and were staying at a hotel. But things would soon return to normal. Meanwhile she was to enjoy herself abroad. He had cabled the number of a Swiss bank account.

'We have plenty of money,' Maria said. 'Enough to travel around the world and back. But the war is on in Europe, so France is out. So are Germany and England.'

'Let's go to America,' Jennifer suggested. 'We could go to New York. I've never been to New York.'

'How? I am not a citizen. Travel is impossible with Europe at war. You might make it on a Red Cross boat – as an American citizen you would have priority – but there would still be the mines and submarines. Anyway, I have no desire to go to New York. We shall stay here for the summer. Hitler will win any day and the whole thing will be over.'

They were to remain in Switzerland three years.

They became lovers the first night. Although Jennifer had been startled at the proposal, she felt no revulsion; in fact, she was even a little curious. Maria was still the exalted school-girl heroine. And Maria's logical explanation removed any taint of abnormality. 'We like one another. I want to make you know about sex, to feel thrilling climaxes – not let you learn about it by being mauled by some brutal man. We are doing nothing wrong. We are not Lesbians like those awful freaks who cut their hair and wear mannish clothes. We are two women who adore one another and who know about being gentle and affectionate.'

That night Maria undressed and stood before Jennifer proudly. She had a lovely body, but Jennifer felt a secret delight in the knowledge that her own was superior. She dropped her clothes to the floor shyly. She heard Maria's startled gasp as she exposed her breasts.

'You are more lovely than I dreamed,' Maria said softly. Her hands stroked Jennifer's breasts lightly and endearingly. She leaned over and rested her cheek against them. 'You see, I love your beauty and respect it. A man would be tearing into it now.' She ran her fingers gently over Jennifer's body. To her amazement, Jennifer began to feel a sensation of excitement . . . her body began to vibrate . . .

'Come.' Maria took her hand. 'Let us lie down. We will have a cigarette.'

'No, Maria. Keep touching me,' Jennifer pleaded.

'Later, I will touch you and hold you to your heart's content. But I want you to feel comfortable with me. I will be gentle . . .'

Maria had been gentle, and very patient – taking more liberties each night, slowly teaching Jennifer to respond, erasing any embarrassment. 'You cannot just be loved, you must love back,' Maria would insist. 'Make me thrill as I thrill you.' Each night Maria urged her on, until at last Jennifer found herself responding with equal ardor and reaching peaks of exaltation she never dreamed existed.

She enjoyed a dual relationship with Maria. At night she was eager for Maria, demanding and ecstatic. But during the day she regarded Maria as a friend. She felt no other personal attachment. When they shopped together or explored strange little towns, Maria was just another girl. She felt no involvement. Often they met attractive men – ski instructors, students – and Jennifer found these encounters quite difficult. Maria remained aloof to their advances, but Jennifer found some of the young men quite appealing. Many times as they danced, she felt her body thrilling to the touch of the strong masculine one that held her close. When a boy whispered an endearment, she found herself longing to respond.

Once she had slipped out for a brief walk with a particularly handsome Panamanian boy. He was a medical student, and he was going to New York after the war for further studies. He wanted her. They kissed, and she found herself clinging to him, responding to his kisses with equal passion. It was wonderful to hold the strong shoulders of a man, to feel a man's chest against her own . . . the strength of a man's hand after Maria's soft, tender one . . . the firmness of a man's lips. She wanted this boy desperately, but she tore away from him and returned to the café. Maria had noticed her absence; there was a slight scene that night when they were alone. Jennifer swore it had been a headache, that she had just wanted some air. At last, in bed, Maria relented . . .

But most of the time it was wonderful. Maria was wildly extravagant. She bought Jennifer beautiful clothes. Jennifer learned to ski. Her French grew fluent and effortless. When they grew bored with Lausanne they moved to Geneva.

After three years in Switzerland Maria's father wanted her to return, but she refused. Then, in 1944, he stopped her checks. She had no choice.

'You will come with me,' she told Jennifer. 'But we will have to cash in your return ticket to America. I have not enough money without it.'

Jennifer knew she was handing in her ticket to freedom. For the past year she had grown increasingly weary with Maria's demands on her body, yet Cleveland and her mother were even less appealing. But Spain! She might find some handsome Spanish man of good family. She was twenty-three, technically a virgin . . . why not?

Jennifer remained in Spain over a year. She met many eligible men. A few were passable, but Maria kept a hawklike watch on all her activities. They were always chaperoned by one of Maria's aunts. Maria repelled all advances and saw to it that Jennifer made no progress. Jennifer grew desperate. Maria's possessiveness was stifling. For the first time she understood her mother's fear of poverty. Money bought freedom; without it one could never be free. In Spain she could live luxuriously and wear beautiful clothes, but she belonged to Maria. If she returned to Cleveland she faced a different kind of imprisonment – marriage to some third-rate man who would also demand the use of her body. Whichever way you looked at it, without money you were someone's captive. But there had to be a way out!

She began lying awake nights. She suffered through Maria's love-making, returning an ardor she did not feel, feigning sleep until Maria's even breathing assured her of safety. Then she would slide out of bed and sit by the window, smoking endlessly, staring at the stars, thinking . . .

Money. She had to have money. The answer was in her body – it would work for her. It had carried her this far. She would go to New York, take a different name, lie about her age . . . maybe she could model. Somehow she'd get money. She'd never be trapped again.

When the atom bomb was dropped, everyone in Madrid was feverish for news. Even Maria sat breathlessly at the radio set, eagerly listening for bulletins. Jennifer took this opportunity to post a secret letter to her mother, instructing her to write and demand Jennifer's presence at home due to illness.

Her mother obeyed and Maria had no choice. They separated with promises of undying devotion, Jennifer swearing to return as soon as her mother recovered. She felt a twinge of guilt when Maria pressed a book of travelers' checks in her hand. 'It comes to three thousand dollars in American money. Try to save enough for your return here, but if you need more, cable me. I live only for the day of your return.' To erase any suspicion, Jennifer left most of her clothes in Spain as further assurance of her return. She had gone directly to New York and checked into a commercial hotel. She sent her mother five hundred dollars and told her to forward any mail from Spain, but under no circumstances to reveal her whereabouts or new name.

In the beginning Maria wrote every day. Jennifer never answered. Through a strange stroke of luck she had run into the Panamanian medical student the first day she was in New York. Fortunately he only recalled that they had met and that he had wanted her. He accepted the new name without question. She went to bed with him every night for three weeks, and then he introduced her to Prince Mirallo . . .

It was seven o'clock – she crushed out the last cigarette. She *had* to sleep. She wanted to be really good with Robby. Then maybe she could get the gown *and* the money for her mother.

NEELY

January, 1946

The New York critics had been unanimous in their raves for *Hit the Sky*. Helen Lawson's public adoration had reached new heights, and Neely had received several excellent notices – none strong enough to incur Helen's animosity, but glowing enough to exceed Neely's wildest expectations.

No one had been more surprised than Neely. One critic had actually called her the freshest new talent to come along in many a season. This accolade, coupled with the new apartment, made her almost believe she was someone.

She couldn't get over the luxury of the apartment. Anne was just fabulous! She just ran into luck, that girl. And it always seemed to be connected with Allen. Only this time it was Allen's father. Gino had dumped his girl friend Adele, who had gotten so mad she had booked herself into the Dorchester Hotel in London as a showgirl. Just before she left, Anne had run into her and gotten her scrumptious apartment. Neely kept touching everything – the bedspreads, the lamps . . . She never dreamed she'd live in a living room that had a white rug.

Of course it was only a sublease. Adele would take it back from them June first. But by then Jennifer would probably marry Tony, Anne might marry Lyon and she would marry Mel. Especially if Mel's new job worked out. What a Christmas present from the blue that was! Johnny Mallon giving him a two-week trial as a writer on a radio show! If he made good they could be rich. Radio writers made as much as five hundred a week, Mel said. Even more. Mel was starting at two hundred, and she was making two hundred – and the show had come in to New York three weeks earlier than planned because they didn't need Boston. Geez, things were just perfect!

She was going to buy some fancy clothes, too. After all, everyone had seen the purple taffeta a hundred times. Geez, the way Jennifer came back from Philadelphia with a closet full of clothes. No wonder she was always broke. She said Tony Polar was tight, but how could she mean that with him giving her that gorgeous big blue ring for Christmas? Jennifer said it was only an aquamarine. Geez, she'd be happy to accept an aquamarine. Well, for a start she was going to get a new winter coat. Ohrbach's was having a big sale.

She and Mel had been invited to Johnny Mallon's New Year's Eve party. But they'd seen the old year out in Helen's dressing room. 'You'll never get out of the theatre and to a party before twelve o'clock,' Helen had insisted, pouring champagne.

Johnny's party had been terrific. Neely had never been to a party packed with celebrities. And they all knew her! That was the big surprise – everyone knew who she was! She couldn't get over it. And then Johnny Mallon had told Mel he 'could consider himself a permanent member of the team.' Geez, that was great. She had to stop saying 'Geez' all the time. Several people had laughed when she said it. Oh, not nasty laughing . . . they'd thought she was kidding. But maybe if she mixed with these classy friends of Mel's she'd learn some good expressions. She never heard anything backstage except words she didn't want to say. And Mel had such a good vocabulary . . . he'd gone to college. Geez, a college man like Mel – in love with her!

She'd never forget that New Year's Eve. Mel said he wouldn't either. She'd hugged him that night when they reached his hotel. 'I'm so happy, Mel – I'm scared.'

'This is really starting off 1946 with a bang,' Mel had said as they got ready for bed. 'But you know, I felt a little sorry for Helen Lawson tonight. She looked so lonely when we left her dressing room.'

Neely had wrinkled her nose. 'Listen, Helen never has a date. Tonight she was lucky she had that faggot designer to take her to a party. Geez, Mel, your hotel is really chintzy – there's no heat and it's practically morning. We get heat almost all night.' She'd climbed into bed and shivered in his arms.

'All right – name the day and I'll move. We can get married any time you like. I'll find us a nice apartment.'

Neely had snuggled up to him, wrapping her legs around his for warmth.

'How about it, Neely? You heard Johnny tonight. I'm set – I'm making two hundred a week.'

'So'm I.'

'Then let's get married.'

'Okay. On June first.'

'Why do we have to wait until then?'

'Because I got the apartment with the girls till then. I'd have to keep kicking in my third of the rent if I left before. We all agreed to that kind of a deal because we're all on the verge of getting married.'

'We can manage it. We'll pay them.'

'Are you kidding? I should pay two rents?'

'But Neely, I want you.'

She giggled. 'You got me. C'mon, take me . . . now . . .'

'But Neely—'

'We'll get married June first. C'mon, Mel, make love to me. No, not that way – I'm not wearing my diaphragm. Do it the other way . . . please. Please, Mel . . .'

February, 1946

Anne and Jennifer stared in speechless disbelief as Neely casually directed the moving men in the placement of an enormous piano.

'I've just signed with the Johnson Harris office,' Neely announced.

'What happened to Henry?' Anne asked.

'Well, we had a long talk yesterday. I told him the Johnson Harris office had come to me, and he gave me a release right away. I'm not really big enough for a manager. I need a big agency behind me. Henry agreed. And look what happened . . .

'They gave you a piano?' Jennifer asked.

'No, but they're paying for the rental. And they got me into La Rouge – I open in three weeks.'

'But you're in *Hit the Sky*,' Anne said.

'I'm gonna double. I'll just do a midnight show at La Rouge. And for that I'll get three hundred a week! Isn't that terrific? And guess what? The Johnson Harris office got me Zeke Whyte and *they're* paying for him – and he's gonna make my arrangements and stage my act. Zeke only works with the biggest stars. When he heard me sing he said with a little work I could be great. He said I'm a cross between Judy Garland and Mary Martin.'

'Well, just don't let any Helen Lawson creep in or we'll throw all three of you out,' Jennifer said with a wink at Anne.

'Isn't the piano gorgeous?' Neely asked, running her hand lovingly across the scarred Steinway. 'Zeke insisted on this one. It does something for the room, doesn't it?'

Jennifer nodded. 'Sure does. Gives it a real air – like a rehearsal hall.'

Neely's childish face looked chagrined. 'Gee – do you mind it being here?'

Jennifer smiled. 'No. I'm just wondering where you plan to put the ballet bar. That does come next, doesn't it?'

Anne laughed. 'Let her be ambitious, Jen. It'll be nice having a star in the family.'

Neely made a wry face. 'I'm doing it strictly for the money. In June, when Mel and I get married, I wanna have enough cash saved to furnish a place as nice as this.'

'When does he get a chance to write for Johnny Mallon?' Jennifer asked. 'He seems to be working full time as press agent for you. I've never seen anyone get so much publicity.'

'Why shouldn't he?' Neely insisted. 'After all, everything I earn is for our future.'

'You really don't care about making it – the star bit?' Jennifer asked.

'For what? To wind up alone on New Year's Eve with some faggot as a date? Oh, I'll keep working after I'm married – but my marriage will always come first. And you're a fine one to talk – didn't you just turn down a contract at Twentieth because of Tony?'

Jennifer shrugged. 'It wasn't a good contract. Only one-fifty a week.'

'But Henry thought you should have taken it,' Neely insisted. 'If it had been bigger would you have signed?'

'Maybe . . . I guess so. But I have no talent, Neely, and you have.'

'Yeah, but it takes more than talent. Hey, let's clean up this place. Zeke will be here any minute.'

169

'It's neat as a pin,' Anne insisted.

Neely ran around emptying ashtrays. 'Jen, you use every ashtray in the place. Zeke says he's glad I don't smoke. Even in a room, smoke hurts a singer's voice.'

Jennifer raised her eyebrows. 'Will cigarettes be barred at your club opening?'

'No, but why do I have to have my home contaminated?'

For the next three weeks Zeke Whyte took over the apartment. He rehearsed Neely relentlessly. Anne and Jennifer never arrived without finding him there. He was femininely attractive, aware of his own importance, a hard taskmaster and an excellent musician. He drove Neely unmercifully.

'What does he want from me?' she'd demand, bursting into the bedroom in tears. 'I never had a singing lesson in my life and I'm doing okay. All of a sudden he's trying to turn me into a Lily Pons – in three weeks! Anne, go in and tell him to get off my back!'

Then Zeke would appear at the doorway. 'Okay, Neely . . . hysterical time over. Let's get back to work.'

'I can't,' she would sob. 'You expect too much.'

'Of course I do. Why be good if you can be great?'

Neely would always go back . . . the scales would continue . . . there would be more hysterics . . . more scales . . . it seemed endless.

But the loudest argument came at the end of the second week. Neely came tearing into the offices of Bellamy and Bellows. 'Where is he?' she demanded of Anne.

'Where is who?'

'Henry! I want him back as my manager. I need him. He's got to get Zeke off my back.'

'Henry's at N.B.C. What's Zeke done now?'

'He wants me to burn all my clothes!'

'What?'

'You heard me. *Burn* them! He says he won't even let me *give* them away, they're so awful. Including this new coat.' She stroked the red fox collar lovingly. 'I paid seventy dollars for it at Ohrbach's.'

Anne hid a smile. 'Well, the coat is a little sophisticated for you.'

'Look, all my life I've worn my sister's hand-me-downs. I have a right to pick my own clothes now.'

'What does Zeke want you to wear?'

'Who knows? I'm supposed to meet him later at some designer's place. That's why I need Henry – to talk to him – to tell him I have some rights.'

'Now Neely, you don't need Henry. You can tell him yourself.'

'No, I don't want to fight with him. He might walk out. Geez, Anne – he's done such great things with my voice. Sometimes I don't even believe it's me. And in just two weeks. You know, for the first time I feel maybe I could be great. I can hit notes I never dreamed existed, and hold them with real power. He's a genius.'

'Then maybe he's right about the clothes.'

Neely sighed. 'Well, I'm gonna let him pick my dress for the opening. It's being specially designed because he's making me dance and move a little on some numbers. But I'll *never* give up this coat . . .'

The following week she sent the coat to her sister, along with the purple taffeta and the six new dresses she had bought since the show had opened. Zeke made her buy an evening dress for the opening, two wool street dresses for everyday and a tailored navy blue coat. She stared at her sparse wardrobe in disgust. She alternated the two dresses, afraid to eat when she wore them – one spot and half her wardrobe was out of commission.

'Imagine, a hundred and twenty-five bucks for this,' she told Mel as she spread a napkin carefully over the blue wool. They were sitting in Sardi's, where Neely now rated a front table – a fact that never ceased to amaze her.

'It's smart looking,' Mel said. 'But it doesn't look like that kind of money.'

'Zeke says I have to create an image and look that way all the time.'

'What kind of an image is this dress supposed to create?'

She shrugged. 'I dunno. What does it do to you? You went to college.'

Mel bit into his sandwich and stared thoughtfully at the dress. 'Well, you don't look like a rising young Broadway star, that's for sure.' He studied her. 'More like a schoolgirl. Yes, that's it – like maybe you're fresh from some fancy girls' college.'

'Is that good?'

'I don't know, honey. I love you in anything – even that awful purple job.'

'Mel You never told me you didn't like the taffeta.'

'You had it when we first met, and I didn't want to hurt your feelings.'

'What about my black coat with the red fox collar?'

'Well, it *was* ordinary looking . . . and sort of old for you.'

'And this plain navy coat is unusual?'

'I don't know, honey, but I think it's right for you. Fags have pretty good taste.'

'Oh, all right.' She sighed and bit carefully into her sandwich.

March, 1946

No one was prepared for the impact of Neely's opening night. Anne was there with Lyon and Henry. Jennifer sat across the room at a large table with Tony Polar, his sister, his writers and some song pluggers. Helen Lawson arrived with an assistant stage manager. She waved hello to Henry and pointedly ignored Anne.

It began as a typical club opening. The newspapermen came because it was an assignment. The celebrities came to be seen by the newspapermen. No one expected very much. It had happened before – a new little girl, using the handle of a hit show to augment her slim pay check. They came respecting her energy and ambition; they left a raving, worshipping cult.

Anne couldn't believe it. She caught Jennifer's eye during the show and they exchanged stares of delighted amazement. Henry Bellamy was sitting on the edge of his seat.

Neely was fantastic. The lighting made the childlike face almost beautiful and the dress – a plain white satin shirtwaist and a short navy satin skirt – showed off her marvelous legs. Anne was surprised she had never noticed them before, or her perfect little figure with its small waistline and childish breasts.

'The star that got away,' Henry whispered. 'Jesus, Lyon – how did we ever let her slip through our fingers?'

Lyon shook his head. 'When we make a mistake, it's a beaut!'

'She's really great, isn't she?' Anne whispered.

'Great isn't the word,' Lyon answered. 'She's unbelievable. There's no one around like her.'

After that, the excitement that generated around Neely made life chaotic at the apartment. The phone rang constantly, and the living room was taken over for interviews, picture sessions, rehearsals. Neely had guest shots on all the radio shows. She signed with a major record company. Metro wanted her. Twentieth wanted her. And Helen Lawson stopped talking to her.

Neely felt awful. 'Imagine. She just cuts me dead,' she told Anne.

Jennifer grinned. 'That means you're a star. She's still adorable to me.'

'I was gonna stay with the show into next season,' Neely explained. 'But I won't now. Gilbert Case offered me a new contract starting June first with bigger billing and a hundred-dollar raise. But I can't work when Helen treats me like this.'

Anne laughed. 'Come on, Neely – you have no scenes together. You're just salving your conscience about leaving the show June first.'

'Why should I feel I owe Case anything? I'd have never got the job if it wasn't for you, Anne – and if Helen hadn't been scared of Terry King.'

She finally signed with Century Productions. 'It's a smaller studio than the others,' she explained, 'but the Johnson Harris office thinks it's best for me. Two of their pictures were up for Academy Awards last year. They're getting all the new stars, and I'll get the real star buildup.'

Mel wasn't happy about her picture deal. 'But it's wonderful,' she insisted. 'I stay with the show till the last day of May. Adele wrote and says she's coming back the middle of June and wants the apartment back anyway, so—'

'What about Jennifer and Anne?' Mel asked.

'Well, *Hit the Sky* will run another year. Jennifer will stay in until she marries Tony, though nothing seems to be happening that way. They just date – no marriage talk.'

'But where will they live?'

'Oh, things are easier now. They might move to the Orwin Hotel temporarily. They can get a suite there fairly reasonably.'

'And what about us?'

'We'll get married – June first, like we planned.'

Mel smiled. 'Gee, I thought you'd never ask.'

She squeezed his hand. 'Then we'll go right to California for our honeymoon. The Head is getting me a house.'

'The Head?'

'Oh, I forgot to tell you about him,' Neely babbled. 'He was in town last week. Cyril H. Bean – but no one ever calls him Cyril or Mr. Bean. He's called The Head. He's a sweet little old man, about fifty, real tan, and nice white hair. He's so kind – and real fatherly. He's renting a great house for me in Hollywood – three hundred a month with a swimming pool, only he told me not to dare get in the sun because I got enough freckles. Then he said if things go great and I make it, I can get a house in Beverly Hills.'

'What's the difference?'

'Who knows? Maybe it's the wrong side of the street. He kind of apologized about the house being in Hollywood. I pretended I understood. But imagine, Mel – a house with a pool.'

'Neely.' Mel reached out and took her hand. 'You know I love you—'

'And Mel, I start at one thousand a week! Just think of all the money we're gonna have.'

'Neely . . . the Johnny Mallon show comes from New York.'

'Give it up.'

'Just like that?'

'Mel, are you crazy? You're only making two hundred a week.'

'I'll make three starting next year.'

'But I'll be making a *thousand*! And that doesn't count my money from records. The Johnson Harris office said I'll make twenty-five thousand just on records alone next year. Imagine!'

'And what do I do, sit in the swimming pool?'

'Mel, you're with me. We're a team. I need you. I need all the publicity I can get – more than ever now.'

'The studio will assign someone to you.'

'Sure they will. But it won't be like you. Their press agent will take care of me and all the other stars. I want you to work for me alone. And Mel, you'll have to handle all the money. I never even wrote a check in my life. Even in the apartment with the girls, they tell me what my end is and I hand it to them in cash. And Geez, I wouldn't know what to say to a maid or cook, or even how to hire them. I never had a house. You'll handle everything. Mel, you've got to come. I'd be nothing out there without you.'

'No, Neely. It wouldn't work.'

'Why? You're responsible for all this anyway. How did I get La Rouge in the first place?'

'The Johnson Harris office booked it.'

'But Mel, the Johnson Harris office only got interested in me because of all the publicity you got for me. They didn't rush and sign me after I opened in *Hit the Sky*. Maybe I wasn't the singer I am today – Zeke did that – but you got me noticed.'

He took her hands. 'Zeke didn't give you your voice, and I didn't make you. It was there all the time. We just helped draw attention to it.'

'Then keep helping me, Mel. I need you . . . I love you.'

'But Neely – I don't know whether it could work. I've never been out to Hollywood, but I know how they operate out there. I'd be Mr. Neely O'Hara. No one would respect me.'

'You don't think I'm gonna go to those fancy Hollywood parties or mix with those people, do you? It'll be just like here. I get telegrams all the time to go to openings, and sometimes we go. They don't call you Mr. O'Hara.'

'It's different here, Neely.'

'But *we're* the same! Look, Mel – I wanna work hard, make money, and maybe in five years chuck the whole thing. Everyone will know you're responsible for me. Please, Mel. I won't go unless you come with me.'

'Now, Neely—'

'Mel . . . please . . .'

He reached over and pressed her hand. 'All right. I always dreamed of having a Hollywood tan. Boy, will I impress everyone in Brooklyn . . .'

JENNIFER

December, 1946

Jennifer stood on a chair and tried to shove the hatbox onto the top shelf of the closet, then ducked as two suitcases fell, just missing her head.

She groaned. 'This closet situation is really impossible.'

Anne helped stow the suitcases back on the shelf. 'I'd offer you my closet, but it's filled – with your hand-me-downs.'

'How does a hotel expect anyone to live with just two small dinky closets? Why couldn't Adele have found some big English lord and stayed in London? God, how I miss that apartment.'

'These are pretty large closets, Jen. It's just that no one is supposed to have all these clothes.'

'And I hate them all.'

'Jen! Don't you dare buy another dress! I have the best wardrobe in town already because you get tired of something the second you've worn it. Lyon's eyes pop the way I keep turning up in new creations.'

'Well, if Tony gives me the new mink for Christmas, you're taking my old one.'

'Old one! You just got it last year!'

'I hate it – it reminds me of the Prince. Besides, it's a wild mink. It would look great with your hair. I want a real dark one.'

'I'll buy it from you then.'

'Don't be silly!'

'I have money, Jen. Henry invested the ring money plus my twelve thousand.'

'How are you doing?'

'Well, we only got twenty thousand for the ring. It's worth more, but they said it wasn't a seller's market. And Henry invested it all in A.T.&T. It hasn't gone up too much, but I get very nice dividends.'

'Well, don't touch your stock.'

'You're a fine one to talk. You've got pictures in *Vogue* and H*arper's* this month and you haven't saved a cent. Honest, Jen, you must earn a fortune since you signed with the Longworth Agency. But you spend it all on clothes. It would be different if you cared about them.'

'Between clothes and sending my mother money, how can I save? The modeling brings in three or four hundred a week, but that's not real money. No, my jackpot is Tony. I'm twenty-six, Anne – I haven't that kind of time or future. Tony is impressed with my clothes, and the newspapers call me glamorous. I think about this as an investment. I'm putting all my money on the line and rolling the dice for Tony. If the number comes up marriage, I'll be independent for life.'

'That's still no reason to give away your mink coat.'

'Everyone's seen me in it for over a year. And if I marry Tony I'll have a dozen. And unless Lyon's book is a freak best seller, you'll wait a long time for a mink.'

'Well . . . I'm keeping everything crossed. He finished it last week.'

'Wonderful! Now you can get married!'

Anne laughed. 'It's not that simple. First it has to be accepted by a publisher. He gave it to Bess Wilson – she's a very important literary agent. If she likes it and agrees to handle it, he's halfway home. A publisher will automatically read a manuscript with more interest if he gets it from Bess Wilson.'

'When will he know?'

'Any day now. He's hoping to hear before Christmas. Hey, Neely's stuck.' Anne rushed to the record player and pushed the needle forward.

'You've worn out that album,' Jennifer said.

'It's so great. I'm so proud of her. I can't wait for the picture to come out.'

Jennifer slammed the closet shut. 'Mind if I turn it off now? I want to read.'

Anne turned off the record player. 'Jen, it's two o'clock. We should both go to sleep.'

'Will my night light bother you?'

'No, it just bothers me that you get so little sleep. Sometimes I wake up in the middle of the night and your bed is empty.'

'I go into the living room and smoke so as not to bother you.'

'What is it, Jen? Tony?'

Jennifer shrugged. 'In a way . . . but I haven't been sleeping for over a year. I *am* upset about Tony, though. In February he goes to California to start a radio show.'

'Maybe he'll ask you to marry him before he leaves.'

'Not as long as Miriam is around. When we're alone, I can make him do almost anything. But we're only alone in bed. I can't very well have a justice of the peace hiding under the sheets.'

'What about eloping?'

'I've thought of that – there's always Maryland. But it's not that simple. In bed he'll promise anything. But the moment he gets out of bed, he listens to Miriam.' She started for the bathroom. 'Now go to sleep. No use both of us worrying. I'll think of something.'

'Try sleeping for a change,' Anne said as she patted her pillow into shape.

'I'll give it a whirl. But first I have to do my exercises and oil up my equipment.' Jennifer closed the bathroom door and wearily took out the cocoa butter. She looked at her face under the harsh bathroom light. A few tiny lines were forming under her eyes. In four years she'd be thirty! *Hit the Sky* would go until June, but she had been in it for a year. Nothing was going to happen. Of course, there was always the stock contract at Twentieth. But if she took it and followed Tony to the Coast she'd never get him. And if he went without her, would he miss her enough to send for her? Not a chance! Miriam would see to it that he was flooded with beautiful girls. Beautiful young girls!

Sure, Tony thought she was twenty. But once he saw a girl who was really nineteen or twenty she might look a little beat. Miriam had been staring at her lately – asking funny questions, trying to trip her with dates about school. Thank God Tony wasn't too bright. She stopped suddenly. It was true – Tony wasn't too bright. Or was it just that Miriam took over so much he never had the chance? He certainly was bright about performing. He knew if the music was off even a fraction. No, it was just that Miriam never gave him a chance to think. Miriam! She rubbed more oil under her eyes. She *had* to sleep.

She returned to the bedroom. Anne was almost asleep. She got into bed and turned off the light.

An hour later she was still wide awake. This was going to be another of those nights. She got out of bed quietly and went into the living room. She *could* sleep – if she had the nerve. She went to her bag and took out the small bottle. She stared at the tiny, bullet-shaped red capsules. Irma had given them to her last night. ('Just take one and you'll sleep for hours.')

Seconals. Irma had given her four. ('They're like gold to me. I can't give you any more.') Irma had replaced Neely in the show. She claimed the little red 'dolls' had saved her life. ('I'd give you more, Jennifer, but you need a doctor's prescription. I can only get ten a week.')

Should she try one? It was a frightening idea, that a little red capsule as tiny as this could put you to sleep. She walked to the small pantry and poured a glass of water. She held the pill for a second, feeling her heart pound. This was dope – but that was ridiculous! Irma took one every night, and she was fine. Irma had been nervous going into the show and she was still nervous seven months later. ('I feel everyone is comparing me with Neely when I sing. She has such a big following with her albums now.')

Well, one pill couldn't hurt. She swallowed it, replaced the bottle in her bag and rushed into bed.

How long would it take? She still felt wide awake. She could hear Anne's even breathing, the clock on the night table ticking, the traffic sounds outside – in fact, everything seemed intensified . . .

Then she felt it! Oh, God! It was glorious! Her whole body felt weightless . . . her head was heavy, yet light as air. She was going to sleep . . . sleep . . . oh, the beautiful little red doll . . .

The following day she visited Henry's doctor. He turned her down cold. She was in excellent condition. What was this nonsense! No, he would not give her a prescription for Seconals. Stop drinking all that coffee. Cut down on cigarettes. She'd sleep. If she didn't, then her body didn't need it.

'That isn't the way to do it,' Irma explained a few days later. 'You can't go to a good doctor and just come out and ask for them. It's best to find a little doctor – one whose ethics are a little shady.'

'But where? Irma, I slept four nights in a row with those blessed red dolls, and it was heavenly. I haven't slept in two nights without them.'

'Look for one of those third-rate hotels on the West Side. You'll see a doctor's sign on a dirty window,' Irma explained. 'But don't just walk in and ask for pills. You have to play the game. Walk in and say you're from out of town – California is always good. Don't wear the mink, or the rates will go up. Tell him you can't sleep. He'll make a stab at listening to your heart, and you keep saying all you need is a few nights' sleep. Then he'll charge you ten bucks and give you a prescription for a week's supply, knowing you'll be back. And he knows he's good for ten bucks a week. But believe me, it's worth it. You may have to try a few doctors before you hit the right one – two turned me down – but you'll find one. Don't go to the Mackley Hotel – that's mine. He might get suspicious.'

Jennifer found her doctor on West Forty-eighth Street. She knew he was the right one when he disinterestedly dragged out a dusty stethoscope and made a half-hearted attempt to feel her pulse. Sure enough, he pulled out his prescription blank. 'Nembutals or Seconals?' he asked.

'The red ones,' Jennifer mumbled.

'Here's a week's supply of Seconals.' He handed her the prescription. 'This should straighten you out. If not, come by again.'

Anne was delighted at the change in Jennifer. She knew nothing about the pills, but she was pleased to see Jennifer sleeping through the night. She wondered if Tony had dropped any encouraging hints.

Then, a few days before Christmas, as Anne was packing a bag for her usual weekend at Lyon's, Jennifer made her big decision.

'This is *it*,' she announced. 'I'm going to get Tony to drive to Elkton tonight, or never see him again. I figured it out last night. If it doesn't work, at least I'll have six weeks going for me. Six weeks that he's in town, where I can show up places looking divine with some other guy and drive him crazy. Crazy enough to relent and marry me. If I wait till he goes to the Coast I'm dead.'

'Where's Miriam tonight?'

'Where she always is. With us! There's a new show opening at La Bombra. I've told Tony I'm going home from the theatre to change and to pick me up here. Miriam will be waiting at La Bombra with his group. I'll have him alone and take him by surprise. And if I play it right . . .'

*

180

She was in a robe when Tony arrived.

'Hey . . . hurry and get dressed. The show goes on at twelve-thirty.'

She came to him. 'Hold me first,' she said softly.

When he broke the embrace, he gasped. 'Baby, let me come up for air. Jesus! I need a blood transfusion just being near you.' His hands stroked her breasts. His fingers fumbled with the buttons on her satin robe. 'Jesus . . . why do you wear robes with buttons?' He pulled the robe off her shoulders, down to her waist. He stood back, his breath coming faster.

'Jen, no one should have boobs like that.' He touched them lightly.

She smiled. 'They're yours, Tony.'

He buried his face in them, sinking to his knees. 'Oh, God. I just can't believe it. Every time I touch them, I can't believe it.' His mouth was greedy. She held his head gently. 'I never want to move,' he mumbled.

'Tony, let's get married.'

'Sure, baby, sure . . .' He was fumbling at the rest of the buttons on her robe. It fell to the floor. She backed away. He crawled on his knees after her. She backed away again. 'Tony, all of this' – she stroked her body – 'is *not* yours . . . it's *mine!*'

He came after her. She eluded him again. She stroked her thighs, her fingers touching between her legs. 'That's mine, too,' she said softly. 'But *we* want you, Tony,' she whispered hoarsely. 'Take your clothes off.'

He tore at his shirt. The buttons ripped and fell to the floor. He stood before her naked.

'Your body is nice,' she said with a slow smile. Then she backed away. 'But mine is nicer.' She stroked her breasts deliberately, almost as if she thrilled to the touch. He stood watching, his breath coming in quick gasps. He rushed to her but she backed away.

'You can look,' she said softly. 'But you can't touch. Not until it's yours . . .'

'But it is mine – you're mine!' His voice was almost a growl.

'Only on loan.' She smiled sweetly. 'And I'm taking it back. Unless you really want it.' She stroked her breasts again. 'Want it for keeps.'

He followed her, trembling. 'I do. Just come to me . . . now!'

'Not now. Not until you marry me.'

'Sure,' he said hoarsely. 'I'll marry you.' He kept following her, but she eluded him, smiling all the while and stroking her own body, letting her hands play with her breasts, sliding them to her legs and touching herself. Her eyes were riveted to him.

'When will you marry me, Tony?'

'We'll talk about it later – right after . . .' He kept after her, hypnotized by this new game she was playing. She let him reach her . . . he grabbed at her breasts . . . his mouth sucked at them hungrily . . . his hands reached between her legs. Then she pulled away.

'Jen!' he gasped. 'Stop it. What are you trying to do – kill me?'

'Marry me, or that was the last time you touch me – ever!'

'I will, I will . . .'

'Now. Tonight.'

'How can we get married tonight? We have to take blood tests . . . we need a license. We'll start that jazz first thing tomorrow. I promise.'

'No. By then Miriam will talk you out of it.'

Mentioning Miriam was a wrong move. It snapped him back to reality. His passion began to dissolve. Quickly, she moved across the room, undulating her body, caressing her breasts. 'We'll miss you, Tony,' she whispered.

He crossed the room quickly and grabbed her.

'Marry us tonight, Tony. We *want* to belong to you . . .' She rubbed against him.

'How can I?' he whined.

'Get your car. We could drive to Elkton, Maryland.'

He stared at her. 'You mean they'd marry us – just like that?'

'Just like that!' She snapped her fingers.

'But Miriam—'

'I'll tell Miriam,' she said. 'We'll call after we're married. I'll tell her. Let her yell at me. You'll be in my arms. All of me will belong to you . . . forever.' She moved her body against him. 'Touch me, Tony – it will all belong to you. You'll be able to do anything you want to me, Tony. Anything – even the things I wouldn't let you do.' She broke away and stood, swaying, her hips moving rhythmically. 'And I'll do all the things you've begged me to do . . . after we're married.'

'Now,' he begged. 'Now, please – then we'll go to Elkton.'

'No. After Elkton.'

'I can't stand it. I can't wait until then!'

She came close. 'Yes you can. Because tonight, after we're married' – she let her fingers caress his body, nibbled at his ear – 'then we'll have a ball.'

His lips were dry. 'Okay, you win. Only for Christ's sake, let's get going.'

She threw her arms around him. 'You won't regret it . . . I'll make you wild.'

There was a sharp knock on the door. Jennifer broke the embrace. 'I'm not expecting a soul. Tony, did you tell anyone you'd be here?'

He shook his head. She pulled on her robe. It was an apologetic bellboy with a telegram.

'It's for Anne. I'd better phone her at Lyon's. It might be important.'

She sat on the bed and called Anne. Tony came into the bedroom. Oh, God, this was a stupid thing to do! She stood up, clutching her robe around her. Where was Anne? Why didn't they answer?

'Hello.' It was Lyon. Yes, he'd get Anne. Tony was fumbling at her robe. She pushed him away.

'Hello, Anne? A telegram just came for you. Sure, one second.' She ripped it open. Tony gently but firmly pushed her on the bed. She held the telegram and the phone and silently tried to push him off. She clamped her hand over the phone. 'No, Tony! Not now. No!' He was on top of her. She looked at the wire. Tony's mouth found her breasts. Oh, God . . . 'Anne . . . yes, I'm here . . . Anne . . . Good Lord, your mother is dead!' She felt Tony enter her, roughly, pounding into her. She clenched her teeth and kept her voice even. 'Yes, Anne. That's all it says. I'm terribly sorry.' She hung up. Tony had fallen across her, panting in satisfied exhaustion.

'Tony, that wasn't fair. That was taking advantage of me.'

He smiled lazily. 'Baby, you were born with the advantages – a pair of them.' He flicked her breast lightly.

'We'd better get dressed. Anne is coming back here.'

He pulled on his shirt. 'Christ, I was hot for you, wasn't I? No buttons left on this shirt. I'll run back to the hotel and grab a new shirt.'

'Pack a bag, Tony.'

'What for?'

'We're going to Maryland – remember?'

He smiled. 'Not now, baby. If we hurry we can still catch part of the

183

show at La Bombra. Now be dressed when I come back – in about twenty minutes.'

'Tony; if we don't elope tonight, I'll never see you again.'

He walked over and chucked her playfully under the chin. 'You'll see me, baby. I'm the greatest. Who could replace me?' He walked to the door. 'Wear something gorgeous – the newspapermen will be there.'

She watched the door close. Damn, damn! What timing. Damn Anne's mother! Damn all mothers! Even in death they reached out and loused you up. She suddenly remembered – she hadn't sent her mother a check this week. And Christmas was coming up. Her mother had seen a Persian lamb coat, and she *had* to have it. She wanted *one* fur coat before she died. She rushed to the desk and scribbled a check for five hundred dollars, stuck it in an envelope and wrote, *Merry Christmas. Happy Persian lamb. Jeannette.* Well, at least her mother would have a merry Christmas. Damn it, when would *she* have one?

She began to dress quickly. She didn't want to be here when Tony came by. She had to force his hand. There was so little time.

She'd go to Lawrenceville with Anne. Of course! She owed it to Anne as a friend. She called Henry Bellamy. His sleepy voice became alert when she told him the news. Of course she was to go along with Anne. Don't worry, he'd handle Gil Case. She was also to hire a car and charge it to his account. It would be easier to drive to Lawrenceville than to bother with train connections. Poor Anne – an aunt and a mother, all in one year.

When Anne and Lyon arrived, everything had been arranged. Jennifer had even packed Anne's overnight bag. 'I put in two black dresses and your gray suit.'

'We can take an early train in the morning,' Anne said.

'No. It's only twelve-thirty, and I never sleep anyway. I'll drive – you can sleep in the car. We'll be there in the morning. I've ordered the car. It should be downstairs any second.'

'I'll come up for the funeral,' Lyon said.

She turned to him. 'No, Lyon. You didn't know Mother. I'll be all right. Use the time on the book.'

'Call me the minute you arrive.'

Jennifer rushed them downstairs. The attendant was waiting with a shiny black sedan. He gave Jennifer the keys and registration, and five minutes later they were on their way. Lyon watched the tail lights disappear into the traffic. It had all happened so quickly. He was amazed at Jennifer's take-charge attitude. He had misjudged her; she wasn't all fluff after all. He walked down the street, just missing Tony Polar, who jauntily pulled up in a cab.

The funeral was held on Monday. Once they were in Lawrenceville, Anne took over and coolly made all the arrangements. It had been a senseless accident, her mother's fault. She was getting cataracts. Aunt Amy had always done the driving, yet after Amy's death she had insisted on driving herself. It had been a rainy night, and she was returning from a duplicate bridge game at church. She hadn't seen the trailer truck. It had been a head-on crash, and her mother had died instantly.

The funeral had been serene and dignified. Lyon and Henry sent huge floral offerings. Miss Steinberg and the girls also sent a wreath. Later that evening Anne went through the formalities of receiving. Everyone in town came to express sympathy and to gape at Jennifer.

On Tuesday morning, Jennifer brought up the subject of returning to New York. They were sitting in the sunny breakfast room. Jennifer had enjoyed Lawrenceville. She had been amused at the town's bulgy-eyed admiration. But most of all she was impressed with the large house that belonged to Anne.

'I have to get back to the show,' she said. 'But I imagine you want to stay here for a while.'

'Whatever for?' Anne asked.

Jennifer looked around. 'Well, this house. You just can't up and leave it.'

'I've already spoken to my lawyer. I told him to put it up for sale, furniture and all.'

'But it's a wonderful house, Anne. Maybe you should keep it . . . rent it.'

'I hate it. I hate this town. I want to cut every tie. If I kept this house, there'd always be a reason to return. If I sell it, I'll know I never, never have to come back.'

'Was your childhood that awful?'

'Not awful. Just nothing.'

'I take it you didn't love your mother.'

'No, I didn't love her. But I didn't dislike her. She never gave me a chance to do either. It wasn't her fault. It was Lawrenceville. Oh, Jennifer, I'd rather live my whole life in that one dreary room I used to have on Fifty-second Street than stay here. Lawrenceville strangles me. I can feel it – closing in on me.' She shuddered. 'Imagine, in all my life here I knew at least thirty girls, but not one became a close friend. I've been in New York just a little over a year and I've got you and Neely and Lyon!'

'Well, you've got Lyon and me. We haven't heard from our movie star in months.'

'Her picture opens in March. Imagine – her first picture opening at the Music Hall.'

'Well, she must be good in it. I read where she's already at work on the second. Wonder when the babies will start. And Mel – do you think he's gained any weight?'

They both laughed, and Jennifer poured some more coffee. 'Well, I've got to leave this afternoon. That will get me back late tonight. At least I can make the matinee tomorrow.' Her brow creased. 'God, Tony probably thinks I've been kidnapped. I left no word at the hotel. Miriam must be celebrating.'

She thought about Tony during the monotonous drive back to New York. Even if things worked out – if they did get married – there'd always be Miriam. It was a blind spot with Tony. 'She's raised me, given her whole life to me,' he'd yell when Jennifer balked at Miriam's eternal intrusion. 'She's the only dame who's a hundred per cent for me.'

But Miriam couldn't go to bed with him. Jennifer's face set. It wasn't just his money and security she wanted. She also wanted to be a good wife. She wanted a child. Tony would get more than he bargained for. She wouldn't cheat on him. Cheat? For what? One man was the same as another. Tony could satisfy her; most men could. Maria had taught her about her body, and she knew how to get aroused. It was easy . . .

Her box at the hotel was crammed with messages. Some were from the Longworth Agency – oh, God, she had forgotten to notify them – but the rest were from Tony. The switchboard operator informed her that Mr. Polar had just called – for the tenth time that day. Jennifer smiled in satisfaction. It was two in the morning. She went to her suite and undressed, but she didn't take a Seconal. She got into bed and waited.

Twenty minutes later the phone rang. She could hear the relief in Tony's voice when she answered. Then he growled, 'Where in hell have you been?'

'Away.'

'No kidding!' Then his tone changed, and in a sudden rush of emotion he said, 'Listen, baby, I've been half out of my mind. Where were you?'

He was not appeased when she told him. Nor was he fully convinced.

'Since when do you go rushing out of town to attend funerals?'

'Anne is my best friend.'

'All right, but you sure stayed away a hell of a long time. What happened? Was one of the pallbearers handsome?'

'They all were,' she said sweetly. 'As a matter of fact, I've never seen so many good-looking men in one town.' She hadn't even talked to a man under fifty.

'Jen,' he said softly. 'Can I come over?'

'Tony, it's almost three o'clock.'

'I could be there in five minutes.'

She forced a yawn. 'Sorry, I'm bushed.'

'Tomorrow, then. Early in the afternoon. I have a recording session at three, but I'll be through at four.'

'I have a matinee. It's Wednesday – remember?'

'All right, I'll come to your place after the matinee.'

'No. You know I keep my makeup on between shows. And it would ruin my hair.'

He groaned. 'All right, all right! I'll come by and take you to dinner.'

'We'll see . . .' She hung up.

She didn't go home after the matinee. She forced herself to sit through a movie between shows. At the evening performance, she told the doorman to say she had gone if Tony arrived after the show to pick her up. She sat in the dressing room until the doorman came by to lock up. Yes, Mr, Polar had come by, and he had given the message like she said. She gave him five dollars and walked home.

187

The phone was ringing when she let herself into her apartment. She let it ring. It rang every twenty minutes. Each time she checked with the operator – it was always Mr. Polar. At five in the morning she finally picked up the phone on the third ring.

He was enraged. 'Where have you been!'

'I went to a movie between shows.' She deliberately made it sound like a lie.

'Oh sure! And tonight? You sure must have lit out of there fast!'

'I was there. The doorman must have made a mistake.'

'And I suppose you've been home all evening?'

'Mmmmm.'

'Well, for your information, I've called every twenty minutes since eleven-thirty. You just got home!' He sounded triumphant.

'I must have been sleeping and didn't hear the phone.'

'I'll bet. Probably with one of those Boston swells you met at the funeral.'

She hung up on him and lay back with a beatific smile. It was working! She went into the bathroom and took out a bottle brimming with red pills. What a windfall! In Lawrenceville she had innocently told old Dr. Rodgers about her sleeping problem. He had been blinded by her sunny smile. He was sympathetic and understanding. Funerals often gave people insomnia. The next day he had appeared with a little bottle crammed with twenty-five Seconals!

She heard the insistent ring of the phone again. Tony would keep at it. She told the operator not to ring any more, to say she was accepting no more calls for the night. As an extra precaution she pulled the safety bolt across the door. Then she opened the bottle of pills. She took two of them. One worked – but two! It was the most beautiful feeling in the world. She put her head on the pillow gently. The soft numbness began to slither through her body. Oh, God! How had she ever lived without these gorgeous red dolls!

She played the cat-and-mouse game with Tony for two more days. Each night she looked at the bottle of Seconals with affection. She never could do this without the dolls. She would have spent sleepless nights, smoking, worrying – and she would have lost her nerve.

On Friday night, Tony was standing at the stage entrance when she arrived at the theatre. He grabbed her arm roughly. 'Okay. You win,' he snarled. 'I have the car. We leave for Elkton tonight – now.'

'But I have a show, and a matinee tomorrow.'

'I'll go in and tell the stage manager you're sick.'

'But they'll read about us in the papers tomorrow if we elope. I'll be fired – maybe brought up on charges at Equity.'

'So what? You'll be Mrs. Tony Polar. You don't intend to keep on working in the show, do you?'

(Of course not! Was she crazy? Besides, Henry would smooth everything over. This was it!)

She grabbed his arm. 'Go tell them I'm sick, Tony. As a matter of fact, I *am* beginning to feel faint . . .'

Jennifer was happy, Tony was dazed. They were married! The Elkton newspapers had been informed. They had posed and smiled for the local cameramen and given statements for the AP and UP. Finally, they had driven off and checked into a small hotel in the outskirts of the city.

Now, as Tony sat on the bed, watching Jennifer unpack, the numbness created by the excitement began to wear off. He was suddenly frightened.

'Miriam will kill me,' he said slowly.

Jennifer came over and put her arms around him. 'You're not a child, Tony, you're my husband.'

'You've got to stick by me when we tell her,' he mumbled.

'I'm your *wife*, darling. I'll always stick by you.'

'But she'll be so mad, Jen.' Tears came to his eyes. Suddenly he buried his head in the pillow and sobbed. 'I'm scared . . . oh, I'm scared . . .'

For a moment Jennifer stood very still. A wave of revulsion sickened her. She felt a crazy impulse to turn and run – but where? And to what? No one would understand. They'd think something was wrong with her. She had to make this work. Tony was a star, and talented people had idiosyncrasies. Maybe that was it – he was just more emotional than most men.

She sat, on the bed and cradled his head in her arms. 'It's going to be all right, Tony,' she said softly.

'But Miriam will be mad. She'll holler.' He looked at her, his eyes brimming with tears. 'It's your fault. You made me do it.'

'I told you, I'll stand up to Miriam.'

189

'Honest? You really will?'

'Yes.' She stroked his head. 'Just remember that I'm your wife.'

He reached out and touched her breasts. Slowly he wiped away his tears and began to grin. He looked at her slyly. 'And now I can do anything I want with you.'

She managed a weak smile. 'Yes, Tony . . .'

He pulled the robe off her. 'Turn over,' he growled.

She ground her teeth in agony as he tore into her. She felt his nails ripping down her back. Smile, Jen, she told herself. You've made it – you're Mrs. Tony Polar . . .

Miriam held the crumpled wire and stared vacantly into space. Elkton! Well, that was it! And she had taken every precaution – two hundred a week she had paid that Ornsby! She picked up the phone, her fat finger tearing viciously at the dial.

'Sorry to disturb your sleep, Mr. Ornsby,' she snarled, 'but it just so happens you're sleeping on my time!'

He was instantly alert. 'I followed him to the stage door at eight. He was waiting for her. She came along at eight-oh-one and they stood talking. It was almost half-hour time and I knew she had to go in so I went off and grabbed a bite. I knew I was safe for three hours – she had the show to do. Then I showed up again at eleven. He didn't come around. If he's gonna pick her up he gets there by eleven-fifteen at the latest. I waited till eleven-thirty, then I took my post at his hotel. I just left a few hours ago. He hadn't come in. I checked all the clubs – he's not around. So I figure maybe she had another date tonight and he shacked up with some other chick. She's been ducking him for several nights, running home alone after each show.'

'Well, she didn't do no show tonight,' Miriam snapped. 'They eloped.'

There was silence at the other end of the line.

'Two hundred a week I been paying you, just to prevent this. What kind of a detective are you?'

'One of the best,' he said sharply. 'But those two are fruitcakes. I've frozen my ass off standing outside his hotel night after night, while they were up in bed all warm and cosy, banging away. But hell, lady, I'm not the F.B.I. I got to eat, and I got to stop sometimes to take a leak. I figure the only time I'm really safe is when that broad is on the stage. Who figures she's gonna skip a show?'

Miriam slammed the receiver down. But he was right. Jennifer had been too slick. She sighed. She had been so careful, and now it would all probably go up in smoke. So far the public and everybody had been fooled. They accepted Tony's childish replies as part of his charm. Some even thought it a clever pose. Only Miriam knew the truth, and she had hidden it from everyone – even Tony. With a woman he functioned as a man, physically. His talent as a performer was a gift. He did everything right when he sang, automatically. But mentally and emotionally, Tony was ten years old.

Now what? As long as she was present at every interview, she could cover for him. But now there was Jennifer.

How much had Jennifer guessed? Actually, she had nothing against the girl. She was probably genuinely attracted to Tony. Why not? He was handsome and talented and quite a stallion. Maybe she hadn't noticed anything. After all, they were never alone – except for the sex. She had seen to that, always being with them, seeing to it that at least one or two of the writers always trailed along. She had trained Tony that way. 'A star always has an entourage,' she had told him repeatedly, and he had accepted traveling with groups as standard procedure. That way no one ever really got to do much talking with him.

Until Jennifer, it had been easy. Miriam knew he had to satisfy his physical needs and she encouraged it, always managing to keep it on a transitory basis. A dancer in the line at a club they played, happy to be with him, out for kicks and reflected glory and satisfied to let him go out of her life with a gift of perfume and his promises of undying affection. That's the way it had been until he met Jennifer. She had done everything to break that up. Every time he went out of town she practically threw the most beautiful girls in the world in his arms. He took them, too – but he always came back to Jennifer. She had been hoping the California trip would finish it. Only two weeks to go – and now this!

Miriam sighed. Most people thought she tagged after Tony to revel in his reflected glory. Some glory! She'd have given anything for a life of her own. But she couldn't leave Tony. So here she was, a forty-four-year-old virgin, masterminding Tony into a spectacular success. Why did it have to be like this? The sins of the father, she thought wryly. Well, they had visited Tony, all right – only he didn't know it. She was bearing the brunt. And it hadn't really been the sins of the father, but their lousy tramp of a mother! So many secrets she had hidden from Tony and from the world. She had spun a beautiful picture of a handsome father who had been killed in a train accident before Tony was born. And a lovely, frail mother, so weakened by the shock that after she had given birth to little Tony, she had quietly smiled and passed into the arms of the angels, leaving the fourteen-year-old Miriam to take care of him. The press believed it. Tony believed it. He had never learned that his real father, like Miriam's real father, had been a mystery, even to their mother.

They had been sired by different fathers, strangers who passed through their mother's arms from night to night. And the one who had produced Tony must have been a beaut! But then her mother ran into a lot of strange ducks. A singing waitress at Coney Island did not exactly draw the Social Register. Her mother had sworn Miriam's father was a nice man from Pittsburgh. Perhaps. But Tony's father – whoever the bastard was – must have been good-looking. Tony had come off with the best of both parents. He had his mother's deep brown eyes with the incredible lashes. His nose was short and straight, his mouth sensuous. And he was tall. Miriam, on the other hand, had inherited someone else's looks. She smiled wryly. That guy from Pittsburgh might have been a very nice man, but he sure was no Robert Taylor. In fact, if she ever ran into a short, stout man with small blue eyes and a bulbous nose in Pittsburgh, she'd holler 'Daddy.'

She had selected the name Polar out of sentiment. The kindest and most permanent lover her mother had known was a man named Polarski. He had genuinely liked the pudgy little girl and had never failed to bring her a present or chuck her under the chin. She had never forgotten him. Years later, as a silent tribute, she shortened his name and took it for herself and Tony.

It hadn't been hard to hide his true identity from Tony or the press. Their mother had been a drifter. Every city has women like Belle, the not-quite-young girl who plays a tired piano and sings in a throaty voice in a local cocktail bar. Belle had started out singing at Tony Pastor's, but that was the only shining hour of her career. Then she floated to the cocktail bars and beerhalls around the different cities, passing from man to man.

Miriam was born in a charity ward in Philadelphia. Belle placed her in a foster home until she was eight. Then Belle fell into what seemed like a job of some permanence in Coney Island and sent for the girl. For a few years Miriam knew the luxury of a two-room flat and the affection of Mr. Polarski, but when Polarski went his way there was a succession of men. Belle was getting older. They were both stunned when Belle found she was pregnant again. Christ! She hadn't had the curse in months – all she needed was a change-of-life kid.

She stayed on the job for six months; then the costume could no longer conceal her condition, and she was fired. They moved to one room. Miriam, now fourteen, quit school and got a job as a counter girl. They had no friends, no neighbors. Then late one night, with the ambulance clanging, Belle was rushed to the hospital with the trembling Miriam at her side. Belle died five minutes after the screaming boy entered the world.

Miriam had taken the baby home. It had been easy to convince the disinterested hospital supervisor that there was a grandmother waiting to take over. And all alone, the fourteen-year-old girl had raised Tony. It seemed impossible when she looked back – the dreadful early weeks trying to make the formula correctly, washing diapers, trying to make the two hundred dollars she and Belle had saved stretch out, counting out pennies for milk, living on cans of soup and big boxes of crackers.

Tony had been four weeks old when he had the first convulsion. Again there was the clanging ambulance, the hospital. Tests were made and all the big doctors studied Tony's case. They kept him in the hospital a year. Miriam was frantic with worry, but at least she was able to get a full-time job and save some money. Then Tony was returned to her. He looked healthy. Then more convulsions and back to the hospital. It went on like that until he was five. Then the convulsions stopped. He went to kindergarten, struggled through the first grade. In the second grade they threw him out. They suggested a special school, but she kept him home. Her Tony wasn't going to be with a lot of crazy kids. Patiently she taught him herself, as much as he could learn.

Yes, it had been an impossible beginning. But at fifteen one can fight for survival against any odds. At twenty one could take on the world. But now the odds were piling up again. And Miriam was tired.

A few times she had even considered going to Jennifer and telling her the truth about Tony, so she would understand the idea of marriage with Tony was senseless. But it was too big a gamble. Suppose the girl had turned on both of them, told the story around town? It would destroy Tony's career – and that would destroy Tony.

She couldn't give up now; she had fought too long and too hard. God, she had even fought the United States Army. Tony had been elated when he received his draft notice – it was like playing soldier to him. His career was just starting, and he never knew about the secret trips she had taken to Washington, the endless red tape and the lack of sensitivity of the Army brass. She had been ready to give up until she met Major Beckman. He had a brother like Tony. He read Tony's medical reports, all bound in the frayed manila envelope from the hospital in Coney Island. He had Tony examined by his chief neurologist. Finally, Miriam received a new collection of reports to add to the manila envelope and Tony was rejected by the Army, quietly and firmly. Major Beckman announced to the press that Tony had been rejected due to a punctured ear drum.

No, she couldn't give up now. She had fought off the Army, the press, the whole damn world – one slinky blonde wasn't going to ruin everything. She'd stick close to them. They were leaving for the Coast in a few weeks, and she'd be living with them. Who knows – it might work out somehow. She pulled the robe around her shapeless body and resolutely organized her thoughts. She had to notify the press, the columnists – who should she give the first break to? No, don't play favorites – the wire services must have picked it up already from Elkton. When they returned, she'd call a press conference, arrange interviews with Jennifer and Tony . . .

ANNE

December, 1946

That night Anne returned to New York. She found everything in wild
disarray. A note written in Jennifer's hurried scrawl was propped on
the night table.

> *It was a tough fight, but I won. When you read this I will be Mrs.*
> *Tony Polar. Wish me luck. Love.*
>
> Jen

She was glad for Jennifer, but Jennifer's victory seemed to emphasize
the dreariness of her own situation.

Lyon had called her in Lawrenceville to tell her his great news.
Bess Wilson loved the book – thought it had great promise – but felt
it needed a complete rewrite before she could show it to any publisher.
Lyon was very enthusiastic. Sure it meant another six months at the
typewriter – but Bess Wilson liked it, and Bess was tough to please.

She had tried to hide her disappointment – six months of rewrit-
ing. And now Jennifer was gone. The hotel suite seemed so empty.

She could carry it alone. She had plenty of money, or would have,
as soon as everything was in order. Unfortunately, severing all ties
with Lawrenceville could not be accomplished just by handing Mr.
Walker the keys. There were endless legal adjustments that required
her presence. The will had to be probated formally. And the furniture – she couldn't just dump it on the sidewalk. Mr. Walker said

every piece was worth something. It had to be tagged and sent to New York or Boston for auction. It'd bring her a good deal of money. Her mother had left her fifty thousand dollars in bonds, cash and stock. Aunt Amy's money also went to her – twenty-five thousand more. Mr. Walker thought he could get forty thousand for the house alone, since it was on an acre and a half of good ground. Yes, she would have plenty of money – well over a hundred thousand, not counting the furniture – but meanwhile there was still the necessity of returning to Lawrenceville for at least another week, perhaps longer. She shuddered. Just being in that house made her feel unreasonably depressed.

She took a quick shower, changed her clothes and took a cab to Lyon's apartment. He was at the typewriter when she arrived. 'Come into the dungeon,' he said, embracing her warmly. He began picking up some crumpled pages he had tossed on the floor. 'Don't mind the rubbish. I've been working every evening. It's coming along swimmingly.'

She forced a smile. 'I'm glad, Lyon. I know it will be a good book.' She picked up a sheaf of the new pages and glanced at them. 'This is no time for me to be trapped in Lawrenceville – but I can take some of it back with me and type it up in a clean copy.'

'What would I do without you? My typing looks like hieroglyphics.' Suddenly he frowned. 'It really isn't fair to you – you've been so patient. And now another delay – this bloody rewrite.'

She smiled. 'I told you I'd wait forever – if necessary. Don't mind me and my mood, Lyon – it's just Lawrenceville.'

Later, as she lay in his arms, Lawrenceville seemed thousands of miles away. As if it had never happened. And it wasn't until later that she even remembered to tell Lyon the news about Jennifer.

'I'm glad for her,' he said. 'But doesn't that leave you in a bit of a fix? No roommate.'

'I have money, Lyon. Mother left me quite a bit.'

'Don't tell anyone. Some fortune hunter will grab you off.'

'Lyon, why can't we get married? I have enough for us to live on for . . . well, for a long time.'

'And you'd get up every morning and go to work—'

'Only to keep out of your hair. It'd be too cramped here with both of us hanging about, but once you made it . . . then I'd work for you. I'd type your manuscripts, handle your fan mail . . .'

'It doesn't work that way, Anne. You know what Bess Wilson said. Even if it's a good book, it might do nothing more than earn me a slight reputation. Then I'd have another year's work, with no money coming in. And don't think I wouldn't like to write full time. These past few evenings have proved something to me – you get a certain rhythm when you keep at a thing hours on end.'

'Then I'm right.' She sat up.

'And wrong. I have some money, Anne. But by the time I was into my next book it would run out. I'd be coming to you for cigarette money. I'd be too humiliated to write. No, darling, it wouldn't work.'

'But what am I supposed to do? Sit around and wait until you win the Pulitzer Prize?'

'No. Just wait and see how this book is received. If it's received at all. I have no real assurance I'll even get published.'

'You will. I know you will. And I'll wait.' She looked thoughtful. 'How long does it take to get a book published, I wonder?'

He laughed and took her in his arms.

Anne paced up and down the wooden planks of the Lawrenceville station. As usual, the local train was late. Poor Lyon. The five-hour train ride to Boston was deadly enough, but to sit on the unheated local for an hour with all those stops . . .

The last three days had certainly been deadly for her. She had even been grateful for Willie Henderson, who had driven her everywhere in his new Chevvie. There was such red tape connected with every detail, and sometimes it seemed that nothing had been accomplished. She would have to remain through part of next week so that the dealer from Boston could come to discuss the furnishings. Everything had to be discussed – every move she made was stymied by slow legal procedure. She was trapped in Lawrenceville.

But Lyon was coming up for the weekend. They'd have two wonderful days together, and for those two days even Lawrenceville would be palatable. For the first time her mother's huge four-poster would hold two people who enjoyed their union. As she tidied it she wondered how many frustrating nights her father had known – how many rejections he had received from her emotionally virginal mother. 'Well, tonight you're in for some surprises,' she told the bed as she gave the comforter a final pat. It responded with a creak, as though in shocked protest.

But now, as she paced the station nervously, she wondered if this had been wise. Everyone in Lawrenceville would know Lyon was here, staying at her house. So what! Once she sold the house she'd never return. Damn the town! Who cared what they thought!

She heard the wheeze of the local as it rumbled down the tracks. She saw him first. A light snow was drifting down, and it settled on his black hair as he walked down the platform. She felt that strange tightening in her chest; she always felt it every time she saw Lyon. Would there ever be a time she would take him for granted and relax in the comfort that he belonged to her? Now, as she saw his quick smile of greeting, she felt the same surge of amazement that this magnificent man *did* belong to her. He had come all the way to Lawrenceville just to be with her!

'I didn't believe I'd ever get here,' he said, hugging her lightly. 'The towns we passed. Good God, I'll bet no one knows there's a Rome in Massachusetts.'

'Or a Lawrenceville,' she said.

'Everyone knows about Lawrenceville – you've made it famous. How do we get to the ancestral mansion, by sleigh?'

She led him to a cab. She snuggled against him as he stared out at the countryside.

'Shouldn't we tell him where to go?' he whispered.

'Mr. Hill knows where everyone in town lives. If you had arrived alone, he would automatically have taken you to the Inn.'

He smiled. 'I like that. A bit different from New York cabbies. Say, this is beautiful country.'

'The snow helps,' she said without enthusiasm.

'When did it start? It was clear in New York.'

She shrugged. 'Probably in August. It snows here all the time.'

He put his arm around her. 'Won't give in, will you? Once you hate something, you're relentless.'

'I gave Lawrenceville twenty years. That's long enough for any small town.'

Lyon leaned forward. 'Do you like Lawrenceville, Mr. Hill?'

The driver cocked his head. 'Aeah. Why not? Born here. It's a right nice town. Miss Anne's just going through some growing pains. She'll change. Once she's back long enough she'll—'

'I told you I was leaving for good, Mr. Hill!'

'I reckon when the time really comes to sell the old house, you'll change your mind. I remember when your mother was born, right in that same house. I bet your little ones will be born there, too. 'Course, now we got that big new hospital right in Weston, just eight miles down the main highway. Better'n a lot of your New York hospitals, too. Why, Boston had to send for our iron lung during the polio epidemic.'

The cab crunched through the snow in the driveway and stopped before the house. Lyon stepped outside and stared silently.

'This is yours?' He turned to her, his eyes beaming with admiration. 'Anne . . . it's beautiful!'

'Picturesque in the snow,' she said balefully.

He paid Mr. Hill, wished him a Merry Christmas, and followed her inside. Anne was forced to admit the crackling fire made the large living room appear warm and inviting. She gave him a complete tour, and his eyes shone in approval of everything he saw. She knew he was not just being polite. He genuinely liked the house.

They cooked steaks in the large kitchen and ate before the fire in the living room. Lyon insisted on building a fire in the fireplace in the bedroom. She was surprised at his agility with the fire irons. 'You forget, I spent most of my life in London where they don't believe in central heating,' he reminded her.

Then he said, 'This is a wonderful house. You've been too close to it to appreciate it. It suits you, you know. You look like you belong here.'

'Don't even say that jokingly,' she threatened. 'I don't regard it as a compliment.'

On Sunday the snow stopped, and they took a long walk. They ran into half the town just leaving church. She waved but did not stop, and she felt a barrage of curious stares as they continued their walk.

When they returned to the house, Lyon worked on the fire and Anne brought him some sherry. 'It's the only thing I could find,' she said apologetically. 'Not an ounce of whiskey.'

'You're a fallen woman,' he said as he sipped his drink. 'I saw your neighbors stare. They'll check at the Inn and find I'm not registered. Looks like I'll have to marry you quickly. Restore your honor in this town.'

'I don't care what this town thinks of me.'

He sat down beside her. 'Come on, my stubborn little New Englander, give in and admit this is really a marvelous house. What a wonderful room! That portrait over the fireplace – isn't that a Sargent?'

'I think so. It's my grandfather. I'm sending it to one of the galleries in New York. They've offered a good price.'

'Hold on to it. The price will go up.' He was quiet for a moment. 'Anne, seriously . . . sitting here, you've never looked so beautiful. This is such a perfect setting for you – and you don't look the least bit depressed to me. Lawrenceville seems to agree with you.'

'Only because you're here, Lyon.'

'You mean, home is where the heart is . . .' He held her close and they both looked at the fire. After a while, still staring dreamily at the burning logs, he said, 'It just might work at that . . .'

'What might work?'

'Us.'

She snuggled closer. 'I always said it would. You might as well stop struggling. It's inevitable.'

'I have around six thousand dollars. Anne, what are the taxes here each year?'

'Here?'

'Couldn't be too steep. Remember, I said I couldn't be married to you and let you support me. But I could accept the hospitality of this fine house. With my six thousand we could manage for a year. And if I get a decent advance on the book, I could start another. Anne – it could work!' He stood up, and rubbing his hands together, looked around the room. 'Good Lord, it would really be marvelous. And I could write here.'

'Here?' The word stuck in her throat.

'Anne.' He knelt on the floor. 'Nothing has been very proper about our relationship. But here, in this very fine and proper house, I will propose in a most proper fashion – on bended knee. Will you marry me?'

'Of course. But do you mean you want me to keep the house so you could come here and write? I'll be glad to – but it would take so long to get here each weekend . . .'

'We'd live here! Anne, it's your house, but I could pay the taxes on it, buy the food. I'd be supporting you. One day I'll make enough money to add to it in some way. That's probably what your father did. Mr. Hill said your mother was born here. We'll have roots, Anne. And I'll make it. I'll be a damn fine writer. You'll see.'

'Live here?' She looked at him wildly.

'I'll go back to New York and give Henry notice for both of us. If you like we can get married in New York. Jennifer is there—'

'*Everything* is there!'

'Nothing we can't live without.'

'But Lyon, I hate it here! I hate this town – this house . . .'

For the first time he became aware of her panic. 'Even with me?' he asked carefully.

She began to pace the room, trying desperately to collect her thoughts. She had to make him understand.

'Lyon . . . you say you could write here. You probably could, perhaps eight hours a day. But what would I do? Join the women's clubs? Play bingo once a week? Renew my so-called friendships with the dreary girls I grew up with? And they wouldn't accept you that quickly, Lyon. You're an outsider. You have to be third-generation Lawrenceville to mean anything in this snobbish town . . .'

His face relaxed. 'So that's what you're worried about? I'd be ostracized. Well, don't worry. I have a tough hide. We'll go to church, be seen around. After they realize we mean to stay they'll loosen up.'

'No – *no*! I won't do it! I won't live here!'

'Why, Anne?' His voice was very quiet.

'Lyon, don't you understand? Just as you have certain principles – you couldn't let me support you in New York – well, I have my blind spots too. Not many – in fact, just one. Lawrenceville! I hate it! I love New York. Before I came to New York I lived here, in this mausoleum. I was nothing. I was dead. When I came to New York it was like a veil lifting. For the first time I felt I was alive, breathing.'

'But now we have each other.' His eyes were direct, questioning.

'But not here,' she said with a moan. 'Not here. Can't you understand? A part of me would die.'

'Then, as I see it, you could only love me in New York. Sort of a package deal.'

'I love you, Lyon.' The tears were running down her face now. 'I'd love you anywhere. And I'd go anywhere that your work took you. Any place but here . . .'

'And you wouldn't even be willing to chance it – a year or two . . .'

'Lyon – I'll sell the house . . . I'll give you all the money . . . I'll live in one room with you. But not here!'

He turned and poked at the fire. 'I suppose that settles it.' Then he said, 'I'd better put another log on the fire before I leave. It's dying.'

She looked at her watch. 'It's early yet.'

'I'd best take the four o'clock train. Tomorrow's a rough day, and with Christmas coming up on Wednesday . . .'

'I'll go with you to the station.' She went to the phone and called Mr. Hill.

The fire was almost out when she returned. Without Lyon the room suddenly looked forbidding and bleak again. Oh, God, did Lyon understand? He had been so quiet on the drive to the station. 'I'll be back on Tuesday,' she had promised. 'Nothing will keep me from being with you on Christmas.'

But when he got on the train he hadn't turned and waved. She felt as if she were going to be sick. Damn Lawrenceville! It was like an octopus, reaching out and trying to drag her down.

Jennifer called the next day. She and Tony were living at the Essex House in a very nice suite. Miriam had taken a room down the hall. And Miriam had acted very nice about the whole thing. They were leaving for the Coast earlier now, January second. When was Anne coming back? They were giving a big Christmas Eve party tomorrow night.

'I'll be there,' Anne promised. 'But it looks as if things will never be settled here. I spoke to Henry a few days ago. He's been wonderful – says to take as long as I need. But I'm coming in for Christmas. When Lyon calls tonight I'll tell him about the party. We'll see you then.'

Lyon didn't call that night. He was probably sulking. This was their first fight, except for that misunderstanding in Philadelphia. Well, she wouldn't give in. But she'd phone him at the office tomorrow and tell him she was taking the train at noon.

She put the call through at ten in the morning. Henry wasn't in the office – neither was Lyon. She spoke to George Bellows.

'I don't know where Lyon is,' George told her. 'No one tells me anything around here. Lyon came in yesterday and took off at noon. Henry left for the Coast on Friday – an emergency with the Jimmy

Grant show. Maybe he sent for Lyon. Like I said, no one tells me anything.'

She unpacked her bag. No use going to New York. She felt disappointment mingled with relief. Lyon had probably left for California – that's why he hadn't called. At least he wasn't angry. He'd probably call that night and explain.

She spent Christmas Eve alone. Lyon didn't call. At three in the morning she tried his apartment. Maybe he hadn't gone to the Coast. Maybe he *was* sulking. There was no answer.

It was the worst Christmas she could remember. And she held Lawrenceville personally responsible. There were no more logs for the fireplace, so she turned the oil burner up. The house was well heated, but cold and dead. She sipped tea. She ate a few crackers. The radio didn't quite drown out the endless chiming of the church bells, and the Christmas carols depressed her even more. This was the day to rejoice. And she was alone. Jennifer was with Tony, Neely was in California with Mel. But she was alone in Lawrenceville.

She spent the next few days with Mr. Walker. Everything was tagged, and gradually some order prevailed. She would be free to leave at the end of the week. But where was Lyon? Five days had passed. In desperation she tracked Henry down at the Beverly Hills Hotel in California.

'Henry, where is Lyon?'

'That's what I'd like to know.' His voice crackled through the wires.

'Isn't he out there with you?'

'No, I assumed he was with you.'

'I haven't seen or heard from him since Sunday.'

'You're kidding!' Henry was suddenly concerned. 'I called the office yesterday afternoon. George said he hadn't been in since Monday. I just naturally assumed he took off to spend Christmas with you.'

'Henry, we've got to find him!'

'Why? Is anything wrong? I mean – what could be wrong? A guy doesn't just disappear. I've tried his apartment three nights in a row. He's not there.'

'I'll be back tomorrow. Henry, find him! *Find him!*' She was suddenly frightened.

'Now calm down. You two have a lovers' quarrel?'

'Not really. A misunderstanding – but I didn't think it was *this* serious.'

'I'll be back tomorrow, too,' Henry told her. 'Unless the weather is bad. I'm booked on a four o'clock plane this afternoon. Now relax. Lyon wouldn't just run out on us. He'll probably be in Monday with a logical explanation. Why don't you relax there over the weekend?'

'Relax! I can't wait to get out of here!'

She arrived back in New York to find a letter from Lyon waiting at her hotel.

Dear Anne,

Thank you for the moment of reckoning. I should say the five hours of reckoning. It was quite a long train ride, and gave me sufficient time to think things out. If I want to write, there's only one thing to do – write. Until now I was constantly searching for excuses. I had to work for Henry, then your house – the perfect setting. Seems I want things tied up in a neat bundle – want the entire world to conform so I can write. Now who the hell am I? Kind of a cheeky attitude, wanting you to slink about like the self-sacrificing little author's wife one reads about. As I see it, at the moment I am in limbo. I am not the driving Lyon Burke that Henry once knew, but neither am I the dedicated writer. I see nothing ahead but half truths – half an author, half a manager, putting off leaving Henry until I am a commercial success as a writer, putting off marriage because I cannot be a full-time husband, putting off writing because I must stay with Henry. Until now I have only given a part of myself to you, Henry and writing. It's obvious I'm not capable of giving to all three. If not, I should at least pull out of the lives of the two people I care most about. I have written most of these same thoughts to Henry. George Bellows is a good man – he is the man for Henry. And somewhere in your wonderful New York, my dearest, there is the right man for you, just waiting for you to find him.

I told you I have a bit of money. I also have access to a large, unheated house in the north of England. It belongs to relatives, but no one uses it. I shall open a few rooms. I could live there for years on a few quid, and I shall write even if my knuckles turn blue. We have only a few hours of daylight during the winter. Lawrenceville is the tropics in comparison. But no one will disturb me.

I have enclosed the keys to my apartment, dear Anne. It is the one practical thing I can do for you. With Jennifer married you are alone, and a flat is still hard to find. And I did inherit this with all the furniture due to your largess. I think it only fitting that you wind up with it. It's not much. I've taken your wonderful gift, the typewriter. But if the flat pleases you, take over the lease. And don't do anything silly like waiting for me. I warn you – I shall marry the first plump English maiden who will cook and tend for me. And years from now, if I do turn out any book that is halfway good, we can both say, 'At least there was one thing he did whole-heartedly.'

I loved you, Anne. But you are too wonderful to accept such a small part of a small person who tried to scatter himself in so many directions. So I shall concentrate on writing – at least in that way I can hurt no one but myself.

Thank you for the most wonderful year of my life.

Lyon

JENNIFER

Jennifer sat beside the pool in the shade. She read Anne's letter again. She sounded happy enough – it was the first letter without a mention of Lyon. Maybe she was finally over it. But how could she live in his apartment? Did she still hope he'd come walking in one day? After five months? Imagine, not one word from him! Just showed, you could never tell what really went on inside a man's head. Take all those pictures of her with Tony. They looked so happy – the perfect young Hollywood couple!

The sun crept under the umbrella. She reached out and bent the framework down to shield herself. Sure – a girl who got hives if she sat in the sun had to wind up in California: She glared angrily at the blazing orange ball. It was always there. It was the one thing in California you could count on. On occasion there might be a slight fog in the morning, but inevitably the lemon disc would make an appearance, timidly at first; then, as if inflating itself, it would brighten and inhale the mist and clouds and emerge triumphant and alone in a china-blue sky.

She sighed. Every day here since her arrival in January had been like the middle of July. How did those damn oranges grow if it never rained? It was May in New York. In the East you appreciated good weather when it finally arrived. She thought about New York. The first balminess must be in the air. The heavy winter coats had been stored away and people were sitting outside the cafeteria in Central

Park. And you could walk in New York! You never appreciated the privilege of walking until you lived in California. You could even walk at night in New York. If you had nothing to do you could walk down Fifth Avenue and look in the stores, or go to a late movie, or walk down Broadway and buy a hot dog. Here, if you walked down Beverly Drive at night, a prowl car picked you up.

Well, at least Anne had New York. According to her letters she was going out a lot, but she never mentioned anyone special. Probably still waiting for Lyon. Well, at least that was something tangible.

But what was *she* waiting for? Another day to pass? There was a party for tonight. It didn't thrill her, but it was better than playing gin with Tony. He couldn't even concentrate on that, because Miriam kept hanging over him, telling him every card to play. If Miriam would only let him think for himself once in a while.

She sipped her Coke. The ice had melted. Why did warm Coke taste like a laxative? She was too lazy to go back in the house for a fresh one. She was too lazy to do anything. And the party – that wouldn't be any fun. It was business. Tony was up for the lead in Dick Meeker's new picture, so she had to be pleasant and polite. 'Pleasant and polite.' Miriam constantly drummed those words into her ears. 'Don't try and be a big personality out here. Out here you're nothing. Everyone is a big shot here, so you just be pleasant and polite.'

She did her best. She floated through parties like a grinning zombie. She made no friends. Miriam was right, beauty was a cheap commodity in Hollywood. There were millions of beautiful nobodies. The girls who hung out at Schwab's were beautiful, the carhops were beautiful – yet most of the big stars were not the spectacular beauties. Jane Wyman was pert looking. Barbara Stanwyck was smart, chic; so was Rosalind Russell. Joan Crawford was striking. Boy, this was a pistol. All these years thinking she had something special because her teeth were good, her nose was straight and she had big boobs. Big boobs weren't even in style. Adrian and Ted Casablanca and all the other big designers had created the broad-shouldered look. Big boobs only got in the way.

It would be another nothing evening. She was no one, just Mrs. Polar, the wife of a promising newcomer. Oh yes, he was on radio, someone might say. But that didn't mean a thing out here. You had to be in pictures – and a wife didn't mean anything. In fact, a wife held the same social status as a screenwriter – necessary but anonymous. Even the starlets rated more attention at parties. Starlets were always available, ready for any kind of action. Starlets knew producers and often had hilarious inside stories to tell – the big screen star who always yelled 'Mother!' when he reached the climax, the movie mogul who wanted his wife to watch . . . Sure, starlets could garner plenty of attention at parties. But a wife – a wife lived in limbo. Too respected to be approached, too unimportant to rate respect. At most parties she wound up at the bar, discussing old times with the hired bartenders, who all hailed from New York, talking nostalgically about Sardi's and Lindy's. It was easier than talking to the other displaced wives, who cared only about the servant problem and tennis.

She couldn't even go on shopping sprees like she had before she was married. She had been allowed to buy *one* evening gown in the five months she had been here. 'You have more clothes than a department store,' Miriam had snorted. Maybe she did, but she got tired of them. Didn't Miriam realize it was important to wear something new? But Miriam had only three dresses, and they all looked alike. Miriam went to parties in a five-year-old blue lace dress and white orthopedic shoes!

Miriam gave her an allowance of fifty dollars a week. She sent it all to her mother, and her mother kept writing that it wasn't enough. She had tried to talk to Tony about the money situation, but she hardly ever saw him. He was either recording, learning new songs or rehearsing his radio show. And at dinner there was always Miriam. At night, alone in the large bed, he was the old Tony, grasping for her greedily. But after it was over, she couldn't reach him. She had tried to explain that if she could be a part of his life and career she wouldn't be bored, but he didn't seem to understand. 'Miriam takes care of all that – talk to her.'

When she mentioned money it was the same: 'Talk to Miriam, she'll give you all you need.' And Miriam had all the answers. 'Whaddaya need money for? I pay for all the food and the booze. You can charge the gas. Fifty dollars is plenty for pin money.'

It couldn't go on like this. How much longer could she just sit by the pool? She had read three books so far this week and it was only Friday. The sun had crept under the umbrella again. She jumped up. She had to do something, go somewhere. Maybe Neely would be home. She had just finished her second picture and the studio had promised her a month's vacation. She went into the house and changed into slacks. She was glad for Neely. Her first picture had gotten raves and Jennifer had seen a sneak preview of the new one – it was great. She hadn't seen much of Neely, though. They talked on the phone occasionally, but Neely had just changed her number again and she didn't have the new unlisted one.

She drove the eight blocks – you just didn't walk in California. Anyway, if Neely wasn't home she'd go over to Schwab's. Maybe Sidney Skolsky would be there and they could sit and talk. Sidney loved Hollywood, but he also understood how she felt.

Mel opened the door. He was in bathing trunks. He had filled out and the tan made him look almost healthy. He led Jennifer to the swimming pool. 'Want some lunch? I'm having a sandwich.'

Jennifer shook her head. She sat down in the shade. Their pool was identical to hers. Same kidney shape, same cabana area, same tennis court and prop bar. She looked off to the purplish hills. Did Mel sit around all day, too?

'Neely's at the studio,' he explained. 'Wardrobe fittings.'

'I thought she had a month off.'

'Sure, a month off before shooting. That means a month of wardrobe fittings, makeup tests and publicity stills. But she should be home any minute. Hey, did you hear? Ted Casablanca's doing her clothes.'

'She's really in the big leagues,' Jennifer said. 'Ted won't design for anyone but the top stars.'

Mel hunched his bony shoulders. 'Only in Hollywood could this happen. Women fainting because some fag deigns to dress them. Any place else, if you pay the money you get the article. In New York does Saks worry if a customer will do justice to their creations? But out here everything is a status symbol. Neely's dieting now – is that a laugh?'

'Why? Has she gained weight?'

'She weighs one hundred and eighteen. She's always weighed that. She's five feet five – that's a nice weight. But this Casablanca – he wants her to lose fifteen pounds. Says her face will be more interesting and the clothes will look better. She takes little green pills . . . doesn't eat a thing.'

Neely suddenly arrived, her old breathless self. She was delighted to see Jennifer. 'Have you heard?' she squealed. 'Ted Casablanca's doing my clothes! Oh, Jennifer, he's divine! I'm going to be beautiful for a change. He's making me some really glamorous things – real understated. Geez, when I remember that awful purple taffeta! Ted says I should have the gamin look, the mischievous little girl. But chic. After all, I'm eighteen now – it's about time.'

'I hear you're dieting.'

'Yeah. Mel, get me some skimmed milk. Want anything, Jen?'

'A Coke.'

'We only have club soda. I don't keep anything fattening around. Mel, make Jen a lemonade. How's that?' Neely watched him leave, then she turned back to Jennifer, her childish eyes wide with concern.

'Oh, Jen, I don't know what to do. He's changed so – he just can't get with it. Everything he does he bungles.'

'I wouldn't say that. He's gotten you a lot of publicity. That story in *Screen World* is a great layout.'

Neely shook her head. 'The studio did that. They told him to butt out. He gets in the way all the time. They don't want him on the set – they say I'm self-conscious when he's around. And Ted Casablanca says he's the joke of the town.'

'I wouldn't take that seriously. You know how bitchy fags can be.'

'Fag!' Neely's eyes blazed. 'Don't you dare call him that! Why, he's – he's wonderful, that's all! He's only thirty and he's made three million dollars. And he's not a fag!'

'Really?'

'Really. What do you think I've been doing today? Fitting costumes? That's what I told Mel. We've been doing it – Ted and I – in every position. In his gorgeous air-conditioned studio. And let me tell you, he's no—' She stopped suddenly. Mel was bringing in the tray with their drinks.

'I've lost five pounds already,' Neely said as Mel handed her the milk. She took out a bottle and popped a speckled green capsule into her mouth. 'What an invention,' she said. 'They're absolutely marvelous, Jen. Really kill your appetite. Only trouble is, they pep me up so much I can't sleep.'

'Try Seconals,' Jennifer suggested.

'They really work?'

'Gloriously. They're beautiful little red dolls that take all your cares away and give you nine blissful hours of sleep a night.'

'No kidding? I'll try them. Mel, Call Dr. Holt right away. Tell him to send me a hundred.'

'A hundred?' Jennifer's voice caught in her throat. 'Neely, they aren't aspirin. You only take one a night. No doctor will give you more than twenty-five.'

'They won't, huh? Wanna bet? Dr. Holt is the studio doctor. He'll give me anything I ask for. Mel, call him right now.' Mel lumbered off to the phone. 'Just one a night, huh?'

Jennifer nodded. She saw no reason to tell Neely she sometimes took as many as three. One would help Neely. Besides, she intended to cut down – as soon as she straightened things out with Tony.

Mel had gone to telephone. Neely watched until he was out of sight. Then she pulled her chair closer. 'I got to get fitted for another diaphragm. Twice last month Mel didn't pull out in time. That sonofabitch is trying to get me pregnant.'

'I thought you wanted children.'

'Not with him. I'm gonna unload him.'

'Neely!'

'Look, he's a drag. Honest, Jennifer, he's changed completely. He has no incentive. I talked it over with The Head, and he agrees. Mel just gets in the way. He insisted I shouldn't lose weight, kept yelling I was fine just as I am. But now that I'm losing weight I'm getting the real star buildup with some glamour. See, Mel is in a rut. He's small time, and he won't get with it and change. But I gotta be careful. See, there's community property out here. Mel could claim half of everything.'

'What will you do?'

'It's all being worked out.' She lowered her voice to a real whisper. 'The Head is seeing to it that Mel gets a big offer in the East. With one of the top publicity offices. I'll make him go. The Head is going to fix it, have him caught – you know – with a girl. And I'll get the divorce.'

'Neely, you can't!'

'Well, what *can* I do? I hinted at divorce last week, and you know what he did? He started crying like a baby. He said he couldn't live without me. Is that a drag? I need a man who tells me what to do, a guy I can lean on, not one who leans on me. And all I'd ever have to do is get knocked up by him and then he'd never leave, not even for New York.'

'How do you know he'll accept the job?'

'I'll make him. I'll tell him that if he makes good – if the job works out – I'll come there and get in a Broadway show and have a baby and live in New York.'

'Would you?'

Neely looked at her strangely. 'Leave California? All this? Are you crazy? I got it made here. After my next picture I'll be a full-fledged star!'

'But you could be a star in New York, on Broadway.'

'A star on Broadway. Big deal! That's chicken feed. When you're a star in pictures you're a star all over the world. Do you know my picture is playing in London? Imagine! They know who I am in London! One movie – and I'm ten times better known than Helen Lawson will ever be. And when you're a star in pictures, you get treated like a star. Everything is done for you. I remember Helen had to ride the train to New Haven like the rest of us and dress in a drafty dressing room. Geez, our toilets at the studio are fancier than a star's dressing room in the theatre. My dressing room is a bungalow as big as Helen's Park Avenue apartment. When you're a hot property – that's what I am – they do everything for you. I just mentioned to The Head – that's what we all call C. H. Bean. He's such a wonderful little man . . . sweet, and you can talk to him like a father. I never knew my father. But as I was saying, I just mentioned to him that I wanted to lose some weight. Geez, know what he did? He had a steam room built onto my bungalow and hired a personal masseuse. And they pay for it. When I have to go anywhere – like an opening – they send a car and chauffeur for me and lend me furs and dresses. And if my next picture is as big as the first two, The Head says he's gonna give me a new contract at a big salary jump – maybe to two thousand a week.'

'That's really big money, Neely.'

'Nah, the Johnson Harris office says I'm worth even more. In fact, they might step in and renegotiate, maybe to twenty-five hundred a week. I could probably get it, too. All I gotta do is snap my fingers and I can have anything I want. The Head says maybe after another year I should dump this rented house and buy one in Beverly Hills. That's classier.'

'Why not take it easy and save your money?'

'Why? I'm not scared any more. Know why? Because I've got

talent, Jen. I never realized it back East. I used to think everyone could sing and dance. But in my second picture I found I could act, too. Did you see when I cried? That was no glycerine. The director just talked to me about the part, the situation the girl was in, and I felt it. And then I really cried.'

Jennifer nodded. 'You made me cry, too. I saw the preview last week.'

Neely stretched her arms expansively. 'I love it here. This town was made for me.'

Mel returned. 'The pills will be here any minute. Dr. Holt said it was a very good idea.' He sat down. 'Want to see a movie tonight, Neely?'

'Can't. Have to be up at six tomorrow. Color tests.'

He stared moodily at the swimming pool. 'I don't have to be up at any time. I'm getting stir crazy just sitting around . . .'

Jennifer thought about Mel as she drove home. She suddenly wondered how Tony felt about her. Was she a drag, too? If Tony didn't get the picture she was going to insist they go back to New York. He could do the radio show from there. But he would get the picture. She knew he would. And she'd be stuck here. Soon Tony would start feeling about her like Neely felt about Mel – if he didn't already. There would be stars playing opposite him in pictures, and young starlets chasing after him. How long could she go on sitting like this? She was almost twenty-seven, and soon it would begin to show . . .

She almost went through a traffic light as the idea hit her. Why hadn't she thought of it before? A baby! She would have a baby! It would bring Tony closer to her, and she'd have something to occupy her thoughts. Something to love. Oh, God, how she'd love it . . . they'd be so close. It would be a girl, it had to be! And she'd be a wonderful mother. She was exhilarated when she got home. It would be her secret.

She dressed with great care for the party. She would start her new project tonight!

September, 1947

She missed her first period in August. At first she was too excited to say anything, but in September, when she missed the second time, she knew. Her waistline had expanded two inches.

She went to a doctor, who verified her hopes and congratulated her. Tony was in a closed recording session, and she couldn't disturb him. But she had to tell someone. She wanted to shout it at the policeman directing traffic; she wanted to go to Schwab's and yell at everybody. But that wouldn't be right. Tony would want to give it a big press release. Neely! She would tell Neely! It was almost five. Neely would be through shooting for the day.

She drove to the studio. The gateman checked and directed her through to Neely's imposing bungalow. Neely was getting a massage.

'Hey, come on in,' she shouted. 'Your timing is perfect. I was going to phone you tonight. Guess what – it's all set! Mel leaves for New York tomorrow!'

'Is it still Ted?'

'Of course! What do you think I am? Some kind of a bum? I'm a one-man woman. Ted and me—' She stopped and shouted at the masseuse, 'Okay, that's enough, scram. I wanna talk to my girl friend in private.'

When the woman had gone, she dropped the towel. 'Well, how do you like the new streamlined Neely? I got a twenty-inch waistline now, and I weigh ninety-eight pounds.'

'Does Ted like you this thin?'

'Does he!' She climbed into a robe. 'He even likes my little boobs. They shrunk some, but he says big ones make him think of a cow. And they look lousy in the broad-shouldered look. We're getting married as soon as this Mel business is settled. And guess what? We're signing a pre-marital agreement. It was The Head's idea . . . this way we'll both know we're marrying for love, and not for each other's property.'

Jennifer managed a smile. 'Neely, guess what? I'm two months pregnant.'

'Oh, Geez.' Neely was instantly concerned. 'Well, there's a guy in Pasadena. He's supposed to be very good. The Head sends everyone who gets knocked up to him. First he tries shots, then if they don't work . . . The abortion is easy. He even gives anesthesia.'

'Neely, you don't understand. I want this baby. I planned it. I'm happy about it.'

'Oh. Well say, that's *marvelous*. You know, it's beginning to show already, now that you mention it. You've lost your *marvelous* waistline.'

'Who cares, as long as I have a *marvelous* baby.' Jennifer mimicked Neely's enunciation of the word.

Neely laughed good-naturedly. 'After it's all over, I'll lend you some of my green dolls to help you get your figure back.'

'They sure worked for you.'

'Yeah, but the trouble is, you gotta keep taking them. The second I stop, I eat like a maniac. But the feeling is great – sets you on fire, like you could dance for hours. And I bless you every night for the red ones. They saved my life. Oh, hey. Have you ever tried a yellow one? They're called Nembutals. If you take one of each – a red and a yellow – wow! You really sleep. I learned it by experiment. The red one puts you to sleep fast, but it wears off in six hours. The yellow works slower, but lasts longer. So I figured, why not try both? I only do it on weekends. Sometimes I sleep twelve hours.'

'I'm not going to take anything now that I'm pregnant. I don't want it to hurt the baby.'

'Yeah, but if you don't sleep, you'll look bad, won't you?'

'For the first time in my life, I'm not worrying about *my* looks. I want a perfect baby. If I lie awake all night, I won't care.'

Neely grinned. 'You sound corny, but I guess I'll feel that way, too. After I marry Ted and negotiate my new contract, then I'll get pregnant. But meanwhile – thank God for those red, yellow and green dolls.'

Jennifer hoped Tony had nothing planned for the evening. She wanted to go to that little restaurant in the Valley – without Miriam – and tell him there.

She saw the extra car in the driveway. It belonged to Delia, the part-time extra maid. Oh, damn! That meant something was on for tonight.

Miriam was waiting for her. 'Tony signed the contract today!' Her homely face was glowing. 'They just seen the rushes of his color test. He's got a five-year deal at Metro, and he starts on the picture two weeks from Monday. Dress real ladylike tonight – the director and his wife are coming for dinner. And the musical conductor and a few others are dropping by later.'

Jennifer dressed carefully. All right, she'd break it at dinner. Publicly! As she struggled with the zipper of her dress she realized she couldn't wait much longer. Tony would notice it soon anyway.

She took a Martini before dinner. Miriam stared at her in amazement. Jennifer sparkled, made small talk with the wife of the director, passed the canapes – was the perfect Hollywood wife. She waited until the wine was served at dinner, then stood up slowly, holding her glass in the air. Carefully avoiding Miriam's hostile stare, she said, 'I want to make a toast – to me.' Then she giggled. 'I mean, to what's *in* me. Tony and I are going to have a baby.'

Everyone cheered, glasses clinked, Tony leaped out of his chair and hugged her. But Jennifer had not missed Miriam's audible gasp and stricken look. When the excitement died down, her eyes met Miriam's. This time the pudgy face held only a pleasant smile.

When the last guest had disappeared, Miriam turned to Jennifer. She was still smiling. 'Run upstairs, little mother,' she said. 'You need all the rest you can get. There's a few details on the picture I want to discuss with Tony, then I'll send the new daddy right up.'

The moment Jennifer was gone she whirled on him. 'I thought I told you to use something.'

'We did.' Tony grinned sheepishly. 'I guess it was an accident.'

'What do you mean *accident?*' Miriam hissed. 'Those rubbers are made strong. I buy you the best. They don't break.'

'Oh, we stopped using them a few months ago. Jen told me I didn't have to. She said she was using a diaphragm.'

'I told you never to *ever* let any girl talk you into that. You could get a disease—'

'From Jen?' He laughed. 'Besides, it feels better without one.'

'A baby will tie you down.'

'Nah. We got enough money, haven't we? And with the picture and all. And I want to have a kid. It'll be fun.'

From the corner of her eye, Miriam saw Jennifer coming down the stairs. She said, 'If you have a baby, you'll have to be home more.'

Jennifer had stopped on the stairs and was listening. Tony, his back to the door, couldn't see her.

'Okay, so I'll be home more.' He shrugged.

'And give up that red-headed singer?'

He looked scared. 'Who told you?'

'Look, there's nothing I don't know. But don't worry – I won't tell Jennifer.'

'Tell Jennifer what?' She walked into the room.

Miriam pretended surprise. Tony looked frightened. 'It's nothing, Jen,' he said. 'Miriam and her crazy ideas. Just because I clown around with Betsy. You know – she's the redhead on my radio show, in the singing group. We clown around, that's all.'

'Some clowning around,' Miriam snapped. 'Three afternoons a week he bangs her in his studio dressing room. He may not be using the rubbers on you, Jennifer, but I buy him a box every week and he keeps running out!'

'Now look what you've done!' Tony whined as Jennifer tore out of the room.

'Look – make her get rid of that kid. You listen to me, Tony. It's no good for your career. There's plenty of doctors who can do it.'

'I want it,' he said stubbornly.

'Tony . . .' She was wheedling now. 'Think of your screen image. A young, handsome leading man – the studio is going to say you're only twenty-four. A kid would hurt the image.'

'Nuts! Sinatra has kids. So does Crosby. You're not going to take it away from us!' He ran up the stairs after Jennifer.

She was stretched across the bed, sobbing, when he entered the room.

'Honey.' He sat down and began to rub her neck. 'Don't mind what Miriam said. We'll have our baby.'

'Not mind!' She sat up, her face streaked with mascara 'Not mind! Let her go on running our lives – even to buy you condoms? And all this time, while I've been sitting in this house, being bored to death and getting older each month, you've been having a ball with some singer! While I just sit – watching Miriam get fatter and bossier every day!'

'What can I do?' he wailed.

'You can tell her to get out. That I'll run the house from now on.'

'I couldn't do that to Miriam. Where would she go?'

'Any place! Just away from us. I don't care if you give her half of everything you make, but just let us live our own lives. Just once, let's be husband and wife – not two children living with Miriam!'

'But who would take care of everything? Who would write my checks and read my contracts?'

'Oh, Tony, other people get business managers – you could too.'

'But why should I get a stranger who would cheat me? My own

sister does better than anyone, and she's always looking out for my interests.'

'But I can't live with her!'

Suddenly he tensed. 'Are you asking me to throw my sister out?'

'Tony,' she pleaded. 'What kind of a life have we got? We don't entertain unless it's business, because Miriam says it's a waste of money to give parties. And now Miriam's talking about buying this awful house. She never asked me if I liked it. Although God only knows what we need the house for anyway. We could do as well in a two-room apartment the way we live. We have no life.'

'I have to rehearse three days a week,' he yelled. 'I have to do my show. I have to listen to new songs and learn them . . . play benefits . . . pose for publicity pictures. What do you want me to do? Sit around and entertain you? You knew what my life was when you married me. Miriam doesn't go out at all. She doesn't go to half the places we go. We went to three benefits last month without her, but do you hear her complain?'

'No, but I heard her on the phone for hours trying to get an extra ticket. We went without her because the studio only sent two tickets. I'm surprised she doesn't sleep with us.'

'Before you came along she devoted her whole life to me. She raised me. She never complains. She's unselfish . . . kind . . . good . . . and you want me to throw her out!'

'It's either me or Miriam, Tony.'

For a moment they both stared without speaking. Then he broke into a boyish smile. 'You don't mean that, honey. You'll have the baby – look, I stood up to her on that, didn't I? Now let's go to sleep.' He began to undress.

In the silent darkness he reached out in bed to embrace her.

'We haven't settled anything,' she said grimly.

'What's there to settle?'

'Miriam.'

'Miriam stays. And so do you.' He ripped off her nightgown – his mouth sought her breasts. She tried to push him away. 'No. I want them. Soon there will be milk in them. Mmmm . . . will you let me suck them then, too?' She began to sob quietly. He looked up. 'C'mon, let's do it. What are you crying for?'

She sobbed more violently.

'Don't tell me you're upset because I gave Betsy a little bang once in a while?'

She jumped out of bed. Oh, God! What kind of a man was he!

He sat up and put on the light. He looked bewildered. 'I don't love Betsy . . .'

She sank into a chair and hugged her nakedness, shivering.

'Then why did you do it?' she sobbed.

He shrugged. 'It was just there, I guess.'

'But I've always been here . . .'

'I couldn't come dashing back to you during rehearsals, and she was always right there . . . But look, it doesn't mean anything. I promise I won't do it with Betsy any more. Hell, I'll get Miriam to fire her tomorrow – how's that? Now come on, get in bed.'

'It's not just Betsy. Tony, it's you – I don't understand you. How do you think, how do you feel?'

'I want *you*, right now. That's how I feel. Come on, honey . . .'

Because she didn't know what else to do, she got into bed and even submitted to his embraces. He satisfied himself, then turned on his side and fell instantly into a deep sleep. Jennifer got up and took three of the red pills. But it was getting light when she finally fell asleep.

The following morning, after Miriam and Tony had gone to rehearsal, she put in a call to Henry Bellamy. She told him the story.

'Looks like you better run for your life,' Henry said. 'Somehow she'll make you lose the baby – if only by aggravation alone.'

'What do I do?'

'Depends. How do you feel about this joker?'

'I don't know any more. Sometimes I feel sorry for him because Miriam has brainwashed him. Other times, like last night, I feel only disgust. But there's a streak of sweetness in Tony. He's not bad. That's the funny part. There isn't anything evil in him. He's just never grown up. It's Miriam's fault. She's made him think the world is his oyster, that he can do anything he pleases just as long as he keeps singing. I think we could find a life together if I could get him to break with her but I can't get through to him.'

'You're young, Jennifer. My advice is to get out while the getting's good.'

'I'm not as young as you think, Henry. I – I lied to you about my age.'

'So what? You've still got a whole life ahead. But you have no life there, the way I see it. If you stick it out there and do manage to have the baby, Miriam will just take it over, too.'

'No!'

'Then come to New York. See if Tony's man enough to come after you. I'll even try and convince him I can run his business affairs as well as Miriam. We'll pension the old dame off, and you can turn him into a real man. If he doesn't go for it, then you've lost nothing.'

'You're right, Henry. It's a cinch I can't go on like this.'

'I'll reserve a suite for you at the Pierre. Leave a note that you've been called to New York to audition for a show. Be sure and leave most of your clothes, so Miriam can't say it's desertion.'

'But Tony and Miriam know I can't take a show if I'm pregnant.'

'Of course they do. But this is just a technicality. And be sure and write an identical note to someone else – write it to Anne – so you'll have proof if you need it. And send me a wire accepting my offer to come East.'

Jennifer followed the advice to the letter. And to her delight, Tony took a plane and followed her to New York. He paced the living room of her suite; he cried; he pleaded; he swore he loved her, that he'd do anything she wanted. Anything except get rid of Miriam.

'But that's the only thing I'm asking,' she insisted.

Tony was adamant. 'She handles my money and runs my career. I don't trust anyone but Miriam.'

'What about me? Don't you trust me?'

'Don't push me, Jen. You're the best lay I ever had, but —'

'*Lay*! Is that all I am!'

'What do you want to be? Jesus! Miriam's right. You want to own me, to dry me out! I give what I have to singing.'

'And what do you give me?'

'My *cock*! And that should be enough'

Tony returned to California. Henry drew up a temporary separation agreement. Jennifer would receive five hundred a week until the baby was born, then she would receive a thousand a week plus expenses and child support. The coming of the baby was to remain secret until her pregnancy was obvious. She would divorce Tony after the baby was born.

Her separation from Tony made front pages. For the first week she holed up at the Pierre, and with the help of the red pills, slept most of the time. Finally Anne became concerned and insisted she move in with her. She forced Jennifer to go to the theatre and she met her for lunch almost every day, but Jennifer remained despondent.

Her only release came at night – with the red dolls.

October, 1947

Jennifer was well into her third month of pregnancy when Miriam arrived. She called from the airport. It was urgent that she see Jennifer right away.

Jennifer's spirits soared. Miriam didn't frighten her now. Maybe *Miriam* was frightened. She had sounded desperate. Tony was probably moping – probably wasn't singing as well – so she was coming to beg for a reconciliation. Well, it would be on *her* terms. Miriam had to leave. And Tony would have to come to her, to apologize.

She hadn't forgiven him, but she still clung to the hope that, away from Miriam, Tony would emerge as a person. And the baby – that *had* to change things. She wanted her little girl to have a father, not to grow up as she had, in a house full of women. Tony would mature . . . he was still young.

When she admitted Miriam to the apartment, she was conscious that she was looking her very best and that the apartment looked clean and neat. She was mistress of the situation. She even managed a smile. 'Sit down, Miriam. Would you like some coffee?'

The woman eased her bulk into a chair and sat tensely erect. Her eyes shot to Jennifer's waistline. 'No coffee. Let's cut the social crap and get to cases.'

Jennifer held onto her smile. 'And what does the case happen to be?'

Miriam's eyes narrowed. 'Is it really Tony's baby?'

'Wait till you see it,' Jennifer snapped. 'I'm sure it will be the image of him.'

Miriam got up and began to pace. Then she turned to Jennifer and said, 'How much do you want to get rid of it?'

Jennifer's stare was icy.

'Look, if it's money you want, I'll give it to you,' Miriam said. 'I'll give you a big settlement. In writing. And you can also have the thousand a week without the baby. Just get rid of it.'

Jennifer felt confused. 'Does Tony know about this? Is this what he wants?'

'No, Tony don't know I'm here. I told him I was going to Chicago to see his radio sponsor and make a better deal. I'm here on my own, to plead with you, before you get in your fourth month and it's too late to get rid of it.'

Jennifer's voice was low and tense. 'You know, Miriam, I never really hated you until this moment. I always thought you were selfish, but at least it was for Tony. Now I know better. You're evil.'

'And you're the All-American Mother!' Miriam snorted. 'You're just dying to walk in the park pushing a baby buggy, I suppose?'

'I want this baby,' Jennifer said earnestly. 'Miriam . . . all my life I've never had anyone who really cared about me. My mother and grandmother just felt I was a drain. All I ever heard was how much I ate, how much it cost to buy me shoes, how I outgrew everything too fast. It got so I was frightened when my shoes got too small. I knew there'd be a scene. Then, when I was older, it was how much money I could bring in – gimme, gimme, gimme. So I married the Prince. Maybe it wasn't a wild love match, but I figured I could support my mother and Gran – and I was going to try and be a good wife. But he didn't care about me – he was using me, too. I loved Tony. All I ever asked was a chance to be a wife, but you never gave me a break. You stepped on me, put me down. But I'll have my baby now. She'll love me and belong to me. And I'll work for her. I'll work hard. I'm saving my money now. I don't even buy clothes. After the baby is born, I'll model . . . I'll save . . . and she'll have everything.'

For a moment Miriam stood silently and stared at her plump fingers. Then she said, 'Jennifer, maybe I misjudged you. If so, I'm sorry.' She sighed heavily. 'All right, come back to Tony. I'll let you run the house . . . we'll try and get along. I'll do everything I can – only you gotta get rid of that baby!'

'Miriam, please leave. I don't want to insult you. I'll have my baby. And I'll get Tony back, too. Once he knows his child is born he'll want to see it. He'll want us both, me and the child – you'll see.'

'Jennifer.' Miriam's voice was almost kind. 'Listen to me, and listen good. You left Tony, and you were the love of his life. Right? So he made one childish stab at getting you back. That's all. He's been out with a different girl every night since then. He's forgotten all about you in just three weeks.'

'Please go, Miriam,' Jennifer said tearfully. 'You've hurt me enough. Why keep at it?'

'I'm trying to help you now,' the woman pleaded. 'If I didn't have some feeling for you, I'd let you go ahead with it. What have we got to lose? Financially the deal is made, and alimony is deductible. So I'm talking for you now. I tried to get you to unload the baby every way I could think of and still protect Tony. But you're stubborn.' She began pacing again. 'Look, why do you think I told you about Tony and them girls? To hurt you? No, to save you from more hurt. Because you never really learn to feel until you hold a baby in your arms. It becomes a part of you, it's a love you never dreamed you could feel – and if anything goes wrong with that baby it hurts more than any guy can ever hurt. Jennifer, hasn't it ever hit you that Tony is . . . well . . . childish?'

Jennifer looked at her strangely. There was something in Miriam's voice she had never heard before. 'Tony may be childish,' she admitted, 'but perhaps you're to blame, Miriam—'

'Jennifer – Tony is a child, mentally and emotionally.'

'Only because you overprotect him.'

'No, that's *why* I protect him. And that's why I don't want you to have his child. For your sake as well as his.'

'I don't understand . . .'

Miriam sat beside her. 'Jennifer, listen to me. When he was a baby he had convulsions. Something was born wrong inside his brain. The doctors at the hospital explained it to me, but I was too young to understand at first. I couldn't believe anything was that wrong. They warned me he would never be normal, but he was just a year old and so beautiful. I refused to understand. But when he was seven and couldn't get past first-grade work, I began to understand. I was older then, and I had all kinds of tests made on him. This time I got the full picture.

'Haven't you noticed, Jen? Tony can barely read comic books. He can't add past fifty. But he has no idea of his inadequacy. I've kept it from him by managing him, letting him think he doesn't know all these things because I handle them for him. That's why I keep telling him his only duty in life is to sing.'

'But you said he had a convulsion when he was little. That probably did it. There's no reason why our baby shouldn't be all right,' Jennifer argued.

'The kind of condition he has is passed on. The doctors don't really know what causes it, but there's a good chance that Tony will be completely insane by the time he's fifty. And his child will be born with the same condition. If it's lucky it might have the mentality of a twelve-year-old, but it could have even less.' She paused, remembering. 'Jennifer, you don't know what it's like. When I found out about Tony I got religion. I used to pray. I went to church – any church – and I dragged Tony along. I got him into a choir. That's when I found out he had a voice. I knew then that it was his only chance. Every dime I made I put into lessons . . .' She sighed. 'But that was a long time ago – this is now. That baby inside you probably won't inherit Tony's voice – but it will inherit his sickness.'

'What about you?' Jennifer asked. 'Will you go insane?'

Miriam shook her head. 'We had different fathers. Tony doesn't know that either. Please, Jennifer – for your own sake – get rid of the baby.'

'How do I know you're telling the truth?'

'I have the medical reports with me.' She fumbled in her bag and took out a bulky envelope. 'I didn't figure you'd believe me. Why should you? I never been especially nice to you.' She handed over the envelope. 'Take these to any neurologist. But do me one favor, Jennifer. Please don't blab this around town. It would finish Tony's career. And that would finish Tony. I know he'll probably wind up in a mental institution some day, but if this got out it would send him there now. That's why I save. You thought I was cheap, but I'm building an annuity for him. I stash every cent I can into it. I don't want him landing in some terrible charity place after I'm gone. I want him to have enough to keep him at a fancy joint for the rest of his days. But meanwhile, maybe he's got fifteen good years – I hope, anyway . . .'

Jennifer handed back the envelope. 'I believe you, Miriam. No one could invent such a terrible story.'

Miriam had tears in her eyes. 'Jennifer . . . I really wish you well.

You're welcome to come back to Tony, but you deserve a better life. And please keep it a secret, for him. You'll find someone else. Please be kind to Tony. Get rid of his baby and forget him.'

Jennifer sat and stared into space for several hours after Miriam had gone. Then she took three red pills and went to sleep.

She never gave Anne or Henry any reason for her sudden decision. She found the doctor by herself, a nice, antiseptic-looking man in New Jersey. There was a clean operating table and an efficient nurse. It cost a thousand dollars. The nurse jabbed her arm with the needle – sodium pentothal, it was called, and it was a greater sensation than even Seconals. When she woke, it was over. Two weeks later it was as if it had never happened. Her waistline returned to normal and she flew to Mexico for the divorce. On her return she entered into the excitement of the new fall openings and went on a shopping spree for new clothes. Dresses were getting longer and everyone was fascinated with an eight-inch screen called television. You couldn't see much except wrestling matches, ball games and roller derbies on it, but everyone went around saying it would kill radio.

Jennifer registered with the Longworth Agency again and began modeling. Soon Anne's closets were bulging once more with Jennifer's discards. The phone was always ringing and Jennifer was firmly entrenched in her new social life, dragging Anne along.

Jennifer saw several men, but she favored Claude Chardot. He was a French film producer – Gallic, charming and amorous. Anne didn't like him, but Jennifer plunged into a violent romance. There were three-hour luncheons, finger kissing, dancing at the St. Regis. He spoke little English, and Anne was amazed at Jennifer's fluent French.

On Christmas Eve, Jennifer and Anne trimmed a small tree. Claude and a few of his friends were coming by.

'He leaves in ten days,' Jennifer said wistfully.

'Do you really care for him? I mean *really*?' Anne asked.

Jennifer wrinkled her nose. 'Well . . . he's different. What do *you* think of him? Now be honest.'

'I can't say. Half the time I don't understand him, and the other half you two are jabbering away in French while I sit trying to understand his buddy's broken English. But I did manage to decipher from his pal François that your Claude has a wife stashed away.'

'Naturally. Probably a mistress, too,' Jennifer said easily. 'Whenever I get stuck on a man you can be sure he's some kind of a louse. He wants me to come to Paris.'

'You're not thinking of going!'

Jennifer shrugged. 'He wants to star me in pictures over there. Says I'd be a smash, looking so American and speaking French.'

'But you've always said you couldn't act.'

'He wants me to do sex pictures. Artistic – but semi-nude.'

'*What?*'

'It's accepted over there, Anne. A lot of the big stars do it.

It means nothing. Oh, I don't mean dirty pictures – I mean movies with a real plot. Only when you take a bath in a scene, they photograph it.'

'But why should you?'

'Why shouldn't I? What have I got going for me here? I was last season's sensation. Soon I'll be twenty-eight, and I have two bad marriages behind me. I won't meet any real guy here. I've got a reputation now. Married to a prince and then to a movie star – men feel I'm too rich for their blood. Maybe Paris is the answer. I know Claude is a phony. He's been giving me this whole romance buildup just to get me to sign with him. He expects to make money with me. But so what? What have I got to lose?'

'But you've only been in New York such a short time – why not give it a chance?'

'I'm too well known. Nothing new is going to happen to me. Oh, I could get into another show, but it wouldn't be a good part. And then what? I'm not that great as a model. I have enough money from my alimony, but I'm sick of Morocco and the Stork and the same stale faces. What about you? Are you still carrying on the love affair of the ages with New York?'

Anne shook her head. 'No, it kind of fell flat after Lyon left. I read in the *Times* that his book comes out next month. He's probably working on his next one.'

'Have you gone to bed with anyone since?'

'No. I couldn't. I know it's foolish, but I still love Lyon.'

ANNE

There was a three-hour luncheon at '21' on the day of Claude's depar-
ture. When Anne arrived the party was well on its way. There was a
large tin of Iranian caviar and the inevitable iced bucket of champagne. Jennifer, looking radiant, played hostess to Claude, his friend
François and another man Anne had never met.

'I'm Kevin Gillmore,' the stranger said.

Jennifer grinned. 'Now, Anne, you must have heard of Kevin
Gillmore. He owns Gillian Cosmetics.'

'Of course. Your products are excellent.' She helped herself to some
caviar.

'Are you going to Paris too?' he asked.

'No, it's Jennifer who's going to be the new French sensation.'

'She will take the town by storm,' Claude said in his thick accent.
'But please, Anne . . . I depend on you to see she get on the boat. She
must be there by the end of the month.'

Jennifer laughed merrily and snuggled close to Claude. 'I'll be
there, as soon as I get my passport and tidy up a few things.'

'Isn't it exciting?' Anne said to Kevin, trying to hide her lack of
enthusiasm.

'I suppose so. Are those your teeth?'

'What?'

'Yours? Or caps?'

Anne smiled. His directness was disarming. 'They're my own. Why?'

227

'And your hair?'

She felt the color come to her face. 'It's natural,' she said quietly.

'I know that. I know enough about coloring to realize that. But is it all yours?' He tugged gently at her long hair. 'I mean, are you wearing a fall?'

'A what?'

'A fall. A false piece under to give it that thickness.'

'Why should I?'

He smiled suddenly. It was a smile completely out of context with his bold questions. A humble smile. 'Because most girls need one to get that kind of look.' He shook his head sadly. 'That's the big trouble in finding the right girl – either they have good hair and lousy teeth or good hair and teeth and a bad nose. I suppose you're pretty well booked. I mean, you wouldn't consider working for us on an exclusive basis?'

'As what?' Anne looked toward Jennifer for assistance, but she was busy whispering some French endearment to Claude.

'Well, you see, with television coming in, I figure radio will be finished in another year – as far as the big shows are concerned. I want a "Gillian Girl." I want to feature that girl in all my ads – hair, nail polish, lipstick, the works. I've seen several girls I like—' He reeled off the names of five of the top models. 'But they make too much money to work for me exclusively. I don't want the Gillian Girl posing for Ted Casablanca's clothes in *Vogue* or for Chanel's perfume in *Harper's*. I want her to be identified with Gillian products only. And all I can pay to start with is three hundred a week.'

Anne sipped at her champagne. She didn't know what to say.

He took her silence for refusal. 'I'd give you a year's contract, with an option for five hundred the second six months. And extra money if we use you when we go on television.'

Jennifer suddenly came to life. 'Did I hear mon-ee?' she asked.

'I'm telling your friend I'd like to make her the Gillian Girl.'

Jennifer's eyes widened. 'But of course! Anne would be perfect.'

'She sure would. She's beautiful, but not too sexy. The All-American Girl,' Kevin said.

Claude threw up his hands. 'There is that word again! You Americans! You don't know what to do with a beautiful girl. You keep trying to make everyone look like the girl next door. If that is what the public want, no one would go to the movies. Take

Jennifer – she will be the big hit because she is not the girl next door – she is the girl every man dreams of having.'

'I agree. But it doesn't work that way in advertising,' Kevin insisted. 'Oh, we use sex – but in a subtle kind of way. Anne is beautiful. But she has the type of beauty women can identify with. A college girl or young matron will think she can look like Anne if she uses our product, but she would never think she could look like Jennifer. You're selling escapism in pictures – I'm selling a product. Anne is right for my product. People won't stop to think that it's her fine bone structure that does it, or the way her eyes are spaced, or the thickness of her own lashes. They'll think if they use the same product it will happen to them. Her kind of beauty doesn't frighten them. Jennifer's would.'

'Well, I'm taking my frightening beauty to Paris,' Jennifer said. 'But Anne, I think you should take Kevin's offer. You need a change. We all need one.'

Anne frowned. 'I'm not a model, and I'm very happy working for—'

Jennifer nudged her and stood up. 'I think it's time to powder our noses. Come on, Anne.' As she followed Anne out of the room, she turned and tossed Kevin a reassuring wink. He nodded and held up crossed fingers.

They sat in front of the large mirror while the attendant stood by, carefully acting bored and disinterested.

'All right.' Jennifer began her attack instantly. 'Why not?'

'I know nothing about modeling—'

'I know nothing about movies, but that's not stopping me. And in Paris, yet!'

'You'll be wonderful—'

'Don't change the subject. What are you making with Henry?'

'A hundred and fifty a week now. But that's not important. I just sold the house and got a wonderful price, and Henry invested that and my stock's gone way up. Money is the last thing I need.'

'But this will be exciting.'

'I can't leave Henry—'

'Henry?' Jennifer's eyes were accusing. 'Anne, you're talking to me, Jen. You mean you can't leave that office because it's still a link to Lyon Burke. But he won't come back to you. Stop dreaming that some day he'll stride in and whisk you off. That's over! Finished!'

'How do you know? I mean, next week his book comes out . . . well . . . he'll have to be here for it. Most authors do, don't they?'

Jennifer studied her bag. She played idly with the handle. 'Anne . . . I wasn't going to tell you, but now I think you should know. He's – gone back to England.'

'Back?' Her mouth felt dry. She was afraid she was going to be sick. 'You mean he was here?'

Jennifer's nod was solemn. 'For a week. To see his publisher. He did a complete rewrite – threw out practically everything he had written here, then went back there and wrote from scratch. That's why it's taken so long. But it's a good book. Henry told me. He saw Lyon.'

'Henry saw him?'

'They met for lunch. Lyon has already started his second book. He got a fairly good advance from his publisher. And he went back to London. He's taking a flat there.'

'He saw Henry . . . he was here . . .' She stopped. The tears ran down her face.

Jennifer threw her arms around her. 'Anne, don't take it that way. Henry said Lyon thinks about nothing but his writing. It's the only thing that matters to him now.'

'But Henry knows how I feel. Why didn't he tell me Lyon was here?'

'Because he's a man, and men stick together. Anne, you owe Henry nothing. And you need a change. This is fate. Claude didn't invite Kevin Gillmore today. He just wandered in alone and joined us. I think it's meant to be.'

'Maybe you're right,' Anne said slowly. 'I've got to get out of the office. It's like a living shrine.'

'Now you're making sense. And unload that apartment, too! Now . . . fix your face. Don't lose the job before you get it!'

At first Henry was upset. But he grudgingly admitted the Gillian offer was excellent. 'This is your doing,' he said to Jennifer, who had come with Anne to break the news.

'You know it's best for her,' Jennifer said merrily. 'Now come on, Henry. How long did you expect to keep Anne chained here? She isn't Miss Steinberg, you know.'

'Okay, but bring the contract to me before you sign it,' he grumbled.

'Let's see if we can't get some extras in the deal. Television is coming in strong. I don't want anything left for later negotiation. If he wants you for his ads now, he has to guarantee to use you on the commercials.'

'But Henry,' Anne protested, 'I'd faint in front of a television camera.'

'It'll be no different from a photographer's camera, and you'll have had about a year's experience by then. Incidentally' – he scribbled a name on a pad – 'start seeing Lil Cole. Take at least two private lessons a week. It's expensive, but you can afford it.'

'Who's Lil Cole?' Anne asked.

'The best speech and diction coach there is.'

'What do I need her for?'

'Because I have a hunch the commercials will wind up being more than just posing. You've got to get rid of that Boston accent.'

'Henry, I'm just going to model, not be an actress.'

'Listen, Anne.' His voice was stern. 'If you're going to do something, do it a hundred per cent. There's no halfway business about any job. You were a great secretary – now, if you're going to be the Gillian Girl, be the best there is. Besides, what else have you got to do? Maybe keeping busy is the best thing for you right now.'

He suddenly looked very tired, as if all the strength had drained out of him. Impulsively, Anne threw her arms around him. 'Henry, I love you.'

He scowled to cover his emotions. 'How do you like that?' he said to Jennifer. 'I've had a giant crush on this girl for two years, and now that she's walking out on me she tells me she loves me.'

'I do, Henry. And I always shall. And please . . . always be my friend.'

'Just try and lose me. You're one in a million, Anne. They don't come like you. Now scram. I got to call the agencies. Who knows, maybe another Anne Welles might walk in.'

'Don't you want me to stay until you find someone? I could help break her in.'

'Nope, beat it. Jennifer's only gonna be here a short time. You two girls live it up. Incidentally, Jennifer, your alimony comes to seven hundred after taxes. Knowing you, I'll take the taxes out right away. This picture deal will complicate things. Do you want your checks sent on to you?'

'No, keep my money here. Invest it. Make me rich like Anne.'

He laughed. 'Two Rockefellers I got here. Whoever said it was a man's world?'

'I'm getting mine the hard way,' Jennifer said grimly.

'Sure. You had to sweat out five months at a swimming pool. Real rough.'

Jennifer flashed her brightest smile. 'Yes, it was all just fun and games.'

'Listen, all I ask in the next life is to come back as a beautiful broad,' Henry insisted. 'And now you got Paris ahead. You'll wind up as the French Lana Turner. But do me a favor – don't spend all your money. You owe me two thousand. I'm deducting it from your alimony. And for Christ's sake, don't send for it. Give me a chance to save some of it for you. Clients like the two of you I sure need!'

'Which reminds me,' Jennifer said sweetly. 'Advance me another thousand, Henry—'

'Oh come on, Jennifer . . .'

'I need clothes. After all, I've got to make a big entrance in Paris.'

February, 1948

Anne rushed into '21' and joined Henry at his usual front table. 'Sorry I'm late, but Lil Cole is a slave driver.' She sat down.

Henry noticed that every man in the room had turned to look at her. Three weeks of grooming with Kevin Gillmore's makeup experts had created an indefinable yet eye-catching change. They hadn't tampered with her natural beauty, yet somehow they had succeeded in heightening it. Before, it used to creep up on you. Now you noticed it immediately. She wore eye makeup and her hair was fuller, like a lion's mane. She still looked every inch the lady, but she was exciting now.

'I got a long letter from Jennifer this morning,' she said, unaware of the stir she had created.

'I got a short one, asking for money. Anne, how fast *can* she spend it?'

Anne laughed and ordered a salad. 'No matter how much she has, she'll always be in debt. Jennifer is a compulsive spender. I don't know why – it's not as if she enjoys the things she buys. She gives most of them away.'

Henry shook his head. 'I hope she finds a guy – a good guy – over there. I don't think she's much of an actress, but she has one hell of a face and body. I hope she makes it pay off. Because that's all she's got, and when that goes . . . that'll be the end of Jennifer.'

'Henry! I gave you more credit. Are you like all the others, taking Jennifer at face value? She's a wonderful girl, but no man ever takes the trouble to find out. I thought you were different. Jennifer is really a fine person . . . a real friend . . . and sweet. She's one of the sweetest girls I've ever known.'

'Sweet? Okay, I'll go along with that. Sweet on the surface. That smile is glued on. But tell me something, Anne. How deep do her feelings go?'

'That's hard to say. Jennifer doesn't open up too much. You know something? I've never really heard her pan anyone. She *is* sweet, about everyone. I know that's a funny word to use about Jennifer, but it's the right word for her. I've lived with her – I know. Now Neely is someone you'd think of as sweet, but she isn't. Neely's sharp and bright, but she isn't sweet. Jennifer is. Do you know she never says anything against the Prince? Just that it didn't work out. No vindictiveness against him, or Tony – or even Miriam. Just says she couldn't take the boredom of California. No, she's basically lonely underneath all that glamour, waiting for a man who'll like her for herself. Because Jennifer really wants just one man, and a normal life and children—'

'So how come she got rid of her baby? That's when she lost me. She called from the Coast hysterical because they wanted her to get rid of it – at least the sister did. And she wanted to keep it. Then, after I knock my brains out getting her a good alimony, she unloads it. You tell me a dame who wants a kid can't live on a thousand a week?'

'She never talked about it, or gave any reasons,' Anne said slowly. 'But somewhere along the line she must have lost her nerve about raising it alone. I'm sure if she ever found the right man she'd settle down.'

Henry looked at her closely. 'And what about you?'

'Oh, things are going fine. We've finished all the test shots. I pose for Gillian's first spring layout next week.'

'I don't mean that, Anne. I mean your future. You know, being the Gillian Girl is going to change things. Once your face starts getting plastered in magazines and on billboards, a lot of excitement is going to come your way.'

'I've been through that,' she reminded him. 'Remember me? Just two years ago I was on the front pages, in all the columns – Allen Cooper's Cinderella girl. But it didn't change me.'

Henry said quietly, 'It did change you. You didn't marry Lyon Burke, did you?'

She studied her plate. 'I wanted to, Henry . . . more than anything in the world. I still want to.'

'Why didn't you? When you had the chance?'

'He wanted me to live in Lawrenceville.'

'That's what I mean,' he said slowly. 'The girl who walked into my office that first day would have gone to the ends of the earth for the man she loved. That's why I took you. I figured you'd be pretty hard to please. You wouldn't fall for just any guy. I hadn't counted on Lyon's coming back. The minute he walked in, I said 'Good-by, Anne – this is it.' Unfortunately Lyon was never capable of really caring for anyone deeply, man or woman. You and me, we're alike – when we care for someone we make gods of them.'

'Lyon loved me . . . I know he did,' she said stubbornly.

'But not as much as he loved himself. A man who could cut every tie the way Lyon does is a man who could never care deeply. Lyon is like Jennifer in a way. They fall in love, the Lyons and the Jennifers, but they can walk away unscarred. Because Number One always comes first. Remember it, Anne, you're young. Keep those eyes wide open. And when you meet another guy who's for real, grab him and run for the hills. Don't hang around the glamour belt too long.'

'I don't think there will be anyone else who really matters,' she said. 'Lyon was it.'

'Lyon's gone,' he said roughly. 'Over . . . done!'

'I understand, but it still doesn't change *me*. I can't just fall for the first passable man who comes along. I want to marry one day and have children. But I want a man I love.' She sighed. 'And I'll never love anyone like I did Lyon.'

'Listen,' he said. 'Don't be a schmuck like me. I loved, too. Only one dame my whole life. Helen Lawson! And I knew goddam well – right from the start – that she didn't love me. She wasn't capable of loving anyone. I taught her everything. And smart as I was, I never stopped loving her. Maybe I never gave myself a chance to find a real girl. So how do I wind up? Alone.'

'Maybe you and Helen could still—'

'Are you kidding!'

'But you said you loved her.'

'I did. I loved what I pretended she was – what I wanted her to be. But now I see her as she really is, and I'm too old to find someone else. It's catching up with her, though. She's beginning to look on the outside like she is inside – Old Ironsides! I'd kill anyone who called her that to my face, but I can say it to you. I'm not really in love with Helen any more, but I can't break the habit. It sneaks up on you, Anne – the habit. And after all emotion is gone and logic takes over, the habit is still there. For the rest of your life. So don't you, at twenty-two, start building any habit. Lyon isn't wasting a moment thinking about you. Believe me. And you stop thinking about him.'

Anne smiled weakly. 'I'll try. I can only try . . .'

NEELY

Neely closed the script wearily. No use going over it again. She knew it cold. She stretched luxuriously in the large bed and sipped some Scotch. Eleven-thirty and she was still wide awake. Maybe she should take another doll. She had already taken two . . . maybe another red one. She had to be on the set at six. She wandered into the bathroom and popped a red pill into her mouth. 'Come on, you little doll, do the job.'

She stumbled back into bed. She noticed her appointment book was open. Was she supposed to remember something? She stared. The words blurred, but she recognized Ted's handwriting. *Come home early today. Bud and Jud's first birthday!*

Oh, God! Geez, it had been today. She hadn't even looked at the book in the morning. She had been so stoned by the pills she had just managed to make it out of bed. She had needed two Dexies to wake up. And now she'd missed the birthday party! Goddam those retakes! She leaped out of bed and tiptoed into the nursery. A wild thrill of pride surged through her as she looked at the two sleeping blond heads. 'Bud and Jud,' she whispered into the darkness, 'Mommy missed your birthday, but she loves you. Oh, God, how she loves you! Mommy didn't see the book or she'da been there – honest.'

She tiptoed out and weaved back to her room. Ted was probably mad, off sulking somewhere. Well, Christ, it wasn't her fault. She hadn't seen the damn book. So he left it open on her night table.

Who in hell can see anything at five in the morning? She lay back against the pillows. They musta had a cake. With a candle. And Miss Sherman and Ted probably sang Happy Birthday to them. A large tear forced its way through the cream on her face. But Geez, they were only babies. They didn't know it was their birthday. They weren't hurt . . .

And now Ted was taking it out on her. Where in hell was he? Probably cruising, the double-gaited sonofabitch. She recalled the first time she had caught him. Christ! With his arms around that English actor and their tongues down each other's throats. She had taken a whole bottle of pills that night. They'd had to pump her stomach. She grimaced at the memory. She'd never do that again.

But Ted had been doubly sweet after. The first night back he had held her close and explained that he had only done it with the guy because he had felt insecure. Her being up for an Oscar two years in a row – even if she didn't get it – it had made him feel insecure, less of a man. That was the night she had conceived. And twins yet! Those two beautiful blond boys in the nursery were hers. They came out of her body! She felt all warm and weak inside. Only twenty-two . . . the biggest star on the Century lot . . . a house of her own in Beverly Hills . . . and twin boys!

The pills weren't working. She wondered whether Jennifer ever took three. She just bet she did. A person would have to take something to make the kind of pictures Jennifer made! Wow! The last one had really caused a sensation. In La Jolla you'd had to stand in line for hours to get in. And there was Jennifer, with her bare tits, spouting French like a native. Maybe they didn't think anything of it in Paris, but subtitles under a bare ass still didn't make it art. And Geez, that big story in *Look* – or was it *Life* – showing Jen in that fancy Paris apartment. It practically said she was living with that French producer Claude Chardot.

She wondered what Anne thought about it all. Geez, she owed her a letter. She should thank her for Lyon's new book, despite those lousy reviews. The trades all said he had gone commercial – or tried to and missed. But hell, maybe he needed money and thought this junk would sell. After all, his first book had gotten raves and didn't make a dime. She wondered if Anne still cared about Lyon. She must feel something if she had to make sure her friends read his books. But then the columns all hinted she was Kevin Gillmore's girl. Geez, imagine Anne being the Gillian Girl. You couldn't open a magazine without seeing her picture. Oh, yes . . . Sunday night. She leaned over and scribbled it in her book. She must remember to watch. Anne was going to do the Gillian commercials on the Big Comedy Hour. Anne on television!

Television . . . Geez, the way everyone in California was acting over that stinking little box. As if it could ever hurt the Industry. But they were all panicking. Contract players in most of the studios were being dropped right and left, and they weren't signing people to long deals any more – just one-picture or two-picture deals. Lucky she was so big. Boy, they had jumped to sign her. Five nice, solid years . . . money coming in fifty-two weeks, for five more years . . .

She wished Ted would come home. She needed him to go to bat for her tomorrow. The dancing sequences were too tough. She could dance, but this was ridiculous. She'd get Ted to say she couldn't dance in the costumes, then they'd have to make the dances easier. She had hardly been able to catch her breath today. Those green pills were beautiful and kept you awake and skinny, but they also made your heart pound so you couldn't practice a two-hour dance routine. Maybe Ted was at his office. Maybe he wasn't mad, just working late. She reached for the phone. No, if he wasn't at his office she didn't want to know. And what the hell – what would it prove? He could be at his office doing it with a guy. Jesus, why did she love him this much? He wasn't even a real man. But then Mel was kinda weakish, too. Why did she get attracted to men like this? They seemed so strong in the beginning – helping her, telling her what to do – real strong. Then they petered out.

She looked at the clock – midnight. The pills weren't working. She needed some more Scotch to help them along. Damn – it was down-stairs. It was lucky she had learned booze helped the pills work. She wondered if Jennifer had found out about that. The dolls without booze were nothing. Well, she'd just have to go downstairs and get some more.

She ran down the marble stairs barefoot. The servants were asleep. The lights were out in the living room. While she was groping for the light switch, she heard a splash in the swimming pool. She walked to the patio doors. Who in hell was in the pool? The cabana lights were on, and their reflection hit the pool. It was Ted! She laughed with relief. Geez, what a nut – swimming nude at this hour. She fumbled at the buttons of her pajamas. She'd jump in and surprise him. No, that would wake her completely, and she had an early call. She was just about to shout to him when she saw the girl coming out of the cabana, hesitating shyly, clutching the towel she had draped around her.

'Come on, drop the towel. The water's heated,' Ted called.

The girl looked up at the dark, rambling house. 'Suppose she wakes up?'

'Are you kidding? With what she takes an earthquake couldn't wake her. Come on, Carmen, or I'll drag you in!'

The girl dropped the towel demurely. Even in the semi-darkness Neely could see she had a wonderful body. Neely squinted her eyes. She had seen this girl somewhere . . . Sure! Carmen Carver. She had won some beauty contest, and the studio was testing her.

Ted swam to meet the girl. Neely heard a squeal. 'Oh, Ted! Not in the water . . . Don't!'

'Why not? We've done it every other way.'

Neely felt her stomach quiver. Oh, God! No – not this! A boy occasionally she had accepted. It was a sickness of Ted's – that's what the psychiatrist had told her. It had nothing to do with unfaithfulness to her. But this!

She grabbed the bottle of Scotch and stumbled up the stairs. She poured a stiff drink and took another pill, then climbed into bed. To hell with Ted and his whore! Geez, she'd be hungover enough tomorrow. And she had to be up at five.

Suddenly she sat up. What would happen if she didn't go in? In her whole life she had never been five minutes late for a rehearsal, a fitting or an interview. And what did it get her? Sure, she was making five thousand a week now – but what did she have to show for it? The house wasn't paid for yet – the studio had loaned her the money. Dr. Mitchell said the house was important for her sense of security, that it would rid her of her childhood instability. Some advice at twenty-five bucks a shot! She'd see him tomorrow – let him explain this! And now that she thought about it, what in hell did Ted pay for? The servants, the car, his office, the food and the booze. Maybe it had been a mistake to sign a premarital agreement. His business was going great. *Vogue* was always giving him big layouts. What did she have? After the studio took out a thousand a week toward the loan on her house, then the agent, the income tax, her personal maid, her secretary . . . Jesus! She couldn't save a dime. Well, in another three years she'd be clear with the house. She gulped down some more Scotch. A feeling of euphoria began to float through her. Once everything was paid for, everything would be all right . . .

All right! Holy Christ! With Ted down there banging some girl in *her* swimming pool? She shot out of bed. She was dizzy and her head was heavy, but she had to throw that girl out of her pool. She held onto the banister as she fumbled her way down the stairs. She groped her way to the light switch and triumphantly flooded the pool with light.

Ted and the girl were scrambling out of the pool as she staggered out, holding a bottle of Scotch.

'Having a good time, kiddies?' she shrieked. 'Fucking in *my* pool? Be sure you drain it out. Remember, Ted – *your* children go wading in it every morning.'

The girl dodged frantically behind Ted. Neely carefully emptied the bottle into the pool.

'Maybe this'll disinfect it,' she sneered. Then she stared at Ted. 'So now it's a girl tramp instead of a boy. I guess Dr. Mitchell will tell me you need this too!'

Ted stood erect and silent, his arms behind him to shield the shivering girl. This protective gesture added to Neely's rage. 'Who are you protecting! A whore who contaminated my pool? You know, honey, you mean nothing to him. He usually likes boys for his diversion. Maybe that's it . . . maybe you have no tits – or maybe you're a Lesbian!'

The girl broke away and fled into the cabana. Ted stood very still. He had a crazy dignity in spite of his nakedness. For a split second she wanted to rush to him, to say that she was sorry, that she loved him. He was so tall and bronze . . . But she couldn't let him get away with this.

'All right, faggot – start explaining!'

He smiled slightly. 'I think you need glasses. I'd hardly say she was built like a boy.'

Her lip quivered. 'I could take that better—'

'I'll bet you could,' he said slowly. 'You drove me to that.'

'*I* drove you!'

'You almost made me think I *was* a queer. Sure, I tried it with a few guys. In some crazy way I felt I wasn't cheating on you. And you made me feel I wasn't desirable to a woman. When was the last time you wanted me, Neely?'

'Why, you're my husband. Whattaya mean, "want you"? I always want you.'

'You want me *around*! To fight your battles at the studio, design your clothes, escort you to openings. But as a man . . . You're always too tired for sex. When did you think about it last?'

'You're nuts!' she yelled. 'Say, don't try and switch things. I catch you red-handed and you stand there with your dingle blowing in the breeze and a naked broad in my cabana, and *you* sermonize with *me*! Who in hell is paying for this pool and this house?'

'Who wanted it?' Nonchalantly, he reached for a towel and draped it around his waist.

'We couldn't live in that apartment you had.'

'Why not? It had eight rooms. But you needed the massage room, the projection room, this whole layout.'

'I never had a house.' She started to sob. 'I wanted one so bad. I really don't mind paying for it.'

'Then why do you throw it up to me ten times a day? And now who's trying to switch things?'

'Well . . .' She could hardly keep her eyes open. His voice seemed to be coming from far away. Damn those pills. *Now* they were beginning to work. She watched him as he sat down casually in a beach chair.

'Ted . . . I come from the studio at six. Tonight I didn't get back till eight. I'm beat. I have lines to study for the next day. I have to have a massage. How can I think of sex?'

'Why did you sign the new contract?' he asked quietly.

'That was six months ago. Are you still beefing about that?'

'Neely, you're big now. And I'm doing great. I was willing to tear up the premarital agreement. You could have made a two-picture-a-year deal with any studio in town and left yourself a chance to live. I make enough money for both of us even if you never worked. But without telling me, you went and signed a new five-year deal.'

'I owed the money to the studio for the house. And Geez, Ted, with everyone panicky about television, I was lucky to get a long-term deal. When you have a long contract with a studio, you belong . . . you have a whole studio behind you.'

'Well, you've got your house and your contract. And I've got my sanity back. I wasn't much of a man living with you. Somehow you drained it all out of me, Neely. But that's over. I'm straightened out now.'

'By that little whore?'

'She makes me feel seven feet tall.'

'Ted, I need you.'

'And *how* you do. But not as a man.'

'Sex! Sex! *Sex*! Is that all you think about? I like sex. But in its place.'

'Like once a month on a rainy Sunday? And it never rains in California.'

'Look, stop with all this. That broad is in there. Get her out!'

'I will.' He put out his cigarette and started for the cabana.

'And come upstairs immediately. I want to talk to you!'

She ran into the house. She opened a new bottle, poured herself a fresh drink and got into bed. Maybe she should overlook this thing. Maybe she had better act more sexy. Christ, she loved him. She adored him. But when you were on the set all day how could you be sexy at night? She looked at her plain pajamas. Maybe she should wear some frilly nightgowns. But Geez, her face was loaded with cream and her hair was sticking out at all angles and gooky. It was washed every morning at the studio, so she had to put lanolin on it at night. Her hair was good and thick, but if she slept in that lacquer they put on it and all the gold powder to pick up the lights, she'd be bald. She had to brush it out every night and load it with oil.

She thought of the naked girl in the pool. She stood up, swaying, and the wall mirror across the room shot back her own reflection. Oh, brother, she thought. I look like Halloween. But Geez, why shouldn't that girl look good? She wasn't pulling in five thousand a week. She wasn't one of the hottest names in pictures. She was just a girl trying to make it. If she was a star, she'd be in bed at nine with the cream and oil too! Tears ran down her face. God, all her life she had dreamed about something like this. A big house, a guy you loved, kids. She had them all . . . only there was no time to enjoy it.

She went to the bathroom and washed the cream off her face. If only she wasn't so sleepy. She fumbled in the bureau. Where were the nice nightgowns? Okay, this yellow one. She slid into it. Geez, her hair! She found a yellow silk scarf and tied it around. Now, that wasn't bad – not bad at all. She got into bed. Ted should be up any second. She heard the scrunch of the car on the gravel in front. Well, the whore had gone home; now he'd come up all sheepish. She'd let him crawl a little, then she'd surprise him. She'd take him in her arms and they'd do it. And she'd be real good, like in the old days, not just lay back. It had been so great when they first met – but she hadn't been so tired then. She was getting sleepy . . . God, where was he! She jumped out of bed and ran down the stairs.

'Ted.' The swimming pool was dark. She threw open the front door. She ran to the garage, the gravel cutting into her bare feet. The car was gone! Maybe he had to take her home. She *had* come here with him; maybe she had no car. Bullshit! He coulda sent her home in a cab! She'd give it to him when he came back. She started to sob. Maybe he wasn't coming back. Oh, Christ! What had she done?

1953

She fought the divorce for three years. He had moved his clothes out after the swimming-pool incident. She hadn't gone to work for a week. The studio had been furious. The hell with them, she thought as she tossed in a barbiturate daze. The hell with Ted! At first she was all for a divorce – he couldn't do this to her! But The Head had opposed it. Bad for her public image. She was the girl next door . . . America's sweetheart with twin boys. They had stories lined up on her home life and picture layouts of her and Ted with the twins . . . the perfect marriage. No, no divorce. The Head didn't care how they felt about each other, just as long as it looked good to the public. She was to try to work it out.

The Head also talked to Ted. He was under contract to Century, so he had to go along. He was to escort Neely to openings, pose with her for screen magazine stories, anything to maintain the image.

It had been a three-year nightmare. One picture after another . . . dieting . . . the dolls . . . knowing Ted was off somewhere with that girl. And he had to be keeping her. She wasn't working. To pacify Neely the studio had blackballed her. The word was out – no other studio would touch her.

The Academy Award had cinched things. It had been the greatest moment of her life. She had never dreamed she'd really get it. When they called her name she had turned to Ted with a gasp. His smile had been warm – he was really thrilled for her. She had run up the aisle. Then the pictures, the photographer and newsreel cameras – and Ted right there, holding her arm. Everything was going to be all right – she had won the Oscar and Ted was at her side, smiling at her.

He had stayed until the last camera had clicked and the last congratulation had been accepted. Then he had driven her home, said good night in front of the door and left her – an Academy Award-winning star – to go to the arms of that tramp! That had done it!

The next morning she had called The Head and demanded he come to her bungalow. She could throw her weight around now. And The Head had come, too! This time *she* announced the terms. She wanted a divorce – immediately – and she wanted Ted Casablanca dropped by the studio. The Head had humbly agreed to her demands. God, the power of an Oscar!

It also made her realize that it wasn't life or death to report for work every day. She was the biggest star in Hollywood, and the Oscar proved it. If she had a bad night, fuck 'em! She was Neely O'Hara! And if she gained a few pounds on caviar, fuck 'em. So it took a week to get it off – so what! Her pictures made them a fortune . . .

She sat in the air-conditioned studio bungalow trembling. It was the third time she had walked off the set in five weeks. Goddam that John Stykes. He might be the greatest director in the world, but he was crucifying her in this picture. She tore off the strip of false eyelashes and violently dabbed cream on her face.

'Miss O'Hara, don't! It will take an hour to get the makeup on again,' the maid pleaded.

'No more work today,' she said grimly, erasing the pancake.

'But we're behind schedule—'

'*We!*' Neely turned on her. 'Where do you get that *we* stuff? Christ! Everybody's in show business!'

There was a knock on the door. It was John Stykes. He was

handsome in a craggy, weatherbeaten way. 'Come on, Neely, let's get going.'

She saw his look of despair at her naked face. 'Yes, buster – no more work for today!' She grinned maliciously.

He sat down. 'All right. It's three o'clock. We'll knock off early.'

'Only I'm not okaying that last take,' she snapped.

'What's wrong with it?'

'You know damn well. All the closeups were on our feet.'

'Neely, the studio is paying Chuck Martin fifty thousand just for that dance he does with you. He's a great dancer. What should we shoot? His ears?'

'No, dammit, you shoot *me*! Body shots – my feet can't keep up with him. I'm not that good a dancer.'

'I can't believe my ears,' he said with mock wonder. 'You mean you actually concede someone might have more talent than you?'

'Listen, Chuck Martin's been dancing in Broadway shows for thirty years. But that's all he can do – dance. He's old enough to be my father. I'm only twenty-five, but I can sing, dance and act. I'll put my singing and acting up against the best of them. No one can touch me when it comes to singing. No one! As for dancing, okay, so I'm no Ginger Rogers or Eleanor Powell. But all Chuck Martin can do is dance. He's almost as good as Astaire. But is that any reason I should look bad?'

'If you admit he's that good, why not let us give five minutes to his feet?'

'Because it's *my* picture. That's something I learned in my first Broadway show, from an expert. No performer feathers his nest on my talent. Look, who needs Chuck Martin anyway? I've used chorus boys in all my other pictures.'

'The Head picked Chuck personally.' John Stykes lit a cigarette. Neely reached for one. He lit it for her. 'Since when did you start smoking?'

'I took one the day my divorce became final. I've found they keep me from eating.'

'Bad for the voice, Neely.'

'I only smoke about ten a day.' She inhaled deeply. 'Well, is it set-tled now?'

The director looked toward the maid. 'Neely, could we talk alone?'

'Sure.' She motioned the maid to leave. 'You're through for the day, Shirley. See you here tomorrow, at seven.'

John smiled when they were alone. 'I'm glad you're not planning to play hookey.'

'Why should I? You just sit up tonight and figure a new way to shoot that scene so that it stars me – not Chuck Martin's feet.'

'Neely, has it ever occurred to you why The Head didn't use a chorus boy?'

'Sure, sure. Television! Everybody panics easily these days. But that's not my worry. If The Head thinks sending for Chuck Martin and paying out an extra fifty G's is gonna lick television, that's his business. Only don't do it on my time.'

'Neely, your last two pictures lost money.'

'C'mon! I read *Variety*. I saw the grosses. They were terrific! My last picture grossed four million and it hasn't played Europe yet.'

'But it cost over six million to make.'

'So what? *Variety* says my picture will be the top grosser of the year.'

'Sure, and it would have made the studio a fortune if it had been made for the two million five it was slated for. The studio's kept the real figures a secret – so far. No one ever heard of a picture running that much over. The Head was afraid to let the reports get published. His stockholders would hold an emergency meeting. He has to make it up with this picture. Your first loss was a small one, but this last one . . . honey, no picture has ever cost six million.'

'I had the flu. People can't help it if they get sick.'

'Neely, you were out ten days with sleeping pills.'

'And then I got the flu.'

'I wasn't on that picture, but I know the facts. You boozed and ate . . . All right, so you got run down and got sick. But when you recovered, it took three weeks to get the weight off you. And even then you still were ten pounds over and all the costumes had to be redone.'

'All right! I was upset. My divorce became final that week. And Sam Burns, my favorite cameraman, got sick. I won't work without Sam. I wasn't ten pounds overweight – I weighed ninety-eight. But the clothes were so lousy I looked heavy.' She stopped, then turned on him violently. 'And that's another thing. They've got to get me a new designer. The clothes stink. Ted would never have let me wear this crap!'

'Ellen Small has won nine Academy Awards.'

'Well, let her make clothes for her Oscars, not for me.'

'Neely, I like you. That's why I'm talking to you instead of The Head. I won't let on that you walked out today. Oh, he'll hear about the early dismissal, but I'll say we were through with the scene earlier than we expected and it was too late to set up the next. But how long do you think he'll put up with this?'

'With what?'

'With your walkouts, your tantrums . . .'

'I didn't work this hard to become a star and have to worry about the front office. Once you're a star, everyone has to worry about you. You rate it. I learned that from Helen Lawson.'

'Helen Lawson is a pro,' he snapped. 'That's one thing you aren't.'

'So where is she now?'

'She can star on Broadway whenever she wants—'

'What's Broadway? That's all she can get!'

'Right. And she knows it. But Helen Lawson was never a second late for rehearsal in her life. She only has one thing – a big voice. And she knows it. She might be careless about everything else, but she's a businesswoman with that voice. She's a different kind of a monster than you are, Neely—'

'Monster! Why you . . . you . . .'

He laughed and tweaked her nose. 'Sure you're a monster,' he said good-naturedly. 'Every star is one. But Helen is a mechanical star, a voice. You have . . . well, sometimes, honey, I think you border on genius. You feel things – too deeply at times.' He leaned over and took her hands. 'Neely, they don't come like you. You're rare. But this is no art form – it's dollars and cents. Stockholders aren't interested in genius, just box-office receipts. Look, baby, we're ten days behind, but if you cooperate, we can make it up. We can shoot the nightclub scene in one day instead of three. I've got it all set for tomorrow. The extras have been called. I know how to lick it. I'll work a few nights . . . do the crowd scenes with your stand-in. We can shoot from the back. Neely, we can do it. We can still bring it in on time.'

She wavered for a moment, then she shot him a metallic smile. 'You almost got to me, Johnny-boy. This was the daddy of all pep talks. But like you said, I'm a monster – and monsters know every angle. Seven years ago if someone had talked to me like this, I'd have jumped and said, "Yes sir, yes sir, yes sir." I worked my ass off, half killed myself . . . and I made the studio a fortune.'

'And you made yourself a star.'

'Yeah, and what does that get me?' she said. She walked across the room and poured herself half a glass of Scotch. 'Want a drink?'

'Beer, if you've got it.'

She went to the bar and got some beer from the small refrigerator. 'This is what I've got,' she said as she handed it to him. 'The best booze in town – only I'm not supposed to drink it. It puts weight on me. I also got a swimming pool I can't use because I'm not allowed to get tan. Bad for technicolor. I got two closets full of clothes and no place or time to wear them because I have to stay home each night and study the next day's scenes. John . . .' She knelt on the floor and sat at his feet. 'How did it happen?'

He rubbed her head. 'You just got there too fast.'

'No, that's not the answer. I kicked around in vaudeville all my life. I'm not some beauty-contest winner the studio had to teach to talk, walk and act. They signed me 'cause I had talent. Sure, they taught me some things. I dance better. I've gone through the reading bit – books The Head thought I should read. You know, the self-improvement bit. Now I don't sound like a moron when I give interviews. But I came with my talent. I'm twenty-five and I feel like I'm ninety. I've lost two husbands. All I know is to study lines, songs, dance routines, to starve, to sleep with pills, stay awake with pills . . . There's got to be more than that to living.'

'Did you have more fun back in your early vaudeville days?'

'No, and I hate people who say it was all so wonderful when they were starving. It stunk. One-night stands, cold trains, dim-witted audiences . . . but there *was* something that kept you going and made you feel good – hope. It was all so lousy that you knew it had to get better, and you dreamed of the big time or security and thought it would be so wonderful if you could just latch onto a piece of it. And that hope kept you going so it didn't seem bad. But when you sit here and think, Geez, here it is . . . this is it . . . and it stinks. Then what?'

'You've got the babies, Neely. Right now you're caught up in the time-consuming job of being a star. But you'll find a right guy again – and then you might have to make a choice between mass love and a private life. It's not easy to give up the love of an audience and settle for one man. Not after you've had it like you have. You'll have to weigh all this and ask yourself if the love you get from your talent is enough to compensate.'

'No, it isn't. I can't enjoy it. I mean, what has this God-given talent given *me*? All I can do is give it to others. Is that the end? I got it, but I have to keep giving it away – and I wind up with nothing. Boy, is this crazy? Wait till I tell this to Dr. Mitchell.'

'Your analyst?'

She nodded. 'I don't need one, really. That's another crazy thing. He was Ted's analyst. Imagine! Me – the most normal girl in the world – I wind up with a headshrinker. I went to see him when something awful happened with Ted, and the next thing you know, I found myself running to him every time something came up. At first it was always about Ted . . . but then he started groping in my past, like maybe it was my fault Ted had troubles. But I went along – and then I did learn a lot about myself. You know, John, I never knew what it was to have a mother's love. He says that's why it's important to me to be a star – I need mass love.'

'That's bullshit!' John was angry. 'Listen, there are plenty of stars who love their mass love and who had some pretty doting parents. You're a star because you have talent, not because you never knew a mother's love. I'm tired of all these fancy doctors who blame everything on the poor mothers of the world. So your old lady kicked off early. Did she do it purposely just to get even with you? Listen, Neely, you'll be a lot better off if you forget your headshrinker. You got where you are on your own.'

'But I *am* neurotic, John. I've found I have all kinds of neuroses.'

'So? Maybe that's why you're a star. If he cures them maybe you won't be you. I got my own kinks, but I'm not about to plunk out twenty-five bucks a throw and have some guy tell me my father mistreated me and I miss my mother's love. What am I going to do about it even if I find out it's true? Go to Minnesota and punch my old man in the nose? He's eighty. Or find myself a gray-haired call girl who'll stroke my head and bottle-feed me? Listen, whatever happened is yesterday's newspaper. It's today and tomorrow – that's what counts!'

She sighed. 'It's all so easy the way you say it. But when you spend that long night alone – God, the nights are awful – and you feel there is one person you can talk to . . . See, John, a psychiatrist has no angles. He's out for you . . . to help you. He's the only one I can trust.'

He stood up. 'All right, see him tonight. But look, Neely. Do yourself a favor. Forget the costumes. Do the nightclub scene tomorrow. Learn the lyrics and let's bring the picture in on time.'

Her eyes narrowed. 'Oh, so that's what this whole big talk was for. Trying to soften me for the kill.'

He banged the glass on the table. 'Maybe you're right – you do need a headshrinker. Is that what this business has done to you? Made you suspicious of everyone? Listen, I've talked to you like a father because I *care* – because I don't want to see you and your talent go down the drain.'

'How can it go down the drain? Just because I won't wear a lousy costume?'

'No, because if you keep making pictures that lose money all the talent in the world won't help you in this business.'

'I'm the biggest box-office draw there is. I was voted number one this year in all the polls.'

'Neely, when the stockholders add up the figures they don't care about the line around Radio City or the movie-magazine polls. What good is it to them to make a big hit picture if it doesn't make money?'

'I don't believe they lose money,' she said stubbornly. 'They're just so worried about television they want my pictures to carry the whole studio. Yeah, sure . . . I'm supposed to work like crazy so The Head can sit in his palace or go to his beach house and screw all the starlets. Who's paying for all this? *Me* and my talent.'

'Neely, last year three low-budget pictures without stars brought in bigger profits than your last two pictures. One cost eight hundred thousand and grossed four million. If you don't believe your picture lost money, ask your agents.'

'Who can trust them? They'd go along with the studio. They got other stars to peddle, so they play ball with the guy who does the hiring.'

'Then trust me. Just try . . .'

'Okay, so I trust you. So does that mean I'm supposed to go on the set tomorrow looking like an ice cream cone in that dress?'

'Neely, you look great in that dress.'

'I look lousy.' She poured herself another drink.

'No, you just want Ted Casablanca's clothes and no one else's designs will ever satisfy you. But you can't have them.'

'That's not true.' She sniveled and dabbed at her eyes. 'Now you sound just like Dr. Mitchell.'

'Well? You trust him, and he's obviously told you the same thing.'

She smiled. 'Okay, maybe you're right.'

'Good girl. You'll be in tomorrow?'

She nodded. He kissed her on the cheek and left the bungalow.

She sat there and poured another drink. It was almost six o'clock. She had called Dr. Mitchell when she walked off the set and made an appointment for nine. Nine – that would take until ten, and she wouldn't get home until eleven or in bed until twelve. If she was going to learn the lyrics of the song for the nightclub scene . . . She called and canceled the doctor and went home.

She sat in bed, her dinner on a tray before her. She tried to memorize the lyrics. Why had she drunk all that Scotch earlier? Her mind just wouldn't function. Maybe she should go to sleep now. Yes, that was it. Be asleep at nine and leave a call for five. She could learn the lines from five to seven easy. With eight hours of sleep she'd feel great.

She sent the dinner tray back untouched. Might as well skip a meal. She had weighed a hundred and three that morning. Besides, the dolls always worked faster on an empty stomach. She took two red and one yellow. Then she poured half a glass of Scotch. The wonderful, relaxed drowsiness began. She sipped her drink and waited for the real reaction, the anesthetic feeling that would seep through her whole body and drag her down into sleep. But it didn't come, just the drowsiness. That wasn't enough. She could still think – and if she thought she'd think about being alone. And then she'd think of Ted and that girl. And she had no one. She was alone – as alone as when she was part of The Gaucheros, touring with Charlie and Dick, alone in strange hotel rooms – with no one who cared about her.

Perspiration made her neck damp and trickled down her back – she felt clammy. She stumbled out of bed and changed her pajamas. Dr. Mitchell was right – she was building up a tolerance to the pills. Maybe one more yellow . . . No, then she'd be groggy and hungover in the morning, and she had to learn those lyrics. Jesus. Today she had needed three green dolls just to get through the morning shooting.

She poured a full glass of Scotch. Maybe one more red pill . . . yeah, they wore off faster. She swallowed it quickly. And she wouldn't drink all this Scotch, just sip at it until the pills worked. Maybe she should read, that always made her drowsy. Anne had sent her another of Lyon's books. This was the arty type again. She skimmed the pages. It had gotten good reviews – but what good were reviews? The book wasn't selling.

Suddenly she wished Anne was with her. Anne always knew what to do. It was a shame Anne had made it so big on TV. If she hadn't she could send for her, give her a couple hundred a week to be a personal secretary. Geez, wouldn't that be dreamy? But Anne must be making a fortune. You couldn't turn on television without seeing Anne demonstrating hairspray or lipstick. But why shouldn't she have made it, especially if those rumors were true about her and that Gillmore guy. But even so, Anne had class. Not like Jennifer. Imagine – the trades said Hollywood was bidding for her, and she was turning them down. Jennifer turning Hollywood down! That broad was making a fortune by showing her fanny and tits in those French pictures. The darling of the art houses. Art houses shit! If Hollywood made pictures like that they would just be dirty pictures. And lately Hollywood was getting so goddam moral. No more low-cut dresses, no soul kissing, moral clauses in every contract. And this same Hollywood was begging Jennifer to come star for them. Sure, they'd cover her tits and her ass. But they'd make her a star, give her the same kind of money real stars were getting just because she had once walked around and showed her boobs!

She took another long swallow of her drink. She wasn't sleepy. She was just getting drunk. And hungry. God, she was starving! She wished she hadn't sent that tray down. There was caviar in the refrigerator. No . . . she mustn't. Damn Ted for teaching her to like it! But the costumes were tight as it was. The booze was doing it. Geez, she never ate a thing, and now, if she ate on top of all the booze— No, it wouldn't be fair to John. He had been so nice today. Funny . . . she had never noticed how blue his eyes were against his tan skin. He must be about fifty, but he was beautiful. John . . . here . . . beside her. Geez, that'd be nice. If he held her in his arms she'd feel protected.

She looked at the clock. Ten-thirty. Maybe John could come over. He could tell his wife it was to discuss a scene. He was probably sitting worrying about her now, wondering whether she'd show. She smiled. No, she wouldn't ask him to come tonight. She'd already rubbed the lanolin in her hair. But tomorrow she'd work like a horse and ask him to come back for a cold supper and work with her. And it would be more than just a quick bang. She'd make him stay and hold her in his arms until she fell asleep. Maybe he could stay often. She'd cooperate. They'd bring the picture in on time. She'd demand that he direct all her pictures. His kids were grown – maybe he could be with her a lot. She'd call him and tell him she was studying. That would be a good start – so at least he'd fall asleep thinking of her.

She called the studio and got his unlisted number. Then she dialed his home. A woman answered. Neely put on her most gurgly voice. 'Is this Mrs. Stykes?'

'No, this is Charlotte – the maid.'

'Oh. Is Mr. Stykes there?'

'No, madame. They are out for the evening. May I take a message?'

'No. No message.' Neely hung up.

Out with his wife! Probably sitting at Romanoff's telling his wife about how he had conned Neely O'Hara. She could just hear him . . . 'I got her eating out of my hand. She's easy – she may be a star, but underneath she's just a lousy little mick who's scared to death. You just have to know how to handle her.' Well, *no one* handled Neely O'Hara! She might have been born a little mick, but she was a star now! She could do what she goddam well liked!

She got out of bed and tiptoed downstairs. Suddenly she stopped. 'What the hell am I tippy-toeing around for? This is *my* house!'

There was no one in the kitchen. She opened the refrigerator and took out a large jar of caviar. 'Neely, we're gonna have a ball,' she said aloud. She took a spoon and ate the caviar from the jar. She finished it off. 'Now what? Come on, Neely, you can have anything you want. 'Cause you're a star . . . a big fucking talent . . . nah . . . a fucking *big* talent. And you can have anything.' She lurched against the refrigerator. 'Lessee. More caviar? Why not? You bought it.' She opened another jar. 'Hah! Now we'll just take some pâté upstairs in case we wanna eat it later. Neely, nothin's too good for you.'

She reached out and took a new bottle of Scotch off the bar and stumbled her way up the stairs. She poured another drink and went to the cabinet in the bathroom. 'Now, Neely, whaddaya want – red, yellow or blue dolls? Anything you want, baby.' She swallowed two red pills. Then she staggered into bed. She picked up the phone and buzzed. The butler answered. 'Lissen, Charlie, cancel the early call. Call the studio tomorrow and tell 'em Miss O'Hara has . . . has laryn . . . laryngitis. And I won't take any calls. I'm gonna sleep . . . and eat . . . and sleep . . . and eat . . . for maybe a week. When I wake up tomorrow I want pancakes, with butter and loads of syrup. I'm gonna have an orgy!'

1956

Neely had dressed carefully. White slacks, a loose blouse that would hide the roll around her waistline. Geez, why was it so hard to lose the ten pounds this time? Wardrobe fittings for the new picture started in a few days. And now, out of the blue, The Head wanted to see her. She wondered what was up. She thought about it all during her drive to the studio.

The call had come late the previous afternoon. Eddie Frank, one of his satellites, delivered the message. Respectful, casual and easy. 'Oh, Miss O'Hara, The Head would like you to have lunch with him tomorrow if it's convenient.'

If it's convenient! Ha! As if anyone had anything more convenient to do if The Head summoned. Boy, they had short memories. Three years ago when she won the Oscar *he* had come to *her*. Well, this new picture would fix things. Geez, what a part. And the songs . . . She'd win an Oscar nomination for sure, maybe even another Oscar.

She sat there across the great expanse of Early American desk, trying to look eager and young. He liked her that way. She decided The Head must have been born old. He never changed – that shock of white hair, the perennial tan that blended with the crusted liver spots. His eyes twinkled merrily and his small hands played with the trade papers on his desk.

'Dearie, do you know why I sent for you?'

'No sir, but it's always a pleasure to see you, sir.' (Oh, she knew all the right protocol.)

'Did you see yesterday's trades?'

(Oh, God, that award. That stinking award.)

'Miss Front Office Poison of 1956 – Neely O'Hara. Not very pleasant, is it?' he asked kindly.

She fidgeted. 'Oh, you know those awards.' She used her little-girl voice. 'I was real hurt when I saw it. But several people told me it means nothing. The press just gets together each year and picks a patsy. Last year they gave it to Stewart Lane and he's Twentieth's top star.'

'No, he is not.' The voice was still kind. 'He never made it back after the war. Every one of his pictures has lost money. But they're committed for two more years so they keep it quiet.'

'Well, my pictures do great.'

'At the box office, yes. For us – no.'

She squirmed. Well, here it was again – the overtime, the missed rehearsals, the pep talk . . .

'This new picture is very expensive,' he stated. 'Prices have soared. We're competing with television, and people won't go out just to see any movie. Not when they can see entertainment for free in their own homes. It's no longer a little box – it's got a big face and it's getting bigger.'

She played with the cuticles on her fingers. What the hell – she hadn't invented the damn thing. Let him go holler at General Sarnoff.

'We're putting more money into *Let's Live Tonight* than any other picture we've ever made. Any overtime and we're dead. Sam Jackson is working on a tight schedule.'

'Sam's one of my favorite producers,' she said.

'I've made a deal with Sam. For every day he brings the picture in *under* the shooting schedule, he gets a thousand-dollar bonus.'

It *was* going to be a rat race.

'And the first time he's one day behind he goes off the picture.'

'You mean you'd take Sam Jackson off a picture?'

'I'll take anyone off who can't meet my demands. Hollywood has changed, dearie. We've let the last of our contract players go. Your present contract has one year to go, and when . . . *if* we renegotiate, it won't be like before.'

You're damn right it won't be, she thought. I'll form a corporation and get a piece of the action. I'll own something. Her tax men had explained this to her.

'No, dearie.' He sighed. 'Everything is changing. Now I can't tell the stockholders to mind their business. Now I have to answer to them – and the only answer they want is profits.'

She nodded and wondered when the interview would end. This was just a routine pep talk! He had a nerve dragging her out here just for this. She was hungry – he could at least have ordered lunch. She hadn't had breakfast and she had only taken one Dexie.

'That's why I'm taking you off the picture,' he said.

She stared at him in astonishment.

'Dearie, I can't afford the risk. Sam Jackson can be replaced if he doesn't work out. But if you're on film I can't replace you. I'd have to start from the top . . . reshoot everything.'

'But you can't replace me before I even begin,' she stammered.

'Why not? Look at you. You're fat again. Fittings are scheduled for next week, and you won't be ready. No, this is too big a venture. I'm putting in Janie Lord.'

'Janie Lord! Why, she's just beginning.' He couldn't mean it. He was just trying to scare her.

'She's made three inexpensive pictures and they all made money. She's got stories in every fan magazine this month. This picture will make her a star, a big one. And I've got Brick Nelson playing opposite her for insurance.'

She had wondered about Brick Nelson. He was expensive, and usually her pictures had no other top-monied stars. She was the star, the whole picture. Her mind raced to her contract. He wasn't kidding. But could he cancel her like this after she had been announced? With no cause?

'There's nothing you can do, legally,' he said, as if reading her thoughts. 'We rewrote the role so it calls for a younger girl.'

'Younger girl! Listen, I'm only twenty-eight. That's not exactly over the hill.'

'You look forty,' he said casually.

'I have no makeup on,' she said defensively.

'You have circles under your eyes . . . the beginnings of a double chin. You're a mess.'

The tears ran down her freckled cheeks. One week of sleep and diet and she'd be as good as new. He knew that. Why was he carrying on like this?

His secretary interrupted to say the Paris call had come through. He picked up the phone, his face beaming unctuous charm. 'Hello!' He was shouting as people usually do when they are speaking across impossible distances. 'Yes.' His voice lost some of its volume. 'I can hear you clear as a bell. Marvelous, isn't it? Yes, Mr. Chardot . . . yes, I received your letter this morning. That's why I put in the call. Your terms are . . . well . . .' He forced a soft laugh. 'Impossible is an understatement. Naturally I want to do a picture with Miss North. And I'm perfectly willing to let you co-produce. But a one-picture deal with you owning fifty per cent of the foreign rights is not feasible. After all, this star of yours – we will be putting her in clothes, covering her completely. How do we know she will have the same appeal? Yes, I realize she was fully clothed in her last three pictures. But let's face it, Mr. Chardot, an actress she's not. What? Well, maybe she did win those awards . . . maybe it's because I don't understand French. But in English, how can we be sure? And your not giving me a second picture option – is that fair? I spend all the money on advertising and then some other studio grabs her for the second picture. I want a three-picture deal, and you can have your terms. She can have her own production setup. The money will be deposited in a Swiss bank . . . How much? . . . Oh, my good man, where are you getting those figures? No one could meet your demands, Mr. Chardot.'

He held the phone silently, a pained expression on his face. 'Mr. Chardot, a Louie Esterwald will contact you this afternoon . . . What? Oh, it's eight o'clock at night there. I never can get over this big difference in time. All right, tomorrow morning. He'll negotiate the fine points. He speaks your language, a very fine French. And can we expect you here in September? . . . Now Mr. Chardot, if we wait until February that brings us into 'fifty-seven. I want to report to my stockholders that we have a Jennifer North picture in the works for 'fifty-six . . . Fine, I'm looking forward to it, too. Have you started shooting on her new picture? . . . You'll do two between now and November – God, I envy you. Between now and November I'm lucky if I get one finished. But you haven't got union problems, and that goddam television. Wait, you'll see – in a few years you'll feel it too. It's like cancer, that television. It spreads to every place.'

After he hung up he immediately placed another transatlantic call. Neely waited patiently while he toyed with a pencil. He slammed the receiver down in disgust. 'A twenty-minute delay!'

Suddenly he seemed to remember her. 'All right, you can leave.' He waved his hand.

'I thought we were having lunch,' she said, stunned.

'You can skip lunch. With that belly, you're better off. I'd think you were four months gone if I hadn't seen you that way so many times. I've got to wait for the call to Louie Esterwald to come through.' He sighed. 'Imagine the deals I have to make and the footsies I have to play to get that naked whore to come make a movie for me. Ten years ago the Industry would have thrown her out. Now every studio is fighting to get her. Something's happening to this country. We're going to go immoral. And television is doing it. I've always stood for clean American pictures, but now we have to fight television with everything we can get – tits, asses, French whores . . .'

'She's no French whore,' Neely said. 'She's an American girl, and very nice. I roomed with her once.'

He was genuinely interested. 'You roomed with Jennifer North?'

'Eleven years ago. We were both in *Hit the Sky*. She was just a glorified showgirl, then she married Tony Polar. She was out here.'

'Of course! He was married to a Jennifer . . .' He shook his head. 'No, it can't be the same girl. This girl is only twenty-three.'

Neely laughed bitterly. 'In French pictures everyone is twenty-three. It's the same Jennifer I roomed with. Jennifer is . . . Geez – I don't know – I was seventeen, and she was supposed to be twenty-one . . .'

'That would make her thirty-two.' He was amazed.

'That's right,' Neely said. 'And you're hollering that I'm old at twenty-eight.'

'This girl must take care of herself. And she's reliable. Two pictures by November.' He shook his head. 'She won some award at some foreign film festival, so now she thinks she's an actress. Just my luck – the French get her when she's naked . . . I have to get her when she's an actress.' He sighed with a rattle that shook his whole body.

'And meanwhile what do I do? Just sit?' Neely asked.

'Sit and take off weight. You're getting paid each week.'

'And when is my next picture?'

'We'll see . . .'

Her eyes blazed. 'Who do you think you are, treating me like this?'

'The head of the studio. And you're just a little snotnose I made into a star – only you haven't paid off lately. So you'll just sit. And you'll learn a goddam good lesson. Watch a few new stars come up like Janie Lord. Maybe that'll knock some sense into your head. Now beat it, I've got more important things to do.'

She rose. 'I could walk out of here and never come back.'

He smiled. 'Do that. And you'll never work anywhere again.'

She sobbed all the way home, racing the car recklessly through the canyons and around the winding hills. She really didn't care. What was she supposed to do? Go home and sit in that barn of a house? Even the twins didn't need her, really. They loved their nurse, and they were going to school. Once the word was out that she was replaced in this picture – and right on top of that Front Office Poison award – then she'd really be alone. No one calls a loser. Geez, how could people be so mean? She had worked so hard, tried so hard – and now everyone was out to crucify her.

She went into the house and grabbed a bottle of Scotch off the bar. Then she went to her bedroom, pulled the blinds to shut out the daylight, shut off her phone and swallowed five red pills. Five red ones hardly did anything now. Last night she had only slept three hours with five red ones *and* two yellows. She undressed and slipped into bed.

It must have been midnight when she woke. She opened the blinds. Night . . . and nothing to do. She wandered into the bathroom and unconsciously got on the scale. She had lost two pounds. Hey, that was an idea – if she just slept and took pills and didn't eat she could take ten pounds off in no time. She took a vitamin pill – that would keep her healthy – then she swallowed a few more red dolls and washed them down with a generous slug of Scotch.

She could see the sun sneaking through the drapes when she woke. She fumbled her way into the bathroom. She was groggy, but not sleepy. No, she wouldn't get on the scale. She'd wait and be surprised. She felt hollow and empty. Better take two vitamins . . . Yeah, they had everything in them. She slapped some cream on her face and put lanolin in her hair. Might as well make this a real beauty cure. She'd look like a living doll when she finally got up. This time she took five yellow pills and then two red ones. That would speed up the action. There was just enough Scotch left for another good drink . . .

When she opened her eyes everything looked too clean and bright. What was that goddam needle doing taped to her arm? And that bottle hanging upside down? Christ! This was a hospital room! She tried to sit up and a nurse rushed over.

'Relax, Miss O'Hara,' the nurse urged in her professionally cheerful voice.

'What am I doing here? What happened?'

The nurse handed her a newspaper. Jesus! On the front page – a picture of her, fresh-faced and smiling, one of her first studio stills. But the large picture beside it – a girl being carried by two men, her head hanging back, her bare feet showing . . . God, it was her! She read the headline, *Star Takes Overdose of Pills*, and the caption, *Accident, Claims Studio Head*. Reading how The Head had come to her rescue, she smiled for the first time. Sure he had been afraid – afraid she might conk out. He didn't dare say he had fired her off the picture. She read on avidly.

'Miss O'Hara and I had a discussion five days ago' – Geez, had she been out that long? – 'and I suggested perhaps she was too tired to rush into production of the next picture. She assured me that she was not, that all she needed was a few days' rest. Obviously this was all she was trying to do. Get in shape for the new picture. If she lives—' The Head had choked up and had had to pause to wipe tears from his eyes. Tears! That shit could turn them off and on better than any star. He was probably just scared she had left some messy suicide note. She read on. 'If she lives, she will play the starring role in our biggest picture. It is not true that we are replacing her with Janie Lord. No one could replace Neely O'Hara. We had been considering changing the script in case Miss O'Hara didn't feel up to it. Then perhaps Janie Lord *could* do it. But all we want is for Neely to come through. Once in a generation a star like Neely comes along.'

She felt marvelous. There were eulogies about her from every star she had ever played with, and from stars she hardly knew. Even the trades had devoted several columns of praise. It was like dying and being able to watch the crowd at one's own funeral. She liked the sensation. Geez, they must have really expected her to die. It must have been close for The Head to put himself out on a limb like this. He *had* to give her the picture now.

'Was I very sick?' she asked the nurse.

'Sick! Until a few hours ago we didn't think you'd make it. You've been in an oxygen tent for twenty-four hours.'

'But I only took a few pills. I really was just trying to get some sleep.'

'It was lucky your butler called the doctor. He came up and found you hardly breathing. He grew concerned about you being without food for three days.'

She grinned. 'I bet I'm nice and skinny now.'

The nurse turned abruptly away. A second later the doctor came in. 'I'm Dr. Keegan.' She recognized the name – The Head's personal physician.

'Well, we made it,' he said briskly.

We sure did, she thought. But knowing The Head would get a full report, she merely smiled weakly.

'Silly thing to do. What does it prove?' he asked.

It got me the picture back, buster. But she held onto her wistful smile and added a few tears for good measure. Then she said softly, 'I . . . I didn't want to live without the picture.'

'Oh, yes . . . yes . . . the picture. We'll have to see. Can't tell whether you'll be up to it.'

She sat up. 'I *am* up to it!'

'You've had a rough time. We'll see. If I don't think you're ready, I'll tell the studio. Can't let you have a relapse.'

So that was it! This was his out! His own personal physician would say she wasn't strong enough.

She smiled sweetly. 'Well, let's hope you find me ready. Because it was The Head's idea that I lose weight, and the faster the better. And as for my not being in shape, it was The Head who first got me the green goof balls – when I was eighteen – to kill my appetite. And I worked many times with *no* food at all for a week at a time – on his orders. So I think you'll find me strong enough. Let's see . . . wardrobe fitting must be in a few days. I'm thin enough, so I can make them. Then I have a whole week to rest before we begin shooting.'

The next day she had her lawyer and her agents at her bedside. It was a cinch. She couldn't be taken off the picture now, not with the statements The Head had given to the papers. It was better than any contract. And public sympathy was riding with her too. But she didn't dare miss one day of shooting. Her agent warned her. 'One day . . . one hour late, and out you'll go. He's mad now, and he'd do it, even at a sacrifice to the picture. You've outsmarted him, and he doesn't like to lose.'

She was nervous the first day of shooting. She saw Sam Jackson standing with the crew, and he seemed nervous, too. Everyone seemed nervous. But she had studied her lines. She knew the scene cold.

'We'll have one run-through and then try it on camera,' Sam suggested. 'Let's start with the dialogue where you address the audience in the nightclub. You beg them for quiet, then you sing.' He turned and shouted, 'Extras in place! Let's get going!'

The scene was set and she ran through it. It went well. But why were they all so nervous? And why was Sam avoiding her eyes? This wasn't like him. Was he embarrassed because he was on trial and could be taken off the picture? Everyone knew The Head was a bastard. She'd talk to Sam at the end of the day.

She watched them set the boom and pull the cameras into place. Was Sam this hysterical for the thousand bucks bonus a day? No one could do an actual take in one shooting. Christ, if they got through one whole scene in a day it would be good shooting.

The lights flooded the set, the slate was snapped under her eyes . . . Jesus, she had never done a scene on camera with just one run-through. No one did.

It went fairly well. She missed a few cues, but for a first take . . . Geez, he might even get a foot of actual film out of it. She turned to him with a smile when it was over.

'You blew the lyrics.'

She shrugged. 'Two lines. The recording is taped already. So I mouthed it wrong . . . next time—'

'All right. Let's do it again. And I want this to be a final take.'

God, he was sick. He'd never get through the picture running this scared. But it was his funeral.

She returned to the set. This time she turned her ankle and lurched over the wires of the hand mike she was supposed to be carrying.

'Cut!' he shouted. He walked over. 'Are you feeling all right, Neely?'

'I feel fine. Hey, relax, Sam. You didn't expect to get an actual take with the second try.'

'I expected to get it the first time.'

'Sam, are you crazy? I know the heat's on you, but don't push the panic button. You act as if we're shooting a quickie. Even The Head would laugh if he heard you expected to do a full scene with one take.'

He ignored her and turned to the crew. 'Get ready for Take Three.'

She started to storm off the set. Then she stopped. Good God, this would be playing right into The Head's hands. She walked back. She was shaking. Neely O'Hara, having to take this shit from a scared director. He knew the entire crew was watching. No one had ever treated her like this, turning their backs on her and walking away. She did the walking!

She forced herself to return to her place on the set. She stood under the lights, trembling, while the girl patched her makeup. The slate snapped – Take Three. She fluffed a line on the opening. The cameras stopped. Take Four. Another fluff. Take Five. Take Six . . .

By late afternoon they were on Take Fifteen. This was ridiculous. She had never done more than eight takes in her life. Sam had done this to her. He was taking his nerves out on her. She couldn't remember a line now if her life depended on it.

'Dinner break – everyone back at seven,' he called.

Dinner break! She hadn't worked at night since her early days. And he hadn't even consulted her. She stalked over. 'I presume you're planning on shooting around me.'

He concentrated on the viewfinder. 'I'm shooting the same scene until you manage to give me a decent take.'

'Not me, buster. I've cooperated. I was here on time and I leave on time. I'm not breaking my ass so you can make a bonus of a thousand a day.' She walked off.

'If you walk off I'll report it.'

'As you like,' she snarled. 'I have some rights!'

The cast and crew arrived back at seven. They waited until ten. A call was placed to Neely's home. They were told she had retired for the night. Sam Jackson stood up and dismissed the crew. 'No call tomorrow. No call until further orders.'

He got into his car and drove out to the beach. He came to a small house and honked his horn. The door opened. A beautiful girl with long black hair, wearing a terrycloth bathrobe, stood in the doorway. She beckoned to him and he came into the house.

'Well, Janie, you got the part.'

She opened her mouth and let the smile show her even teeth. 'Oh, Sam, you swung it! I'm so glad!' Then she turned to the little man with the white hair who was sitting in a chair, smoking silently. 'Did you hear? Sam pulled it off.'

The little man smiled. 'Good.' He stood up and pulled the string of her loose robe. It fell open, revealing her perfect body. The little man, who barely reached the young goddess's shoulder, ran his suntanned hand lightly over the arched breasts.

'Take a good look, Sam. But don't touch – this is mine.'

Sam nodded. 'Yes, sir.'

'I just want you to know. You're a young guy – you might get ideas.'

The girl turned and hugged the little man. 'But I love you, you know that.'

The man nodded. 'All right, Sam – good work. Now beat it. Call everyone back day after tomorrow. I'll send out the releases. And send a wire to Neely telling her not to report. Sign my name.'

Sam nodded and walked out. The white-haired man turned to the beautiful girl. 'Okay, now you'll be a star, Janie Lord. You'll be *the* Miss Lord – just so long as you remember . . . I'm *your* lord!'

'Yes, sir.' And she fell to her knees and began making love to him.

ANNE

Anne hung up the receiver thoughtfully. Kevin Gillmore reached across and took her hand. 'Neely again?' She nodded. He patted the bed. 'Lie down here with me and we can talk it out.'

She lay back on her own bed. 'It's not that simple, Kevin.'

'I heard you squirm on the phone. I assume she wanted to stay with you.'

When Anne was silent, Kevin laughed. 'You're still the New England prude, aren't you? Why didn't you come right out and say, "Yes, Neely, I do have twin beds, but my guy often spends the night with me."'

Anne picked up the script she had been studying. 'Because there was no reason to say that. Kevin, I'm worried. Neely's in a bad way.'

'Why? Because they didn't pick up her option? She's been sitting on her fanny for seven months drawing a lot of money. It's no disgrace to be without a long-term contract today. No studio is giving them out any more.'

'But she sounded odd . . . desperate. Says she has to get away.'

'She can have her pick of offers. The minute she hits town every Broadway producer will be after her. She could do television – anything she wants.'

'But I've heard funny rumors . . .' Anne reached for a cigarette.

Kevin reached across and held her hand back from lighting it. 'Come on over here with me so we don't have to scream.'

She smiled. 'Kevin, I *will* scream if I go before the cameras and don't know these lines.'

'Use the cue cards.'

'It's better when I don't. I like having them there just in case, but it's better if I know what I'm saying.'

'Do you really care about me, Anne?' he asked.

'I care very much, Kevin.' She put down her script and waited patiently. It always started like this.

'But you're not wildly in love with me.'

She smiled. 'That's a young kind of love, reserved for one's first romance.'

'Still torching for that hack writer?'

'I haven't see Lyon in years. The last I heard, he was writing some movie scenarios in London.'

'Then why haven't you fallen in love with me?'

She reached out and took his hand. 'I enjoy your company, Kevin. I enjoy you in bed. I enjoy working for you. Perhaps this is love.'

'If I offered to marry you, would you love me more?'

Her words were measured. 'In the beginning it mattered terribly. I didn't like being known as someone's "girl." But now the damage is done . . .' She spoke without emotion – they had gone through this so many times before.

'What damage? You're famous. You're known everywhere as the Gillian Girl.'

'*And* Gillmore's Girl. But it doesn't matter now. I wanted a child . . . I still do . . .'

'Anne.' He got out of bed and began to pace. 'You're thirty-one. That's late for children.'

'I know women who had their first child at forty.'

'But I'm fifty-seven. I have a grown son and a married daughter – and a two-year-old grandchild. How would it look if I married you and had a child younger than my grandchild?'

'Many men marry late in life and start a new family.'

'I was married twenty-five years to Evelyn – may she rest in peace – and I went through the whole business – summer camps, nurses, braces, measles. I haven't the patience to go through it again. Now

266

that I have a little freedom and more money than I could ever spend, I want an easy life and no encumbrances, and a girl who will be free to travel with me, to have fun. I never had any fun in marriage. It was all a struggle then. I was starting the business and Evelyn was raising the kids. We never went anywhere, except maybe a weekend in Atlantic City, and then she was always worried that the maid wasn't reliable or that one of the kids would get sick. And then, when I made it big and the kids were grown, it was too late. She was sick. I had five years of it – five years of watching her die. Then I met you – one year to the day after her death – and I knew right away you were the girl for me.'

She managed a smile. 'I'm glad I fit in with your plans. But a girl doesn't plan on just being someone's girl – she hopes to be a wife and mother.'

'I've thought about it, Anne – but my kids wouldn't like it.' He sat on the edge of her bed and said lightly, 'Besides, I'm more sure of you this way. Once we were married, you'd take me for granted.' He went back to his bed and picked up the newspaper. Soon he was lost in the financial section of the *Times*.

Anne went back to her script. In a few months he would bring it up again, and again it would end like this. Kevin felt guilty about not marrying her, but it really didn't matter to her any more. Maybe it was too late to think about children. And a marriage certificate certainly didn't insure fidelity or happiness – look at Jennifer. And look at poor Neely.

It was true that everyone knew she was Kevin's girl. But she was also the Gillian Girl . . . and he had made that possible. She enjoyed her work. It was lucrative and kept her busy. She liked Kevin, too – no, it was more than just liking him, perhaps it *was* love. Not love as she had known it with Lyon – there were no Cloud Nines with Kevin. Their physical union left her completely untouched, and very often she wondered what attraction she held for him. When she recalled the wild abandon with which she had given herself to Lyon – their deep kisses and feverish embraces, lying locked in each other's arms all night – her relationship with Kevin seemed absolutely antiseptic.

In the beginning, it had been strictly a business relationship. Then gradually they had drifted together socially. She had enjoyed his company, and she found dating one man easier than resisting the advances of many. She was an asset to his company, and he was patient with her inexperience before the cameras. It was his patience that had enabled her to achieve her success. He hovered around every rehearsal, checking every light, working with her on her delivery, helping her choose the right dress. She grew to rely on him, to seek his advice and judgment. She was aware of the pretty little models who flung themselves at him, and she saw wealthy divorcees and visiting starlets seek him out. She knew about the frantic invitations he received from the chic, famous fifty-year-old ex-movie queen. Yes, Kevin Gillmore could write his own ticket. But he wanted her. She held him off for a year, but she met no one who kindled any excitement or romantic image. So, finally, she gave herself to Kevin.

She recalled their first union. She had been unable to do more than submit. She allowed him to take her, to satisfy himself – nothing more. And he never asked for more. Sometimes she forced herself to respond in a tepid way, and Kevin seemed to accept this for passion. Soon she realized that with all his worldliness, he was totally unsophisticated about the act of love. Obviously he had been quite pure when he married his wife, and she must have been equally chaste and unimaginative. They probably had never progressed beyond a few limp kisses and the mechanical act of intercourse. After his wife's death there must have been girls, and some of them must have gone all out – but he probably related this kind of sex to girls of loose morals. Anne was a lady, as his wife had been. And so he accepted her frigidity as the normal attribute of a lady, and being a gentleman, he expected nothing more.

No, with Kevin there were no highs or lows, but perhaps this was what mature love was like. Sometimes she told herself she was fortunate. Many girls never knew the Lyon Burke kind of love, and few achieved the solidity of Kevin's kind of love. Even his unwillingness to marry her presented no real problem. She had never forced the issue, though she knew she could make Kevin marry her – all she had to do was threaten to leave him. No, she was perfectly content with their present status. She knew Kevin would always be there.

Neely arrived the following week. Anne managed to conceal her shock at Neely's transformation. She had gained weight, her face looked puffy, and even though she wore an expensive suit, she looked seedy. Her nail polish was chipped, there was a run in her stocking and she seemed rumpled. But most of all, there was something dead in her whole countenance. Neely didn't sparkle any more. Her eyes didn't seem to focus when she talked.

Anne remained the attentive listener as Neely poured out her entire diatribe of woe – the diabolical schemes of The Head, the broken marriage, the evils of Hollywood . . .

About herself, Anne offered very little information. She talked about her work and her close friendship with Kevin, and when Neely asked with a trace of the little-girl voice if she were 'doing it,' Anne smiled and nodded. That seemed to please Neely.

Kevin played the gracious host. If Neely infringed on his private life he hid his irritation well. He escorted both girls around town to the shows and the nightclubs. Neely caused a sensation wherever she went. She blossomed with the acclaim. There were no lost days, no endless bouts of drinking. She bought new clothes, dropped ten pounds in two weeks and rarely took more than three pills a night. She sparkled again – and became the bouncing girl Anne had always known.

One hot September evening, as they were leaving a theatre, a large crowd deserted the stage door and rushed to Neely, cutting them off from their cab. Laughing, waving, signing books, Neely was buffeted by the friendly mob until Kevin, assisted by a policeman, managed to clear a path to the curb.

In the taxi Kevin mopped perspiration from his face and shook his head in wonder. 'It's fantastic! If they're that crazy just to *see* you, what would they do if you sang?'

'Pass out in sheer ecstasy.' Neely laughed. 'But my public has always been hot for me,' she added, her round eyes suddenly growing serious. 'There were lines at Radio City for all my pictures. They just cost too darn much money to make. But I never had a picture that died. I always did big business—'

Kevin stared at her as though what she had been saying had just penetrated. A note of excitement made his voice tremble. 'You're right. Your pictures always sold out. Your public is still with you. They want you. Neely – let's do a spectacular! I'll present it – I'll buy an hour of prime time on one of the networks. My God – it would be a sensation!'

'Are you kidding? Me do TV? A whole hour live with no retakes? Geez, I'd die.'

'If you sang all the songs you've introduced, you wouldn't need retakes,' Kevin insisted. 'No gimmicks, no other acts – just you standing out there singing.'

'Forget it,' Neely answered. 'I heard what those television cameras do to you – they add ten pounds and twenty years. And besides, what do I need it for? The Johnson Harris office is trying to work out a three-picture deal with Metro right now.'

As Neely's appearances in public continued to generate new excitement, Kevin became obsessed with the idea. 'Work on her,' he pleaded to Anne. 'I'd give her four weeks of rehearsal. We'd introduce a new product. The publicity would be worth millions for Gillian.'

'I can't force her if she's afraid,' Anne insisted. 'If something went wrong I'd feel responsible.'

'What could go wrong? It's not as if she's a no-talent hothouse flower created by the Hollywood cameras. Neely grew up in vaudeville, she played Broadway – she's a trouper. Television's loaded with no-talent performers. Every day someone you never heard of jumps into television and becomes a star, and only because the real talents like Neely are holding out. It's not as if I'm asking her to do a weekly series. Just one shot, a spectacular – and she'd do herself a lot of good, too.'

'I agree, Kevin. But you're the super salesman – it's up to you to convince her. I'm her friend, and I intend to remain just that.'

Kevin brought up the subject several times, and each time Neely good-naturedly turned him down. She was enjoying her first real holiday, her first contact with the adulation of the fans, a long-overdue payment for the years of cloistered grind in the studio factory.

Kevin seized every opportunity to get Neely involved in watching performers and reliving her own past. He bought tickets for the opening night of Helen Lawson's new musical, hoping that seeing Helen would reactivate Neely's ambition and revive the excitement of working to an audience.

Helen's opening was a major event. She had disappeared from the Broadway scene in another unsuccessful attempt at marriage, this time as mistress of a large estate in Jamaica. She had retired with ecstatic interviews. She had found 'the only true love of her life.' There had been pictures of an overblown Helen clinging to the arm of a nondescript, gray-haired man. She was selling her New York apartment and furniture and going to Jamaica to live a wonderful life as a simple housewife. The wonderful life lasted six years. Then Helen returned, and there were more front-page stories. Jamaica was 'a tropical small town filled with rich, idle people and bugs.' There was nothing to do but drink and gossip. The wonderful man was 'a louse who drank too much and had "liaisons" with other women.' She got a Mexican divorce and immediately accepted the starring role in a new musical.

It was a typical Helen Lawson opening. All the right people were in the audience, waiting to cheer her, to welcome home the Queen. The applause had been deafening on her entrance, but after ten minutes the air was heavy with 'flop sweat.' Kevin had felt a surge of hope as Neely sat on the edge of her seat, mentally taking every bow with Helen. But his hopes were dashed when Neely whispered, 'I thought she was old when I first met her. Geez, she was a kid in comparison.'

Kevin had to admit Neely was right. Helen was no longer skirting middle age; she *was* middle-aged. She had put on a good deal of weight. But her legs were still good, and she still tossed her long mane of black hair.

'Boy, has she been dipping into the dye pots,' Neely whispered. 'I like black hair, but she must be kidding with that color. It's ebony.'

'She should use Gillian's color black,' Kevin commented. 'Gives a more natural look.'

'Nothing could help her,' Neely hissed. 'And now she hasn't even got a good script going for her. Why did she ever take this show? She's got loads of dough.'

'What else is she going to do?' Kevin said carefully. 'An actress is only alive when she's on stage.'

'Eh!' Neely waved him aside. 'That's an old cliché.'

'It's just started,' Anne whispered. 'It might get better.'

'It's a flop. I can smell it,' Neely answered.

Neely was right. Anne watched Helen struggle valiantly. She felt a surge of sympathy for this blowsy-looking middle-aged woman trying to play a romantic role. Her voice was as vital as ever, with only the trace of a vibrato; but either the lyrics missed or the tune wasn't there. As the show progressed her energy increased, as if she were trying to put her own life's blood into the dying show.

There were numerous curtain calls. The first-nighters gave the Queen dutiful homage. But the comments as they filed out of the theatre were more truthful. 'Helen's first flop.' . . . 'It wasn't Helen's fault, it was a bad book.' . . . 'The direction was lousy.' . . . 'Ah, but the old Helen would have pulled it out. Remember *Sunny Lady*? No book or score – just Helen, and it was enough.' . . . 'Listen, everyone is entitled to one flop.' . . . 'Yes, but at her age it's too late to make a comeback. Why didn't she let well enough alone?' . . . 'They're kinder to racehorses – at least they put the champions out to stud.' . . . 'Yeah, and from what I hear, that's what Helen would really like.' . . . 'But who's the old bag going to stud with?' . . . 'Aw, she still has great legs and magnificent hair.' . . . 'Well, she's got to have *something* left.' . . . 'And my dear, *I* studied voice in college. There *was* a vibrato.' . . .

'I can't go backstage,' Neely said. 'I know she musta heard I was out front, but Geez, what can I say? Like maybe the sets were great?'

'Want to go to Sardi's?' Kevin asked. 'She'll come there to take her bows.'

'Wanna bet?' Neely answered. 'Listen, no one knows better than Helen what a bomb this was. She doesn't want to be sitting around Sardi's with egg on her face when those early editions of the *Times* and *Tribune* come out. Besides, Franco Salla is opening at the Persian Room tonight. He was a sensation at Ciro's. I went every night. I wouldn't miss his New York opening.'

Wearily, Kevin called the Persian Room and booked a table. It was mobbed with the same columnists and many of the same people who had attended Helen's opening. When the captain saw Neely, a new table was placed ringside in front of a disgruntled group who had tipped lavishly to insure an unhampered view. A surge of excitement ran through the audience as Neely entered.

Kevin ordered champagne, but Neely barely sipped at her glass. Anne watched the crowd and thought about the new commercial she was to do the following day. It was late, and she could see the show was not going to start on schedule. Tomorrow she'd have to use the 'idiot cards.' She watched the people milling at the door. Nothing ever changed at openings – the same impatient people waiting to be shown to their tables, offering folded bills for better locations, the same perspiring busboys scuttling around placing makeshift tables at ringside, trying to ignore the complaints of the occupants of tables they eclipsed.

People who had started at ringside were now three rows back. The dance floor was half its original size. And just as it seemed impossible to squeeze another person into the room, Anne saw a busboy rushing another platter-sized table to the ringside. It was placed directly opposite them.

Helen made her entrance, accompanied by a slim young boy. He was a minor dancer in her show, effeminately beautiful and ignorantly proud to be the center of attention. Helen must have known all about his 'roommate,' but he played his role of escort with flawless perfection. He held her hand, listened raptly to everything she said, laughed on cue and reveled in the introductions Helen engulfed him in as she turned to the tables around her and loudly greeted friends. The captain answered her bellowed summons with a look of patient resignation. Anne could hear her across the room as she shouted, 'I know this is one of those fancy-Dan rooms that don't serve booze while the act is on, so set up a few bottles of the grape fast, before it's too late.'

The lights finally dimmed. Franco Salla was introduced. He was a strong singer, especially good in his Italian numbers. The audience had read his out-of-town notices and was eager to make him a star. He was forced to do several encores. Then, after a charming speech of gratitude, enhanced by his accent, he turned gravely to the ringside, and with an air of solemn awe, introduced 'the giant of musical comedy, the queen of them all, the great lady who has been a star for decades . . . Helen Lawson!'

Helen forced a mechanical grin. She rose and waved good-naturedly to the audience. The applause was loud and hearty with respect.

Then Franco turned and looked at Neely. The audience followed his gaze. His voice was soft and his eyes grew tender with admiration. 'And now, the once-in-a-lifetime star . . . the girl everyone loves . . . the singer every singer worships . . .' He stopped, groping, as if there were no superlatives strong enough to describe Neely. Then he smiled and said, simply, 'Miss Neely O'Hara.'

The applause was deafening. A few people stood up to cheer. Then, suddenly, in a body, the entire audience was on its feet, clamoring, applauding, demanding a song. Kevin stood, too. Anne didn't know what to do; everyone was standing except Helen Lawson and her young dancer. Helen sat there with a glassy smile clamped on her face and clapped noiselessly. The dancer stared at her dumbly, awaiting any command.

Neely finally rose and walked to the microphone. She thanked everyone graciously and tried to beg off. When the audience stormed an insistent demand, she shrugged helplessly and turned to the orchestra. After a quick discussion of key and chords, she took center stage and sang.

She was brilliant. Her voice was clear and soaring, and the audience reacted with the frenzied adoration of worshippers at a revival meeting. She did six songs before she could beg off. She returned to the table ecstatic, her eyes shining with tears of excitement. Columnists came over to congratulate her, and well-gowned women demanded autographs 'for my daughter.' Neely good-naturedly signed menus, cards and bits of paper. When the deluge finally died down, she gulped a glass of champagne. 'You know, I could get to like this,' she said.

'Singing in a supper club?' Kevin asked hopefully.

'No, drinking champagne. It's good.' She poured another glass. 'It's safer to stick with Scotch or vodka, but tonight is an exception. Only I better not make a habit of it – too fattening. Look at Old Ironsides over there – all that blubber is solid vintage wine.'

'Neely, you were great tonight,' Kevin began.

'Sure. It's easy to be great with old standards. They don't write songs like that any more.'

'But that's what you'd do on my spectacular.'

She grinned. 'Oh, we're back to that, huh?'

'Neely, the public adores you—'

'Sure. They adore my movies, too. Is it my fault that unions and costs are so high they can't break even in Hollywood?'

'They say it's not just the costs and unions, Neely.'

Her eyes narrowed and lost some of their good humor. 'And what *do* they say, Mr. Bones?'

'They say *you* run the costs up . . . that you're unreliable . . . that you've lost your voice.'

Anne shifted nervously and tried to catch Kevin's eye to signal a warning, but he ignored her and riveted his gaze on Neely.

Neely managed a smile. 'Well, you just heard me sing. So don't believe everything you read in the papers.'

'I *don't* believe it, because I heard you tonight. And no one in this room believes it. But that's only a handful of people. The public believes what they read, Neely. So do a lot of movie producers.'

Her smile vanished. 'Listen, Mr. Killjoy, I'm having a perfectly marvelous time. I got up and sang for my supper. What do you want from me?'

'A spectacular.'

She sighed. 'Here we go again, Charlie.'

'I mean it, Neely. You convinced everyone here tonight that you can still sing like an angel. Why not convince the world? Do you know how many people you'd hit with one big television program? I'd give you national publicity for weeks in advance – the whole country would be watching—'

'Forget it.' She reached for the champagne. 'Hey, the bottle's empty. Let's get some more.'

Kevin signaled for another bottle. Anne looked at her watch. Neely caught her glance and grabbed her arm good-naturedly. 'Come on, don't be a crepe hanger. This is my big night.'

'But it's one-thirty and I have a show tomorrow, with a very early rehearsal.'

'So what?' Neely laughed. 'Anne, they *are* only commercials. It's not like you're starring in a De Mille epic. Besides, I know your boss – I'll put in a good word for you.' She winked at Kevin. 'We'll just finish off the new bottle . . . please? But first, let's go fix our faces.'

Anne sighed and trailed along to the powder room. The attendant gushed over Neely, and a few of the women who were patching their makeup fell on her with endless platitudes of praise. Neely managed a gracious modesty. Anne stood by patiently while the room slowly emptied out. Finally Neely sat down in front of a mirror and started to comb her hair.

'Listen, Anne, get Kevin off my back. He's very nice and all that, but he's like a broken record. Tell him once and for all I'm not gonna do a television show!'

'You can't blame him for trying,' Anne said.

'Well, enough's enough already. Besides—'

The door opened and Helen Lawson swept in. For one tense moment she stared coldly at Anne; then, with a sudden change of

275

heart, she nodded and said, 'Good to see you, Anne. I hear you've become a big television star.'

Anne managed a smile and tried to think of an answer. Helen spared her the problem. She sat down beside Neely and patted her heartily on the back. 'You were great out there tonight, girl. Wish I had some Cole Porter or Irving Berlin in that turkey I did tonight. I heard you were out front – why didn't you come back to say hello?'

'Ah . . . we were . . . ah . . . rushing to get here. You know how hard it is to hold a reservation,' Neely stammered.

'C'mon, don't give me that shit,' Helen said. 'But what the hell, no one likes to come back after a flop. Why I ever let myself be talked into doing this dog . . . But that's the story of my life. I was trying to give two unknown composers a chance.'

Neely's grin was friendly. 'Someone has to give them a chance. And if you can't put them across, nobody can.'

'I always take a chance – that's how someone like you gets born. I took a chance and unloaded a used-up nightclub singer to give a young kid a break. But no one ever thanks me – you included, sweetheart.'

Neely's smile faded. 'It wasn't your show that got me to Hollywood, Helen. It was my nightclub appearance.'

'And how'd you get that? By using me as a springboard.'

'All right – thanks, Helen. As I recall I used to thank you every night – but thanks again. I'm grateful. C'mon, Anne.'

'Don't be so lah-de-dah with me. I read the papers. You're a girl without a contract now. You've gone far for the little guttersnipe I gave a break to, but—'

Neely jumped up and stared at Helen with blazing eyes. The attendant moved closer, thrilled with this unscheduled break in the monotony.

'Come on, Neely,' Anne said quickly. 'Kevin is waiting.'

Neely brushed Anne's arm aside and glared at Helen. 'What did you call me!'

Helen stood up and faced her squarely. 'A guttersnipe. What else were you? A third-rate vaudeville tramp who never even went to school. I was surprised you could even read the lyrics. I only gave you that break because of me and Anne being so buddy-buddy.'

'Buddy-buddy! All you cared about was having her pimp for you,' Neely snapped.

'You're fulla shit! Anne and I were real good friends. We had a misunderstanding, but I was only being a friend, trying to keep her from getting involved with some limey bastard. I did it for her own good.' She turned to Anne. 'He did turn out to be a bastard, didn't he? I was right, wasn't I, Annie? I've always thought of you as one of my real friends.'

'Come on, Anne,' Neely said. 'This hearts-and-flowers bit is getting me here.' She patted her middle.

Helen ignored Neely and flashed the remnants of her old smile at Anne. 'I mean it, Anne. I never had a real friend. Everyone uses me and walks out. I always liked you, angel, and I'm so thrilled about your success. Now that I'm back in town, let's see each other and do a little hooting, like in the old days.'

'Anne, let's go!' Neely snapped.

'What's your rush?' Helen said innocently. 'Where've you got to go? From the way I hear it, you've got nothing but time on your hands.'

'After the reviews come out, you'll have a lot of free time too,' Neely answered.

Helen shrugged. 'My show may get lousy notices, but I'll have six new offers by noon tomorrow. What's on your agenda? More free concerts like tonight?'

'With that vibrato you got, in a little while you won't even be able to sing for free,' Neely replied. 'And I didn't hear any clamors for your services tonight.'

A slow flush spread up Helen's neck. When she answered her voice was shrill. 'What would a washed-up little hasbeen like you know about a vibrato? I've been on top for thirty years and I'll stay on top as long as I like. But you better keep singing for free, because that's all you'll get. Sure you'll get applause – any audience will applaud for something extra they get for nothing. But you're finished, washed up.

'Now, out of my way, has-been. You may have no place to go, but I got a guy out there waiting for me.'

'Guy!' Neely laughed derisively. 'You call *that* a guy? But maybe you better not keep him waiting at that, because from here on in all you'll be able to get is a fag to take you out – that is, if you pay the tab.'

'You should know all about that! You were married to one,' Helen snapped. 'Christ, you couldn't even hold your faggot. Not even with twins as a bargaining point. Hey – are they faggots too?' She started to leave, but Neely blocked her way.

'What did you say about my children?' Neely's voice was quivering.

'What's wrong with having little twin faggots? I hear they're very good to their mothers. Now out of my way . . .' She shoved past Neely and headed for the door.

'No you don't, you old bag!' Neely shouted. She leaped after Helen and grabbed her by the hair. Helen pulled away, but Neely held fast.

Suddenly Neely let out a gasp of amazement and stood staring at the thing in her hands. At the same time Helen's hands flew to her head in horror.

'A wig!' Neely yelled, holding the long black hair up for Anne to see. 'By God, her hair's as phony as she is!'

Helen reached out for her wig, but Neely jumped back.

'Give me back my hair, you little bitch,' Helen yelled. 'It cost me three hundred bucks!'

Neely put it on and danced around the room. 'Hey! Dig me as a brunette!'

Helen chased after her. 'Give me that, damn you!'

'It looked awful on you, Helen. I think you're much more interesting this way – crew-cut.'

Helen fumbled with her own short, ragged hair. 'I'm letting it grow in,' she said sullenly. 'Those lousy operators in Jamaica didn't know how to use dye, and when I got a permanent here, it all broke off. Now come on, Neely – give me that wig!'

In a sudden quick movement, Neely dashed to one of the enclosed toilets. Helen lunged after her, but Neely was too fast. She locked the door. In a moment they heard the toilet flush.

'Hey – what the hell are you doing?' Helen screamed. She turned to Anne. 'Jesus, she's throwing it in the can, I bet. I'll kill her, that little bitch!'

Helen shouted oaths while Anne and the attendant tried to reason with Neely. Their only answer was the ominous flushing and reflushing of the toilet. Helen pounded on the door. Inside, Neely giggled and flushed the toilet again. This time there was a strange gurgling, followed by the splash and gush of overflowing water. A pool rushed out from under the door and spread across the room.

278

The door opened and Neely tiptoed out gingerly, giggling hysterically. 'Oh . . . hell . . .' she gasped. 'The silly thing won't even go down the crapper!'

The attendant gingerly held up the sopping wet mass – it looked like a drowned animal.

'It's ruined!' Helen shrieked. 'Now what can I do?' She turned to Anne, her face streaking with tears. 'How can I go out there now?'

Anne stared at her, speechless, as the water spread across the room.

Then, in the silence, the attendant cleared her throat. 'Miss O'Hara – that wasn't nice. You've probably ruined the plumbing.'

Neely laughed. 'Send me the bill,' she said. 'It was worth every penny of it.' She picked up her purse and rummaged in it, pulling out a five-dollar bill. 'Here,' she said, 'you run the best john in town.' She turned to Anne. 'Come on, let's leave the old bald eagle to cry in peace. I hope your faggot doesn't get cold out there all alone,' she said sweetly to Helen.

Anne followed her through the door. Outside, she said, 'That wasn't fair, Neely.'

'Fair! I should have murdered her.'

'But it wasn't right. She actually *can't* come out of there until everyone goes.'

'Okay, so she's stuck for tonight. Tomorrow she can buy another wig. But tomorrow I'll still remember the things she said about my kids – and me. So I'm washed up – I can only sing for free, huh? Why, that miserable . . .' She strode over to the table. 'Kevin, you still want me to do that spectacular?'

Kevin's face broke into a big grin.

'All right. You got yourself a deal,' Neely said. She slumped into a chair and poured herself some champagne. 'Draw up the contracts and let my agents and lawyers okay them.'

'First thing tomorrow,' Kevin said happily.

As they talked about the show, the room began to empty out. Neely and Anne watched the anxious young man sitting at Helen's table, his eyes fastened on the door.

'I wonder what happened to Helen Lawson,' Kevin said as he paid the check. 'Probably got involved with some of her fans.'

'Yeah, maybe one of them scalped her,' Neely said innocently.

As they passed the powder room, Anne looked back across the

nearly empty room to Helen's table. The young dancer was hysterically searching his pockets, trying to forage enough bills to pay the
check the captain had presented. Kevin squeezed Anne's arm happily.
'You won't have a change of heart about this television deal, will you,
Neely?'

She tucked her arm gaily into Kevin's. 'Nope. I'll sing my heart out
for you and your little old product – but you're gonna pay me a lot of
money.'

'With pleasure,' Kevin answered. He looked at Anne with mute
gratitude. Women sure were funny – you could talk your head off and
get nowhere, but then let them spend ten minutes alone together in
a powder room and anything could happen . . .

Kevin flooded the newspapers with stories about the coming television spectacular. Neely was interviewed by several major magazines,
and television columnists heralded it as a major breakthrough. The
medium was coming of age. At last the viewers would be given genuine talent.

Kevin engaged a top choreographer, a top director and producer.
He stepped up production on new products to be introduced on the
show, and special sets were built for Anne to demonstrate the new
glamour line. The show was to be aired the beginning of November.
It promised to be the most spectacular event on television that season.

Neely moved into a hotel, installed a piano and spent the entire
month of October between her hotel suite and Nola Studios, rehearsing, dieting, working with the old discipline. She was determined to
show them in Hollywood and make Helen Lawson eat her words.
Washed up, was she? Unreliable, only able to sing for free? She'd like
to have seen Helen's face when she read the papers. Every paper stated
it was the largest single salary ever paid on television. They also
applauded Neely's courage for leaping into the new medium.

Neely had no fears. True, there were no retakes on a live show.
Well, all the better. She'd show Hollywood – she'd show them all. In
interviews she played the gurgling, nervous, eager young Neely. 'Sure
she was scared' . . . 'sure she was biting off a lot.' But secretly she knew
it was a cinch . . . a wrap-up. How could she miss – twelve standards,
six of them songs she had introduced; no untried material and not
even one scene to learn – you just read all the lead-ins off idiot cards.

Geez, if those Hollywood squares knew it was this easy, they'd be crowding the networks. But these opinions she kept to herself.

Neely took three Seconals the night before the great day. Dress rehearsal was scheduled for ten in the morning, and she arrived on time, well rested and eager to begin. The first hour was spent in testing her makeup. Then at eleven-thirty the actual rehearsal began. She did the opening dialogue smoothly, with youthful enthusiasm. Then she started her first song. She did three bars and the director called, 'Cut.' He walked out of the booth and down the aisle. 'Neely, you were singing to the wrong camera.'

'I don't get you,' she said nicely. She was supposed to sing. The camera was the cameraman's problem.

'Camera One was on you for the opening. But for your song you turn to Camera Two.'

'Which is Camera Two?'

'The one with the red light. You do the first half to it, then shift to Camera Three for the chorus, then wind up the last eight bars at Camera Two again.'

'Geez, I'd have to go through M.I.T. to figure that out. Why do we need all those cameras?'

'Honey, it sounds tougher than it actually is. Just remember the red light – that's the camera that's on you. You can't miss.'

She began again, carefully watching the cameras. It went all right, but she lost her place on the cue cards. Next time she focused on the cue cards and missed Camera Three.

'Don't worry about the cards,' the director pleaded. 'He'll follow you. You just follow the cameras.'

'But I'm used to the camera following me,' she wailed.

The director was patient. 'You'll get it. Now let's try again.'

There were two more rehearsals. The director's face took on the haggard look of quiet desperation. 'Neely, you walked past the chalk marks twice, out of camera range.'

'But I have to move when I sing.'

'Fine, baby. But let's mark it out so I can plan it with the cameras.'

'I *can't*. I move as I feel it, and each time I feel it differently.'

And so it went, hour after hour of grueling camera rehearsals. Neely's makeup began to run and her hair went limp. At five o'clock they had not done one complete runthrough.

The director called a dinner break. He came to Neely and carelessly threw his arm across her shoulder. 'At six we'll go through it straight from the top. Keep going even if you make a mistake. I've got to time it. Then I'll give you the mistakes and changes and cuts, and you'll have time to fix your makeup and take a breather before airtime.'

To Neely the final dress rehearsal was a nightmare. The red eye of the camera seemed to be leaping constantly off and on, and the cue cards with the lyrics seemed to blur under the hot lights. She would be into a song, feeling it deeply, hitting notes she knew were perfect . . . Her eyes would close, then fly open in panic. There was no wonderful Hollywood camera following her around, waiting to record every move; no one to splice and put all the best shots together. No, just those red-eyed monsters *she* had to follow, and those constantly shifting cardboards with the words. She lost them – she shouldn't have closed her eyes. Where were they? She hummed a lyric. He said to go on . . . God where were the cards? And which camera? On the left – yes, the red eye was on. Thank God, the song was over. Jesus, now what? What was the card saying? Oh yes, introduce Anne and the product. Oh thank God! Anne was talking now – she had a breather. Jesus! She should have rushed to the wings! There was the frantic maid, waving her arms – this was the three-minute change. Only three minutes to change her dress, and Anne was half through already . . .

'I can't!' she screamed. 'I can't do it! I can't really make a song come alive if I have to worry about chalk marks, cameras and quick changes. If I want to shut my eyes, I *have* to shut my eyes. I feel it that way. I can't do it – I can't!'

Kevin had been in the control room. He dashed down the aisle and joined the director. Together they tried to calm her.

'I won't go on. I'll make a fool of myself!' Neely's voice broke.

'Neely, you're a pro,' the director begged. 'Once that audience fills the theatre and you hear the applause, it will all come to you.'

'No,' she sobbed. 'I'd need a week of this camera rehearsal. I can't follow eight things at once and be good. I can't stand on certain chalk marks and watch for cameras and cue cards. I can't do it – I'll blow higher than a kite!'

'Neely.' Anne put her arm around her. 'Remember in Philadelphia,

282

how you jumped into a part in *Hit the Sky* with just a moment's notice?'

'I had nothing to lose,' Neely cried. 'I was a kid. I had no reputation at stake. I'm a star now – if I look bad or blow up I'm through.'

'You'll be fine,' the director kept repeating.

'No, *no*! I'm not doing the show!'

'Neely, you've got to,' Anne insisted. 'The time is paid for . . . the show goes on in an hour.'

'I can't do it,' she sobbed.

'Then you'll never work again,' the director suddenly snapped.

'Who wants to? If I never set foot near a television studio again, it's too soon for me!'

'I mean in any medium,' the director said coolly.

'Who says?'

'AFTRA. If you walk out on a show like this, it's breaking a contract. All the unions are affiliated in upholding the rules. AFTRA, SAG and Equity.'

'What would happen if I suddenly dropped dead?'

He smiled coldly. 'Unfortunately, I hardly think that's likely.'

'Couldn't you just announce that I developed a sudden case of laryngitis?' she pleaded.

The director sighed. 'Neely, the network doctor would insist on examining you. The network went co-op on all the ads – they've spent a fortune. Now look. You've got an hour – don't even think about the show. Go to your dressing room and relax.'

Neely went to her dressing room. She made a hurried phone call and contacted a bellboy at her hotel. He arrived ten minutes later. A twenty-dollar bill and a small bottle exchanged hands. Neely stared at the bottle. 'You little red dolls,' she said softly. 'Now for God's sake do your work. I'm relying on you. I can't even help you with the booze – they'd say I was drunk.' She quickly swallowed six. 'Come on, babies,' she cooed as she lay down. 'Come on . . . I haven't eaten anything. You little dolls can work fast on an empty stomach.'

In ten minutes she began to feel the familiar light-headed reaction. She let it seep through her. It wasn't enough. They'd be able to rouse her with black coffee. She staggered over to the sink and took two more. 'Come on, dollies, make Neely groggy so's she can be sick . . .' She heard the muffled sounds of the audience filing in, the musicians tuning up. She gulped down two more. Dimly she heard someone calling her name, but she was floating far away . . .

The network had to run a kinescope of a past show. They announced that due to technical difficulties the Neely O'Hara show would not be aired. Kevin did not bring charges against Neely, but the network did. Neely had to be a test case, they said. Too many big names had been scheduled for spectaculars in the new season, and if Neely got away with it there might be other disasters. She received a one-year suspension from all work – pictures, stage, nightclubs and television.

At first she didn't care. She went back to California and holed up at her pool. The newspapers and trade papers attacked her without mercy. They called her temperamental; they hinted that she had been drinking; they unanimously declared she was washed up.

Sometimes she spent day after day in bed, until her housekeeper would force her to the pool. Sometimes at midnight she'd leap into her car and head for a bar. There she'd stand, with a bandana around her hair and no makeup, unrecognized, lost in soft anonymity, sipping beer, happy to be with people. She didn't care; she had enough money; she could sit out the year. It would blow over, and then she'd get back into shape and maybe do a Broadway show. That would be fun. She'd show them. Meantime she could eat anything she wanted . . . and drink. There were always the wonderful red and yellow dolls – and now there were even some new blue-striped ones!

Anne was badly shaken by Neely's behavior. Her first instinct had been to follow her to the Coast. Neely was in no condition to be left alone. But her own television commitments could not be ignored . . . and there was her loyalty to Kevin, too. She felt a personal guilt about the Neely walkout, which had been very costly. He had been forced to pay for the time, the advertisements, the musicians and the overtime, with no high-rated program to show for it.

But as the weeks passed, her anxiety about Neely was submerged in the constant daily crisis of live television. New color tests were being done, and sometimes the hot lights were almost unbearable. Yet she never thought of quitting – there was nothing else she particularly wanted to do.

Sometimes items about Neely – blind or real – appeared in the columns. Everyone seemed convinced that Neely was going through some kind of deliberate self-destruction, yet it was impossible for Anne to reconcile the image of the nervous, tortured Neely with the bright-eyed child who had once lived below her on Fifty-second Street. *That* was the real Neely. This phantom that Hollywood had created would eventually disappear and the real Neely would return.

It seemed impossible that a place could really change people. More than a decade had passed, yet in some ways she felt no different than she had when she first arrived in New York. If she sat and analyzed herself she knew she would find New York was no longer a pulsating fairyland. Broadway was a Coney Island arcade and Forty-second Street was a tenderloin. Fifth Avenue no longer thrilled her. Even the giant tree at Rockefeller Center at Christmas was no longer a spectacle. An opening of a show or nightclub brought out the same stale faces.

But it was still a better world by far than the world of Lawrenceville. In Lawrenceville people hibernated and life passed them by. At least she was on the scene, where things were happening. Yet something was lacking. Sometimes she looked in the mirror very closely and tried to see herself objectively. Had she changed? She used makeup now – had she really gone to El Morocco in those early days with just a dab of powder and lipstick? Now she felt undressed without the subtle pancake, the eye shadow and mascara. And her clothes – she still insisted things be simple and muted in color, but name designers created the well-cut suits and she had long since discarded Jennifer's mink coat for one of her own, designed by New York's leading furrier.

But once, for a fleeting moment, the passage of time was wiped out by the expression in Allen Cooper's eyes. They met accidentally at the Colony. She was with Kevin. Allen introduced his wife, an attractive young girl who wore a large emerald-cut diamond, identical to the one Allen had given her. At the moment a crazy idea hit Anne – maybe he had a drawer full, in all sizes for the proper occasions.

She had often wondered what she'd do or how she'd feel if she ran into Allen. And like most long-anticipated meetings, the actual happening was uneventful and far from dramatic. Allen was losing his hair, but he still wore striped ties and he still traveled with Gino. Age had suddenly caught up with Gino. He had developed the palsied fragility that afflicted so many elderly people. He seemed to be shriveling away before her eyes.

She knew Allen had wanted to be indifferent and curt, but the old admiration welled in his eyes. 'Anne . . . you look marvelous.'

'You look well too, Allen.'

'We see you all the time on television, don't we, Gino?'

'Yeah, sure,' Gino answered.

There was a pause. God, was there nothing to say after ten years?

'Allie always points you out when you do those commercials.' This was Allen's wife.

'I'm glad to hear that you watch. Most people run to the refrigerator for beer while I'm on.'

'No, I always watch, even though I don't use the Gillian products. My beautician says—' She stopped suddenly, alerted by the pressure Allen put on her arm.

Kevin came to the rescue. 'I'm sure anyone so young and lovely doesn't need much help from cosmetics.'

The girl blushed with pleasure and giggled.

'What's with our table?' Gino complained shrilly. 'If we'da gone to Morocco instead of this fancy place we wouldn't be standing around like this.'

The captain motioned to Kevin that his table was ready. There were mumbled good-bys. Anne and Kevin walked away as Gino went into another tirade about the lousy service and why didn't they go to Morocco.

Anne felt sad. People parted, years passed, they met again – and the meeting proved no reunion, offered no warm memories, only the acid knowledge that time had passed and things weren't as bright or attractive as they had been. She was glad Lyon was in England. She'd hate to run into him like this, to find that his hair had thinned or that the girl he dated was too young, too insipid. It was better to keep a memory intact.

She wondered about Jennifer, too. Was Jennifer afraid to come back? At the last minute she had turned down Century's offer and remained in Europe. Was she afraid of Hollywood? How could she be? She was the biggest star in Europe today, and her pictures were equally popular in America. She looked magnificent on the screen. Anne was well aware of the tricks and wonders of lighting, and of course Jennifer was thirty-seven, even though she was ten years younger in all her publicity releases and in her American image as well. Perhaps she was smart remaining in Europe. If Neely was any example, Hollywood could be frightening.

JENNIFER

1957

Jennifer *was* scared of Hollywood – scared to death. Half a bottle of Seconals and a stomach pump had forced Claude to reconsider and not sign with Century the year before. But this year brought another fantastic offer, and this one was just too lucrative to pass up. A three-picture deal and one million dollars deposited tax free in a Swiss bank! Of course Claude would split it with her, but half a million clear! She couldn't turn that down. And at thirty-seven her looks were still intact – the right lights dissolved all the tiny lines. Claude would have the entire say on everything, and he would see about the silk on the camera and the soft lighting.

Of course, there were the candid photographs to contend with. There would be reporters at Idlewild in New York, and there would be an even bigger reception in Hollywood. Flash cameras couldn't be fooled, but Claude would think of something. Maybe she could stage a Garbo-like entrance – hide from the cameras.

Early one morning, a week after she had signed the contract, Claude arrived at her apartment.

'I just got the cable – the money is deposited.'

'Separately?' she asked.

'Yes. Here is your number – put it in a vault. I have my own.'

She stretched in bed happily. 'Isn't it wonderful? I can have a three-month vacation before I leave. Maybe I'll go to Capri, and then New York. I'll wear a black wig. I'll see all the shows with Anne

288

and really have some fun. God, it will be good to speak English again.'

Claude threw back the covers and yanked her out of bed. Then he flung open the windows and let the daylight in.

'Are you crazy?' she asked.

'Stand just as you are – at the window.'

She shivered. It was September, but the sun was weak and cold as it grudgingly forced its way through a clouded Paris sky.

He sighed. 'Yes, it must be done.'

'What must be done?'

'The face lift.'

'You *are* crazy!' She pulled away from him and threw on her robe.

He dragged her to the mirror. 'Here, look at yourself in the daylight. No! Don't hold your head up and smile – look at yourself in repose.'

'Claude . . . I'll always be in makeup. And I know my best angles. Who would ever get a chance to see me like this?'

'Hollywood! The makeup men, the studio hairdressers . . . word will travel fast.'

'But I'm still not exactly a hag. I look pretty good for thirty-seven.'

'But you don't look twenty-seven!'

She stared in the mirror. Well, there *was* a little slack under her jaw. Not much, really . . . if she held her head back and smiled, it disappeared. But in repose it was there.

A wattle, Claude called it. Yes, she saw what he meant – that indefinable slackness in the skin that tells the difference between the twenties and the thirties. No actual lines, but the taut, young look was gone. No one noticed these things in a café, or with flattering lighting . . . but they were there. Maybe he was right. But Jesus! Face-lifting at thirty-seven! She had always thought of waxen-faced old crows of sixty when she thought of face-lifting. She recalled the heavily mascaraed, white-faced monstrosities she had seen in New York, with someone always whispering, 'She's sixty-five. Had her face done, but it doesn't help.' No, it was too risky.

'Claude, don't let Hollywood panic you. I've been there. It's not as rough as you think. Everyone is scared of everyone else. I'll get by.'

'I don't want you to just get by!' he thundered. 'You are *the* sex goddess of Europe. All Hollywood is waiting to see how you measure up to *their* sex symbols – Monroe, Elizabeth Taylor – and those girls are young.'

'I'm not Liz Taylor or Marilyn Monroe. I'm Jennifer North. I'm *me!*'

'And *what* are *you?* A face and a pair of breasts! That's all you are . . . all you've ever been!'

'I haven't done a nude scene in my last seven pictures!'

'Because the image is planted. You could wear a burlap bag, but everyone knows what's under it. They know every inch of your body by heart, and they see it no matter what you wear. Don't ever get it into your head that you have anything else to offer.'

'Then the image exists in America, too. They've seen all my pictures.'

'Jennifer, don't you trust my judgment?' His manner changed and he tried a gentle smile. 'You do have something else. There are plenty of naked stars in Europe, but they cannot touch you. Because you have one extra ingredient. A sweetness, a youthful sweetness that no French girl seems to have. They can be piquant, mischievous, naive – but you have that American freshness. And that freshness can only be retained with youth. A young face. Despite the golden hair and the sexy breasts, there is something about your looks that conveys an impression of innocence, of girlishness . . . almost of purity. Now, we have no problems with your body. It's still marvelous – but you've got to drop ten pounds.'

'Oh no you don't! That's what happened to Neely. As it is, I take three or four sleeping pills every night to keep the circles away. You're not going to get me on the pep pills. I weigh one-eighteen and I'm five foot six – that's thin enough.'

'For nude scenes, yes. But not for the high fashions they will put you in. But you will not take pep pills. I have it all arranged. You will go to Switzerland for the sleep cure.'

'The sleep cure. That's for nervous breakdowns, isn't it?'

'Also good for weight. I've informed them you wish to lose ten pounds. They'll put you to sleep for eight days. You sleep . . . and you awake thin, rested and beautiful. After that, there will probably be more slack to your face. Then you will have the lift.'

Traveling through the hills of Lausanne, she thought of Maria and wondered about her. It all seemed such a lifetime ago, yet she remembered it with such clarity.

The clinic was beautiful. She entered under an assumed name, and only a handful of trusted people knew her true identity.

'You must not worry,' the head physician said. 'You will sleep. But we will awaken you for your meals, and at all times a nurse will be in constant attendance. You will eat without realizing it, you will be walked around the room and taken to the bathroom, but you will not be aware of any of this. However, this bit of exercise is necessary to keep the lungs from filling. A nurse will change your sleeping position every hour. And when you wake up, you will have lost your ten pounds.'

Jennifer smiled. 'But I'll also have lost a week of my life. Besides, I was under the impression the sleep cure was for emotional disturbances.'

'True. Of course, it cannot cure a deep-rooted disturbance, one that took years to form. For that we need psychiatric therapy and possibly even electric shock. But it is excellent for the situational depression. Let us give you an example. A married woman from Hollywood is here now. Her husband is a big director. One of their small children wandered into the swimming pool and was drowned. She is inconsolable. She could not face the days ahead. Her husband and friends were sympathetic, and she knows time will heal, but meanwhile she cannot go on. She feels she cannot live through the necessary months or years that will ease the memory. That is where the sleep cure helps. You see, the brain has little niches. Each niche is a thought or a memory. If we think of the same thing repeatedly, the niche grows deeper and the thought is ingrained. It is the way an actor learns his lines. But when the thought stops, the niche begins to fill in like a cut. And in time it is erased. The deep tragedy and love for the child is cut deeply in this woman's mind. Three weeks of the sleep cure will help the gash to heal over. When she awakens, she will be aware she has lost her child, but the hurt and inconsolable ache will be gone. The release that five years of time might give will have come in three weeks – saving her years of anguish.'

Jennifer grinned. 'Well, if I'm ever a fat, unhappy girl, I'll take the three-week job. Now I just want to lose ten pounds.'

He nodded. 'Eight days will do it.'

It was that simple. A smiling nurse brought her a glass of champagne, 'for the good sleep and happy thoughts.' She sipped it slowly.

Soon a young doctor appeared. He checked her pulse and blood pressure, then gently slid a hypodermic needle into her arm. She put the glass down. She had never experienced such a feeling. It began at the tip of her toes; it eased through her legs; it rushed through her hips . . . and then suddenly she floated off into space and she felt nothing more.

She must have slept through the night, she decided. The sun was shining when she opened her eyes. The nurse appeared with a breakfast tray. Jennifer smiled. 'They said I'd sleep through the meals, but I'm wide awake.'

'But you *did* sleep.' The nurse was grinning.

'How long?'

'Eight days.'

Jennifer sat up. 'You mean . . .'

The nurse nodded. 'Mademoiselle weighs twelve pounds less – one hundred and six.'

'Oh, how divine!' Jennifer exclaimed. 'God, what an invention!'

She returned to Paris and Claude was delighted. 'I have arranged the face-lifting,' he said. This time she did not argue. The drastic loss of weight had made her look haggard. Suddenly he said, 'Undress.'

She stared at him. 'Claude – that's been dead between us for years.'

'I have no desire to make love to you,' he said with irritation. 'I want to see if the loss of weight has hurt your body.'

She slid out of her clothes. 'Nothing's happened. Besides, what difference does it make? I'm not doing nude roles in America.'

He inspected her breasts clinically. 'I have arranged for you to take a series of hormone shots to maintain the firmness of your breasts. They will be given while you recuperate from the face lift.'

'And where does all this gloriousness take place?'

'It was not easy. But it is arranged. You go to the Clinique Plastique tomorrow, under an assumed name again.'

Claude had been right; it had not been easy. The operation itself had been uncomfortable, but it was the recuperative period that had taken the most out of her. Six weeks of isolation; staring at her swollen, mottled face, her bloodshot eyes, the hideous black stitches behind her ears; wondering if she would ever return to normal, terrified that she had made a mistake. But gradually, as time passed, the stitches were removed and the scars went from a bright, angry red to a light pink that she knew would eventually fade.

The swelling went down, and her spirits soared. Claude had been right all around; it was an unqualified success. She doubted if she had looked this perfect at twenty. She didn't look twenty, but she looked magnificent. Not a line in her face, and the tautness of the skin gave it a flawless appearance. She was sure she could pass Hollywood's harshest scrutiny.

She arrived at Idlewild on a bright day in December. When the cameras flashed and the reporters crowded in, she was suddenly grateful to Claude. She noticed several women reporters eyeing her closely, and she smiled with easy confidence. She was not afraid of the strong sunlight or the close glances. She knew she looked perfect. And the newspapers noticed it, too. Every one of them commented that she was even more beautiful than her screen image.

She insisted on remaining in New York for a week while she renewed acquaintances with Anne. They spent long hours catching up on Jennifer's adventures and many transitory romances. At last Anne told of her relationship with Kevin.

Jennifer sighed. 'I don't care how nice you say he is, he's a louse for not marrying you.'

'It doesn't matter,' Anne insisted. 'I'm not *really* in love with him. It's better this way.'

'Still looking for the stars-in-your-eyes kind of love?' Jennifer asked. 'You know, Anne, I guess a woman can either love or be loved, but it's almost impossible to have both.'

'Why?'

'I don't know, but it just doesn't seem to work out that way. You should know. Allen loved you, even wanted to marry you. And Kevin loves you. Yet you could walk away from either of them and feel nothing. *You* loved Lyon . . . and he was able to walk away from you.'

'No, *I* was stupid about that. If you knew how many nights . . . Even now, I still lie awake and relive it in my mind. How I *should* have handled it. How it *could* have worked.'

'By going back to Lawrenceville?'

'Yes. It wouldn't have been forever. His career as an author would have been the same. His first book would have gotten great reviews and made no money. Then he would have written that terrible commercial one – that was a gesture of defiance – then a few more, and finally movie scenarios. That's what he's doing in London. The same thing would have happened here. Only he'd be in New York writing for television, or out in Hollywood. Anyway, we'd be together. I just panicked. If only I had thought it out . . .'

'But a man who could walk away like that . . . Anne, he never really cared.'

Anne set her jaw firmly. 'He loved me. I *know* he did.'

'Sure, just like Allen thought you loved him. Like Kevin thinks you love him. He's so sure of you he doesn't even feel he has to marry you. Anne, if you really feel Kevin loves you, make him marry you. It's a pretty rare thing to be loved. It's never happened to me.'

'Oh, come on now, Jen. All of Europe loves you . . . and now you've got America as well.'

'They love my face and body. Not *me*! There's such a difference, Anne.' Then she shrugged. 'Maybe I'm just not very lovable.'

'I love you, Jen – really.'

Jennifer smiled. 'I know you do. It's a pity we're not queer – we'd make a marvelous team.'

Anne laughed. 'If we were, maybe it wouldn't work out this way. As you said, one loves and the other is loved. Or maybe it's different with Lesbians.'

Jennifer had a far-off look. 'No . . . even with queers, one loves and the other is loved.' She studied her face in the mirror. 'Well, you've got Kevin – and I've got Hollywood.'

'But you *are* enjoying your success, aren't you?' Anne asked.

Jennifer shrugged. 'At times. But I hate the work. I never was a career girl. I'm no dedicated actress. And I always had my share of the limelight, first with the Prince and then with Tony. And it all adds up to the same thing – I really didn't earn any of it – the Prince, Tony or my career. My face and body got it for me. Oh, God, I'd give my life for someone who would just love *me* . . .'

'If that's what you really want, Jen, you'll find it. I'm sure you will.'

Jennifer reached out and grabbed Anne's hand. 'Pray for it, Anne. I want to get out of this rat race. I want a man to love me . . . I want a child. It's not too late. Pray that I meet the right guy so I can tell Claude and everyone else to go drop dead!'

294

ANNE

Kevin Gillmore suffered a serious heart attack in the spring of 1960. For two weeks he lay gray and lifeless in an oxygen tent. The moment he was strong enough to speak, he reached for Anne's hand. 'Anne, am I going to make it?'

He seemed reassured when she squeezed his hand and nodded.

'Promise me one thing,' he whispered. 'If I do make it, will you marry me?'

She forced a noncommittal smile. 'Don't talk, Kevin. Just rest and get well.'

Tears came to his eyes. 'Please, Anne. I'm afraid. I can't face it alone. Please . . . I'll make it if I know that you'll marry me . . . that you'll always be there.'

'Kevin, you must rest. You're going to be fine.'

'It's too late for those children you wanted, Anne, but I'll give you everything else. I'll sell the business . . . we'll travel. Just say you'll marry me and never leave me.'

She smiled. 'All right, Kevin. I promise.' She kept her vigil at his bedside for six long weeks. As he grew stronger, he talked incessantly about their marriage, about the things they would do, and how he would make everything up to her. She grew resigned. Why not marry Kevin? What was she waiting for? She was thirty-five – Good Lord, thirty-five! How did it happen? You felt the same inside, but suddenly you were thirty-five and time was racing on. One year blended into another. So much had happened – and yet so little. She had blown her chance for the great love and for children. But there were other compensations. She was independently wealthy. Her original investments had more than doubled, and Henry had put her in several other successful ventures. Each year Kevin had given her several hundred shares of stock in the company – and the stock was due to split two for one any day. No, money would never be a problem. If she never worked again – and without Kevin's help – she was a rich woman.

But then, money had never been a problem. Even in the beginning there had been the five thousand in the bank. She had never been like Jennifer . . . Jen, who *had* to send her mother money; Jen, who *had* to make it. She was very proud of Jennifer's whirlwind success in Hollywood. She had made five pictures – five beautiful, technicolor pictures, with someone singing for Jennifer. Someone else danced in the long shots, but it was always Jennifer in the closeups. And she was miraculously beautiful. Her name had been coupled with a director and a leading man, and her latest conquest was a producer. But from her letters and phone calls, Anne knew Jennifer was still searching.

Toward the end of his stay in the hospital, Kevin began planning their honeymoon. 'You're sure you won't mind giving up your work?' he asked anxiously.

'My work?' she laughed. 'Kevin you handed me the whole thing on a silver platter.'

'No, Anne. I started you modeling, but you did the rest. You're good. You're an asset to the company.'

'Well, you can take the asset away from the company any time you like. I think both will survive.'

His hand clutched hers. 'I love you, Anne. I'll sell the company . . .'

She nodded. 'Now you get some rest. Plan our honeymoon while I'm gone.'

He clung to her hand. 'Must you go?'

She made her voice light. 'I'm still working for you, and there's a show tonight.'

'Anne . . . You know – there won't be any sex. Not for a long while, maybe never again.'

'Don't worry about it, Kevin.'

He started to sob. 'I'll lose you, I know I will!'

In spite of herself, she felt revulsion. The terrible strength of illness – it robbed a man of his dignity. She patted him gently. 'I'll be with you, Kevin. I promise.'

Kevin was back at his desk in August, strong, vital, with his old 'take-charge' power. The fear-ridden days in the oxygen tent were a dim memory. Sure, he had had a little coronary, but it hadn't gotten him down. He was better than ever. The rest had done him good. And he was going to marry Anne. Of course, being alone frightened him at times. If anything should happen at night . . .

'I want to make the best possible deal for the company,' he told Anne. 'I'm holding out for twelve million and an honorary chairmanship of the board. As long as the company bears my name, I want to be sure it keeps its class. I figure I can wind up everything by the first of the year, February at the latest. Is that okay? But if you like we can get married right now . . .'

She smiled. 'We've waited this long, let's do one thing right. I want to get married and go on a honeymoon.'

'February then! That will be the deadline I set for myself. Then marriage and a long honeymoon trip. We'll go around the world.'

'Really around the world? I mean, not just London, Paris and Rome? But the Orient, India, Greece, Spain?'

'The works.' He looked at her closely. 'I noticed you threw in Spain. Okay, we'll search Spain from top to bottom. We'll find Neely – I promise you we will.'

She worried about Neely constantly. After the television shambles, Neely had sat out her year of suspension. Then, with another fanfare of publicity, she had been signed to star in a big technicolor picture at a major studio. She was thin, radiant and exuberant, the center of attention. It was a major event – Neely O'Hara's comeback. But after a few weeks of filming, the usual uneasy rumors began to drift into print. Neely was holding up production . . . Neely had a bad back . . . Neely had laryngitis. Then came the bombshell – the picture was to be scrapped, at a loss of half a million! Once again Neely was branded unreliable and uncooperative. There were even rumors that she had lost her voice.

Ten days later, with no warning, she had arrived at Anne's apartment. She had no money, but her lawyers were arranging for the sale of her house – then she'd have a bundle. Anne let her move in, though she dreaded the disrupting influence. Television had forced her into a highly organized way of life. There were certain hours set aside to study scripts, set times for fittings, time put aside for complete rest and a facial before facing the cameras.

Neely's invasion was cyclonic from the start. The phone kept ringing; newspapermen came in a steady stream, demanding interviews; fans were found prowling around the building. But Anne knew Neely needed her, and it would only be for a few weeks.

But the weeks stretched into months. The apartment was always in a shambles. Three maids quit. Neely broke a lamp and an end table lurching around in a semiconscious state. Anne kept emptying bottles of pills down the drain, but Neely seemed to have an endless source and endless hiding places. When she wasn't in a drugged sleep she was underfoot, bleary-eyed, carrying around a bottle of Scotch and screaming curses at Hollywood.

It was Kevin who insisted she move. He put her in a hotel suite. She could stay there as long as she wished, as his guest.

When her money for the sale of the house came through, Neely mysteriously checked out of the hotel. A few weeks later she turned up in a Greenwich Village police station, arrested on a charge of disturbing the peace, based on complaints about the loud parties she gave. She had been almost unrecognizable in the newspaper pictures – fat, blotchy, red-eyed, her hair falling into her eyes.

Anne had rushed to her. Neely was holed up in a fashionable building on lower Fifth Avenue, but the apartment looked like a tenement. It was littered with empty whiskey bottles, and most of the furniture was broken, stained or burned from careless cigarettes. The rumpled line on the bed looked as if it hadn't been changed since Neely had taken occupancy.

'Lemme come and live with you, Anne,' she mumbled. 'I got lotsa money. I just can't stand being alone. That's why I always give parties. And look what those slobs have done – this place was gorgeous when I sublet it.' She looked around ruefully. 'The lady I got it from is suing me for damages, so I gotta get outta here . . .'

'Neely, you've got to pull yourself together. I spoke to your agents. You are still a big name – you could do a Broadway show.'

'Nope. I'm unreliable. They're afraid of me.'

'Not if you straightened out – if you did a show and proved you *are* reliable.'

'I can't sing, Anne. I lost it.'

'No one could sing living like this. And you shouldn't smoke, Neely. You smoke more than I do. Look, why not check into a hospital for a few days—'

'No! That's what Dr. Gold said. He's my new headshrinker. Wants me to go to Connecticut to some fancy funny farm. Costs a thousand a month. But I'm not a nut – I'm just unhappy.'

'I agree. I meant a regular hospital – like Mt. Sinai or Doctors. Let them get you off pills, regulate your life—'

'No. Lemme move in with you. I'll be good. No pills. I swear.'

Anne had heard this oath before, but she promised to think about it. When she left she called Neely's doctor. He was deeply concerned. He agreed a few weeks in a hospital might help, but it wasn't the solution. Neely needed drastic psychiatric help.

That night Neely disappeared. Perhaps she feared commitment. No one knew. She had over a hundred thousand dollars, but the way she was spending it even this sum couldn't last long. She turned up in London, and the British press gave her a front-page reception and an enthusiastic welcome. She attended parties and basked in acclaim. She was booked into the Palladium, but at the last minute cancelled out. Then, suddenly, there were stories of her exploits in Spain. She seemed to have settled there. She made a picture – the advance publicity was excellent, but it was never released – and after a time she gradually disappeared from the news. Anne's letters were returned stamped 'address unknown' – Neely seemed to have vanished.

JENNIFER

Jennifer arrived in New York late in November, without publicity. Her call came as a complete surprise to Anne.

'I've got to see you,' she said eagerly. 'I'm at the Sherry.'

'I'll come right over. Is anything wrong?'

'No, everything's perfect – divine! Anne, I read that Kevin was selling the company. When is the marriage date?'

'We're trying for February fifteenth.'

'Good. Maybe we can have a double celebration.'

'Oh sure, we'll— *What?* Jen, what did you say?'

'Come on over. I'm talking on a hotel wire, remember?'

Jennifer was waiting impatiently when Anne arrived. 'I've got sandwiches and Cokes all set up. We can have a real old-fashioned gab session. Have you got time?'

'The whole afternoon. Jen, who is he? Tell me!'

Jennifer's eyes were shining. 'Oh, Anne, I'm so happy! I don't even care that I'm going to be forty next Friday. I still get the curse, so I can still have babies, and . . . well, being forty doesn't matter now.'

Forty! The word hit Anne with a sudden jolt. Jennifer forty! She looked marvelous. She recalled how she had thought Helen Lawson old at forty, and her own mother – dried out at forty-two. But Jennifer still had the incredible figure and the firm skin. She looked twenty-five.

'Remember when I attended the big Republican rally in Washington – right before the convention?' Jennifer asked.

Anne laughed. 'Remember it! Kevin swears you're responsible for the Democrats getting in.'

Jennifer grinned. 'Well, it was a studio publicity thing. I was willing to do anything for them after they got me my release from Claude. It cost them plenty, but they did it to make me happy.' She shuddered. 'I'd had it with his dictating to me. I was nothing but a saleable piece of flesh to him. Not that the studio doesn't regard me the same way, but at least they're more delicate about it. They even pretend I have talent.' She laughed outright.

'Now, Jen – you were excellent in your last picture.'

'I thought I wasn't too bad. It was my first serious role. But the picture's dying everywhere.'

'That doesn't mean a thing. The biggest stars come up with a loser now and then. You were listed number three at the box office in last month's polls.'

Jennifer shrugged. 'Listen, if I hadn't met *him*, I'd be in a state of shock. The studio is hysterical about the picture laying an egg. They're rushing to get top writers for my new picture . . . the top director . . .' She shrugged. 'But I couldn't care less. This morning I found two new lines under my eyes and even *that* didn't bother me.'

'Who *is* he?' Anne demanded.

Jennifer pushed away her untouched sandwich and sipped at her Coke. 'Well, you remember the shindig in Washington? He was there. We met at all the cocktail parties. He was always nice, but he didn't fall all over me like everyone else did. He was remote, polite, but . . .'

Anne was exasperated. 'Jen, *who*?'

Jennifer's eyes narrowed. 'Winston Adams.' She waited for Anne's reaction.

Anne almost exploded. 'You mean the *senator*?'

Jennifer nodded.

'*You* . . . and Winston Adams!'

Jennifer leaped up and spun around the room. 'Yes! Winston Adams. Senior senator, Social Register, millionaire – comes from generations of millionaires. But Anne, if he didn't have a dime, I wouldn't care. I love him.'

Anne sat back. Winston Adams! He was about fifty – attractive, brilliant and immensely popular. 'But Jen, I heard he was the Republicans' big white hope, that they're grooming him for—'

Jennifer nodded. 'They are. And he's willing to give it all up for me.'

'How did it happen?'

Jennifer's eyes grew soft. 'Well, like I said, we met. I met dozens of senators and had my picture taken with all of them – you'd be surprised how obliging some of those senators can be. They're bigger hams than actors. Except Winston Adams – he refused to be photographed with me.'

'Good for him!' Anne said. 'That's one way of attracting your attention.'

Jennifer shook her head. 'He meant it. On the day before I left, when all the hoopla was over, he phoned me. He said he wanted to talk to me – asked me to dinner. I went to his apartment that night. I thought maybe it was a big party, but it was just us.'

'He must be a democrat at heart,' Anne said, smiling.

'No, nothing happened. I mean, no sex – he didn't even try. He had a servant who was there all the time – not hovering over us, but you knew he was there. He explained that he hadn't meant to be rude in refusing to pose, but that he just didn't go for that kind of thing. Then we talked. He asked me a lot of questions, and he actually listened to me. We talked about Paris. He went to the Sorbonne when he was young, and he wanted to know how Paris had changed since the war.'

'Why have you kept it such a secret?' Anne demanded. 'He's not married.'

Jennifer grinned happily. 'It's not going to be a secret any longer. Last week marked two years since the death of his wife. He felt it wouldn't have looked proper until now.'

'Oh, that's right. They *were* very devoted.'

'Only on the outside. It was one of those arranged marriages, like you would have had if you had stayed in Lawrenceville. Both from good snooty families with money. Oh, he thought he loved her at the time. But she was the frigid type – hated sex. But that's not the important thing to him with me,' she said quickly. 'He went with me for two months without even trying. We'd sneak and meet in out-of-the-way places – Kansas City, Chicago . . . I'd wear a black wig. Then he came to California for a week – and we did it! Anne, he's divine. He's so gentle. He loves me, but for *me*! He was stunned when he saw

302

my boobs – he had always thought they were padded! He had never even seen any of my foreign films. Anne, he's the first man who ever fell for me, not just my body. And he was so *shy*. At first he was even afraid to touch my boobs. But I've taught him, and now – wow!'

'He's discovered sex,' Anne said with a smile.

'Discovered it – he acts like he *invented* it. But don't you see, I don't mind it this way, because he was originally attracted to me without it. And Anne, he wants children. His wife was the flat-chested, horsey type from Maryland, and she never had any.'

'But Jen, he's not really young – and what makes you so sure you'll conceive just like that?'

'Well, I've had seven abortions. My insides are ready, willing and able all the time. And when I told Win I wanted to get out of pictures and have children he was so happy he cried. He actually *cried*, Anne. He felt life had passed him up on all the things he really wanted – a girl he could love, children. That's why he buried himself in his work. He doesn't give a damn if I louse up his career. He says the Republicans won't get a President in office for at least eight years, and they can't fire him from being a senator just because he marries a movie star. He just wants what I want – a home and kids.'

'Does Winston know your real age?'

Jennifer nodded happily. 'He was delighted. Of course, I didn't tell him about the little tucks behind my ears. I mean, let's not scare the man. He's liable to think I'm something out of Shangri-La. But he was glad I wasn't in my twenties. He thought I'd think he was too old. And once when I visited him on his farm, I sat around all weekend in pigtails and no makeup and he said I was gorgeous. Oh, Anne – it's all so wonderful. I'm going back to the Coast next week to drop the bomb. I'll finish the next picture – they've already shot the exteriors and fitted the costumes – but that's it! Let them scream. So I'll never work again, who cares? I'm through with the whole scene.'

'When will you get married?'

'Well, starting tonight we're going out publicly. We're going to the theatre, then to a supper party at "21" with Senator Belson and his wife. We'll probably make all the papers tomorrow, and Win will shyly admit we're engaged.'

Anne smiled. 'I'll probably see you tonight. We're going to "21" too. It's a late dinner, so we'll probably be there when you arrive. This

303

will be one of those long dreary ones, with some of the people who are buying Kevin's company.'

Jennifer impulsively pressed Anne's hand. 'Oh, girl friend, isn't it wonderful! We've both wound up at the top, with success, security and a man we love and respect.'

Anne smiled, but she felt the familiar weight descending.

When she saw them at "21" that night, Jennifer was glowing, and she had to admit that Senator Winston Adams was an imposing-looking man. He was tall, with clipped steel-gray hair and a flat stomach that suggested daily workouts at the athletic club. Jennifer stopped at their table. Introductions were exchanged, and the Senator went out of his way to be gracious. 'I feel as if I know you,' he said to Anne. 'I've seen you so often on television – and of course, Jennifer talks about you constantly.'

She watched Jennifer all evening. Jennifer's eyes never left the Senator's face. They were adoring, the eyes of a girl genuinely in love. Anne envied her. She looked at Kevin. Thank God he had recovered. He was so good and kind. Oh, God, why couldn't she feel *anything* for him? If she had, she would have been married to him ages ago. Look how she had pestered Lyon, even offered to support him. But with Lyon there was more to it than just sex. She had wanted to be close to him every second, to crawl inside his thoughts . . . Oh, God, what am I doing, she thought. There is no Lyon. Like Henry says, I'm in love with an image . . .

Jennifer was on all the front pages the following day. And Senator Winston Adams acknowledged they would marry early in 1961. In a flurry of ecstasy, excitement and headlines, she returned to the Coast to make her final picture.

1961

Jennifer returned to New York the first week in January. Senator Adams was detained in Washington for a few days, and Anne went with her as she bought her trousseau.

'Everything must be different,' she insisted. 'Striking, but – you know – subdued. You've got to help me, Anne.'

They were in the fitting room at Bergdorf's when Jennifer suddenly leaned against the wall. 'Anne . . . have you an aspirin?'

She was ashen and the pupils of her eyes were dilated. The fitter rushed for the aspirin. Jennifer sat down. 'Stop looking so terrified, Anne.' She managed a smile. 'It's the curse. It came early, from all the excitement, I guess. I get stabbing pains.'

Anne relaxed. 'You scared me to death.'

Jennifer lit a cigarette. 'It's passed now. But that pain – it was a real bonecrusher. I guess that's what labor feels like. If this is a sample, I'm going to find a nice painless doctor when I have my babies.'

The fitter returned with the aspirin and the head saleslady came rushing in, visibly concerned.

'I go through it too,' the woman said. 'I crawl up walls. Thank God it only comes once a month.'

'You're lucky,' Jennifer said. 'Lately I've been getting it every two or three weeks.'

The salesgirl shook her head. 'It's better than my girl friend. She's beginning to go through the change. She skips whole months and worries herself sick.'

Jennifer selected three dresses. The salesgirl thanked her, got her autograph for her niece and wished her luck.

Later, when they were sitting at the Palm Court having a drink, Anne said casually, 'By the way, Jen, when was the last time you had a checkup?'

Jennifer was thoughtful. 'Let's see, the last abortion was in Sweden – it's legal there – that was four years ago. The doctor said I was sound as a rock.'

'Well, it wouldn't hurt you to check. My doctor is excellent.'

Jennifer nodded. 'Maybe I will.'

Dr. Galens was calm and easy as he made out her card. The internal examination was over; she was dressed and seated across the desk from him. 'How long has this been going on?' he asked.

'A few months. I wouldn't even have thought about it, but Anne's been on my neck. And then, when the curse continued – it's been ten days. I'm getting married next week, so I wanted to be sure everything was in order. After all, I intend to start having babies right away.'

He nodded. 'Is the Senator in town now?'

'No, he's in Washington. He'll be here next week.'

'Well, then suppose you check into the hospital tonight.'

'Tonight?' Jennifer crushed out her cigarette. 'Is anything wrong?'

'Absolutely nothing. If you weren't planning on getting married next week, I'd say let's wait and watch your next period. You have polyps in your uterus. It's very common. You go in for tonight, have a scraping tomorrow and leave the hospital the following day. You will stain for a few days, but if you go in now you'll be fine for your wedding day.'

Alarmed, Anne checked with Dr. Galens. He was hiding nothing from Jennifer. It was a simple 'D and C.' She helped Jennifer pack a bag and went along to the hospital with her.

Anne sat in the empty hospital room after Jennifer was taken up. She was glad it was nothing serious – Jennifer wanted a baby so much. And she deserved one. Funny . . . as close as they were, Jen had never explained why she had gotten rid of Tony's baby.

Dr. Galens was down in an hour. Anne sensed instantly that something was wrong.

'She's sleeping off the anesthesia,' he said.

'What is it?' Anne demanded. 'I can tell – something's wrong. It wasn't just polyps.'

'It *was* just polyps – exactly as I thought. There's nothing wrong with her insides,' he said. 'But while the anesthetist was checking on her heartbeat, he found a lump in her breast the size of a walnut. She must have known about it.'

Anne felt weak. 'But lots of lumps mean nothing. I mean – some are only cysts, aren't they!'

'I took the lump out,' he said quietly. 'It was a simple, tiny incision that wouldn't leave a noticeable scar. I had an immediate biopsy performed. Anne, it's malignant. She must go up tomorrow and have the breast removed.'

Anne went cold with horror. Oh, God, why Jennifer? And why now? She felt tears running down her face. 'You tell her,' she sobbed. 'I can't!'

Jennifer opened her eyes slowly, struggling to wake. It was over. She smiled at the hazy figure of the nurse beside her. 'Is everything all right?'

'Here's Doctor Galens now,' the nurse said brightly.

He touched her forehead gently. 'Coming out of it?'

'Mmmm . . . tell me, it was just as you thought – polyps – wasn't it?'

'Yes, everything is fine in that department. Jennifer, why didn't you tell me you had a lump in your breast?'

Instinctively her hand reached to her breast. She felt the small bandage.

'I took out the lump. How long have you had it?'

'Dunno . . .' She was getting drowsy again. ''Bout a year . . . maybe longer.'

'You go back to sleep. We'll talk about it later.'

Through the haze of anesthesia she felt the fear. She reached out and grabbed his arm. 'Talk about what later?'

'I'm afraid I'll have to bring you up here again tomorrow . . . to do a little more cutting.'

'Cutting? Like what?'

'We're going to have to perform a mastectomy. Dr. Richards will do it. He's one of our top breast surgeons.'

'What's a mast – what you said?'

'We have to remove your breast, Jennifer. That lump was malignant.'

She struggled to sit up. 'No! *Never!* Oh, God – *no!*' She fell back, her head spinning. Something was shot into her arm.

She fell asleep, fitfully, waking some time later and clutching at the nurse, pleading, 'It was a dream, wasn't it? I just dreamed it under gas, didn't I – what he said about my breast? Tell me . . .'

'Now, now . . . relax,' the nurse said softly.

She saw sympathy on the woman's face. It was no dream. Oh, God, it was true!

Anne had rushed to Kevin's office and sobbed out the story. He had listened in silence, then asked. 'Did Dr. Galens say the prognosis looked hopeful?'

Anne stared at him impatiently. 'Hopeful? Haven't you heard a word I've said?'

'I heard everything. She must lose her breast. It's dreadful, but it's not the end of the world. Anne, do you know how many women live long and happy lives after successful breast surgery? The point is to catch it in time.'

She looked at him gratefully. That was Kevin. Always taking hold, finding the hopeful side of everything. He got Dr. Galens on the phone. The doctor said he had every reason to believe the prognosis would be good. Dr. Richards had agreed. It was a small tumor, and the survival rate in breast surgery was high. If there was no metastasis, the prognosis would be excellent – but that could not be determined until the breast was removed and the lymph glands examined.

Somewhat reassured and calmed by Kevin's matter-of-fact reaction, Anne returned to the hospital. Jennifer was wide awake and oddly emotionless. She reached out and clutched Anne's hand. 'Dr. Galens called Win,' she whispered. 'He's flying here immediately.'

'Did he tell him?' Anne asked.

Jennifer shook her head. 'I told him not to say a word. I feel I should be the one to tell him.' She smiled weakly at the nurse. 'I'm all right. Would you leave me alone with my friend?'

'Don't let her drink any fluids for at least two hours,' the nurse said. 'Do you want a special nurse ordered for tonight?'

'No, the operation isn't until tomorrow and Dr. Galens ordered round-the-clock nurses starting then. I'm fine – please just leave us alone.'

She watched the nurse leave – then she jumped out of bed.

'What are you doing?' Anne asked, alarmed.

'I'm getting out of here – right now!'

Anne seized her arm. 'Jennifer, are you crazy?'

'Look, they're not going to disfigure me. How could Win want to come near me!'

'You said yourself he fell in love with *you*, not your breasts. Now don't be ridiculous.'

But Jennifer was at the closet, pulling out her clothes. 'I'm getting out of here. I'll take the chance. He got the cancer out – he's not taking off my breast!'

'Jennifer – it's the only way they can be sure. It might have spread to another part of the breast.'

'I don't care! It's bad enough that I won't be able to give Win any children, but I won't come to him deformed.'

'It could be suicide if you leave. Do you think that's fair to Win? To marry him and perhaps a year later put him through this? His last wife was sick. And what has this got to do with having a baby? You can still have children. Dr. Galens said you were fine inside.'

'But I mustn't get pregnant. Dr. Galens said so. A pregnancy might stir up some malignancy in the ovaries. There's some direct connection with the breast and ovaries. In fact, he said after the operation he may give me some X-ray treatment on my ovaries to insure sterility! What would I have to offer Win? No children, a maimed body . . .'

'You offer him *you*! That's all he really wants. Look – you said you were sick of living for your body. Well, prove it. And if you want children you can adopt them.'

Slowly Jennifer climbed back into bed.

Anne rushed on. 'No one need ever know – just you and Win. He'll love you and won't mind about the babies. I'm positive of that. And if you adopt a child it will be the same as your own. And the operation will be nothing. Honest, Jen, with the pain killers today – and with the wonderful falsies you can buy – Jen, it's not the end of the world.'

Jennifer stared at the ceiling. 'You know, it's funny. All my life, the word cancer meant death, terror, something so horrible I'd cringe. And now I have it. And the funny part is, I'm not the least bit frightened of the cancer itself – even if it turns out to be a death sentence. It's just what it'll do to my life with Win – not being able to give him children. And the disfigurement.'

'It won't show, Jen. Some people have automobile accidents, have their faces disfigured. Some women are naturally flat-chested, and they manage. You're the one who's been saying all along you didn't want to live for your body. Well, have some guts, some belief in yourself – start proving it. And start believing in Win.'

Jennifer smiled faintly. 'Okay, then I'd better get out of this hospital gown. And get me my makeup. I want to look my best when I tell him.' She sat up and combed her hair. As she slipped into the filmy nightgown, she stared down at the breast with the small bandage. 'Good-by, Sam,' she said. 'You don't know it, but you aren't going to be around much longer.'

Kevin joined Anne, and they were both there when Winston Adams arrived at seven. Anne had arranged the lights. Jennifer looked every inch the movie star, and she was almost cheerful. After a brief exchange of greetings, Kevin and Anne left.

The moment they had gone, Winston dashed to the bed and took

309

Jennifer in his arms. 'God, I almost died of fear. The doctor was so strange on the phone – said you needed an operation, hinted that the wedding might have to be postponed. And now, to see you looking so beautiful . . . What kind of an operation, darling?'

She looked at him closely. 'It's pretty drastic, Win. I'll be scarred and won't be able to have any children . . . and I'll be—'

'Hush . . . not a word.' He looked at her with adoration. 'Shall I tell you something? I was going along with the whole thing because of you. The children, I mean. At my age, I really didn't care one way or another. But I wanted to please you. You seemed to want it so much, so I pretended it was important to me. All I care about is *you* – can't you understand—'

She held him close. 'Oh, Win!' Tears of relief ran down her face.

He stroked her hair. 'You weren't afraid you'd lose me? Oh, my beautiful girl – you'll never lose me. Don't you realize I'm just beginning to live because of you?' He kissed her breasts through the filmy nightgown. 'You're all I want – not babies, *you* . . . you're the only woman who ever stirred anything in me. God, Jennifer, before I knew you I often wondered if something wasn't lacking in me. I blamed it on Eleanor. Poor Eleanor – it wasn't her fault. She roused nothing within me, and I probably left her cold, too. But with you . . . At first, when we met, I turned away from you – remember?'

She nodded and stroked his head as he lay against her breasts. He kissed the firm skin of her neck. 'But you changed me, made me realize I wasn't running from you, that I was just afraid, running from myself. And the moment you walked into my apartment, I knew. I knew somehow everything would be different. Jennifer, you taught me how to love. I could never give that up.' He caressed her breasts. 'These are my babies,' he said softly. 'These are the only children I want, to lay my face against their perfection each night . . .' He stopped as his finger stumbled against the small bandage. 'What's this? What have they done to one of my babies?'

Her smile was frozen. 'It's nothing . . . I had a small cyst . . .'

'There won't be a scar!' He was genuinely horrified.

'No, Winston – they drew it out with a needle. No scar.'

'That's all that matters. Let them take out your ovaries – I couldn't care less. That's not you – I've never met your ovaries. But as long as they never harm my babies . . .' He caressed her breasts again. 'Why did that doctor sound so grim when he phoned? Wouldn't tell me a thing – just told me to come quickly.'

'He – he knew I wanted children – and . . .'

'Why didn't he just say you needed a hysterectomy?' He shook his head. 'Those doctors – they're all crepe hangers. But I'm glad I came. Now I can go back thinking of holding you in my arms.' He held her close. 'I want to hold this memory. I won't be able to return until Friday.' Then he wrote down a number. 'Have Anne call me the moment the operation is over. If I'm not there, they'll reach me.'

He stopped at the door and looked at her, his eyes roving over her as though he had never really seen her before. 'I love *you*, Jennifer . . . only you – you believe that, don't you?'

She smiled. 'Yes, Win. I know . . .'

For a long while after he had gone, the smile remained frozen on her face.

Dr. Galens stopped in at midnight. 'We'll go up at eight in the morning,' he said cheerfully. 'And Jennifer – it's going to be all right.'

She smiled. 'You bet it will.'

It was three in the morning when she slipped out of bed. She opened her door quietly. The hospital corridor was dimly lit, but she saw the nurse near the elevator. She closed the door and dressed quietly. Thank God she had worn slacks and a trench coat – that had been to fool the photographers. She took a bandana and tied it over her hair. Then she tiptoed into the hall.

She crept against the wall, then hid herself in an arch that held the water cooler. The nurse on duty was sitting under a bright light, writing in her book. There was no way to get to the elevator without passing her. She had to stand there and pray that sometime during the night the nurse would leave her post. She also had to pray that no one discovered her hiding there.

The large clock ticked loudly on and on, while the nurse wrote endlessly in her book. Sweat ran down her neck. She felt waves of heat, as if she were near a furnace. Damn – it was a radiator. Suddenly a buzzer sounded. Oh, thank God! A patient was ringing. But the nurse continued to write. Was she deaf? The buzzer rang again, seeming more insistent this time. 'Go answer it!' Jennifer screamed inwardly. As if taking a cue, the buzzer rang again, and kept ringing.

The nurse rose lethargically, looked at the room number the arrow pointed to and headed down the hall.

Jennifer watched her disappear into a room, then ran swiftly to the elevator. No – it might take too long in coming and make too much noise. The stairway . . . She ran down eight flights of stairs. When she reached the lobby, she was out of breath. She looked around warily. No one paid any attention to her. The elevator man was smoking, talking to the cashier. She ran out into the street and walked a few blocks before hailing a cab. She reached her hotel at four in the morning.

When the nurse found her room empty the following morning she notified Dr. Galens, and he called Jennifer's hotel immediately. When her room failed to answer, he had the assistant manager open the door.

She was lying on the bed, in her most beautiful dress and full stage makeup, clutching an empty bottle of sleeping pills. There were two notes. Anne's read:

> *Anne – No embalmer could make me up as well as I do myself. Thank God for the dolls. Sorry I couldn't stick around for your wedding. I love you.*
>
> *Jen*

The note to Winston Adams said:

> *Dear Win – I had to leave – to save your babies. Thanks for making it all almost come true.*
>
> *Jennifer*

Senator Adams offered no explanation about the note. When cornered by the press he muttered a terse 'No comment.' Anne was just as tight-lipped. Dr. Galens refused to discuss the nature of Jennifer's ailment. She had gone through a minor operation the previous day, and there was nothing he could add.

The funeral was a nightmare. Frenzied mobs clustered outside the church, blocking traffic on Fifth Avenue. Mounted police were called to enforce order and to unsnarl crosstown traffic. Newspapers ran Jennifer's life story, Anne's picture made the front pages – and to complicate the frantic confusion, Jennifer's mother arrived, eagerly giving out the Cinderella story to every attentive reporter, sobbing on cue, and demanding an itemized account of all of Jennifer's clothes, furs and jewelry.

Anne might have been able to handle Jennifer's mother, but the appearance of Claude Chardot caused new complications. He produced a will, and while Henry Bellamy frantically searched for a later will, proclaimed himself the rightful heir. Then, to climax things, Neely arrived.

She was frantic that she had missed the funeral. She had been in Spain. She moved in with Anne and took over the spotlight. The newspaper stories eased away from Jennifer and played up Neely, who was painfully thin and glamorous. She was eager to work – but of course not until she got over this awful thing about Jennifer.

Somehow Anne managed to get through her appearances on television. She was taping the commercials now, and the new owners of the company were pleading with her to stay on at a large increase in salary. Her involvement in the publicity about Jennifer had increased her name value. Jennifer's tragedy had postponed her own wedding. April was now the new date.

It took three weeks for the publicity to ease off. Then, after two days of quiet, two days without any mention of Jennifer in the papers, violent new headlines erupted. Senator Winston Adams had resigned from office. He was suffering a mild breakdown and intended to travel for a year.

Jennifer's suicide was revived amidst new speculations. Dr. Galens was harassed. Yes, he had told the Senator the nature of Jennifer's illness – after all, as her fiancé he had a right to the facts. But the facts were for the Senator, not the press.

Anne taped several commercials and fled to Palm Beach with Kevin. It was one of the nicest weeks she had known in years. And she had also been able to avoid the hysteria of Neely's first television appearance. Neely's new agent had booked her on a top variety show as the guest star, at a fantastic fee. It was to be taped, so Neely felt secure.

Anne watched the show in Palm Beach. Neely was superb. Everything caught fire – her voice was perfect and she glowed, with eyes like large coals. Neely was no longer a child, but the impish quality was still there. The trembling lip, the nervous laugh, the girlish desire to please – all this came through. It seemed incredible, but she was better than ever. Once again there were shouts of 'genius' . . . 'a living legend.' It was a spectacular comeback. She signed for a picture in Hollywood.

Neely was back on top.

NEELY

Neely carelessly tossed things into a bag. 'I'll get new clothes out there,' she told Anne. 'Geez, I've left most of my stuff in Spain – now can I leave some with you?'

'I'll probably be married before you return, Neely, and I'm going around the world. I might sublet the apartment.'

'Well, I guess I'll take this along. I'm like a gypsy, all spread out. But it's good this happened. I was just about busted. Hey, what happened to Jennifer's money?'

'It will all go to her mother. That Paris will was a phony – Henry found some peculiarities in it. Claude will get fifty per cent on any reruns of her pictures made while she was still under contract to him. But the rest goes to her mother. That's mostly jewelry and furs. And they're reissuing her pictures. But there wasn't any real money.'

Neely shrugged. 'Listen, for a girl with no talent, she lived pretty good. Why do you think she did it? The Dutch act, I mean.'

'I've told you, Neely, I really don't know.'

'Well, I've figured it out. I don't think she had anything wrong with her like some of the rumors – some people think it was TB and I even heard a crazy rumor of incurable cancer. I think the real reason she took a powder was because she was losing her looks.'

'That's ridiculous! Jennifer was more beautiful than ever.'

'But her last picture was a bomb. Oh, this new one will make money because of the publicity, but I heard that wasn't too hot either. She was slipping, all right.'

'Neely, she was retiring. She was going to get married.'

'Yeah, I read all that jazz in Spain, how she suddenly found true love and all. But come on – the Senator was no Rock Hudson. Jen got pretty bored sitting around just being married to Tony, and he was young and gorgeous. Nope, I think she just couldn't face it. She was getting older, and her looks had to go soon, and she couldn't settle for just the Senator. So she took a powder. Now me, I never have to worry. I have talent, and fat or thin it doesn't matter. Look at Helen Lawson. She wasn't like me, of course it was mechanics with her, and now that her voice is gone she's going to the Coast to play a character role in some television series. But even with her voice gone she'll survive, because she had a talent.'

'Helen will survive,' Anne said slowly, 'because she has no real emotions. Any unhappiness she has is like a child's unhappiness. It can be erased with a new toy. But any voice – even yours, Neely – must be taken care of.'

'No, my voice comes from inside, from the way I feel things. And I've learned something – guys will leave you, your looks will go, your kids will grow up and everything you thought was great will go sour. All you can really count on is yourself and your talent.'

Three weeks later Neely returned. She was in a state of near collapse. 'Anne – my voice – on the third day of recording, it went! I can't sing!'

Anne tried to calm her. There were wonderful throat men . . . things like this happened to singers all the time.

'No, I'm through,' Neely wailed. 'I was examined by every doctor. I haven't even got a nodule. They say it's nerves, but it's not. God is punishing me for talking about Jen the way I did. And they had to scrap the picture. I'm through for good – they'll never touch me out there.'

'God doesn't work that way,' Anne said soothingly. 'If anyone is punishing you, you're doing it to yourself.'

'Oh sure, that's what my last headshrinker said – that I have a self-destructive urge and that I'm always punishing myself for some imaginary guilt. That's a lot of shit! I've never done anything wrong.'

Neely found a new psychiatrist. Dr. Massinger was highly recommended. Anne insisted that Neely live with her. She was positive that intensive therapy and a friend's support would pull Neely out of it. She had always snapped back before.

And Neely tried. She tried to be neat, and she didn't clutter the apartment. But she never slept. She went out with musicians, came home and sat in the living room until dawn, gulping Seconals and listening to her old records.

One morning, Anne awakened and found Neely huddled in the living room with tears running down her face. 'I'm through, Anne. I tried to sing with my records, and I can't make it.'

'But Dr. Massinger says it's nerves. Your voice will come back, Neely.'

'He said Hollywood gave me nerves. That's why I tried tonight, for the first time, here, alone, with no cameras and no Hollywood. Anne, my throat closed. I can't sing.'

'It's only been a few weeks, Neely – give it time.'

Neely stood up. 'Maybe.' She wandered into the bathroom and swallowed a few pills. 'Got some Scotch, Anne? The pills won't work without it.'

Anne handed her a bottle. It was going to be one of those days, with Neely bombed out on pills. It was Sunday, and she had planned to stay in. She had invited Kevin to dinner and she had meant to cook her one dish, a crabmeat casserole. But now Neely would sleep all day.

She phoned Kevin and arranged to spend the day at his place. Later they could go down to Lüchow's for dinner.

Neely heard the door close. She wasn't asleep, but it had been easier to pretend to sleep. Anne got so nervous when she drank and took pills – was always afraid she'd set herself on fire or something. Neely sat up and poured herself another stiff drink. She lit a cigarette. Christ, it was the last one. And you could be sure Anne had stashed all the rest away, just for safety. Well, she'd fall asleep soon.

She refilled her glass, then realized she was drinking too fast. Better sip it, with a few more pills. She reached under her pillow – she had hidden three red dolls there. She swallowed them and sipped the Scotch slowly. The pills were finally working – she felt lethargic. But she couldn't sleep. She refilled her glass. Damn, the bottle was nearly empty. And no cigarettes. Well, maybe a few more dolls. But she had taken so many – and that could be dangerous. Dr. Massinger had warned her that one day her tolerance might not be as great as usual. So what! If her talent was gone, why not? What was there to hang around for? She only had ten thousand dollars left. Geez, no – there *had* been ten thousand when she left the Coast, but she had sent a check for the twins' school – that was twelve hundred – and then twenty-five a day to the headshrinker for three weeks, and her trip in was a few hundred. And she had been writing checks for cash right and left! Maybe there was only five thousand left. How long could that last? And she couldn't stay with Anne forever – Anne was getting married next month. Geez, where was she gonna get money? The house was gone – no insurance . . . maybe she should just swallow the rest of the bottle. Ted would have to take care of the kids, but they didn't really care about her – when she saw them on the Coast it was just 'gimme, get me, buy me.'

There was no one who cared if she lived or died. No one cared about her. Maybe God did, if there was a God.

'Hey, God, are you really up there?' she said. 'Are you a big white-haired man with a beard? Do you understand me? Tell me, what went wrong? I never asked for too much. Geez, all I wanted was an apartment and a guy to love me. I tried – why did you fuck it up all the time? Why in hell did you give me a voice if you didn't want me to be great? Why did you take it away?' She poured the last of the Scotch and dropped the bottle on the floor. 'Hey, Jen – are you up there? I know you're not flying around with big wings or any of that jazz, but if there is another life and you are somewhere, then maybe you can hear me. Did you feel like this? Geez, I'd love to be with you . . . it's got to be better than this. What's here for me? Another day, another night to get through – go to Jilly's with guys who are nothing, who want to be seen with me while I sign the tabs.' She drained the glass.

'Geez, I'm thirty-two . . . that's not young any more. There's got to be some kind of a crazy heaven . . . not the jazz with harps and angels, but maybe like Earth without problems. Sure, it's got to be. After all, look at all the bright people who believe, like the President and Clare Booth Luce. Maybe I should become a Catholic or something. I guess I was born one, but I never got to go to church. But there has to be a heaven, Jen, because look at all those babies who got killed by Hitler.

And look at all the people born deaf and blind like Helen Keller. If there wasn't something after, then it wouldn't be fair. Why should a nice lady like Helen Keller never be able to see or hear and someone like you have everything if it wasn't gonna be evened up later on. Sure, there's a heaven. Look at my sister, living with that dope Charlie. Why should I be so successful and my sister be stuck in Astoria with nothing if there isn't a heaven later on? Sure. Hey, Jen, does it hurt before you die? Were you scared? Stay with me, Jen . . . I'm gonna get some more pills – I'm gonna join you.'

She ran into the bathroom. She had hidden the bottle behind the bath salts. Only six left! She swallowed them quickly. Six wouldn't do it, though. Maybe aspirin? Maybe a whole bottle of aspirin on top of the pills? Shit! Only five aspirin left. She swallowed them. No more Scotch, but there was some bourbon Anne kept in the bar for Kevin. That on top of the Scotch . . . She started out of the bathroom, lurched – and the glass she was carrying crashed to the tile floor. Oh, Geez . . . Anne got so mad when she broke things. She stopped to pick up the fragments. It was just a bar glass, but knowing Anne, it was probably crystal or something. She picked up a long sliver. Boy, this would do it – one slash across the wrist and she'd have a funeral like Jennifer. Would they fight over her too? Would Ted Casablanca demand she be buried out there, or would her half-assed sister come to life and demand to take over? Geez, imagine spending the rest of your life in some stinking cemetery in Astoria. Anne would fight for dignity, but she wanted the biggest funeral ever . . . even bigger than Jennifer's. Well, nothing could be bigger than that. Okay, *as* big as Jennifer's. But what if there was no heaven or God? Then she'd be dead, but she couldn't enjoy it. But – she held the sliver – if she were *almost* dead, there would be the same fuss. Like before in Hollywood . . . maybe they'd even plead with her to come back, and everyone would be sorry. Then, if she wasn't nervous, maybe she could sing, and everything would be wonderful again . . .

'Well, let's get some bourbon first,' she said, wobbling to the bar. She found the bottle and a glass and poured a stiff drink. Still holding the sliver of glass, she made her way back to the bedroom. She got into bed, took a deep swallow of the bourbon, then studied her wrist. If she cut the side – not the big vein, because that could really kill you, but just a little nick on the side . . . just enough to bleed. She dug the glass in deep – make it about one inch wide, but not over the main vein – good, the blood was coming. She lay back and watched it ooze. Geez, it was a lot of blood and really coming fast. Hey! Maybe she really cut something important! Geez, it wouldn't stop! She picked up the phone. Where in hell was Anne? The blood was coming faster, and now those goddam pills were working. It was the bourbon that was doing it . . .

She dialed Operator. An impersonal voice answered.

'I'm Neely O'Hara,' she mumbled. 'I'm dying . . .'

'What is your number?' the operator asked.

'My number?' She looked down at the phone. Everything was getting fuzzy. 'I don't know . . . it's unlisted . . . I can't remember. Please help. I cut my wrist . . . the blood . . .'

'Your address?'

'East Sixty-second Street near Park. Apartment belongs to Anne Welles . . .'

'The television star?' The operator was no longer impersonal.

'Sure . . . sure . . .' Neely let the receiver fall and her eyes began to close. She forced them open. God, she had ruined Anne's sheets. Her arm was dangling lifelessly over the side of the bed and the blood was spotting Anne's gold carpet. Geez, Anne would never let her stay here again. 'Please, operator, hurry . . .' All that blood, and it was still coming . . . but she wasn't going to die. You can't die if you can think this clearly . . . I'm sleepy . . . not dying . . . just sleepy . . . damn the dolls . . . of all times, *now* they have to work . . .

Neely opened her eyes and closed them quickly. It smelled like a hospital. That meant she was alive! She began to remember. The bells, the ambulance . . . She opened her eyes again. Anne was sitting across the room with Kevin. Anne sprang up. 'Oh, Neely, you're awake! Thank God!'

Neely smiled weakly. 'I'm sorry about the apartment.'

'Forget it.'

'Where am I?'

'At Park North Hospital.'

Neely wrinkled her nose. 'Why not Doctors? I hear that's divine.'

Kevin crossed the room. 'Listen, young lady, you're damned lucky to be here. Do you know where they were taking you when we arrived at the apartment? Bellevue!'

320

Neely struggled to sit up. 'Oh, Geez, that's all I'd need.'

'It's lucky we decided to come back. Anne wanted to look in on you. We found the ambulance and the police. They were taking you to Bellevue. It's a law – all attempted suicides have to go to Bellevue and *stay* there for a period of observation.'

'Geez!'

'It was Kevin who saved the day,' Anne said. 'He pointed to the broken glass and insisted it was an accident.'

Kevin frowned. 'I had to spread around a lot of twenty-dollar bills to make them see it my way. And we had no time to pick hospitals – you were pretty far gone, and this was nearest.'

'It wasn't really suicide,' Neely said.

'Well, it will do until the real thing comes along,' Anne said.

'Did I make the papers?'

'Front page.' Anne pulled a chair up to Neely's bed. 'Neely, we've got to do something about your life.'

Tears came to Neely's eyes. 'What's there to do? I can't sing any more.'

'It's all up there.' Kevin tapped his head. 'There's nothing wrong with your throat.'

'So go tell that to my throat. I'm willing, but the notes won't come.'

'All right. You'll be out of here in a few days. Then what?' Kevin demanded.

Neely's eyes filled with tears. 'I'll leave Anne's apartment – don't worry. I'll check into a hotel.'

'It can't go on like this, Neely . . . all the pills and booze. The next time you won't be so lucky.'

Neely stretched out. 'If I could only sleep, really sleep – like for a week – then I'd be all right. This way I never get more than a few hours. It's been so long since I had a real night's sleep . . .'

'The sleep cure!' Anne said suddenly.

Both Kevin and Neely stared questioningly. 'Yes, the sleep cure,' Anne insisted. She explained how Jennifer had taken it in Switzerland to lose weight, but that it was created to help with emotional disturbances.

Neely was enthusiastic. 'A week of sleep! Oh, God, then I bet I'd sing. But Switzerland – that would cost a fortune.'

'If it's a legitimate treatment, I'm sure we have it here,' Kevin declared.

Dr. Massinger was against it. Yes, he knew about the sleep cure. But Neely's disturbance was too deeply rooted. It was his feeling that she needed at least a year in a sanitarium. 'This is no situational depression,' he insisted. 'This girl is deeply disturbed. From her records it is obvious she had suicidal tendencies ten years ago. I recommended a sanitarium the moment she came to me, but she refused to go. She's been going on sheer nerve and pills ever since. But now she has no choice. She must go away.' He recommended several sanitariums.

Neely would have none of it. 'Me go and live with kooks? No siree. I want the plush treatment, like Jennifer had. Champagne for starters, a sympathetic nurse, a lovely needle . . . and sleep, beautiful sleep.'

After frantic calls, Kevin finally located a large private sanitarium in upstate New York. Yes, they knew about the sleep cure. They would be delighted to accept Miss O'Hara and administer it to her. Yes, it would be done with the utmost secrecy – the newspapers would never know.

On a balmy Sunday in March, Kevin and Anne drove Neely to Haven Manor. Anne felt confident when she saw the spacious grounds and well-tended lawns. Neely had fortified herself with a few dolls for courage.

They entered a large, ivy-covered Tudor mansion and were ushered into a drawing room lined with paintings of late benefactors. Dr. Hall, the chief of staff, greeted them. He shook hands with Neely. 'I'm a great admirer of yours, Miss O'Hara.'

Neely smiled weakly.

'Now, if you'll just complete these forms . . .'

Neely signed her name to several papers. 'Okay, let's get to the sleep cure,' she said brightly.

Dr. Hall pressed a button. A large, stout woman in a white coat appeared. 'This is Dr. Archer, my assistant. She will take Miss O'Hara to her room.'

Neely grasped Anne's hand. 'I can't thank you enough. You'll come for me in a week?'

Anne nodded. Neely turned to Kevin. 'I know you're paying the freight for this. Thanks a lot.'

He shook his head. 'I offered to, but Anne is taking care of it. She insisted.'

Neely looked at Anne with a shy, sleepy grin. 'Annie . . . always there, huh? Thanks.'

'Just get well, Neely,' Anne said.

'I jus' wanna sleep for a *long* time.' She went out, leaning on Dr. Archer's arm.

Anne rose to leave. Dr. Hall cleared his throat. 'Miss Welles . . . and Mr. Gillmore. Could we talk about this?'

'About what?' Anne sat down again.

'This so-called sleep cure. I've been on the phone with Dr. Massinger, and I have Miss O'Hara's past records here. He sent them on. A sleep cure is not the answer, you know.'

'But you said—' Anne was nonplussed.

'I said we could give it. But I hadn't seen her records or talked to her doctor at the time. We still can, but I would hardly recommend it. Oh, she might come out of it refreshed. She might even function for a few weeks, a month – then she'd return to her old habits. Eventually she would kill herself. She's bent on it, you know. She's a great talent – we owe it to her to cure her.'

'But how?' Anne asked.

'Not with sleep cures or pills. This girl is an addict now. Sleeping-pill addiction can be as serious as any other addiction and harder to cure, because unfortunately it's quite easy for a patient to get pills on the outside. It's a little tougher to get cocaine, heroin or morphine. Did you know that on the day of the suicide attempt she had taken fifty pills? I checked with her druggist. Her prescription had been filled the night before. And Dr. Massinger never gave them to her – each prescription had a new physician's name on it. And that bottle of fifty pills was empty when she was found, that and a good supply of liquor – a dangerous combination. Yet she still needed to cut her wrists to accomplish the act. Her tolerance is the tolerance of an addict.'

'What would you recommend?' This was Kevin.

'I'd like to try deep psychiatric therapy. Not shock – not yet, anyway. I hope she won't need it. But I think, with real work, we can return a bright-eyed, talented girl to the world.'

'How long would it take?' Anne asked.

'At least a year.'

Anne smiled ruefully. 'You'd never convince Neely. She'd leave immediately if she didn't get the sleep cure.'

Dr. Hall's smile was tired. 'She signed this.' He tapped a paper. 'She committed herself. Of course, she thought she was just signing in. But this states she must remain here for at least thirty days.'

'Thirty days,' Anne said thoughtfully. 'But I know Neely. You'll never convince her to stay beyond the thirty days.'

'If we can't, you can commit her.'

'I?' Anne was horrified. 'Never!'

Dr. Hall smiled. 'Then we could have her certified.'

'What's that?'

'If our psychiatrists agree that she needs further treatment, we present the case in court. Three outside psychiatrists are called in. If they concur, the court commits her for three months – and every three months she is automatically committed again. We often do this,' he said easily. 'It takes the feeling of guilt away from relatives and friends.'

'But this is like railroading her,' Anne protested. 'She thinks she's going to have a week's sleep. We promised her . . .'

'Miss Welles, I admire Miss O'Hara. She's a great talent. It costs fifteen hundred dollars a month to stay here, and there is a waiting list from all over the country. We took Miss O'Hara ahead of the others because she *is* an artist – she must be cured. I beg this chance for her. I beg it from you.'

'But Neely was so against a sanitarium—'

'Miss O'Hara is in no condition to make any decision about her future. In fact, if left to her own devices, she won't have a future.'

Kevin suddenly took over. 'I think Dr. Hall knows best. Let's at least give it a try.'

Anne nodded dumbly. 'When can we see her?'

'Not for two weeks. But you may call me every day, and I'll report her progress. I guarantee you'll find her much improved when you visit her.'

Anne was silent as they drove back to the city. 'Fifteen hundred a month for a year?' Kevin said to her. 'Anne, you'd better let me take over.'

'No, this is my responsibility. Kevin, I was thinking . . . If I signed with Gillian . . . they're offering me two thousand a week . . .'

'What about our marriage? And our trip?'

324

'It's waited this long – what's a few more months? Besides, I can't leave on a long trip with Neely at Haven Manor. I'll have to visit her.'

'You don't want to marry me, do you, Anne?'

'I do, but—'

'No. That's why you're paying Neely's bills. You don't want to feel obligated to me.'

'Kevin, you kept me waiting many years before you decided you were ready for marriage. I think we at least owe Neely a few months.'

'So we don't go on a honeymoon till Neely is set – okay, I'll buy that – but why can't we get married? And why should you keep working?'

'If I want to pay for Neely, I'll have to work. I talked with Henry Bellamy the other day. He told me I was worth close to a million dollars. Of course, a great deal of it is paper profit, but it's blue-chip paper. But I couldn't carry Neely without touching my capital, and that would mean selling off some stock. Henry doesn't want me to do that – he thinks A.T.&T. will keep soaring, that there will be a split. But if I sign with Gillian for another twenty-six weeks, I can afford Neely. That would bring us to next October, and by then Neely should be well on her way to recovery. Then we'll get married and off we'll go. I promise.'

Kevin stared off into the distance. He had to go along. Goddam that little brat – whenever she came to town she caused nothing but trouble.

Anne sighed. 'Poor Neely. I guess they've broken it to her by now. I wonder how she's taking it.'

At first Neely had been patient. She sat in Dr. Archer's office, monotonously answering the questions the woman asked, lighting one cigarette after another and waiting for the blessed needle that would give her the wonderful sleep. Dr. Archer's phone finally rang. Neely guessed it was Dr. Hall, giving orders. Dr. Archer answered with a terse, 'Yes, Doctor. Of course, Doctor. I'm so glad. I'm in full agreement.'

Neely yawned. Fine. They agreed. That was nice. Now come on, get with it. Dr. Archer pressed a button. Neely stared at the woman's orthopedic shoes. Now why couldn't they be nice white shoes? Why did they have to be thick, ugly oxfords? Geez, she was probably born

325

that way – wore orthopedic booties when she was a baby. Neely laughed out loud at this thought, and Dr. Archer turned in surprise. Then a new pair of white shoes, topped by a white uniform, entered the room.

'This is Miss O'Hara,' Dr. Archer said. 'Take her to Building Four.'

'Is that where the sleep cure is given?' Neely asked good-naturedly as she followed the nurse. The nurse merely smiled and led her through a series of underground corridors. At each entrance she took out a large set of keys and unlocked a door, then immediately locked it when they had passed through.

'Hey – where is this place? In New Jersey? We been walking a mile.'

'Haven Manor has twenty buildings, not including the gymnasium and occupational therapy building, and although they are all separate buildings, there is an underground passage that connects each one. We have passed from the administration building through Buildings Two and Three, and are now approaching Four.' There was a note of civic pride in her voice.

Building Four was like a private cottage. Neely spotted women of various ages watching television in a large room. They all looked perfectly normal, she thought. The nurse led her down a long hall past many tiny cubbyholes. Geez, some crappy bedrooms. Her bedroom on Fifty-second Street had been three times the size. Each room had a bed, a window, a bureau and a chair. But maybe she was going upstairs to a deluxe suite or something. Obviously this was not the sleep-cure department.

The nurse stopped at a tiny cubbyhole at the end of the hall. 'This will be your room.'

Neely started to protest – but what the hell, she was going to be asleep. What did it matter if there was no view? She flopped down on the bed. 'Okay, bring on the needle.'

The nurse left the room. Minutes ticked by. She looked at her watch. Where in hell were they? She called out, 'Hey . . . what gives?'

Two nurses suddenly appeared. 'You want something, Miss O'Hara?'

'You bet I do. I'm supposed to be put to sleep.'

The nurses exchanged a curious glance.

'I'm here for the sleep cure,' Neely repeated.

326

'You're in Building Four. This is the adjustment building.'

'Adjustment for what?'

'All new patients come here for a few days while we evaluate their cases. Then they are transferred to the building that best suits them.'

Neely walked to the bureau and opened her bag. She took out a cigarette. 'Call Dr. Hall. There's been some mistake.'

One of the nurses leaped over and grabbed Neely's matches.

'Hey, what are you doing?' she yelled.

'You are not allowed matches in here.'

'How am I supposed to light my cigarettes?'

The nurse took her bag. 'You can't smoke. There are certain hours when you are allowed to smoke – under supervision.'

Neely tried to snatch her bag back, but it was two against one. 'Call Dr. Hall!' she demanded.

'These are Dr. Hall's orders,' one nurse said. 'Now come on, Miss O'Hara. At five o'clock you get two cigarettes. Let's go out and meet the other patients.'

'*What?* Me socialize at a funny farm? I'm Neely O'Hara – I pick my friends. Call Anne Welles, or Kevin Gillmore. This is ridiculous. I'm leaving!' She started for the door.

One of the nurses detained her. 'She's still wearing her watch,' the other one said. She unstrapped it, forcefully, from Neely's wrist.

'Hey, that watch cost a thousand bucks!'

'It will be put in the safe. You'll get it back, along with your other personal effects, when you leave.'

Neely began to panic. She had never felt this helpless kind of fear before. 'Look, call Anne Welles,' she pleaded. 'She'll set things straight.'

Another half hour passed. Neely alternated between anger and fright. She wanted a cigarette. The two Seconals had worn off, and she was wide awake and terrified. She rang. A nurse appeared. The nurse was polite but evasive. Miss O'Hara could have a cigarette right now if she came into the lounge. In fact, she had better hurry. If she missed this smoking period she couldn't smoke again until nine o'clock.

'Who the hell are you to tell me when I can smoke?' she screamed. 'This is no charity ward. This place costs money – I want to be treated with respect.'

'We respect you, Miss O'Hara. But in turn, you must respect the rules of Haven Manor.'

'I don't follow rules. I *make* the rules! I'm Neely O'Hara.'

'We know that. We all admire your work very much.'

'Then do as I say!' she demanded.

'We follow orders from Dr. Hall and Dr. Archer.'

'Well, call Dr. Hall!' She turned her back on the nurse. She felt a gnawing terror. Maybe this Dr. Hall was trying to pull a double cross. No, she was just scared, that's all. There was just some mixup. Dr. Hall wouldn't dare. Why, if Anne and Kevin found out there'd be hell to pay!

Ten minutes later the nurse returned. 'Miss O'Hara, if you'd like to smoke before dinner, please come out. There are only ten more minutes left.'

'I won't join those kooks!'

The nurse disappeared. Neely began to pace. Boy, she sure needed this sleep cure. She needed some dolls – her hands were shaking. Geez, lately it was getting so she needed a couple of dolls every hour just to keep calm. But the sleep cure would break the habit. Dr. Massinger thought she had just built up this tolerance. Geez, after Spain, what were twenty or thirty dolls a day? But it was lucky she'd left, or she mighta really gotten sick. Damn that Dr. Madera – he had given her that first shot of Demerol . . . Oh, God, that was an exquisite feeling. It had removed all cares. After the first shot, she had lain in bed for six hours, feeling a silken happiness and a sense of well-being such as she had never known. She felt she could sing better than ever; reach notes that weren't even there; remain thin without the green dolls; act better than ever.

Of course, when it wore off she felt lousy. How could she face another day, another lover, another party? But there was always Dr. Madera to fix her 'bad back.' She had learned that on the movie set in Hollywood – claim a bad back. X-rays can't pinpoint it; studio doctors can examine you and can't dispute it. It had often brought her a few days' release from work. It had worked with Dr. Madera, too – only Demerol was Dr. Madera's contribution. They never gave *that* in Hollywood. And Dr. Madera had been very generous with the Demerol. Gave her three shots a day for a whole wonderful year.

After a short time she didn't just lie in bed. She could function with the Demerol. She'd get up and go nightclubbing, and sing – she never sang better. The picture she had made in Spain – Geez, if only it had gotten an American release. She had reached a new peak in it; she had been thin and vibrant – you didn't want to eat as long as you had Demerol – and her eyes had been like burning coals. Sure, that was because the pupils went so big and black, dilated from the Demerol. But her voice . . . clear and pure.

Then there'd been the money situation, the wire from California. Ted was going to sue for custody of the twins if she didn't return and take care of them. As if she'd let her sons live with that whore he married! And then, to top everything, Jennifer's suicide. She had had to leave Spain – and the Demerol. The dolls helped, but now she needed so many – at least thirty a day. Thirty Seconals . . . God, she had only had about six today, and the last had been two hours ago. Where in hell was Dr. Hall? When did this thing begin?

A nurse came to inform her that dinner was being served. Would she please come to the dining room? She would not! 'I want a cigarette and some Seconals – at least six – to last until Dr. Hall starts this sleep cure.'

She flopped on the bed. Her throat was parched. Geez, a drink, anything . . . This two-by-four cage was beginning to crowd in on her. If something didn't happen soon she'd just walk out of here. They couldn't stop her – it wasn't like she was in jail. She heard footsteps. She sat up. Maybe now they were going to put this show on the road. A nurse appeared, carrying a dinner tray. 'Miss O'Hara, if you wish to eat in your room—'

The nurse never had a chance to finish the sentence. Neely's patience snapped. She picked up the tray and hurled it across the room. The nurse ducked. Another one came running. Neely exploded with rage. 'I don't want to eat and I don't want to socialize. I just want to sleep. Now get me my cigarettes – and give me the sleep cure this minute or I'm leaving. I've had enough!'

One nurse, who seemed more important than the others, took charge. 'Miss O'Hara, there is no sleep cure.'

'What do you mean?'

'I have checked with Dr. Hall. No sleep cure, no barbiturates. You are going to get well with psychiatry and therapy.'

'I'm leaving!' Neely started for the door, but she was restrained by four arms.

329

'Get your filthy hands off me!' she screamed. 'Let me alone!' She started flailing at them with her fists.

A nurse started shouting orders. 'Take her to Hawthorn!'

'I'm going home!' Neely screamed. More nurses appeared, and Neely found herself being dragged down a hall. It couldn't be happening! She, Neely O'Hara, being dragged by four nurses. And this unearthly screaming – it was coming from *her*! But she wasn't having a fit, she was just goddam mad at this doublecross.

She fought them all the way – through halls, while doors were locked and unlocked, into another building, down another entrance hall. Two new nurses leaped to take charge. She was dragged down another hall, to another two-by-four room – but even in her fury she noticed the difference. This one had no carpet, no drapes, no bureau. Just a bed – like in a cell! She was deposited on the bed. Her slacks were torn. Thank God she had packed another pair.

A young nurse came and sat down beside her. 'Come on now, Miss O'Hara, let's have some dinner.'

'I want to go home!' Neely shouted.

'Let's have dinner. Come on and meet the other patients.'

'I want to sleep.' Neely began to sob. She was trapped. She had never felt so trapped in her life. She looked toward the window. No bars . . . that was something. Just a screen, and screens could be cut – but with what? She dashed out of the room, ran into a large lounge. There were patients sitting around, quietly watching television. She looked around wildly. What would cut through a screen? She looked at the bookcase. It was stacked with books, puzzles . . . a chess set! She grabbed a pawn. It had a small head . . . if she poked it hard enough, it might cut through the screen. She ran back to her room clutching the chess piece.

The nurse was sitting on the bed, calmly watching. Let her watch, Neely thought. I'm stronger – let her try and stop me. She opened the window. The nurse didn't budge. She tried the chess piece on the screen, poking, slashing, sobbing all the while. There must be a weak spot where it could poke through and rip. There had to be . . .

'It's a steel screen,' the nurse said calmly. 'And even if you broke out, you'd be on our grounds. We have twenty-five acres here. And the main gate is locked.'

Neely dropped the pawn. She sat on the edge of the bed and sobbed.

The nurse tried to calm her, but her sobs grew more violent. She thought of Anne and Kevin. They were back in New York, probably thinking she was blissfully asleep. She thought of Anne's apartment. Why hadn't she stayed there? You could walk around there, light a cigarette whenever you wanted, take as many dolls as you wanted, have a drink . . . She thought of Hollywood. The Head . . . who was he dictating to now? And Ted . . . It was earlier in California, maybe only three o'clock – and it was warm and the sun was shining. Ted was probably at the pool with his wife. And *she*, the great Neely O'Hara, she was locked in a fancy fruit farm! She sobbed louder.

She must have sobbed for an hour, because when she finally looked up it was dark outside. The head nurse appeared. She had a pin on her starched uniform that stated her name was Miss Schmidt. A big bull dyke – that's what she looked like, Neely decided.

'Miss O'Hara, unless you get hold of yourself, we'll have to do something to calm you.'

Okay, so that was the answer. She *could* get a few dolls or a needle. She'd show them! So they never gave barbiturates here. Well, Neely O'Hara would change that. She'd break their fucking rule! She began to scream.

In no time she had some action. The husky nurse reappeared.

'Come, Miss O'Hara, this has to stop. You are upsetting the other patients.'

'Let them all go fuck themselves!' Neely shrieked. Her screaming increased in volume.

Miss Schmidt gave a quick nod to the two nurses. They took Neely's arms and hauled her down the hall. She fought, kicked, screamed – but she was outnumbered and overpowered. She found herself in a large bathroom. Miss Schmidt and the two nurses told her to undress.

'What! And give you dykes a big thrill!' she shouted. Miss Schmidt nodded her head and the two nurses forcibly undressed Neely. Naked, screeching, she was forced into a bathtub. A huge canvas top was hooked over it, leaving just her head exposed. A pillow was placed behind her head. A nurse sat at a table nearby, poised with a notebook and pencil.

Neely continued to scream. Actually the bath felt very good. She loved baths as a rule, loved to lie in one until her skin became water-logged. And this bath was something special – water kept coming in

331

and going out, bubbling all around her. The sensation was relaxing. She sifted these thoughts as she continued to scream.

Miss Schmidt returned and knelt at her side. Her eyes were kind. 'Miss O'Hara, why not try and relax and let the bath do its work?'

'Get me out of here!' Neely screamed.

'You will stay in this tub until you stop yelling – or until you fall asleep.'

'Hah! There's not enough water in this whole goddam state to put me to sleep!' Neely took a breath and shrieked into Miss Schmidt's face.

'We've had patients in the tub for as long as fifteen hours,' Miss Schmidt answered. She stood up. 'I'll drop by in an hour. Maybe you'll be more relaxed by then.'

In an hour! Neely felt hoarse. Her throat hurt. She wanted to lie back and relax, but that's what they expected, what they wanted. She was hungry . . . she wanted a cigarette, and some dolls. Oh, God, some dolls! She began to scream, cursing Dr. Hall, the nurses, the hospital . . . When she ran out of oaths she broke into sobs. But she noticed the little nurse at the table stopped writing when she sobbed. So that was it – write down every word the patient says so the great Dr. Hall can read it. Relax now, huh? Well, there would be no relaxation for anyone – not as long as Neely O'Hara was here.

She began to scream again. She used her most vicious language and noticed that the little nurse turned scarlet when she recorded the obscenities. In some part of her mind she felt sorry for the nurse. The girl was young – maybe nineteen – and it wasn't her fault . . . she hadn't made the rules. But she kept screaming all the oaths she had ever learned. Meanwhile she worked at the canvas with her knees, though they were getting scraped. Suddenly she found a way of slipping her head under the canvas. She dived down.

The little nurse sprang over and pulled her head out, then leaped back and rang a bell. Others came, and the neck opening was made smaller. Neely screamed louder . . . the nurse wrote faster . . .

While she had been under the canvas she had spotted a small hole near the faucet. As she continued to scream and the nurse continued to write, Neely worked at the hole with her big toe. It grew larger – soon she could put half her foot in it. She kept hurling violent oaths to keep the nurse busy writing. Then, with a superhuman effort, she put her foot in the hole and yanked her knee up to her chest. There was a loud rip and the canvas split open. Neely leaped out of the tub. The nurse sounded the alarm. A battery of nurses came charging in, led by Miss Schmidt. A new canvas top was placed on the tub, but Neely did have the small satisfaction of hearing one nurse whisper, 'No one has *ever* torn a canvas!'

She must have been screaming forever. There had been a change of nurses. This one was young too, but Neely's profanities didn't make her bat an eye. Neely was hoarse . . . exhausted . . . her back ached . . . her knees hurt . . . her toe felt like it was broken from ripping the canvas – but she continued to scream. The door opened. A doctor entered. He pulled up a stool and sat near the tub.

'Good evening, I'm Dr. Clements. I'm making the rounds tonight.'

She noticed the hour on his large watch. Nine o'clock. She must have been in this tub almost three hours.

'Can I help you?'

I'm not crazy, they are, she thought. Here he is, sitting here, like maybe we're passing the time of day, me with my head sticking out of this frigging tub, and he casually asks if he can help me.

'Is there anything I can do?'

She turned to him, and the tears began to stream down her face. 'What kind of a psychiatrist are you?' she gasped. 'Can you help me? God, every doctor in this place knows why I'm here. You all know I was double-crossed. I was promised a sleep cure, and because I want my rights I get dumped into this tub!'

'A sleep cure?' His surprise was real.

'Yeah, that's why I came here. For eight days. To sleep. That stinking Dr. Hall promised. Then the moment my friends left, wham! Everything changed.'

He looked at the nurse. The nurse shrugged. He looked back at Neely. 'I just came on duty. I know nothing about your case. I'm just making the rounds. I'll hand in my report tomorrow, and I'm sure everything will be straightened out.'

'Just like that, huh?' She didn't scream. She had sensed a look of concern in the young doctor's eyes. Maybe she could reach him. 'You're supposed to help me,' she begged. 'Is this why you studied? Is this how you help? Make a notation about me, then go home and

333

sleep in your own bed while I lay here waterlogged? If you were a real human being with compassion, you'd give me a cigarette . . . something to eat . . . a few Seconals . . . not just make a note in your book and walk away.'

He left the room. She renewed her efforts at screaming. Her throat was sore and she was tired. If she could only stop . . . The water was bubbling at an even temperature. Maybe she could sleep at that – but then they'd win! Everyone stays in the tub till they sleep. Not Neely O'Hara! If she lost the first battle, she'd lose them all. She screamed louder . . .

An hour later the young doctor returned. He was accompanied by Miss Schmidt. He opened his bag, poured something into a glass and handed it to Miss Schmidt. 'I spoke to Dr. Hall at home. He agrees the main thing is to get her to sleep. Tonight, at any rate.'

Miss Schmidt held the glass against Neely's lips. 'Drink it.'

Neely turned her head away. 'I do nothing till I get out of here.'

'Drink it,' Miss Schmidt said softly. 'You'll fall asleep right away and we'll take you out. I promise.'

Neely understood. They had said she wouldn't leave the tub until she fell asleep, but they were giving her something to *make* her sleep. It was her victory. No barbiturates, huh? Well, what the hell was that smoky-looking stuff, an ice cream soda? She let Miss Schmidt pour the drink down her throat. She drained the glass dry.

Jesus! Now *this* was a recipe! She felt the effects instantly. It was marvelous! She stopped yelling. The most incredible feeling had come over her. They were taking off the canvas top . . . someone was rubbing her body with a Turkish towel . . . she was helped into a nightgown . . .

'We're full at Hawthorn,' Miss Schmidt said. 'Miss O'Hara, can you understand? There is no private room left. We have to put you in a dormitory.'

Neely waved her hand. A bed . . . sleep . . . that's all she wanted and she didn't care where.

It was dark when she woke. Where in hell was she? In a long room with a lot of beds. Oh Geez, the funny farm! What time was it? She got out of bed. The nurse who sat outside the door jumped up. 'Yes, Miss O'Hara?'

'What time is it?'

'It's four in the morning.'

'I'm hungry.'

Some milk and crackers were immediately produced on a pretty tray. They let her sit on the bench in the hall. God forbid she should wake the other kooks. She finished the milk – now could she have a cigarette? She could not. They were polite, but she could not have a cigarette. Well, what were they gonna do? She wasn't sleepy; besides, someone was snoring in the room. Miss Schmidt apologized. A private room would open in a few days.

Neely returned to her bed. A few days! She would leave as soon as it was daylight. They'd have to let her put in a call to Anne.

She must have fallen asleep, because the next thing she knew there was great activity. Everyone was up. A nurse came in, a new one.

'Good morning, Miss O'Hara. Get up and make your bed. The bathroom is down the hall.'

'Make my bed!' Neely snapped. 'Not at these prices, sister. I haven't made my bed in fifteen years, and I don't aim to start now.'

'I'll do it for you.' A nice-looking girl with sandy hair rushed across the room. 'My name's Carole.'

'Why should you make my bed?' Neely asked as she watched the girl whip the sheets into order.

Carole smiled. 'They'll give you a black mark if they find it unmade. This is your first day. You'll get with it.'

'What do I care about a black mark?' Neely asked.

'Well, you don't want to stay in the Hawthorn Pavilion forever, do you? You want to move to Fir next, then Elm, then Ash, then the out-patient clinic.'

'Sounds like school.'

'It is in a way. This is the most disturbed ward. I was all the way up to Elm, but I . . . acted up. I've been at Hawthorn two months now. I hope to get transferred to Fir soon.'

Neely followed Carole into a large bathroom. There were about twenty women there, brushing their teeth and chattering. They were all ages. Some were in their forties; there was one lovely-looking woman about seventy; Carole was about twenty-five. There were six or seven girls her own age, and several who were even younger. They chattered like students in a school dormitory. Neely was given a toothbrush, and an attendant came over with a large box. 'All right, girls, here's your lipsticks.' Neely couldn't believe her eyes. In the box were twenty lipsticks with names taped on. She saw her own; it had been taken from her bag and taped neatly. She used the lipstick and then handed it back to the attendant.

Then she was herded in line to get her clothes. An attendant handed her a bra, pants, flat loafers, skirt and blouse. To her amazement, they were *her* clothes, all name taped. She hadn't packed them. Anne must have sent them by messenger during the night.

That meant Anne knew she wasn't taking the sleep cure!

Her fear made her numb. She dressed slowly, trying to get some order out of her jumbled terror. She followed Carole into the large recreation room. The sun flooded through the windows, creating a false air of cheer. She looked at the clock. God, it was only seven-thirty! How could she get through this day?

Miss Schmidt had been replaced by a day nurse, Miss Weston. She was built on the same lines as Miss Schmidt, and the five or six young nurses leaped at her commands with the same alacrity. Neely joined everyone for breakfast. The dining room was bright and cheerful, with four women to a table and scurrying waitresses. She had decided not to eat, but the first whiff of the bacon and eggs reminded her she was hungry. She ate a large breakfast and trudged back with the others to the recreation room.

They were obviously well-bred kooks, she decided. She knew they recognized her, but they smiled at her politely and warmly, without making her feel self-conscious. She looked dreadful. The skirt needed a belt – there had been a belt, but they had removed it. Her hair was in strings and her knees were scraped, mementos of the night in the bathtub. She wished she felt the warm camaraderie and good humor the other girls seemed to share. They acted as if they liked the place!

Carole introduced her around. Geez, everyone seemed so sane and normal. She sat down, wondering what happened next. A nurse entered, and everyone surged around her. She was holding a box, and she called out every name, even 'Miss O'Hara.' Neely went over. Geez, were they organized – even her package of cigarettes was labeled. The nurse handed each girl two cigarettes, and another nurse stood by to light them. Neely settled back and puffed gratefully at the first cigarette she had had in over twelve hours. The first draw made her dizzy, the second was satisfying and the third cleared her head. Imagine going without a cigarette since yesterday afternoon, she who smoked over two packs a day. She got up slowly, stabilized by the cigarette, and walked over to the desk where Miss Weston was sitting.

'I'd like to make a phone call,' she said. 'Where do I go?'

'Phone calls aren't allowed,' Miss Weston said pleasantly.

'Well, how do I reach my friends?'

'You are allowed to write letters.'

'Can I have a pen and some paper?'

The nurse looked at her watch. 'I think it had better wait. The doctor is coming to see you in five minutes.'

'Dr. Hall?'

'No, Dr. Feldman. This is just a routine checkup.'

He was a medical doctor, not a nutcracker. He took some blood from her finger and her arm and checked her heart.

She asked a nurse to light her second cigarette. An attractive, dark-haired girl came over. 'Don't let the checkup bother you. They do that to make sure you're healthy. It would be embarrassing to have you die of cancer or something while they were taking care of your brain.'

Neely looked at the girl. She could be beautiful with proper makeup, she felt. Her bone structure was good and her black eyes flashed. She must have had a good figure once, though now she was quite heavy. Neely judged her to be about thirty years old.

The girl sat down. She was holding a square box. 'I'm Mary Jane. Let me break you in – when you get to gym, buy a box of writing paper. It costs a dollar.'

'But I have no money.'

Mary Jane smiled. 'You charge everything – it's put on your bill. But you can use it as a kind of pocketbook.' She opened her box. There was writing paper in it – and a pack of cigarettes.

'Where did you get—'

The girl silenced her with a quick gesture. 'On visiting days, you're allowed to sit with your visitors and chain smoke. Get whoever visits you to bring a carton. Then you hide it, and in smoking periods you can smoke a dozen.'

'But they light you up. They'll notice if you smoke more than two.'

'The nurses are wise. You can always cadge a light from someone else's cigarette. That's allowed. It's just matches we loonies aren't allowed to have. But the nurses don't care how many we smoke. They figure we have to have some pleasure in life.'

Neely smiled. 'You're not a loony, are you?'

'No, I came here to get even with my husband, only it backfired. He's a bastard – loads of money – and he got himself another girl. He wanted a divorce, so I pretended to go ape – you know, have a nervous collapse. It was the biggest mistake of my life.'

'Why?'

'All I did was take a few pills – three pills – and leave a phony suicide note. The next thing I know, I'm in Bellevue. Boy, you could really go crazy there. Real nuts around you, screaming and carrying on. I guess then I actually flipped from fright. I began to scream and wound up in a straitjacket. So, since my husband could afford it, I came here. Signed myself in. Then, when I wanted to leave, he had me committed. I've been here five months. I was at Elm House officially, which was pretty good. You can smoke there and wear belts, even use more makeup. But when I learned he had committed me, I got hysterical, threw a tantrum. So here I am at Hawthorn. And I warn you – play ball with them. I didn't. I threw tantrums every day, refused to eat, refused to cooperate. I spent three weeks in the damn bathtub. You have to play along. There's only one way – *their* way. I'm being an angel, and soon I'll get moved to Fir. A while there, then Elm, then Ash, then the out-patient cottage . . . then out for good.'

Neely was suddenly cold with fear. 'But that sounds like months.'

'It'll take about a year,' Mary Jane said cheerfully.

'And don't you mind?'

The girl shrugged. 'Sure I mind. I cared enough to scream and shout for a week. But you can't fight them. They show the record to your lawyer, or husband, or whoever is responsible for you. It looks bad on paper – "Patient had hysterics. Patient had to be restrained. Twelve hours in the tub." Then they say to your lawyer, "Now just sign her in for another three months. Don't you want a bright-eyed, healthy girl returned to you and to society?" Sure, for fifteen hundred a month they can afford to take their time. So I've decided not to fight it. I'll sit it out. Besides, what have I got to lose? I've got no place to go. Hank – that's my husband – he's with his girl. But at least he can't marry her. And it costs him fifteen hundred a month for me.'

'But I only came here for eight days – for a sleep cure.'

'A what?' Mary Jane looked at her strangely.

Neely explained the sleep cure. Mary Jane smiled. 'They never give it here. They won't even give you an aspirin.'

'They gave me something last night,' Neely said proudly.

Mary Jane laughed. 'Boy, we had to hand it to you. Did you really tear the canvas? Everyone heard you did.'

Neely nodded. 'And I'll get out of here, too.'

Mary Jane smiled. 'Okay, I'm all for it. Show me how it's done. Look at Peggy – they've brainwashed her husband.'

Peggy walked over. She was twenty-five, blonde, attractive. 'Telling her all our gruesome case histories?' Peggy asked.

'Why are you here?' Neely asked.

'Because I was nutty as a fruitcake,' Peggy said cheerfully.

'No she wasn't,' Mary Jane said. 'She lost two babies in a row, still-born. Anyone would go into a depression.'

Peggy managed a smile. 'All I know is I'd begin to cry if I saw a doll in a store window. When I got here it was worse. I've had forty shock treatments. I'm just beginning to feel human again.'

Neely's throat swelled in horror. Shock treatment! Mary Jane read her thoughts. 'Don't worry. Even if they think you need it, they still have to get permission. Whoever is your nearest of kin or is respon-sible for you.'

Neely relaxed. 'Anne would never give permission.'

Mary Jane smiled. 'Unless they brainwash *her*, like they did Peggy's husband. When Dr. Hall and Dr. Archer start to work on them, the first thing you know they agree to anything. Peggy's husband arrived the first visiting day. She was fine – just wanted to get out. He was so thrilled. He said he would go right to the office and sign her out. Ha! That was it! He didn't come back for two weeks. And the following day Peggy started her shock treatments.'

'But why?'

Peggy sighed. 'I don't blame Jim. At first I did, but now I can understand. They showed him my chart. I was depressed, I didn't sleep, I cried a lot – all signs of a manic depressive. Who wouldn't cry after losing two babies and being stuck here? But they convinced Jim that if I went home I'd crack up again, and maybe for good. Naturally Jim wants a happy wife, so he signed the papers and committed me.'

Neely listened. Everyone had a similar story. No one was nuts; in fact everyone seemed more normal than the people she knew on the outside. She was in the middle of listening to the seventh life story when the nurse called, 'Come, ladies!'

'Now what?' Neely asked.

'Gym,' Mary Jane explained.

They followed the nurse in a double file. They went through corridors; doors were unlocked and relocked; they finally entered a large gymnasium. There was a badminton court, Ping-Pong tables – even a pool table. A group was leaving when they entered. Mary Jane waved to a few girls.

'That's the Fir group. They use the gym from eight to eight-thirty. Those girls I waved to – they were just promoted last week, from Hawthorn to Fir.'

Neely sat on the sidelines while the others chose sides for badminton and Ping-Pong. She bought a box of writing paper, but she refused to be fitted for gym shoes. She was not staying long enough, she told them. The writing paper? Well, she had to write to Anne. She must not get panicky. Mary Jane said if she showed fear, they'd mark it against her.

They left the gymnasium at nine-thirty as another group entered. They were led to another building – occupational therapy. All the girls rushed to their projects, and the teacher explained that she could do mosaic work, or knit, or anything she wished. She wished to do nothing! She sat in a corner. Oh, God, how did this happen? She looked out the window. Patches of grass were beginning to get green. She saw a little rabbit bound across the grounds. At least he could go where he chose. He was free. The feeling of confinement was more than she could bear. She stared at the teacher, who was patiently helping the girls. Sure – at five the teacher was free to go, to do as she wished. She needed a cigarette. *She needed a doll!* Oh, God, anything for a doll. She felt the perspiration come to the back of her neck. Her hair was damp and her back was aching, really hurting now. She was going to black out! She moaned softly. The teacher came rushing over to her. 'My back,' she complained.

'Did you hurt it in gym?' The instructor was all attention.

'No, I have a history of a bad back. It's acting up now.'

The instructor immediately lost interest. 'You'll have a session with your psychiatrist this afternoon at two. You can tell him.'

So the day went. By two, when she saw the doctor, she was ready to scream.

He was a thin, red-faced man named Dr. Seale. He wrote as she talked. She poured out her wrath – the injustice of the double cross, the promised sleep cure, the way she was being pushed around. She chain smoked cigarettes. During sessions with psychiatrists patients were given all the cigarettes they wished.

'My back really aches,' she pleaded. 'Please give me a few Seconals.'

He kept writing. Then he said, 'How long have you been taking Seconals?'

She lost her patience. 'Oh, come on – don't make a federal case out of that. If everyone who took them was in a loony bin, you'd have half of Hollywood and all of Madison Avenue and Broadway in here.'

'Do you think it's normal to take sleeping pills in the middle of the day to ease pain?'

'No, I'd much prefer a shot of Demerol,' she said. She was pleased at the angle his eyebrows shot up. 'Yes, Demerol.' She smiled. 'In Spain I got it all the time. Two or three times a day. And I functioned just fine. I even made a picture. So you see, two lousy little Seconals are like appetizers for me. Now come on, get me a few. If I can have two every hour, I might be able to get with it around here.'

'Tell me about your mother, Miss O'Hara.'

'Oh, shit! Don't tell me we're gonna start with that Freudian jazz. Look, I went through all that way back in California. It took me five years and twenty thousand dollars to convince him I didn't remember my mother. If we're gonna start back there, I'll be an old woman before I get outta here.'

'I'll send for your records from California,' he said.

'I won't be here that long. I'm writing to my friend tonight.'

'But you must stay at least thirty days.'

'Thirty days!'

He explained the paper she had signed. She shook her head. 'What a racket. They think of everything. When you're coming here, who figures you need the William Morris office to check the fine print!'

He stood up. 'I'll see you tomorrow, same time.'

She shrugged. 'Okay, so I got a thirty-day hitch. I might as well enjoy it.' Then she said suddenly, 'I *can* leave in thirty days, can't I?'

'We'll see,' he said vaguely.

'What do you mean, we'll see?'

'At the end of the period we'll evaluate our findings. If we think you're fit—'

'*We?* What is this *we* crap? *I'm* the one who's here, and *I'm* the one to say I want to go. How can anyone stop me?'

'Miss O'Hara, if you insisted on leaving and we didn't think you were fit, we would talk to the people who are responsible for you – in this case, Miss Welles. We'd ask her to commit you for three months – that is, if you didn't agree to sign yourself in.'

'Suppose Anne refused?'

'Then we could take means to have you committed – present your case to an impartial board . . .'

She was rigid with fright. 'A nice little racket you got here.'

'It's no racket, Miss O'Hara. We want to cure people. If we released someone before she was cured and she took her life a few months later, or harmed someone else . . . well, it wouldn't give us a good name. If you had an operation in a medical hospital and you wanted to leave before the incision had healed, the doctor would have a right to restrain you. At Haven Manor, when we release a person, they are ready to take their place in society.'

'Sure – in the old-age home.'

He smiled. 'I think you have a long, productive life ahead. A year or two here will not be wasted.'

'A year or two!' She began to tremble. 'No! Listen . . . thirty days, okay – if I'm stuck. But that's all!'

He smiled again. 'You take your Rorschach test now. That will tell us more.'

Neely grabbed his arm. 'Look, Doc, I don't know about tests – maybe my inkblots will show I'm some kind of a nut – but I'm not *like* other people. That's why I'm a star. You can't get to where I've gotten unless you *are* different. Why, if you threw a butterfly net over Sardi's and Chasen's and gave them Rorschach tests, you wouldn't release any of them for years. Don't you see, it's just our little kinks that make us what we are.'

'I agree. And they're fine if they work *for* you. But when they turn and work toward self-destruction, then we have to step in and change the course.'

'I'm not self-destructive. Everything just went wrong. Look, when you have a studio treating you like you were Jesus Christ for so many years, taking care of everything, I guess it becomes a big mother image. They do *everything* – get you plane tickets, write your speeches, take care of the press . . . they even fix traffic tickets. And you gradually fall into a way of depending on them. You feel like you belong, like the studio is protecting you. Then, when you're thrown on your own, it's like a big rejection. It's scary. I felt like I was just Neely again.'

'Who is "just Neely"?'

'Ethel Agnes O'Neill, who had to do her own dirty work, wash her own underwear and make her own breaks. Neely O'Hara had things done for her. She commanded respect. It should work like that, if you're a real talent, so that all you have to do is concentrate on your work. That's why I lost my voice – I couldn't do both.'

'But Ethel Agnes O'Neill obviously did both at one time,' he said.

'Sure. At seventeen you can do anything. You have nothing to lose. You start with nothing, so you can attempt anything. I'm thirty-two now. I haven't worked recently, but I'm sort of a living legend. I can't afford to risk my reputation. That's why I really froze on that picture in Hollywood. It was a one-picture deal – no studio was behind me, building me for the future and guarding me. They were using me, hoping to make a quick buck on my name. I knew it was a lousy picture and they knew it, too, but they figured it would make money. So I lost my voice – I *really* lost it. Dr. Massinger explained that to me. But the studio marks me as uncooperative and unreliable so they can get off the hook.'

'But I thought you said the studio was the mother image.'

She sighed. 'That's gone. Television changed everything. Even The Head. He's a frightened old man who has to report every move to his stockholders. They're trying to dump him, I hear. Everything is changed.'

'Then you have to change with it, grow up.'

'Maybe,' she agreed. 'But it doesn't mean I have to run scared. I'm a star. I have to act like one, no matter what happens.'

He led her to the door. 'We'll talk tomorrow.'

'When can I see Anne?'

343

'In two weeks.'

Two weeks! Neely returned to the main recreation room. She slipped six cigarettes into the writing-paper box and returned the pack to the nurse. No matches, but she'd figure a way.

There was a recreation period. The girls wrote letters, played cards. Then there was a smoking period, and everyone seemed to be chain smoking. Neely wrote a long, outraged letter to Anne, telling her everything that had happened, ending with a strong demand for instant release. She folded it into the envelope and began to seal it. The nurse labeled 'Miss Weston' came by. 'Don't seal it,' she warned. 'Just write your doctor's name on the corner where the stamp should be. He'll read it, and if he approves of it he'll mail it.'

Neely's jaw dropped. 'You mean Dr. Seale gets to read everything I write?'

'It's the rule here.'

'But that's not right. A person should have some privacy.'

'It's done to protect the patient,' Miss Weston said.

'Protect the patient! You mean protect this creep joint!'

'No, Miss O'Hara. Very often a patient is depressed and takes her hostility out on the one she loves. Let's say a woman is put here by her husband. She's always been a true and devoted wife, but while she's here she gets hallucinations and writes to her husband that she hates him, that she's been untrue to him – even mentions friends of his who were her lovers. None of it is true, but how is the husband to know? That's why the doctor reads the letter before it goes out.' Miss Weston smiled as Neely fingered the letter. 'Look, if you've written that you hate it here, or even uncomplimentary remarks about Dr. Seale, don't worry. He'll understand, and the letter will be posted. All he's interested in is protecting you – that's why the rule was made.'

Neely handed over the letter. So Dr. Seale would read that she thought he looked like an eggplant – served him right, him and his rules! She put her head in her hands. Jesus, she had to get out!

Mary Jane tapped her on the shoulder. 'Don't sit that way. They'll write that you're in a depressed state.'

Neely laughed aloud, bitterly.

'Don't laugh that way,' Mary Jane warned. 'That's hysteria. If you laugh, laugh normally. And don't stick by yourself. They'll write that you're withdrawn, antisocial . . .'

'Oh come on!' Neely exclaimed. 'This is too much.'

'It's true. Why do you think they keep six nurses for just twenty of us? We're always under C.O. – constant observation. Twice a week the head nurses meet with the doctors and give reports on you. Everyone gives reports on you – the occupational therapy instructor, the gym instructor . . . You've got two bad marks already – you sulked in gym and refused to cooperate in O.T. Didn't want to make one of the darling little ceramic ashtrays. You've got to remember, Big Brother is everywhere, always watching.'

When they returned to occupational therapy later in the afternoon, Neely began making a cigarette box. 'I'll point to it as my fifteen-hundred-dollar cigarette box,' she said to herself. She worked feverishly with the sandpaper, smoothing down the wooden surface. She hoped the teacher was watching.

At five, everyone was taken to the massage room – showers, massage, Swedish hose. It could really have been quite nice, but she hated every second. She envied the girls who acted as if they were away at summer camp, enjoying the whole thing as a social event. Maybe for some of them this was escape from dull lives, but it was no holiday for her. Her back was murder and her hands were shaking. If she didn't have a doll soon she'd scream. Waves of nausea broke over her. She mustn't get sick – it would be a bad mark. She clenched her teeth, finally rushed to the toilet and vomited secretly. She came back and took the Swedish hose. Okay, she'd play ball . . . until Anne came. Then she'd convince Anne that she was fine. She *had* to get out in the thirty days. God, a year in this joint with the badminton and arts and crafts and she'd really be crazy!

At six o'clock they returned to Hawthorn Pavilion. Everyone sat around. There were plenty of books to read, and everyone offered her candy. No wonder they had all gained weight. Mary Jane confided she had put on twenty pounds in five weeks.

Suddenly Carole, the nice girl who had made her bed, stood up and screamed. 'You've insulted me,' she shouted at the girl beside her.

The girl looked up in surprise. 'Carole, I was reading. I haven't said a word.'

'You said I was a latent homosexual,' Carole insisted. 'I'll kill you!' She lunged at the girl.

Two nurses separated them instantly. Carole kicked and screamed and fought the nurses, and hurled oaths as she was dragged out of the room.

'Two days in the bathtub will calm her down,' Mary Jane commented.

'Did the girl say anything?' Neely asked.

Mary Jane shook her head. 'Carole's a paranoic. An awfully nice girl. She can go for weeks being absolutely divine, then out of the blue she imagines something. I don't think she'll ever get well. She's been here two years.'

Two years. You'd have to go crazy by then. Neely's terror was now absolute. Her back was twitching with pain . . . her throat burned . . . but she had to hold on. She had to! Was this really happening to her? Jesus, other stars did crazy things, and you read about them going to sanitariums. It sounded so nice, so easy, like they could come and go. Were they trapped like this – had they gone through this terror? Or was she the only one who had been railroaded? Look, Neely, she told herself. You'll make it. You started with nothing, and got to the top. You'll get out of here. Just hold on, girl.

Dinner was served at six-thirty. Then they took showers, and afterward everybody sat around in pajamas and robes. Some looked at television. Idly, she watched a movie, recalling that she had once had a brief affair with the star. God, all those lucky people in the outside world. If she ever got out she'd act fine. No more fits, no more tantrums – just two dolls a night. She needed a cigarette – she had smoked the cache she had hoarded. Mary Jane slipped her a few more. Several girls told her their life stories, and she tried to appear interested. No one was crazy – everyone was here by mistake.

At ten o'clock everyone went to bed. She lay in the dormitory, and soon she heard the regular breathing of all the other girls. Who in hell could go to sleep at this hour? And every half hour a nurse came in and flashed a light at each bed. She kept her eyes closed and pretended to be asleep – they might say she was disturbed if she didn't sleep. She heard the clock strike twelve, then one. She thought of all the luxuries everyone took for granted, things she couldn't have, like the luxury of being able to turn on a bed light and read, of lighting a cigarette. She wouldn't even mind not having the dolls or the booze – but just to lie here like this was ridiculous. Geez, if she got through this night then she was really strong. Nothing could ever kill her.

Two o'clock. She had to go to the bathroom. Would they write it down as a neurotic act? Christ, taking a leak was normal. She got up and walked down the hall. Two nurses leaped to her side. 'Anything wrong, Miss O'Hara?' No, she just wanted to take a leak. She often took a leak during the night.

She went to the community bathroom while a nurse posted herself outside the door. Oh, God, not even to take a leak in private . . .

ANNE

Anne sat by the window and smoked. It had been an awful visit. Neely pleading and sobbing, begging to be released; Dr. Hall and Dr. Archer and Dr. Seale all reading reports to her, arguing that Neely was definitely disturbed, that she was having a 'walking nervous break- down' with suicidal tendencies, that to take Neely out now would be signing her death warrant. Before talking to the doctors she had promised Neely to get her out immediately, but the reports spoke louder than Neely's tears.

How could she face those haunted eyes and tell her she had to stay at least three months? She had signed the commitment. Kevin had insisted. God, had she done the right thing? The doctors said Neely should have been in a sanitarium long ago, that there was no stigma about it today, that when Neely got better, she could go on to bigger and better things. It would be rough for Neely, but in the long run it would pay off. And it wasn't as if she were in some dreadful place – the hospital was beautiful. For fifteen hundred a month it *should* be beau- tiful. But those pleading eyes kept stabbing her conscience. It must be awful to be locked up, no matter how plush the cell. She would visit Neely again in two weeks. Perhaps she'd be more adjusted.

At the next visit, Anne found Neely in good humor. She had been moved to Fir House. 'I'm promoted!' she shrieked when Anne came in. 'I've graduated to eyebrow pencil and I have a bureau. I get a pack- age of cigarettes every other day. Did you bring the carton? Good. I'll stash them away. We still have to be lit up, but the night nurse at Fir House is a fan of mine. Last night she snuck me out of my room into her lounge and let me watch an old movie of mine on the late show. We both smoked like crazy.'

Neely had gained some weight, but she looked well. Her back still hurt, she complained, and she never slept. But she would sit it out for the three months. She understood – they had brainwashed Anne. They did it to everyone. She hated the place, but the girls were nice. Only she had found out they were not as normal as they seemed. Mary Jane was an alcoholic, and Pat Toomey – the society girl who claimed she was only there because her husband was trying to get the children – had no children! She had been in and out of institutions since she was sixteen. The night nurse had told her. 'I'm as normal as apple pie compared to these cats,' Neely exclaimed. 'But on the surface, they all seem fine.'

In May, Neely had a setback. Through her friendship with the night nurse, who had consequently been fired, she had stolen a bottle of Nembutals. They found the half-empty bottle under her mattress. She had fought violently when they tried to take them away – she'd screamed oaths and gone into a frenzied rage that required a ten-hour siege in the bathtub. She was put back in Hawthorn. When Anne visited her, she was sullen and uncommunicative.

Anne continued to visit her every week. She had signed for the new season with Gillian. Kevin had sold the company, but he hung around the studio, and his silent presence was worse than a shrieking protest.

Secretly, Kevin blamed everything on Neely. He was secure in Anne's devotion, he told himself. Anne belonged to him, married or not. Look how long she had stuck when he had been against marriage. He knew it was wrong to hang around like this – the new owners were in full command and everything was running well. But he had nothing to fill his time. An occasional visit to his brokers, his daily shave, lunch with his lawyer . . . but this could not fill a day. So he found himself coming to the studio, watching Anne tape the commercials. And each time he came, he promised himself it would be the last.

He was telling himself this again. It was a cold, rainy day, unseasonable for June. He sat outside in the hall while Anne rehearsed in the studio. Well, in three more weeks the show would go off for the summer. Anne had promised they'd take a vacation together – but it would probably be Dune Deck in the Hamptons, so she could still visit Neely each week.

Jerry Richardson, the director, brought a stranger over. 'Kevin, I'd like you to meet a friend of mine, an old buddy. We were in the war together. Kevin Gillmore, Lyon Burke.'

Kevin froze at the name. It had to be the same one – it wasn't a common name. He looked more like an actor than a writer. A good build, too, and that tan . . . Kevin suddenly felt pasty and old. He was also suddenly aware of his own thinning hair. Burke's hair was coal black, heavy, just getting gray at the temples. And the big grin the bastard had. Kevin smiled nervously and shook hands with Lyon.

'You joining the outfit?' he asked.

'No. Just got into town a few days ago. Had lunch with Jerry, and he told me an old friend was working here – Anne Welles. I dropped by to say hello.'

'I'll see if she's free,' Kevin said quickly. 'I discovered her . . . made her the Gillian Girl. Come on, she's in the studio.' He took Burke's arm. He had to be there, to see Anne's reaction.

She was going through the final dress rehearsal, so Kevin and Lyon sat in the audience. He knew she couldn't see them behind the strong lights and cautiously fastened his attention on Lyon, watching his reactions. Lyon watched the rehearsal with interest. 'She's really excellent at this,' he said to Kevin, as if making a surprising discovery.

'She was great right from the start,' Kevin said carefully.

'This is the first time I've seen her. I've been in Europe.'

'They're breaking now. Want to come around and say hello?' Kevin made his voice casual.

'By all means!' He sprang up and followed Kevin.

Anne was discussing some changes with the producer when the two men approached. She saw Kevin and smiled intimately, with a wink that said, 'This will be finished in a second.' At first her glance passed over Lyon – then it returned in startled disbelief.

'Yes, it's me,' he said with a bright smile. He walked over and took both her hands.

She smiled weakly. She actually felt her lips tremble. Lyon, more overpoweringly attractive than ever . . . Somehow she found her voice and said it was good to see him.

'Can we sit a bit?' he asked. 'It's devilishly hot under these lights. Or must you continue?'

'No, as a matter of fact I'm through until taping time.'

'I have some things to attend to at the office,' Kevin said. 'Why don't you both run off for a while – you must have a lot of catching up to do.' He nodded and walked away. Anne knew it was the most dif-ficult move he had made in his life.

The pain of his grandstand play of pride and dignity was revealed in the stiffness of his shoulders. Her heart went out to him. He was scared – but he was fighting for a show of courage. She was also fight-ing as she led Lyon to her dressing room. He's back – just like that, she thought. And am I supposed to forget fifteen years of silence and hold out my arms to him? Yet that's exactly what I want to do. I can hardly look at him without wanting to reach out and touch him. But there's Kevin now . . . Where would I have been without Kevin? And where was Lyon all these years!

In her dressing room they sat down. She let him light her cigarette and deliberately waited for him to speak.

'Well, it looks as if you were right,' he said.

'About what?'

'New York . . . your real love.' He waved his hand, taking in every-thing around her. 'You liked it here, and you've made it, Anne. I'm terribly proud of you.'

'You made it too, Lyon.'

'Not in dollars and cents, or in high-styled success. But yes, you could say I made it, because I am doing what I really wanted to do. And I believe you're the same girl who once told me that everyone owed himself that chance.'

'What are you doing in New York?'

'We're terribly fascinated with your commercial television and the quick buildup of your artists. One of our newspapers has assigned me to write a series covering all the aspects of your television – the girls who make millions with one hit record, the cowboy stars who wind up owning factories – and the girls who become financial wizards sell-ing nail polish.'

She laughed. 'Don't you have that over there?'

'Not yet. Oh, I suppose it's coming – we're about ten years behind you – but at least I can prepare the British Isles for the invasion that *will* come.' He smiled. 'It's a far cry from the writing I set out to do, but it's a windfall. Pays well, and also gives me a chance to visit the States.'

'How long will you be here?'

'About six weeks, I should think.'

'Have you seen Henry?'

'We lunched yesterday. Henry's tired. He wants to sell the business. George Bellows is trying to raise the money, and if not, the Johnson Harris office will buy him out.' He lit a cigarette. 'I saw George, too. He's quite prosperous looking. But I don't envy him. It's the same rat race.'

'Nothing comes easy, Lyon.'

'No, not even this bit of journalism I'm going to take a shot at. There's research, and a lot of bloody figures that must be checked and rechecked. I can't just write it off the top of my head. But I enjoy it.' He leaned across and took her hands. 'And what about you? No marriage – or babies – Henry says you're still single.'

She looked away and hoped the heavy television makeup covered her self-conscious flush.

He held her hands firmly. 'I've come up zero too,' he said. 'It's my one regret. There is no one like you, Anne – there never could be.' He paused. 'I'd like very much to see you while I'm here. I'll understand if you can't – Henry says you and this Kevin Gillmore—'

'You can see me, Lyon,' she said evenly.

'Marvelous! When shall it be?'

'Tomorrow night, if you like.'

'Great. Where can I reach you?'

'Let me call you,' she said quickly. 'I'll be on the outside on some appointments during the day.'

He scribbled down his hotel and number. She noticed he was staying just three blocks from her apartment. She smiled and promised to call him at six.

'We'll plan on dinner,' he said easily. He stood up. 'I'll leave now – I'm sure you want a chance to freshen up before you tackle this thing on camera. I'm terribly proud of you. Till tomorrow, then . . .'

For a long time she sat very still. Lyon was back. Nothing had changed. But it had – she was no longer twenty, and the years had brought changes. There was Kevin, who had given her love, trust – and

352

her career. Kevin needs me, she thought, and in walks Lyon, just for a visit, and I act like an idiot, ready to kick over the traces and forget all the years without a word. Tomorrow I'll call him and say I'm busy. Or maybe I won't even call. Let him wait, like I waited so long.

But she knew she would see him.

Kevin didn't mention it until they had finished dinner. Then he casually asked what Lyon was doing in New York. She explained his assignment. Kevin listened intently as he studied his brandy glass. Then he said, 'Well, now that I've seen him, I can understand. A girl of twenty would be attracted to a man like Lyon. Of course he's a bit too obvious – his looks and that phony English charm – but I suppose a young, impressionable girl would find him attractive.'

'Yes.' She sipped her drink. 'But part of Lyon's charm is his unawareness of his looks—'

'Ha! Don't kid yourself!' Kevin said with a trace of irritation. 'That bird knows his power. He operates on those looks. There's not a wasted movement. He also knows how to make men like him. I'd have liked him, if he wasn't your Lyon Burke.'

She smiled and reached for a cigarette.

'Anne.' His tone was urgent. 'Say something. I'm trying to play it cool, like they do in movies, but for God's sake, help me, give me something to grab at – tell me he left you cold.'

'No, Kevin. I'd be lying if I said that.'

'You're not going to see him again?'

'If you tell me not to, I won't.'

'But you want to?' He was pleading for a denial.

She avoided his eyes. 'It might be wiser if I did. Wiser for both of us. I might find everything I thought attractive about him kind of childish now. As you say, his appearance hits one hard – but I don't know what Lyon Burke is like now. Maybe I never knew . . . maybe I dreamed him into an image. Henry warned me about that. But if we want any chance at happiness, you and I, then I have to find out.'

'You mean I could blow the whole thing because this sonofabitch got some newspaper assignment? If he hadn't, you'd never have seen him again. You know that!'

'Of course I do. Kevin, I care for you . . . deeply. We have years together that can't be dissolved. But Lyon was something that ended on a high note. Maybe I'll find it ends with a flat one after all, but I've got to find out.'

'Don't, Anne. Don't see him!' It was a harsh croak.

'Kevin . . . please . . .' She looked around the restaurant uneasily.

'Anne.' He groped for her hand, almost spilling a glass of water. 'Anne, you're my life. I can't live without you!'

'You won't have to, Kevin.'

His eyes held hers. 'Is that a promise?'

She saw tears in his eyes. 'Promise,' she said miserably.

She couldn't come to terms with herself the following day. She reached for the phone a dozen times to call Lyon and cancel the date. But she never finished dialing. Maybe it *would* fall flat. Maybe she *could* just walk away. That would solve everything. She had promised Kevin she wouldn't leave him, but she hadn't promised not to see Lyon. She had to see him.

They met at the Little Club at seven. He was sitting at the bar when she came in, and he sprang to his feet and led her to a table. 'You're just not the type to sit at a bar,' he said. He looked at her intently after they had ordered a drink. 'Anne, you look marvelous. You haven't changed a bit. No, that's not true. You are much more lovely.'

'You've held up fairly well too,' she said wryly.

'I often wondered about you,' he said. 'Sometimes when I longed for you I'd console myself with crazy fantasies. I'd tell myself you were fat, with six or seven sniffly little brats clinging to your skirts. At least it got me back to the typewriter.'

She laughed. 'Oh, Lyon – and I used to pretend you were bald.'

It was easy after that. She told him about Jennifer, carefully skirting the real truth. Somehow she felt that Jennifer's legend must be kept intact – that the body beautiful should not be blemished by cancer. They discussed Neely. Henry had told him about that, but he couldn't believe it could happen to the bright-eyed Neely he had known.

'She's such an enormous talent,' he said. 'She's frightfully popular in England. Her pictures were quite wonderful for Hollywood products. In spite of all the tinsel and sugar candy they surrounded her with, she still emerged as a true artist. She will come out of it, won't she?'

Anne's eyes clouded. 'They say she's bent for self-destruction, that her kind of illness is never really cured. It may be arrested, and with help she might be able to function again. But she'll always have that self-destructive urge. At least, that's what the doctors say.'

He sighed. 'Perhaps that's why I never made it big. Sometimes I think all great artists are a little barmy. I'm much too normal. I fall asleep the minute I hit the pillow, don't drink to excess and never even take an aspirin.'

She laughed. 'I guess I'm second-rate too. Perhaps I smoke too much, but I'm still a one-drink girl, and although I'd never admit it, I sometimes fall asleep right in the middle of the late movie.'

He laughed back. 'No, Anne, you're first-rate – there's no one like you. There really isn't, you know. Every girl I met, it always washed out. They just couldn't stand up to your image.'

They talked through dinner about New York and the changes he noticed. He introduced her to Irish coffee and she became an instant devotee. She was still praising it when he suddenly turned to her. 'It's all the same, Anne. I want to take you in my arms this moment. I feel as if we've never parted.'

'I want to *be* in your arms, Lyon.'

He grinned. 'It's a deal. But I think it's best if I paid the check and we got the hell out of here!'

It was unbelievable. To be lying beside him, watching the smoke curl into the light of the bed lamp . . . There had been no hesitation, no bridges to cross; they had come together in a fusion of love and desire. This was complete fulfillment. When she held him in her arms she suddenly knew it *was* important to love – more important than *being* loved. And she knew this was a decision she had to make. Lyon loved her, in his own way. Was it enough? Would she miss Kevin's tender, unselfish devotion, the one-sided way he lived for her? With Lyon she would have to be on her toes every second. Was she up to the give and take of this kind of love?

He reached out and stroked her bare back. 'It was wonderful, Anne. It always was.'

'For me too, Lyon – but only with you.'

'Anne, there *is* Kevin Gillmore,' he said quietly. He felt her stiffen and stroked her head. 'It's common knowledge, darling. And everyone knows he wants to marry you.' He paused. 'You know I didn't just happen on the set yesterday, don't you? I made it a point to look up Jerry Richardson. I wanted to meet this Kevin Gillmore – and I wanted to see you.'

She pulled away and sat up. 'What was I supposed to do? Sit around all these years and pray for your return? Lyon . . . not a letter, not a word . . . nothing.'

'Hush.' He put his fingers across her lips. 'Of course I understand. I *wanted* to write – oh, God, the letters I wrote and never mailed – but that bloody pride of mine . . . Each book would do it, I'd tell myself. Then I'd return the conquering hero and take my girl away from whatever guy she was with. But I'm *not* the hero – and Kevin Gillmore is *not* just a guy. He's a good man, Anne, and from what I hear he's head over heels about you.'

She was silent.

'If I had any character, I wouldn't see you after tonight,' he said.

'Lyon!' There was fear in her voice.

He laughed aloud. 'I said *if* I had any character. I'm afraid I never had very much. And seeing you made whatever shred I had go up in smoke.' Then he said very seriously, 'I'll be here, Anne, for the taking, any time you want me. But that's all it can be.'

'What does that mean?'

'I return to London after this assignment. I have a new book in the works. The first draft is written.'

'Couldn't you write here?'

'Possibly. But I couldn't live, at least not as well. I have a nice flat, and I pick up extra money doing articles. It's a different life, Anne, but I like it.' Then he added, 'And I earn just enough to make it possible to spend those bleak hours at the typewriter, writing what *I* want to write. It's a lonely existence, but there's always the hope that perhaps *this* is the book that will do it. I believe in my writing and what I'm trying to do, and I have you to thank for this. I've lost you because of it – but then, it probably couldn't have worked any other way . . .'

'Why not?' she said stubbornly. 'If I hadn't opened my big mouth that day in the Barberry Room – if I hadn't insisted that you write – you might have been the biggest manager in town and we'd have children and—'

'And hate one another. No, Anne, a marriage hasn't a chance when you're scrambling for success. And it probably wouldn't have worked if you had meekly submitted to that wild idea about living in Lawrenceville, either. I'm just cut out to be a loner, I guess. But I am so very glad to have this chance to be with you again. I'll cherish every second you give me, and stretch out all the memories for those rainy British nights when I'm home again.' He took her in his arms, and her hurt evaporated in the incredible wonder of loving him.

It was dawn when she reached her apartment. As she slipped the key into the door, she noticed the sliver of light.

'How did you manage to tear yourself away so soon? It's not morning yet.' Kevin was sitting in the living room, smoking.

She walked over and snatched the cigarette from his mouth. 'You haven't smoked since your heart attack. What are you trying to prove?'

He sneered. 'Why the big concern for my health? Seems to me that after tonight I have very little future.'

'Kevin, why did you come here?'

'Because I knew you were with him. Tell me about it. Did he release all those inhibitions? Did you both swing from chandeliers?'

'Stop it! It's not good for you to carry on like this. Come on – if you want to stay the night, go to bed.'

'Would you go to bed with me tonight?' He saw her stiffen. 'If you did, you'd be a wet deck. That's the name for a girl like that. Well, would you?'

'Kevin . . . we haven't had sex since your heart attack. It's not that I've minded – I understand about your health and . . .'

'And my age – go on, say it.'

'Whatever happened tonight is between Lyon and me. It has nothing to do with my feeling for you.'

'Am I supposed to take that? Let Lyon play the stud, and I play the doddering faithful retainer?'

'You are my friend, part of my life . . . someone I love deeply. Lyon is something . . . different.'

'Well, I won't stand for it. You'll have to choose.'

'All right, Kevin,' she said wearily. 'If you force me . . .'

He grabbed her. 'No – no! Anne, don't leave me!' He began to sob. She wanted to pull away; instead she stroked his head. It was so terrible to see a man fall apart. Was she responsible, or was it his failing health and his age?

'Kevin, I won't leave you.'

'But you'll go on seeing him. Do you think I can go on like that? Knowing you come to me from his arms?'

'Kevin—' She groped for the right words. 'We both know I was with Lyon. But he's going back. And he knows about you. He even said you're quite a guy.'

'That's the English in him. Don't you know that? All the English are decadent. He'd probably get a kick out of sharing you.'

She sighed patiently. This wasn't Kevin speaking. It was his hysterical fear. 'Kevin, I'm staying with you.'

'Why? Doesn't he want you?'

She turned and went into the bedroom and began to undress. It was unbelievable. History repeating itself. Kevin had suddenly looked like Allen Cooper – the same cowlike expression and the same childish rage. And once again it was Lyon who was sitting back, demanding nothing and promising nothing, while she was being torn in two. How much did she really owe Kevin? Her relationship with him had been far from thrilling. Yet throughout the entire time she had never given him cause for jealousy or concern. There had been many chances – many men younger and more attractive than Kevin – but she had ignored every advance. She had given him fourteen years of happiness – shouldn't that balance any obligation she owed him? Yet Kevin needed her. He had sat there all night, smoking. She knew how it was to sit and wait for someone. Suddenly she felt a great surge of tenderness and pity for Kevin. Oh, God, he had looked so old, so vulnerable. She couldn't hurt him.

She returned to the living room. He was sitting there, staring into space – crumpled, defeated.

She held out her arms. 'Kevin, I love you. Get undressed, it's late. Get some sleep. I'm here – I'll always be here, as long as you want me.'

He stumbled toward her. 'You won't see him again? You won't?'

'No, Kevin. I won't see him ever again.'

For two weeks she fought against calling him. She tried to blot him out of her thoughts. Although he never called her, she knew he was there, waiting. But she called on every bit of self-discipline she had ever known and managed to hold out. There were nights when she was alone, obsessed with the need to phone, to race down the three blocks to his hotel. She'd stand on her terrace, breathing in the balmy night air and looking at the stars. A night like this was made for love – to be with Lyon, not to stand alone like this. And invariably there'd be a call from Kevin, casually checking up on her. He had never done that before, but now he had taken to calling at odd hours. Often he'd leave her and say pointedly, 'Well, my girl, back to my bachelor quarters. Tonight it's going to be a warm bath and bed for your old man.' Three hours later he would silently let himself into her apartment. 'I couldn't sleep,' he'd say. 'May I spend the night here?' She'd smile and pity the relief that flooded his face at finding her home, alone.

She was at '21' with Kevin and one of the new owners of Gillian when Lyon walked in. It was the end of June, one of those sticky, hot nights that suddenly arrive with no warning. The temperature was in the nineties. She had taped commercials all day, and she was tired. And bored. She looked up and saw Lyon swing into the room. He was with what Kevin would call a 'dish,' and he didn't see her as the captain led him to a different section of the room. From her seat she could watch him without being observed. The girl was about nineteen, with coal-black hair that hung to her shoulders. Her tan was heavy, and it was obvious that she had worked at it systematically. She had a pretty face, and her sleazy white dress clung provocatively to her youthful body, its tiny shoulder straps showing an expanse of decolletage. Her hand, with its outrageously long silver fingernails, kept entwining itself in Lyon's. She hung onto his words. She tossed her hair. At one point she said something and Lyon threw back his head and laughed. Then he leaned over and planted a light kiss on the tip of her nose. Anne felt physically ill. How many nights had he spent with girls like this? All those nights she had lain awake, wanting him, thinking of him, picturing him alone and thinking all she had to do was call . . .

It was the worst night she had known in a long time. The depths of her unhappiness frightened her. She had not felt anything so deeply since the old days with Lyon, but now it was as if all her senses had suddenly been awakened – all the emotions she had thought were part of her youth – they weren't dead, they had just been sleeping, waiting to be activated. She kept her eyes riveted on Lyon and the girl, grateful Kevin was deep in some discussion of stock options.

At last the endless evening was over. As she left she shot a final glance at Lyon. He was giving his undivided attention to a story the girl was telling.

She pleaded a headache, but Kevin insisted on coming up. The moment they were in the apartment he said, 'I saw them too.'

'Who?'

'Your lover and the beautiful girl. You sat there, eating your heart out, didn't you?' His voice was nasty. 'Now maybe you know how I feel!'

'Kevin, I'm tired.'

'She could be your daughter, Anne.'

'Come now, Kevin – I'm only thirty-six.'

'Lots of girls have babies at eighteen. Oh, she could be your daughter, all right. See, my pet, your Lyon is still roaring. He can have his pick. In fact, did it ever occur to you that maybe he just laid you for old times' sake? Out of pity, like you pity me. Well, cheer up – we're a set, you and I. Two discards. And in a way I'm beginning to pity you. You're probably still dreaming of that wonderful night of love. Well, it was only a night he tossed to you out of sympathy and guilt.' His anger grew as he noticed her eyes darken with pain. 'Sure, that's all it was! Did he plead with you to leave me, to marry him? You bet he didn't! When he marries it will be a dish. You've had it, my lady. Sure, you're a beautiful woman – in your late thirties. But he liked you when you were twenty, and even then he walked out on you. And it was good old Kevin who picked up the pieces. Kevin who made you rich and famous.' He started for the door, then stopped. 'You know, I could get a girl of twenty if I wanted. Oh, don't worry, I'll stick with you – but the shoe is on the other foot now. I call the shots from now on. Tomorrow you hand in your notice. I'm not sitting around next season while you work. And we'll take that round-the-world trip we planned – only I'm not sure there's any point in getting married first. I'll have to think about that.'

She had been staring at him while he spoke. When he finished, she said, 'Kevin, you don't mean any of this. This isn't you.'

'Yes, lady, I've finally gotten my balls back. All along I've been so grateful for your favors – until I saw you tonight. God, what jealousy does to a person. You disintegrated before my eyes. You suddenly looked faded and washed out beside that dish. The lines of anxiety in your face . . . My goddess suddenly toppled. I saw a faded blonde gazing in open envy at a stud she'd lost to a better filly.'

'Kevin, please leave. You can't mean these things.'

'Don't play the *grande dame* with me. That's over. You're a reject now! Want me to prove it to you? He should be home by now – he couldn't wait to get that dish in the kip. Would you dare phone him now? Phone him and tell him you want to see him. I'll clock it. You'll get the fastest brush in town.'

She started into the bedroom. He ran after her and spun her around. 'I'm not through talking. Don't you walk out on me. Haven't you been listening? That's all over, that *grande dame* act.'

'Kevin, you really hate me, don't you?'

'No, I feel sorry for you. Like you have for me.'

'If you mean that, please leave – for good, Kevin.'

'Oh no.' He smiled with confidence. 'Not until I see you really go down the drain.' He picked up the phone. 'Call him. I'm sure you've memorized his number. If you don't, I will. I'll tell him you didn't eat any dinner, that you were sick with jealousy. Sure, I've memorized his number too. We've both been thinking of him for two weeks, haven't we?' He picked up the phone and started to dial.

She pulled the phone away from him. He shoved her and grabbed it back.

'Kevin!' He had actually dialed and was asking the hotel operator for Lyon Burke.

'All right.' He handed her the phone. 'Talk to him. Go on – or I will.'

She took the phone. They were ringing his room. She prayed he wasn't there. This couldn't be happening. It was a nightmare. She heard the click . . .

'Hello?' It was Lyon.

'Lyon?' Her voice faltered.

There was a pause. 'Anne?'

'Go on,' Kevin hissed. 'Tell him you want to come over.'

She shot him a beseeching look, and he made a motion to grab the phone. She pulled away. 'Lyon . . . I'd . . . like to come over.'

'When?'

'Now.'

There was a fraction of a pause. Then, in a bright voice, he said, 'Give me ten minutes to reorganize things a bit, then come directly.'

'Thank you, Lyon. I'll be there.' She hung up and looked at Kevin. His face was pasty.

'Sure,' he shouted. 'I should have known. It'll be a threeway bit – you, Lyon and the broad. I told you the English were decadent . . . And you'll go along – because you have no choice!'

'Oh, Kevin,' she moaned. 'What have we done to each other?'

'I just found I've wasted a lot of years of my life on a bum! A bum who's been passing as a lady.' He walked out, slamming the door.

For a moment she stood motionless, as her anger gave way to mingled feelings of sorrow and relief. Kevin had made the decision. God, what a terrible thing jealousy was – it could transform a strong man like Kevin into an emotional cripple. But she felt no animosity. She was suddenly flooded with relief. She felt almost light-headed, as if a great weight had been lifted. No matter how it turned out with Lyon, she would never have to marry Kevin. That was finished . . . she was free!

She freshened her makeup and quickly walked the three blocks to Lyon's hotel.

The door swung open. 'I was beginning to give up hope,' Lyon said.

Her eyes quickly swept the room.

'She left,' he said quietly.

She pretended not to understand.

'I saw you when you were leaving "21." My glorious little date squealed, "Oh, isn't that Anne Welles!" She adores you on television.'

'Yes, I saw you, Lyon.'

'Good, at least it brought you to me!' He crossed the room and mixed two drinks at a card table that served as a makeshift bar. 'You know, it's a new kind of show business today,' he said. 'I confess I don't understand it. But mine is not to reason why. Connie Masters' last two records sold in the millions, and the British public adores her. So I have to write about her thrilling life.'

'Who is Connie Masters?'

'The charmer I was with tonight. Don't tell me you've never heard of her?' Anne shook her head and he smiled. 'We're the lost generation, you and I. We both think of Dinah and Ella or Neely when someone mentions singers. But Connie Masters is today's sensation. She's nineteen, and every picture company is after her, but I can't listen to one of her records without a stiff drink.'

She smiled. 'I know. Every day I hear of people I never heard of before. I guess the teenagers support them.'

'Well, I've done my bit for the British press and the music lovers of the world. And your call kept me from serving beyond the call of duty.'

'You mean you would have made love to her?'

'Why not? It gets very lonely sitting and waiting for your call that never comes. Oh, I understand . . . I really do. But there she was, all curled up on that very chair you are sitting on, telling me she just *adores* older men. What was I to do? Turn her out into the hot night?'

Anne laughed. 'Come on, Lyon, you're not that helpless.'

'No, but this new breed catches one off guard – the young barracuda.' He crossed the room and pulled her to her feet. 'Now, you're beautiful, glamorous and dangerous, yet I feel safe with you.' He kissed her and held her close. Their embrace was suddenly shattered by the ringing of the phone.

She smiled. 'The barracuda.'

He picked up the receiver. She saw his eyes narrow. Then in a cold voice he said, 'I suggest you speak to the lady herself.' He turned to Anne and extended the phone. In answer to her mute question, he said clearly, 'Kevin Gillmore.'

'I don't want to talk to him.' She backed away.

'I suggest you do,' he said, and she was aware that during this exchange he had made no effort to cover the phone. Kevin was listening.

She took the receiver gingerly, as if it had a physical power of its own. 'Kevin?'

'Anne! Anne, forgive me! I just told Lyon Burke, something happened to me tonight. I went crazy. Anne, tonight never happened. I didn't mean a thing I said. Anne, are you listening?'

'Kevin, it's no good. It's over.'

'Anne, please . . . come home. I didn't mean a word. You can go on working . . . you can do anything you want—' His voice broke. 'I'll marry you tomorrow – or whenever you choose. I'll just hang on. You call all the shots. I'll do anything. *Please!* It was just seeing you look so unhappy because he was with that girl – you never looked at me that way – I guess I went crazy. I wanted to hurt you like you hurt me.' He was actually sobbing. 'Please, Anne . . . I know I'm old. If you want to see Lyon Burke on the side, I'll even let you do that – just don't tell me. You can do anything, just forgive me and don't go out of my life.' He began to choke.

363

'Kevin, is anything wrong?'

'No. I guess I walked too fast. I'm at your apartment. I ran all the way. Anne, please . . . To Lyon you're just another lay, but to me you're my whole life!'

'Kevin . . . we'll talk tomorrow.'

'Anne, I won't sleep. Not tonight, with you there, knowing what you're doing—' She heard him gasp again. 'Anne . . . please. Tonight . . . just come back tonight. Let me sleep in the next bed. Just so I know you're back. From here in I won't check on you. Just stay with me. Please. Anne . . . I can't fight him – I'm not young or healthy. Please . . . please!'

'All right, Kevin.' The phone was like lead in her hand.

'You'll leave?' The hope in his voice was even more heart-rending than his tears.

'Yes . . . right away.' She hung up and turned to Lyon.

'In the middle again?' His back was to her as he freshened his drink.

'Lyon, what should I do?'

He shrugged. 'I'd say it was a matter of whom you wish to please. Yourself – or your conscience. What are you searching for? Happiness – or peace of mind?'

'Aren't they the same?'

'No. Peace of mind does not always come with love. I'm sure you'll have peace of mind with Gillmore, and a good conscience. With me, you might have to battle that conscience. But then, love is always a bit of a struggle, isn't it?'

'Are you saying you love me?' she asked.

'Good God, must it be put in neon lights to get through to you? Of course I love you!'

'But how could I know? You've never called me during these two weeks, or tried to convince me.'

'I'm talking about love,' he said hotly. 'Not begging! Love shouldn't make a beggar of one. I wouldn't want love if I had to beg for it, to barter or qualify it. And I should despise it if anyone ever begged for *my* love. Love is something that must be given – it can't be bought with words or pity, or even reason. I shall never beg you, Anne. I love you. You *must* know that. I shall always love you—'

'Lyon, you know I love you. I always have . . . I always will . . .'

364

'Then why are we standing here batting the subject around? You're here, and I want you here.' He smiled but remained across the room.

'But you're returning to England . . .'

'And Kevin is in America.' He smiled. 'I was talking about love – you are talking about geography. It sounds very familiar, somehow.'

'But love means planning together . . . *being* together.'

'Love is an emotion. To you it's a contract with unbreakable riders and rules attached to it.' He took her hands. 'Anne, it's too late for that. Yes, I will return to London, I've made my way of life there. You have all this. Perhaps you should go to Kevin. He fits in with your kind of life. The best I could offer you is a few more weeks.'

'Maybe *I'd* like London, Lyon. Did that ever occur to you?'

'Anne, I'm a writer – maybe not the best, but I work at it. You're not the eager twenty-year-old girl who typed up my manuscripts. You'd be bored in time, and you'd grow to hate it.'

She turned and ran out of the room. She raced down the hall and rang for the elevator. Perhaps he'd come after her. If he did— The elevator opened. She turned and looked back at his closed, silent door, then stepped into the elevator.

She walked slowly back to her apartment building. When she got there, she deliberately walked past the entrance. She had to think this out. Lyon loved her, but he was offering her no future. Kevin needed her, and was offering her a lifetime of devotion. Kevin put things into contracts, with all the riders she wished – but what good was a contract that paid off in a devotion she didn't want? She was always forcing Lyon's hand, crowding him. So what if he didn't ask her to come to London? She could always follow him. London wasn't the end of the world. But that would be begging – Lyon would hate that. 'Love has to be given' – not pursued.

She returned to the entrance of her building. Kevin was up there, and he needed her. How could she hurt him for just a few weeks of happiness? But suddenly all the wasted years with him came to mind – and all the years just like them that would follow after Lyon left . . . But Lyon was here now – and she had the chance to be with him. Yes, that was the solution. Don't crowd Lyon – take the few weeks he had to offer and let it end. Then if Kevin still wanted her, all right – they'd be as he said, two rejects. But meanwhile, there was Lyon. And she was going to be with him – every second, every minute – as long as she could!

365

She turned and walked quickly. Then she began to run. She never stopped running until she reached Lyon's hotel. The elevator ride was agony. He opened the door – he threw his arms around her and held her close. She clung to him. 'Lyon, as long as you are here, I'm here. No questions, no tomorrow – just every second that we can have together now is what will count. I love you.'

He held her face in his hands, looked into her eyes and said quietly, 'We'll make every moment into an hour. I love you, Anne.'

She met with Kevin the following day. He looked haggard. She tried to explain how she felt, that she had to see Lyon. After he left, if Kevin still wanted her . . . If not . . . well, she would understand.

Kevin stared at her silently. Then his face became splotched with color. He paced up and down her living room. 'Why, you're as decadent as your English stud!' His anger seemed to flood him with strength. He slammed out of her apartment, shouting that he would make her pay for this humiliation.

This time Kevin did not call back with tearful entreaties. In the days that followed he took childish pains to appear everywhere with a variety of well-known glamour girls. Kevin, who hated nightclubs, now sought the most prominent ringside table and made a delayed entrance with the most flamboyant-looking girl he could find. The moment a new starlet arrived in town, her name was linked with Kevin's. There was an inside joke around that Kevin read *Celebrity Service* and rushed to meet the planes to book a date with the newest arriving celebrity.

His final and most desperate act was his attempt to cancel Anne's contract with Gillian. Since he still sat on the board of directors, he insisted he had a right to protect the image of the company he had created. He claimed Anne was 'over the hill,' that the Gillian Girl should be younger, fresher, a new face.

His protests forced a board of directors' meeting. It was an unfortunate move for Kevin. He was outvoted, and Anne received a new two-year contract with a ten-thousand-dollar raise. And it was an exclusive television contract – another victory for Anne, who had been fighting against continuing with the strenuous schedule of newspaper and magazine advertising.

Anne was aware of Kevin's actions, but she could never hate him.

She felt nothing now but pity – and a heavy sadness that it had to end this way.

In the weeks that followed, the excitement of her relationship with Lyon surpassed any emotion she had ever experienced. Lyon enjoyed her casual fame, the instant recognition by fans, but she played it down and concentrated her attention on his work. How was the series coming? She listened to his ideas on the way he hoped to present them. He didn't want to pan television in America, but he wanted to do the articles in a tongue-in-cheek style. She read his copy and often offered valuable suggestions.

Although they maintained separate residences, Lyon spent every night at her apartment. One night he said, 'I shall pick you up at seven, but first I must go to the closet for a change of clothes.' From then on they jokingly referred to his hotel room as The Closet. But as the weeks passed, she knew his assignment was drawing to an end. He hadn't mentioned leaving, but she knew the time was slowly running out. She felt the desperation closing in on her – heavy and oppressive.

And then, one evening in July, she was suddenly filled with new hope.

They were having dinner in a garden restaurant in the Village. 'This was a wonderful suggestion,' Lyon said. He looked at the clear sky and smiled. 'This is what I miss about New York when I'm in London – the marvelous weather. We could never be sure of an evening like this – there is always the inevitable rain.'

'It's the first nice thing you've ever said about New York.' She kept her voice light.

'I love you so much I'm beginning to see some of its finer points,' he said. 'But how do you feel about rain? We have a great deal of it in London, you know.'

It was happening! He didn't want to leave her. She had to be careful – she mustn't force anything. It had to be his idea. She studied the ash on her cigarette. 'I've never been to London.'

'Think about it.' And that was all he said.

It was all she *could* think about. She discussed it with Henry.

'It would never work,' Henry insisted. 'I've seen Lyon's flat. I visited him last year. He thinks it's a palace, but there's no central heating, Anne, and only four tiny rooms – a walkup.'

'But I have all the money in the world. We could have the best apartment—'

'Haven't you had your lesson?' Henry said sternly. 'No one pays Lyon's way – you'd have to live on what he makes.'

'Then I will,' she said with determination. 'I'll live wherever he wants – I can't live without him, Henry. I'd be happy with him anywhere – even Lawrenceville.'

'What about your contract with Gillian? If you broke it you could never work on TV again.'

'Henry, how much am I worth?'

'Over a million.'

'Then why should I work?'

'And what will you do in London?'

'I'll be with Lyon.'

'Look, Anne – you're not a kid about to plunge into a new life. Neither is Lyon. He's set in his little world over there. You'll have no friends – he sits at that typewriter all day – what will you do?'

'I don't know – I only know I can't live without him.'

Henry was thoughtful for a moment, then he said, 'There's only one solution. You've got to keep him in New York.'

'But how? His assignment is finished. And he likes London.'

'Stall for time. Each day that he stays here, he gets more used to New York. Let me think. I'll call a few guys I know at Barter Publications – maybe we can get him an assignment to write a few articles for their magazines. Only it has to look like an accident.'

'What good would that do?'

'He'd stay on for a while, and time will work for you.'

It was Neely who accidentally came up with the idea. Anne had driven out for her bi-weekly visit, and they were sitting on the well-kept grounds and talking. It was uncomfortably warm, but Neely wanted to be outside. She was fat, but she seemed undeniably well on the road to recovery. She was at Ash House, only one step removed from the outpatient clinic.

'When I get there,' she said happily, 'I'll be able to come to New York for weekends.'

'Neely, do you think that's wise?'

'Sure. It has to work that way. Geez, you can't be penned up like this for six months and then suddenly be turned loose. They got to do it gradual. First you get to the out-patient cottage. Then, after a month there, they let you go into the local town one night to a movie or to the beauty parlor. Then, if that goes all right, they try you with one weekend back in New York. You have to come back here on Monday and they check you to see if you're disturbed. After a while, they let you go home for a week. Then they let you go for good, but you still have to see a headshrinker they assign you to every day. It's the pressure that hits you on the outside that you have to worry about.'

'You mean your work?' Anne asked.

'No, I mean just pressure. Here, there's no such thing. If I sleep, I sleep. If I don't – so what? So I won't make a gorgeous mosaic ashtray in O.T. and I might be off in my badminton game. And I eat what I please. Geez, I weigh a hundred and sixty, but who cares? And Anne – I sing. Christ, I sing like a fucking canary.'

'Oh, Neely, I'm so glad. I knew you would.'

'The darndest thing happened. Once every month they have a dance. It's a real camp. The male kooks get all caked up, and we get all caked up, and we meet in the gymnasium – under supervision, of course. I go because I have no choice. If I refuse I get a bad mark. Well, they have a threepiece band, and one night I got up and fooled around a little. It wasn't great, because the piano player is a school-teacher from the village who plays melody with both hands. But I sang, and suddenly a real sick kook – a guy all gray, with a nutty look – shuffled over. He was a chronic, and I'd never seen him before – the chronics rarely come. They're the incurables, the ones who are kept here for life on a custodial basis. Boy, you have to be a rich kook for that – and we have some. Cottage Eve is for the women incurables and Cottage Adam for the men. Naturally, they're separated from us by twelve acres – in fact, we never see a male kook except at the dances. Well, anyway, this real burnt-out looking male kook shuffled over. One nurse rushed to get him, but Dr. Hall was there and motioned to let him alone. Turned out he hadn't talked in two years, and the doctor wanted to see what he was up to. So anyway, he ambles over to me – I'm singing one of Helen Lawson's old numbers – and he just stands there.

'I keep singing – I start doing some of my old songs – and suddenly

369

he begins singing with me, in the greatest harmony you ever heard. It was so wonderful I wanted to die. Anne, my spine tingled – this cat could really sing. And there was something familiar about him. We sang together for an hour, and everyone clapped like crazy – even Dr. Hall and Dr. Archer. And when it was over, this kook touched my cheek with his hand and said, "Neely, you always had it – we both did." Then he shuffled off. I just stood there. Then Doc Hall came over to me and said, "He's been here two years, deteriorating all the time. It's been a well-kept secret, but I see you know one another. Please don't talk about it. We call him Mr. Jones." Well, I had no idea who he was, but I've gotten cagey in this creep joint, and I can outsmart Doc Hall by now. So I played along. I said, "What shall I call him? He calls me Neely." And Doc Hall says, "Oh, you can call him Tony, but stick with the Jones.'"

'Tony?' Anne didn't understand.

'Tony Polar!' Neely exclaimed. 'He's got some kind of a brain illness he was born with. Lucky he and Jen never had a kid – it probably would have gone nuts too.'

The abortion! Jennifer had known! It was a secret she had never revealed. Tears came to Anne's eyes.

'Neely,' she said. 'Jen never told anyone, but she must have known. Please – don't you tell anyone.'

'Why? He's not married to Jen. She's dead – remember?'

'But she died without ever telling anyone. She wanted it to stay a secret. For her sake and his . . . please.'

'Okay, who would care anyway?'

'Well, when you get out of here it might make great gossip. But don't. Tony just faded from the scene. It's been rumored that he's in Europe, but no one knows and by now they don't care. Let's keep it that way.'

'Sure,' Neely said agreeably. 'But it's sure no secret about me. I got an offer to do a two-part story for a magazine. They'll pay me twenty thousand for it. George Bellows is going to get someone to ghostwrite it for me.'

'George Bellows? How did *he* happen to get in touch with you?'

'Well, you've seen the columns. They've been hinting that I'm fat and can't sing, or that I'm thin and can't sing. So I wrote in that they were half right – I'm fat and never sang better. Then I got Doc Hall to let me make a tape here and I sent it to Henry Bellamy and asked him to play it for the press. He musta turned it over to George, because the next thing I knew George came to visit me. And he got me this offer. He wants to handle me when I get out. He's trying to raise the money to buy Henry out, you know.'

'Lyon says the Johnson Harris office is going to absorb Henry's company.'

Neely shrugged. 'If Georgie can meet the price of Johnson Harris in a few weeks *he'll* buy the company. He might manage it, if he can con that alcoholic wife of his into parting with some loot. She's worth millions.'

Anne's head was spinning. 'What alcoholic wife? George isn't married.'

'George is a cozy one. He was married from the very start – when we first met him. He's been married to this dame for twenty years. But he did it for the business, he said. He thought she'd conk off in a few years. But even though her liver is shot, she's still on the scene and controlling the money. I don't know where he'll get it – unless he gives her a nudge over the hill in the next few weeks. And if I know George, he's not above it. I've always hated the bastard.'

'At least he got you this offer.'

'Well, he'll get his commission. I told him I could use the twenty G's. You've been paying my freight here, and I have to pay you back. And I'll need some money when I get on the outside. But I still hope George doesn't wind up with Henry's business. He gives me the creeps.'

The idea began to form when she left Neely. As she drove home it became a certainty. Henry said she needed time, and this would help. She brought the car to the garage and put in a call to Henry. She had to see him for dinner, right away, and they agreed to meet at a small restaurant on Fifty-third Street.

'Why not?' Henry said, after she told him. 'Lyon would be a natural to write Neely's story. He knew her from the early days. And it would buy you another month, at least.'

'But you've got to sell George on the idea, and George has to present it to Lyon so that I have nothing to do with it.'

Lyon was delighted with George's offer. But he refused to visit Neely. He wanted to remember her as she was, as the fresh-faced

371

child. He had to, he insisted, to write it from that angle. He spoke to her on the phone and sent her copy to approve, and Neely was ecstatic with the way the story was shaping up. The writing went well, and Lyon was ready to do the final rewrite by the end of September.

Early in October, Henry met Anne at '21' after another hurried summons. Her eyes were sparkling as she presented her newest proposition. He listened carefully, then threw up his hands. 'You're a real Panzer division – but it won't work.'

'Why?'

'He doesn't *want* to own an agency. I know it. Lyon likes writing.'

'But Henry, you can try. Tell him you don't want the Johnson Harris office absorbing a business you've put your life's blood into. Please – try.'

'But Anne, even if I tell him that I'm making the loan, he has to find out eventually.'

'I'll worry about that when the time comes. Henry, there isn't a moment to lose.'

Lyon sipped his coffee thoughtfully. 'I'm flattered, Henry . . . but I'm not your man.'

The waiter refilled Henry's coffee cup. He waited until the man moved away before he answered. 'Look, Lyon, I gave my life to this outfit. The Johnson Harris office doesn't deserve the roster of stars I've built up. George Bellows doesn't deserve going down the drain either. Oh, they'll take him on, make him a vice president. But they'll kick him upstairs to such an unimportant position he'll be forced to quit. I tell you I haven't slept nights. That's why I'm offering to lend you the money to buy the agency with George.'

'But why me? Why not lend George the money?'

'Why do you think George hasn't been able to raise it?' Henry asked.

'It's a big bundle, I suppose.'

'No. The word is out – George can't handle it alone. He's a great businessman, but he's not good with people. Half the stars will leave. But if I appoint you – if we do it right, with big publicity . . . start with small column rumors at first . . . how I sent for you . . . then let it build . . . Listen, enough people still remember how great you were.'

Lyon shook his head. 'I appreciate it, and I'm flattered. But I have

372

to pass. I'm happy in London. I don't want the pressure of an agency. I hate the rat race, and I enjoy writing.'

'And what about Anne?'

Lyon studied his cigarette. 'She's the only consideration. Does she know about your offer?'

'No.' Henry hoped he sounded convincing. 'Because I think Anne would want you to make the decision without pressure.'

'But it's such a whopping loan, Henry.'

'I don't need the money. I just want out. My last electro-cardiogram convinced me. But I'd like to see the agency continue. You can pay me back a little each year. I'm not worried.'

'Would you feel very badly if I refused?'

'Yes I would, Lyon. You walked out on me once when I needed you. I need you now. I want you to carry on the agency with George.'

1962

On January second, 1962, Bellamy and Bellows officially became Bellamy, Bellows and Burke. George was president, Lyon was vice president and Henry retired completely, but Lyon was adamant about keeping his name in the firm. There was a champagne party for the press and clients, and this turned into a double celebration when Lyon announced that he and Anne were getting married the following day.

When the party was in full swing, Henry took her aside. No one noticed their little conference.

'He'll have to find out the truth next year,' Henry whispered.

'Why does he ever have to know?'

'Anne, next year you'll have to file joint taxes. Then he'll learn that you loaned him the money to buy the business. After all, he's paying interest on the loan, and you'll have to declare it.'

'But why couldn't you lend him the money then? And I'd lend it to you, and—'

'And we'd all wind up in trouble with the Bureau of Internal Revenue. Anne, I don't have the kind of money sitting around that you have. I haven't made two thousand a week clear and been given large blocks of stock in Gillian. And I didn't have a guy like Henry Bellamy invest a hundred G's in A.T.&T. a long time ago and watch

373

it double. If I'm taking a capital gain I can't invest my own money – oh, what the hell, you wouldn't understand. But I can't use my own money to buy my own business. By the way, I sold out all your Gillian. It's for the best – it's gone up to triple what the company is worth and is due for a big drop. I also had to unload half of your A.T.&T. You'll never starve, but you've got a lot riding on this business. So it's no little toy. Lyon and George better make good – three quarters of your savings are in it.'

'Next year, when Lyon finds out, how do you think he'll take it?' she asked.

'Depends. If he's happy, if the business is going well and he's back in the groove, he'll probably laugh it off. After all, how can a guy be angry because a girl he loves tricked him into marrying her by secretly loaning him money?'

'The only thing that worries me is his gratitude to you,' she said. 'He keeps saying he can't let you down and talking about how much you must believe in him to make such an offer. He said he really didn't want to take over the company, but your belief in him made it impossible to turn you down.'

'Nuts. I notice he didn't waste much time in asking you to marry him. I'm sure that was the deciding factor.'

'Maybe. Anyway, at least I've got a year before the trouble starts. And as you say, there might be no trouble. But I don't care if there is. I can't live without him, Henry. I tried for fifteen years, and it wasn't living. I'd bribe, lie, cheat, anything – just so long as I have Lyon. That's all that counts. Just pray for me when the big secret comes out.'

'Listen, if I know you, you'll be pregnant by then, the business will be booming and Lyon will be secretly delighted that you pulled some strings to make his dreams come true.'

They were married in Henry's apartment the following day. Judge Hellman, a close friend of Henry's, officiated, and George and his wife were witnesses. Anne and Lyon rushed off for a four-day honeymoon in Palm Beach. It was agreed they would live in Anne's apartment. Lyon and George were each to draw seven hundred dollars a week and expenses; the profits would remain in the company, with bonuses distributed at the end of each fiscal year.

Within two months Lyon had signed several of the top English stars. They had also taken away some performers from other agencies. They took on some added manpower. Lyon wanted to set up a California office, but George was more cautious.

'Let's evaluate it carefully,' he said. 'I'll agree that we're loaded with clients. But the really big money comes in putting together television packages. We have to get a few jumbos, sell them on TV and tie up the package. We need a Carol Burnett, a Danny Thomas, a Judy Garland . . .'

'I agree,' Lyon said quickly. 'But we can't get them. They've all got excellent management. Besides, that's the easy way. I think we should build our own jumbos – that's real management. Henry did that with Helen Lawson. Now if we create a star, every other star will want to sign with us.'

George looked over the list. 'There's no one with us that has the potential.'

Lyon was thoughtful. 'If Peter Shay's picture with Metro is as good as the shooting script, we're bound to get a three-picture deal after that. Perhaps we could build him into—'

George shook his head. 'He's a character comedian. We need a guy with romantic appeal, or a big comic, or a woman. Besides, Peter will keep commuting between here and England – you know the English. No insult,' George added quickly. 'But no matter how well they do here, they run back to that wet little island with our loot.'

Lyon smiled. 'That wet little island is a swinging place. One can be quite happy over there.'

'Sure. Home is where the heart is. But that doesn't help us. Now, I have a germ of an idea. Someone we could get, and if we built her into a star we could really write our own ticket. Neely O'Hara.'

Lyon grimaced. 'Nothing is worth that. Besides, she's still at Haven Manor. And let's face it, George, she's washed up.'

'Someone like Neely is never washed up. The public identifies with a loser. They feel they've gone through all the tragedies with her. She destroyed herself at the height of her talent. People talk about her as if she's dead. They think she can never make it again. That's all to our good. Because if we bring her back and put her on top, then we make it, because we've accomplished the impossible. Then you watch how the stars leave GAC, CMA, William Morris, Johnson Harris. They'll figure if we could do this for Neely O'Hara, think what we could do for them. Stars are a funny breed – they're long on talent and short on gratitude.'

Lyon was not convinced. 'But with Neely, we're not dealing with just a has-been, we're dealing with a girl who is emotionally sick, who could fly apart at any time. Anne says she's quite overweight – and she's not exactly eighteen.'

'She's thirty-three, and I'll go along with everything you say. *But* – she's also the goddamdest talent around. I've got some tapes she made just last week at a local recording place up there. She's an out-patient now, and she came to stay with my wife and me last weekend. She's fat as a pig – but she can sing!'

Lyon shrugged. 'But it will take a year to slim her down, and she might crack under the strain. She did before.'

'She doesn't get thin. That's the point. Let her stay fat. She sings – that's all that matters.'

'And what do we do with a fat singer?'

'We book her in concerts. Do you know the money in one-night concerts all over the country? Lena Horne, Garland, Liberace – they all clean up. People will come to see Neely if for nothing more than curiosity. In one year her concerts alone will pay for our office. Our other clients will be gravy. And if we keep her functioning for a year, the stars will come to us begging.'

'If you want to give it a whirl, go ahead,' Lyon said. 'But it's your baby. I'll take care of the office while you launch America's new sweetheart.'

'It's not that easy,' George said slowly. 'She's not crazy about me. And my wife isn't a good influence on Neely.' He paused. 'My wife has a drinking problem. But Neely likes you, and she's under heavy obligation to Anne—'

'One second,' Lyon said quickly. 'Anne works hard. Neely O'Hara is the last thing we need in our life.'

'All I'm asking is for you to make the pitch to her to sign with us, then I'll do the dirty work. I'll handle the publicity and set up the bookings. I'll travel with her. All you have to do is make the original offer. She's ready to leave the fruit farm any time now. We'll get her a hotel suite. She has no money, so the office will pay for it – in fact, we'll pay for everything, including her arrangements and rehearsals. We'll keep a maid with her night and day – I know just the dame, a

Danish masseuse who's strong as an ox – and we'll keep books on every dime spent. When she starts to work we'll deduct it from each pay check until we get back every cent we put up. If she flops on us – well, it's a legitimate tax deduction.'

'It's a pretty big gamble.'

'We've little to lose, and the publicity would probably be worth the few thousand it will cost. Besides, if she hits big she'll be able to pay Anne back. You realize your wife has been footing her bills. She owes Anne close to twenty thousand dollars.'

Lyon shook his head. 'I don't like it, but if you want to go through with it I'll go along. With the understanding that it's your ball game. I'll make the initial offer, but from there on, you take over.'

George nodded. 'Watch me. I'll send our little blimp all the way to the moon – and she'll carry us along.'

Anne let herself into the apartment and switched on the air condi-tioner. She was sorry it was the maid's day off. It was hot and humid, a record-breaking heat wave. She rushed to the bathroom and was violently ill. Then she put a cold towel on her forehead. She smiled wryly. Everyone gets morning sickness, she thought – *I* get evening sickness. She was positive she was pregnant. Ten days late. Of course, she couldn't be sure. She had been two weeks late in February, and she and Lyon had celebrated – then she had awakened with the familiar cramps. This time she hadn't told Lyon. And just yesterday this nausea had begun, at five-thirty both days. Oh please, God, let it be true, she prayed. Everything was so wonderful – and now a baby! It would be a girl baby – a girl who looked just like Lyon.

She was frightened about her happiness. No one had a right to be this happy. Her only tinge of uneasiness was the thought of income-tax time, when Lyon would learn the truth about the transaction. But the business was going well, and she'd have the baby by then. Henry was sure he'd forgive the deception. But there was never anything about Lyon one could take for granted.

They had gone out together to see Neely, and Lyon's enigmatic smile had barely concealed his shock when Neely waddled forth to greet them. She was distorted with weight – her eyes had disap-peared in the explosion of her cheeks, and she had no neck – but she sparkled with the enthusiasm of the old Neely. It was incongruous to see the childish eagerness break through the mammoth mass of flesh.

Neely had signed immediately. She'd wrinkled her nose when Lyon refused all credit and named George as the genius of the operation. She didn't like George, but since Lyon was a full partner and Anne was her best friend, she had been delighted to sign. Within one week she was set up in a small midtown residential hotel with Christine, the enormous Danish watchdog. Christine was not fat, just immense – she looked capable of swimming the Channel. And she had vowed she would pummel Neely into great shape.

'Neely doesn't have to get thin,' Anne had said quickly. 'There must be no pressure about Neely's appearance. All she has to do is concentrate on singing.' Christine had also been warned to watch for pills and alcohol – and for two hundred dollars a week, Christine promised twenty-four-hour service. So far she seemed to be keeping her promise.

Anne left the bathroom. She switched on the light in the living room and poured herself a drink of brandy, hoping it would steady her stomach. Neely was working hard, rehearsing four hours a day, and George had already launched the publicity buildup. Neely's first concert was booked in Toronto, which was far enough from the local critics so that no bad reviews would reach New York. Neely would have a chance to break in her act.

She looked at the apartment wistfully. It was beautiful, but if she was pregnant they'd have to move. And she'd be let out of her contract with Gillian on the 'act of God' clause. She'd be glad to be free. It would give her time to find a new apartment and furnish it. How would she do the nursery? A surge of excitement made her almost dizzy. Oh, God, let it be true!

Two weeks later her hopes were confirmed. At first Lyon took the news with mixed feelings. He was delighted, but it would revolutionize their way of life. Anne would have to stop working the end of June – the baby was due in the middle of January, and her waistline had already thickened an inch. But once she assured him how easily everything would run, his doubts vanished and he joined in her enthusiasm.

In the middle of June they flew to Toronto to hear Neely's concert. Anne sat in the darkened auditorium sick with fear. So much rested

on this appearance. George and Lyon were thinking of their investment, but she realized what a setback it could be for Neely if the
engagement was not a success. Neely had seemed relaxed and calm
backstage. She laughed and said she had nothing at stake, nothing to
lose – she could always go back to the funny farm and make ashtrays.
George was knuckle-snapping with nerves, and Lyon's eyes were narrowed with anxiety.

The lights went down and a full orchestra broke into Neely's
theme, a hit song from one of her pictures. The heavy curtain parted
and Neely came out on the bare stage. She was in a plain, black,
street-length dress. Her legs were still good, and the black dress partially concealed her vast bulk. But there was an audible gasp from the
audience, who had unconsciously envisioned her in the image of her
early movie days. Neely heard it and grinned.

'I'm real fat,' she said heartily. 'But so are a lot of opera singers.
Only with me, you're not gonna get opera. I'm just here to sing my
heart out for you – and my heart is big and fat too, so if you like, I'll
do a lot of singing.'

The applause was deafening. Neely was home before she began.
Her voice was clear, true and haunting. A mass hypnotism took hold
of the audience. They went into a frenzy welcoming Neely back into
their hearts. Anne had never heard such an ovation.

It was the same in Montreal. She broke all house records. In
Detroit she was sold out weeks before she arrived. By then the New
York newspapers were filled with accounts of her comeback, but
George wisely kept her on the road. He traveled with her until
September, while Lyon handled the office in New York. Anne had
obtained her release from Gillian, and she used her new freedom to
furnish the large apartment she had found. Her pregnancy was obvious now, but each fluttering movement of the life within her added to
her happiness. Gillian had wanted to give her a leave of absence, but
she had insisted her resignation be permanent. And even though her
mind was on the future, she felt a small thrill of satisfaction when they
decided on the policy of using different girls every week. It had been
impossible to replace her.

At last George felt Neely was ready for New York. The opening
was set for November. They took over a legitimate theatre and booked
her on a two-a-day policy, a one-woman concert on Broadway. A

week before she opened, her entire three-week engagement was sold out.

Neely's New York opening was traumatic in its sentimental excitement and success. The audience cheered in damp-eyed hysteria, welcoming back their wayward child. And Anne noticed that some of Neely's features were once again beginning to emerge from her face. She was still fat, but no longer grotesque – Christine had pummeled off thirty pounds. Her neck was once more in evidence, though she still had two chins. But after one song, the magic of Neely's voice made everybody forget everything else.

The trouble began the second week of the New York engagement. George and Lyon were trying to sort out the most lucrative offers. There were television guest shots, a picture offer and proposals for several Broadway shows, but Lyon insisted they stick with the concerts. 'Another year at least,' he argued. 'Maybe we can take off twenty more pounds. We'll never get her sylphlike again – we can't chance her dieting – but the rigors of performing, plus Christine, can accomplish wonders. Then we can discuss pictures and television.'

'We have to take a picture or a Broadway show,' George said doggedly. 'She refuses to travel any more.'

'But I just booked Los Angeles, San Francisco and the Palladium in London,' Lyon said.

George shrugged. 'We had a big hassle last night. She's on top, so let's face it – she's a shit-heel again. The old star sickness is beginning to appear. No more gratitude, just power. She told me she wants to stay in one place. Which I suspect really means our girl wants to get laid.'

'Good God, who would want her?' Lyon asked.

George laughed. 'Listen, that's been my headache all these months. We forget, our blimp is still a human being. Maybe they fed her saltpeter on the funny farm, but she's raring to go now. For a while we had a sax player who must have dug distortion. He kept her happy until he left the band. Left? I think he ran for his life. She found a few one-night stands, but now she's had it. She told me she wants an apartment and a steady guy, one who'll always be around when she wants him. I have a hunch the Johnson Harris office is behind this. They've probably sent one of their Steve Stunnings in the black suits and tight pants to kiss her hand and make with the compliments. I think she's looking for an out with us.'

Lyon smiled. 'Let her go. If the Johnson Harris office wants to buy out her contract, let's take it – for half a million.'

'I thought of that,' George said, 'but we can't throw away the bait when the fish are nibbling. I have a lunch date with Paul Elsom tomorrow.'

Lyon whistled. 'That would really start the ball going.'

George nodded. 'His last two pictures have outgrossed everything around. If we get him, we get half the stars in Hollywood. With MCA unloading talent management, the field is wide open. All their stars have made short-term agreements everywhere. I've put out feelers, but Neely is our bait. We've got to keep her.'

'Well, go in there and pitch,' Lyon urged.

'I've pitched. Look, Lyon, let's face it, she's never liked me. That's for openers. She had no choice in the beginning. Now she's hot, so now she can afford not to like me. She called me a greasy pig last night. Imagine that cow calling me a pig. No, Lyon – it's your turn now.'

Lyon sat in Neely's dressing room. The matinee was almost over. He stared at the telegrams pasted around the mirror. Every great star in the business had sent congratulations and good wishes. He heard the stupendous applause, the orchestra playing the curtain-call music. He tensed himself for battle.

Neely was happily surprised when she found him in the dressing room. 'Thank God that pig partner of yours stayed away. We had a whopper of a fight last night.' She accepted a large glass of beer from Christine and gulped it down. 'Whew! That tasted just great. Want some, Lyon?'

'No thanks. How about dinner?' he asked.

'Great. Anne joining us?'

'No, just the two of us.'

She laughed merrily. 'Georgie sent in the first team, huh? Well, I'm still not gonna travel any more. But I'll have dinner with you. Where can we get decent escargots?'

'Let's go over to Louise's. Louise can make anything.'

'Great. Can I dunk there? I want gobs of garlic butter and I want black toast and I want to sop it up. That's the nice part of doing a one-woman show – I have no leading man who will cringe at the smell.'

Then she added sadly, 'And I have no guy to worry about after the show, either.'

'That will come soon enough,' Lyon said. 'You've got New York at your feet.'

'That's just it. But I've got no one in my arms. I want a guy. And I'm gonna be choosy from now on. I'm not exactly a size ten, but I'm not a freak. And it's not just getting laid – I want someone who cares about me, someone I can respect . . . someone to love.'

'Let's talk about it over the escargots,' he suggested.

Neely ordered two dozen escargots. Lyon toyed with six and listened to her complaints. He had to admit she had an honest gripe – she had no life other than performing.

'Neely.' He reached out and took her hands. 'I can see your side of it. Just do Hollywood, Frisco and London. Then we'll settle you here, and perhaps take a picture or a Broadway show. I'll hustle around. If we find the right vehicle we could open in the fall. A Broadway musical would be a perfect move.'

'Who'd go to California and London with me?' she asked.

'George, naturally.'

'Forget it,' she said with determination.

'Now look, you and George have had words, but he's not a bad sort. Neely, your entire success was his idea.'

'There'd have been no success if I hadn't had the talent,' she said sullenly.

'Naturally, but George had the vision to see it, to believe in you.'

'And you didn't?'

'To be honest, no. I was doubtful.'

'You thought I didn't have it any more?'

'I didn't think of the talent part. I thought of the grind. To me, your comeback brought visions of dieting, strain and nerves. It was George who insisted the public would accept you as you were. And he was right.'

Neely dropped the piece of bread she had been about to sop in the butter sauce. She pushed the plate away. 'You talk about me as if I'm a freak.'

'Come now, Neely, you know what I mean. I think you're marvelous – a great talent and a delightful personality.'

'But a fat slob, huh?'

'No, but not quite reed thin. Not like you were in pictures.'

'I guess no man could really fall for me looking like this,' she said. 'I know the twins stared at me when they came to Detroit. God, they're handsome kids. I'm glad they live with Ted. It almost killed me when he got custody while I was in the funny farm, but I guess he's straightened out pretty good. His marriage seems to be working. I still think he's a switch hitter, but the boys don't know. I'll never forget their faces when they saw me, though. Bud – he's the taller one – he said, "Gee, Mom, we saw one of your pictures on the Late Show, but you sure look different now."'

'You don't need to be thin,' Lyon insisted.

'I could be thin if I had a reason to be,' she said sadly. 'I can't get thin under pressure from a studio – but I can for love. Like when the studio yelled at me to stay thin, I became a sneak eater. But when I first met Ted and fell for him and he said to drop fifteen pounds, I did, just like that. Because I *wanted* to, to please him. That's why I want to stay here, Lyon. I want to fall in love, to find a guy. I hate what I see in the mirror.'

'Neely, your voice and personality are what make you, not a waistline,' Lyon insisted.

She shook her head. 'I love pretty clothes. I don't want to keep wearing a plain black dress on the stage. But I have to, this way. It kind of hides things. But I have no incentive to get thin. I have to find a guy – then I'll get thin and love myself.'

'Do Hollywood, San Francisco and London,' he urged. 'The rest will come.'

She was thoughtful for a moment. Then she said, 'Okay . . . if you come along instead of George.'

'Neely, how can I?'

'Look, I can't stand George. If I have to look at that moon face of his day in and day out, I'll vomit. He can't even play gin rummy. Do you play gin?'

'Like Nick the Greek. But Neely, I can't leave. Anne is terribly pregnant. The baby is due in six weeks.'

'Oh . . . I forgot.' Suddenly she brightened. 'Postpone my dates. Book 'em after the baby is born. I could stand a little rest anyway.'

'I couldn't leave Anne then. Not with a new baby.'

'Anne could come with us. Listen, I had twins. I know. A good nurse is all they need the first few months. They don't even see until they're three months old.'

'Let me think about it,' he said.

It was easy to put off the Palladium. Lyon switched the booking to the middle of February. But the Los Angeles and San Francisco dates were impossible to change. Neely had to open there over Christmas and New Year's. Lyon feverishly tried to keep the problem from Anne, but Neely told her.

She had dropped by to see the new apartment. Everything was finally in place. Anne, looking ungainly in her pregnancy, showed Neely every room with pride, especially the nursery.

They settled in the den. Anne sipped some sherry and Neely had a beer. A light snow had begun to fall, and Anne started the fireplace going. 'Our first fire in the fireplace,' she said. 'Make a wish, Neely.'

'Why!'

'You always make a wish on something you do for the first time.'

'Then I wish you'd have your baby tonight,' Neely said.

'Why? I'm not due for at least a month.'

'I know, but I won't go to Los Angeles unless Lyon goes, and he won't leave until the baby is born and you can come.'

Anne knew there was trouble between Neely and George, but this was the first she had heard of the change in bookings. She listened while Neely explained.

'But I wouldn't go to London, even in February. I couldn't leave my baby,' she said.

'Sure you can,' Neely argued. 'It won't even be human by then.'

'It's human to me now,' Anne said hotly. 'Every time it moves inside me I mentally blow it a kiss.'

'They're just blobs the first few months, Anne. Honest. All that crap about them smiling at you – that's just gas. The doctor told me. They just see light and blurs. They don't recognize you or focus until they're about three months old. A good nurse can handle a new baby better than you can.'

'I've waited too long for this baby, Neely. And it's been worth the wait, just to realize I have something of Lyon inside me that we've created out of love. I'll never leave our baby.'

'Suppose Lyon has to travel? After all, he can't stay put in New York forever.'

'Then we'll travel together, the three of us.'

'Well, I won't go to California without him.'

'Neely, please . . . I can't be without Lyon on Christmas. And it's too risky for me to travel.'

'What about me?' Neely asked. 'Does everything have to be for you? You've got everything. You've always had everything. You wind up with money, the man you love and now a baby. I've got nothing – just work. I've made it again, but that's all I've got. And I'm working to pay you back.'

'Neely, I've never asked you for the money,' Anne protested.

'I know, but I told George and Lyon I wanted to pay you back. After the California date, you'll be paid in full. Meanwhile, I'm making money for your husband's office, and you're getting the benefits of that too.' She looked around the apartment. 'I live in a lousy hotel suite with that bull dyke Christine, who acts like my keeper. I'm alone, and all I'm asking is for Lyon to go to Los Angeles with me for ten lousy days. I can't face Hollywood alone. It'll be my first time back. Maybe you think it's easy to step out there and know they're all staring and whispering, "Look how fat she is." And then having to grin and win them over. Sure my talent gets 'em – but I have that first awful minute to face, when they're gasping. I need someone to give me a pep talk before each show. I *need* it, Anne. If I didn't have a friendly face I'd take a Dexie – or a drink. A real drink, not beer. And that would be it. They told me at the funny farm that the minute I start with pills or booze, good-by Charlie!'

'If Lyon wants to go it's all right,' Anne said.

'You put it that way and you know damn well he won't,' Neely snapped.

'No, Neely, I mean it. It will be all right with me.'

'It has to be more than all right or he won't go. You've got to make him go. Otherwise, I just won't play the date. I can always get laryngitis.'

Lyon refused to leave Anne. And he deeply resented Neely's blackmail tactics. 'No fat little pig is going to run our lives,' he said angrily. 'She may be important to the office, but not quite that important.'

'But you're on the verge of getting several big stars,' Anne argued. 'George told me things are really popping. But they'd fall through if Neely left the office – and she could. She could break her contract by saying you refused her personal representation when she most needed it.'

'Then she's free to leave. If George and I have to pin our entire future on this bag of blubber then we really haven't much faith in ourselves. I don't know about George, but I'm getting damn tired of hearing how we need Neely to get the others. Maybe *he* doesn't believe he has anything to offer a client, but Henry Bellamy believed in me enough to offer me the loan. Henry Bellamy would never have let a Neely O'Hara dictate his life.'

'Helen Lawson did her share,' Anne reminded him.

'He was in love with Helen. That made the difference. We resurrected Neely. That should be enough for the trade. And Henry's belief in me is enough for me to chance letting Neely go. I'll not be dependent on anyone.'

The following day Lyon came home earlier than usual. His eyes were cold with anger. He took off his coat and stared at Anne peculiarly. She pulled her bulky frame out of the club chair and started to mix a drink. She sensed some crisis . . . something must have gone wrong at the office. He took the drink silently.

'Was George difficult?' she asked.

He sat down and took a long swallow. Then he looked at her intently. 'Tell me, Anne, do you think I should go to California with Neely?'

She hesitated. It suddenly seemed to be a loaded question. She didn't like the way he was looking at her. 'I don't expect the baby until the middle of January. Of course, I don't want to be without you on Christmas, but I'm trying to be objective . . .'

'Tell me what to do, Anne,' he said in that same strange tone.

'It's for you to decide,' she answered. 'I'll understand, whatever the decision is.'

'No, you decide. You've decided everything else. Tell me, what will our baby weigh? I know it will be a girl, because you decided that. Is there anything you don't control?'

'Lyon, what are you talking about?'

'You! And the Bellamy, Bellows and Burke Agency. God, I must be the laughingstock of this town. I was bought by Anne Welles. I suppose everyone knows but me. I just found out – Neely told me.'

'Neely? How could she know?' Anne was frightened. She had never seen this look on Lyon's face.

'I know, it was supposed to be a secret. Henry explained. But it would have come out soon anyway. All those weekly checks I've been sending Henry have been endorsed by Henry and sent to you. They'd show up in the tax returns.'

'But how did Neely find out?'

'Henry told her. It seems she went to him and told him how things were, hoping he'd convince you to let me travel with her. And that's when Henry gave it away. He said he was sure you'd want me to do whatever was best for the business, since it was your money at stake. Neely couldn't wait to rush to the office to tell me. Of course, George put on the proper act, pretended he was surprised. But everyone has known all along, haven't they?'

'Lyon, no one has known. Henry shouldn't have told Neely. I was going to tell you when the time came. I only did it because I loved you, to keep you from going back to England.'

'And you accomplished it. You can buy what you want! Is that what you learned from Kevin Gillmore? Everything has a price – just find out the amount.'

'But my money is your money.' She fought her panic. 'I only did it because I loved you. I wanted to marry you and have your baby – can't you understand?'

'No. I only understand that George stood there with a smirk and said, "Cheer up, Lyon, we're in the same boat – our wives own the business." But I'm not George Bellows. And by God from now on the business will always come first. Your money is at stake, and I'll get it back for you – every cent. But something more important than money is at stake now – my pride and self-respect. There's only one way to get it back – by doubling your goddam investment.'

'Lyon!' She threw her arms around him, but he remained stiff and unyielding. 'I did it out of love. Do you understand?'

'I understand only one thing – the Bellamy, Bellows and Burke Agency is going to be the biggest agency in town . . . in the world! You bought it for me, my girl, and you're going to get your money's worth. I'll show you. And the first thing I do is book reservations to take our pig of a star to Los Angeles. Christmas be damned – full speed ahead!'

Jennifer Burke was born New Year's Day. She burst into the world two weeks ahead of schedule and gave Anne and the doctor quite a frantic New Year's Eve. She took fifteen hours to make her entrance, but when she finally arrived, red and squalling, Anne saw no wrinkles or wizened newborn face – she saw only the miracle and beauty of the little life she had borne, and her strength surged back at the wonder of it all.

She had been lonely with Lyon gone. Although he called every day from California, the rift was there. She felt it in his casual terms of endearment. It stood between them like a steel gate. But when the baby came, the gate opened. As she came out of the anesthetic haze he phoned, and she said, almost apologetically, 'It *is* a girl . . .' He laughed heartily. 'I'm delighted! I'm much too old to learn to play football with a son. I'll have more fun teaching a teenaged daughter how to dance.'

He called her two and three times a day while she was in the hospital. Neely's triumph in Los Angeles had been record-breaking, and now she was ready to go on to San Francisco. Would Anne mind dreadfully? It meant three more weeks away.

'Of course not,' she said quickly. She did not want to chance reviving any discussion of the firm or Neely's work. Not now, when everything was wonderful again. 'Jennifer Burke will be an old lady by then, but I'll try to keep your memory alive,' she teased.

'George said he'd take some Polaroid pictures of her,' Lyon said. 'Send them to me as soon as they dry.'

'I've just sent the one they took at the hospital. She looks like a little old gnome. But really, she's going to be a beauty, Lyon. She has dark hair – what there is of it.'

Lyon flew into town at the end of the month. Little Jennifer weighed nine pounds and had lost her wrinkles. She was all pink and white, and he was delighted with her. He smiled gently as he studied the tiny face. 'I'm terribly afraid she resembles me,' he said with a frown. 'Anne, you should have concentrated harder. I wanted a carbon copy of you.'

'I did concentrate, and it worked. *I* wanted her to look exactly like *you*.'

He had rushed straight from the airport to the apartment to see her and the baby. Now he had to go to the office. 'We'll celebrate the heiress's arrival tonight at dinner,' he promised.

That night Miss Cuzins, the baby's nurse, helped her squeeze into a waist nipper. It was uncomfortable, but after so many months of being ungainly, she wanted Lyon to see her slim and chic again. Not too bad, she thought, studying her figure in the mirror. Actually her weight had returned to normal; it was just her waistline that was off, and the nipper did the trick. After all, it was only a month. But thank God she would finally be able to go to bed with Lyon that night. It had been so long – not since her seventh month. Poor Lyon. The doctor had warned her there might be some pain at first, but it didn't matter. To hold Lyon in her arms again, to feel his body against her own – that was all that mattered.

His secretary called at six. Lyon was at a screening; would she meet him at seven o'clock at Danny's Hideaway? She hung up, slightly disappointed. She had envisioned cocktails together at home, then a quiet dinner somewhere off the beaten track, where they wouldn't run into everyone they knew. She liked Danny's, but it meant everyone stopping by the table to talk about business. Normally she didn't mind shop talk, but tonight was to be special.

She sat at a table near the bar and waited. It was a quarter to eight and she was on her second Scotch when she finally saw Lyon. He was with two of his assistants and Bill Mack, a television director.

He rushed to her and kissed her lightly. 'Forgive me, please. We were looking at a tape at N.B.C., and the bloody thing split and had to be rerun. Oh, darling, you remember Jim Handly and Bud Hoff,' he said as he brought the two young men over to the table. 'And of course you know Bill.'

They sat at a large table and talked about the tape they had seen, a format of a new situation comedy show. From the conversation, Anne deduced that Bill Mack owned it and that he wanted to sign with The Three B's, as Bellamy, Bellows and Burke was beginning to be known. He wanted them to sell the package. Lyon was enthusiastic. He was sure he could interest C.B.S. or A.B.C., and perhaps redo it with Joey Kling in the lead. Joey had just signed with the office. He was the new comedian of the year.

'He's going to be at the Palladium with Neely,' Lyon explained. 'As a matter of fact, he should be here any second. I told him to pick me up.'

'Pick you up?' Anne turned in surprise.

'Oh, my angel,' he said with genuine concern. 'This all happened three hours ago. Joey is going to Washington to break in his act.'

'But you don't have to go, do you?'

'Don't I ever! Neely thinks she's doing a one-woman show there tomorrow night. I have to explain how important it is for Joey to share the bill with her.'

'I don't envy you,' Bud Hoff said.

Lyon smiled. 'Neely knows there will be other acts on the bill with her at the Palladium, but she hasn't shared the bill with anyone in the States. So far it's been a one-woman show. But when I explain that we've just signed Joey . . . Neely's really a good sort, if you explain things right.'

He was leaving tonight! The realization kept spinning through her head. He was leaving tonight!

'When will you be back?' she asked.

'In two weeks. I'll phone first thing in the morning. Perhaps you could fly down over the weekend. Could little Jen spare you?'

'Must you go tonight, Lyon?'

'I must. I hadn't planned to leave until tomorrow. But I have to get the publicity set on Joey, and I'd best be on hand early tomorrow morning.'

He had only planned to stay in town one night!

Joey Kling suddenly poked his head in the door. Lyon waved. 'I've got the car waiting,' Joey called out. 'And we're double-parked.'

Lyon sprang up. 'Sign the tab to the office, Bud. Good night, my angel – I'll phone you tomorrow. Oh Bud, you will see Anne home, won't you?'

She didn't go to Washington over the weekend. Miss Cuzins had said it would be fine, of course she could go. But Lyon never brought it up. And on Friday he merely said, 'I'll ring you tomorrow, same time.'

'Why don't you just come out and ask what's wrong?' Henry said.

Anne stared into her coffee cup as if expecting some miraculous answer to be revealed in its dregs. 'Because basically nothing *is* wrong,' she answered. 'There's just this intangible difference.'

Henry Bellamy sighed. Anne looked pale and much too thin. She had sounded desperate when she demanded he take her to dinner. He was also afraid of the questions she would put to him.

'Henry, the baby is three months old. Lyon has spent exactly four days with her. One between California and Washington, and three between Washington and London. He's been in London a month now. Neely's a smash. I know she's being held over, but there's no reason for him to remain.'

'What does George say?'

She smiled. 'The same old line. That Neely won't stay there alone. That Lyon is like a god to her, the only one she'll listen to. That she's bringing big money into the office.'

Henry's smile was sad. 'This is the story of being a successful manager. The wife always suffers.'

'But they've gotten several big stars now. The office is doing great. How long do they have to play wet nurse to Neely? She seems all right now. I think she can stand on her own two feet.'

'They're new in the business, Anne. Everyone's watching them. George never was a live wire. Oh, he's a hell of a businessman, but Lyon is the personality boy. And there will always be a Neely or some star to wet-nurse. You might as well face up to it.'

'You mean I go through life like this?'

'It gets easier as time goes along,' he said.

'Not for me it won't!'

He was silent for a moment, then he said, 'Anne, you can't have everything. I've seen your apartment. A layout like that costs money. And Lyon is one of those guys who must pay his own way.'

'But Henry – why doesn't he ask me to join him in London?'

Henry studied his cuticle. 'You've never been abroad, Anne. Perhaps he feels he'd like to be able to show you around. But he's trapped in the theatre all the time. It wouldn't be much fun for you hanging around like that.'

'If he explained it that way I'd understand. And I'd go along with it. I could sightsee . . . catch other shows. As long as I saw him a little.'

'Let it be. He should return any day now.'

'He'll be back in a week. But then what? Who knows where Neely will be booked by then? And off he'll go.'

'Take each problem as it comes,' Henry suggested.

*

Lyon returned ten days later. But he could only stay a week. Neely was going to make a picture in Europe. It would be shot in France and Italy with a top cast. 'She's not making a fortune out of it,' he explained, 'but it will prove to Hollywood and television that she's reliable, because I intend to see that the picture is brought in ahead of schedule.'

'Lyon, take me with you,' she said suddenly.

'Wouldn't work.'

'Why not?'

'Neely can be a monster, you know. Her success in London was staggering. You don't know what it's like when you make it over there. They have a loyalty that's unbelievable. They shout her name when she walks down the street and they queue up for hours just to catch a glimpse of her. Two guys from the Johnson Harris office flew over with a big television offer. Everyone is trying to grab her. And all this is getting to her.'

'But she has to have loyalty to you and George – you rescued her.'

'She's also paid off every cent she owes, to you and to the office. She's making money – and she's making *us* money. The shoe seems to be on the other foot. She thinks we ought to be grateful to her.'

'But what's that got to do with my coming over?'

'It would be a distraction. Neely would resent it.'

'Neely would resent it! I'm your wife. And I'm her best friend. How could she resent me?'

'She's a power again, and she knows it. Don't forget, she allowed Joey Kling to share the bill, and we've gotten Joey a big TV deal for next season out of it. The package will go for a hundred and fifty thousand a week, and we represent that package. That's fifteen thousand a week for thirty-nine weeks. And Neely was directly responsible for it. Next year we'll get Neely a special – once a month, for two hundred thousand each. So right now everything revolves around Neely. If you are there, naturally I'll be splitting my time. I'd want to show you Paris, Rome – I'd want to be with you. I would neglect Neely. Please, my darling, bear with me. In another year I shall be able to pay back your loan in the business. But for the moment, Neely is still the backbone of The Three B's and must be handled with care.'

'But I'm sure Neely wouldn't resent me. She was the one who told me I could leave the baby and travel.'

'Neely is . . . well, she's different now. All she thinks about is Neely. You've got to understand that, Anne. You were never close to her when she was doing well. She always came running to you when things went wrong. She was human then – now she's impossible. I have to watch her every second to keep her from alienating people, to make sure she reports on time. She's regained her feeling of power. She's even started with the tantrums again. Luckily I can control them, and let's hope it keeps that way. But I must devote all my time to her.'

The next three months were impossible for Anne. She spent so much time with little Jennifer that the nurse felt idle and complained. Reports kept coming in about Neely's fantastic success abroad. Lyon wrote sporadically and phoned once a week. The picture was going great, although they had had to reshoot the beginning because Neely had lost so much weight. He'd be home the end of June. Then a week passed without any word at all.

She placed a transatlantic call on July fourth. The operator at the George V announced he had checked out exactly a week ago. No, no forwarding address. She believed he had returned to the States. Yes, Miss O'Hara had checked out at the same time.

She was dumbstruck. Could he have come back by boat? But why, if he was eager to see her and the baby? She called George. He sounded evasive. Yes, Lyon and Neely were due back; no, he had not heard from them in five days.

That night she lay in bed and tried to watch television. Nothing held her interest. She finally turned off the set and settled down with the morning papers. Suddenly an item in one of the columns stood out like a neon sign:

What legendary singing star who has made a phenomenal comeback attributes it, along with her shapely new figure, to her new love? But the star's love story may not have a happy ending. Her love is her manager, who is very much married to a television beauty.

Her stomach lurched. It couldn't be! But Lyon *had* said that Neely had dropped a lot of weight. She felt that she was going to be sick – or faint. Wait, she told herself. All right, maybe Neely has fallen for Lyon. That's not hard. But it doesn't necessarily mean Lyon cares about Neely. Lyon might be holding her at arm's length. Perhaps he realized all along that this would happen. That would account for his reluctance to have her join him in Europe. He might be trying to protect her. It might be that Lyon was having a dreadful time . . . But where was he now?

She reached for the phone and on an impulse placed a person-to-person call to the Beverly Hills Hotel in California. She prayed she was wrong. She got the operator at the other end. Yes, Mr. Lyon Burke was registered – he had checked in three days ago. No, he was not in. Yes, Miss O'Hara was also registered. Her room did not answer. It was only nine o'clock in California – did the party wish to try later? Anne canceled the call and fell back against the pillows. He had been in California three days! He hadn't phoned! She threw on some slacks and rushed out into the night.

Henry took ages to answer the door. 'Jesus, what's up?' he said sleepily. He tied the sash of his robe and led her into the living room. Switching on the lights, he motioned toward a chair. 'Sit down. What's the matter?'

Anne was hysterical. 'You saw it!' She pointed to the morning papers on the floor. 'Henry, don't play dumb with me. I just found out Lyon has been back for several days. He's in California with Neely. He hasn't even called me.'

'Let's have a drink,' Henry suggested.

'Henry . . . help me!' She sank into a chair and began to sob.

He calmly mixed a Scotch and brought it to her. 'Now let's cut the hysteria and face facts. You want to save your marriage, don't you?'

'Then you believe it too!'

'Of course. I've known it for some time.'

She couldn't speak. She stared at him as if the last friend in the world had betrayed her.

'Now grow up,' he said. 'This was in the cards. You have several alternatives. One, you can walk out with your pride intact. Or two, if you want him badly enough and have enough guts, you can ride it out and get him back.'

'I can't live without Lyon,' she sobbed.

'Then start getting some control. Make scenes with him and you throw him right into Neely's arms.'

394

'But she's fat as a pig. He can't care for her.'

'Not any more.' His voice was weary. 'I just got back from the Coast last night. I ran into Neely and Lyon at Chasen's. She looks marvelous. She barely weighs a hundred pounds.'

'Neely?'

'Love can do it, I guess. She dropped about ten pounds in Los Angeles on her first trip, maybe ten more in Frisco and Washington, and the three months in Europe did the trick. She doesn't eat a thing. I watched her. She looks like she'll go up in smoke any second. But she's insane about Lyon. She doesn't take her eyes off him – clings to him every second . . .'

Anne buried her face in her hands. 'Henry, stop it! What are you trying to do – kill me?'

'No, I'm trying to give you the truth. Once you know the facts, maybe you'll know how to fight. Surprise could defeat you. So you might as well have it straight. Now – grit your teeth. This is really the bonecrusher – Lyon is not exactly fighting her off.'

'No . . . no . . .' It was a wail.

'Now stop the hysterics and let's figure out a plan.'

She looked at him in total disbelief. 'Henry, you must be mad! It's finished – over.'

He shrugged. 'Fine. I'll handle the divorce for you. Lyon will have to pay plenty of alimony, and child support. I'm sure he'll agree to everything.'

She began to sob more violently. 'No . . . no . . . I won't give him up.'

'Then pull yourself together. Drink your drink and let's figure this out. You're not the first girl whose husband balled around, and you won't be the last. You just have to figure out what means the most to you, Lyon or your pride.'

'But it could never be the same.'

'No, it won't. Some of the stardust will be gone. But you'll have him. And if I know you as well as I think I do, a little of Lyon is better than no Lyon at all.'

'Henry, how could he respect me if he knew I accepted this?'

'That's just it,' he said impatiently. 'He must never *know* you know. If he did you'd *have* to ask for your freedom. That's just what Neely's gunning for. Look . . . Lyon entered into this innocently. You must realize that. But it's pretty heady stuff, being a Svengali, and the timing was right. Lyon needed something like this for his ego. He's a creative guy, Anne. He feels you sold him down the drain creatively and tricked him into this new career. Which is bullshit – if he really had it, no one could stop it. But now he's creating again. From a large mass of blubber he's etched a slim, vibrant star, a star who seems to depend on him for the very air she breathes. He's not just a manager now, he's a creator. He feels larger than life. It's a great feeling of power. No man can resist it. And Neely plays into his hands by acting helpless. She's as helpless as a cobra, but that's not the way it appears to him. To Lyon you're the strong one, the tycoon – *his* Svengali. Actually, Anne, you're not half as strong as Neely – the Neelys of this world are indestructible – but with your poise and self-confidence you make Lyon feel less a man than Neely does. He probably feels that you castrated him – and not once, but twice. The first time when you refused to give up a city for him, and now by buying him an agency.'

'If you only hadn't told Neely,' she moaned.

'It was the end of December. You and Lyon were happy, and Neely was your best friend – or so I thought. She came to me because she knew you listened to me. She wanted me to convince you to travel after the baby was born. She sobbed, swore she wouldn't go without Lyon, carried on . . . She said you wouldn't listen to reason because you were a millionaire and didn't give a damn about the agency, that you probably wanted Lyon to retire. So I explained she had the picture all wrong, that it was *your* money at stake. After all, I was going to have to tell Lyon in a short time anyway. How did I know Neely of all people would use it against you? Christ, do you know how many times she's told me she owed her whole life to you? You got her put back in *Hit the Sky* by having Lyon intercede. *You* talked to Gil Case about her replacing Terry King. *You* paid the freight for her at Haven Manor. I never thought of Neely as a girl who would turn against you, let alone as a rival for Lyon. It was a big mistake on my part, but done with the best of intentions. And now the thing for you to do is face facts. With you Lyon didn't feel like a big man – then Neely came along and built him to new heights. You'll just have to wait till it levels out.'

'How?' she begged.

'By sitting tight. Stop playing God and be a woman for a while. Let the cobra in Neely come out. Lyon's no fool.' He paused. 'You know, this thing with you and Lyon – it was wrong from the start. But you wanted him. All right, you've got him. And you've gone through too much to throw in the sponge now. Your cue is to act as if nothing has happened. It's not going to be easy – in fact, it may be almost impossible at times, because this thing with Neely will get hotter before it cools down. But if you can hold out the cycle will reverse itself. And he's got to wind up hating her. She'll castrate him – she does that to all men. You ought to hear Ted Casablanca sound off on her. She's all syrup and softness in the beginning, but like all stars, she's solid steel underneath. In time, if you can ride with the punches, you'll wind up as the soft female he has wronged, and he'll feel protective and guilty about you. The marriage will be bruised a bit, and you may not even want him by then – but if you do you'll have him. It's going to be a battle of nerves, but I think you can do it.'

'I'll try,' she said wearily. 'Henry . . . my world's just collapsed. I think tonight I may take my first doll.'

'A what?'

'A Seconal.' She smiled faintly. 'Jennifer and Neely called them dolls. I've never taken one in my life, but I think I've earned one tonight. I wonder where I could get some.'

He went to his medicine cabinet and returned with a bottle. 'Here . . . there's a two-month's supply. I just took one out for myself.'

She smiled faintly. 'You too?'

'For twenty years. It's standard equipment for this business. Take one and get into bed. Don't smoke. If you've never taken one before it will act quickly.'

She took the bottle and left. Her legs felt leaden, and during the cab ride unwelcome pictures of Neely and Lyon flashed through her mind.

At home she stood in the bathroom and stared at the bottle for some time. It was packed with gleaming red capsules. She took them out and counted them. Sixty-five. Henry certainly trusted her. Well, why not? She wasn't about to throw in the towel. She had a child who needed her and a husband she had to get back. All she wanted was a few hours of escape, a few hours to blot out this nightmare that had suddenly erupted. She swallowed one of the capsules. 'All right, little doll. Let's see what all the shouting is about.' She got into bed and picked up the papers she had tossed on the floor. She began to read. In ten minutes the print began to blur. It was fantastic . . . her head grew light . . . her eyes closed . . . It *was* a doll . . . she was going to sleep. Tomorrow she'd think it all out.

Lyon arrived a week later. He said they had taken the polar route home and stopped off in California. She pretended surprise. He looked at her peculiarly. 'You mean you didn't know I was in Los Angeles?'

'How would I know?' she asked. 'I assumed you were detained in Europe.'

He turned away, but not quickly enough for her to miss the surprise in his eyes. He had returned expecting trouble, loaded with explanations – and none were required. They had dinner at The Colony, then spent their first evening alone. She was tender and devoted in their lovemaking. It was difficult; she wanted to reach out and claw him, to leave evidence that he belonged to her. She was tortured with visions of him and Neely in bed, but somehow she pushed the thoughts away and returned his embraces with passion.

They had five wonderful days together. She almost began to believe that nothing was wrong, that whatever had happened was in the past. Then Neely arrived. She was signed for ten monthly television specials, and she would have to begin taping in August, since the first show went on in September. But there was still half of July with nothing to do, so she came to New York looking for action.

It was a Thursday. Anne knew nothing about Neely's arrival. She and Lyon had theatre tickets and a date afterward at the Copa with the agent of a new male singer. It seemed that every agent in town was trying to get his client a guest shot on Neely's show.

At five o'clock Lyon's secretary called. Mr. Burke had been called to a meeting with the sponsors, and he would not be able to make it to the theatre. He was sending Bud Hoff to escort her. He would join them later at the Copa.

It never occurred to Anne that anything was amiss. She played with the baby, had a leisurely bath and dressed. Bud arrived and took her to the theatre. They went to the Copa, where the agent was waiting, holding a choice table on the balcony. Anne explained that Lyon was detained and would join them.

The agent nodded. 'I was afraid he'd get tied up with Neely arriving today.'

She felt her face grow warm, but she managed an impassive smile. 'Oh yes . . . that's right. What time did Neely get in, Bud?' she asked, trying to give the impression that the news was no surprise.

Bud seemed uncomfortable. 'About noon, I think. Anyway, that's when the first call came in.'

Anne ordered a drink. 'Poor Lyon. He was hoping she'd stay in Arizona with her sons.' Was there an exchange of glances between Bud and the agent or did she imagine it? How many people actually knew the truth?

She forced herself to watch the show and comment favorably on the singer. Lyon's empty chair seemed to smirk at her. The smile was glued to her face as she made wifely excuses for his absence. She could see how disappointed the agent was, but his misery was no match for her own. 'Probably something came up about Neely's show – she relies on Lyon so much. I'm sure he feels dreadful about missing the show, but Bud will give him a full report, won't you, Bud?'

Of course Bud would. Again there seemed to be an exchange between the two men.

It was three in the morning when Bud dropped her off at the apartment. She knew Lyon would not be there. She tiptoed in and kissed the baby and covered her. Darling, darling little Jennifer, with her father's black hair and blue eyes. She was so beautiful. She felt the tears begin with the closing of her throat. No – she had to be calm when Lyon came in. No tears. She had to swallow whatever story he gave her.

At five o'clock she tiptoed into the living room. Perhaps he had come in and didn't want to disturb her. Maybe he was sleeping in the den. But the living room and den were empty. Oh God, Lyon, why? And Neely – how could you do this to me? She walked to the bathroom and took a red pill – she had taken one every night for a week until Lyon had returned. She had the feeling that it had been the only thing that had saved her sanity. She hadn't taken one since his return. But here we go again, she thought. Thank God for the lovely red dolls. They made the nights bearable. It was easier to get through the days; there was the baby, and she could usually have lunch with Henry or casual acquaintances.

She knew many women who lunched at '21' or The Little Club and who were equally frantic to fill their days, wives of Lyon's assistants, or of directors or clients. But she had never formed a close friendship with any girl since Neely and Jennifer. Close friendships with girls come early in life. After thirty it becomes harder to make new friends – there are fewer hopes, dreams or anticipations to share. Still, there was always someone to fill an afternoon, to lunch or shop with. But the nights! Long after little Jen and Miss Cuzins were asleep she'd find herself awake, thinking of Lyon, seeing his face, his smile – and imagining him with Neely. When it was more than she could bear, she would dash for release in the form of the faithful little red doll. Soon Neely and Lyon would be blotted into nothingness by a dreamless sleep. That's how it had been that week.

And now it was all starting again. She lay in bed and wondered how long Neely was planning to stay. Perhaps it would just be for a few days. The room began to slip away. Thank God the pill was working.

She did not know how long she slept, but she was vaguely conscious of Lyon's presence, his quiet movement in the room. She forced her eyes open . . . It was daylight. He was in the bathroom.

'Lyon?' She sat up. She saw the clock – eight o'clock! Had he just returned? She saw his suit lying on the chair.

He came out of the bathroom in his shorts, smiling. 'Sorry I woke you.'

'What time is it?'

'Eight. I'm getting dressed.' He walked across the room and quickly sat on his untouched bed to hide the freshness of the sheets. He was actually trying to pretend he had been here!

'What time did you get to sleep?' he asked casually as he put on his shoes.

'About three,' she lied. Damn the pill – she was so groggy.

'I came in about four,' he said lightly. 'You were dead asleep.'

She fell back against the pillow.

'Neely got into town,' he said as he put on a clean shirt.

'Yes, Bud told me.'

She knew he was watching her reactions. She kept her eyes shut.

'She joined me and the sponsors. There are some changes she wants made in the format, and a few problems that had to be ironed out. She wants more strings in the band and wants them to pay for it, and she insists that the network absorb half the below-the-line costs. It took hours to work out.'

Till eight in the morning? She kept her eyes closed.

'Then I went on to a late dinner with the sponsors. I had to soothe them – and that Ted Kelly . . . you know how he likes to drink. Oh, that's right, you haven't met him. He's with the agency. I sat with him at P.J.'s till three-thirty, calming him. I wanted to call you at the Copa, but he would have insisted on joining us and he was terribly drunk then, so I just sat nursing him along. Thank God P.J.'s closes at four. I came directly home.'

Oh, God, I can't stand this, she thought. I've got to scream. But she bit her lips and remained silent.

'Are you awake, dearest?' When she nodded faintly, he smiled. 'You must have had a bit yourself to be this done in. By the way, tonight try to arrange something with some of your girl friends. I have to take Neely and some agency people down to the Village and catch some acts.'

She was wide awake now. 'Can't I go along?'

'You'd hate it,' he said quickly. 'And it's business. None of the chaps are bringing their wives. If you came it would put a social connotation on it, and then they'd all bring their wives and we'd have a big party. One can't rush from spot to spot with an entourage.'

'But Neely will be there,' she argued.

He looked surprised. 'But of course. It's her show. She must approve any act that goes on.' Then he smiled and said, 'I hear Jennifer. I swear it sounds like she said "Dada." I think I'll join our beauty for breakfast. Now you go back to sleep.'

She didn't see him for five nights, though she heard him come in early in the morning to change. Sometimes she'd wake and pretend to go along with the idea that he had just awakened. He took care to muss the bed when he came in, and there was always a valid excuse – more acts to see, a meeting with the agency, a recording session with Neely, listening to songs for Neely's new album. And each night she'd take the red pill and sink into merciful oblivion.

On the sixth day she faced a new crisis. He had just gone. He had been out with Ted Kelly again, he said. Just the two of them. She had pretended to swallow it, and now sank back against the pillows. But she couldn't go back to sleep. She walked into the bathroom and took another red doll.

It was one in the afternoon when she woke. She rang for the maid and said she wasn't feeling well, that she'd take some coffee and toast in bed. The maid brought the tray and the afternoon papers. Idly, she opened one, turned to the rotogravure section – and was struck by a large picture of Neely and Lyon. 'Miss Neely O'Hara dancing at El Morocco with her personal manager, Lyon Burke.'

Neely looked good. With a start she realized she hadn't seen Neely in . . . how long? Before the baby – maybe eight or nine months ago. Neely wasn't even trying to hide her affair with Lyon. No, not the way she looked – radiant, smiling into Lyon's eyes. And Lyon looked happy too. Oh, God, now what? He was caught in a lie. If only he hadn't told her he had been with Ted Kelly. She dialed Henry.

'Throw the paper out,' he told her. 'Don't confront him with it. It's possible you wouldn't have seen it.'

'Henry, I can't go on like this,' she sobbed. 'I can't . . .'

'Come on over, Anne,' he begged. 'We'll talk about it.'

Henry paced back and forth. 'I admit it's rough,' he said. 'I didn't think she'd be this brazen. I thought it would only be on tour. I figured you might be lonely, but I didn't figure you'd have it shoved under your nose like this.'

'What can I do? I must be the laughingstock of the whole town. I can't even go to lunch now. I said as late as yesterday that Lyon wished Neely would return to California, that he hates playing wet nurse. I said this in front of three women at lunch – and I knew they were snickering. Now I can't even save face.' She picked up the paper.

'Shall I call Lyon?' he asked. 'Talk as a friend, without letting on you're here . . . see what I can do?'

She shook her head. 'Lyon would know. He knows you're the only one I trust.'

Suddenly he reached for the phone. 'What are you doing?' she demanded.

'I'm going to call Neely,' he said. 'I'll pretend I'm offering her advice, which she needs. You go into the bedroom and listen in on the extension.'

She watched him as he wasted a few minutes complimenting Neely on her new figure, her various successes. Finally he forged ahead. 'Neely, I just saw the afternoon paper. What in hell is this about Lyon Burke?'

Anne didn't like the expression on his face. She went into the bedroom and quietly slipped the receiver of the extension phone off the hook.

Neely was speaking. 'Listen, Henry – I love you, but butt out.'

'Neely,' Henry said quietly, 'I don't care how you feel – even if you feel you owe no loyalty to Anne, there is still your public image to protect. Everyone knows Lyon is married to Anne. So far there've been just a few veiled hints in columns, but this . . . After all, your sponsors certainly wouldn't want a scandal, and Lyon *is* living with Anne.'

'Like hell he is,' Neely snarled. 'He just goes home in the morning to change his clothes. He's waiting, hoping she'll catch him. But she's always asleep.'

'Maybe you only think he wants to be caught, Neely.'

'Nuts! He's been with me every night. When they snapped us at Morocco last night, he even said, "Maybe it's for the best – if the picture breaks it will all come out." That's exactly what he said. He's just afraid to break it to Anne, afraid she might fall apart. And . .' Neely hesitated. 'Well . . . he does love that kid of theirs.'

'Neely, this will all come back to you,' Henry said. 'You can't just reach out and take what you want without worrying about the feelings of others. Everyone gets paid back.'

'*I'm not everyone!*' she cried shrilly. 'And it's about time I take what I want. You know why? Because all my life I've *given*. Even as a kid . . . those fucking Gaucheros couldn't dance, it was *me* who held the act together. My brother-in-law is a checker at Macy's now – he never got an act together after I left. I made the studio money and they kicked me in the ass. But nothing could destroy me. You know damn well there's no one like me. I don't have to live by the stinking rules made for ordinary people, because I'm not ordinary. Nothing can destroy me, I tell you. Demerol, pills, a funny farm, weight – nothing. But Lyon makes me tick. I don't need to eat when I'm with Lyon. I can drink now and take skinny pills and even sleeping pills and it's all right. Dammit, Henry, my talent makes the world happy. And Lyon makes *me* happy. Don't I have a right to be happy? I need Lyon. Who the hell is Anne?'

'Only the best friend you ever had!'

'Oh sure. Listen, she was lucky I gave her the time of day. Why shouldn't she have liked having me around? I'm colorful. I'm a star. Who in hell is she when you get down to it? Even when I was a kid I had more on the ball. Sure, she had some fancy manners, but that was all. And who is she now? A skinny nobody who sold nail polish on the air and who slept with some old bastard for years. So she used his money to buy Lyon, and now she wants to play Miss Pure Mouth. The Virgin Mary with the baby. Well, I didn't get my money handed to me because I had good cheekbones, I earned it with my talent. She's gone through life on a pass long enough because of her goddam classy looks. She's around thirty-eight now, and I'm thirty-four, but my looks don't matter. I never got by on looks. If you're a friend of Anne's, tell her to give Lyon his freedom. Then she can have her face done and maybe Kevin Gillmore or some other slob will take her on. She was always good at attracting millionaires!' Then, with a snort, Neely slammed the phone down.

Anne slowly replaced the phone in its cradle. She walked over to the mirror. The fine lines under her eyes were deep today, and there were small lines evident around her mouth. Funny, she'd never really thought about her looks in connection with Lyon, but—

'Get away from that mirror!' Henry had come into the room. 'That little monster has dark circles under her eyes down to her chin. And I'm glad to hear she thinks she can drink. Her liver is shot.'

Anne began to shake. Henry grabbed her and held her close. 'Come on . . . she was only talking for effect. She knows I'll talk to you.'

'Maybe she's right, Henry. Maybe Lyon does want out.'

'Lyon hasn't said anything. Listen, Anne – you told me he rumples the bed. At least he's still lying to you. He's still making excuses.'

'Be thankful for small favors,' she sobbed.

'Hang on, Anne. Neely said nothing can ever destroy her talent. Nothing can except Neely. She'll destroy herself – you watch.'

She shook her head. 'It's the end of the line. I can't stick it out.'

'Yes you can! And you will. You've got class, and you can be as strong and as tough as that little snit.'

Lyon didn't even phone in an excuse that night. He just stayed away. She was about to take the pill at midnight when she heard the baby cry.

Jen was a good baby – she usually slept through the night. Something must be wrong. Oh, God, and it was Miss Cuzins's evening out. She rushed into the nursery. The baby was red-faced and screaming. Anne lifted her tenderly out of the crib. She searched for an open safety pin. Jen was wet, but no pins were sticking into her. She changed her and offered her some water in a bottle, but Jen refused and screamed louder. Her skin felt hot. She was teething – it could be that. She rubbed some paregoric on the little gums. Miss Cuzins swore by it. But the baby remained fretful and sobbed. Then, for reassurance, she took Jen's temperature. 103! Carrying the baby, she rushed down the hall and banged on the maid's door. The sleepy woman obligingly put on her robe and held the squalling baby while Anne tried to reach the doctor.

It was Friday, and the service said he was out of town for the weekend. They gave the number of the relief doctor. His service said he had not checked in, but he might be reached in an hour. Oh, God, she thought, what do I do? Where was Lyon? She called Henry, but the endless buzz told her he was out, too. Of course, he had a place somewhere in Westport. Was everyone away?

Resolutely, she dialed the hotel where Neely was staying. She announced herself to the operator. After a pause Neely answered.

'Hello, Neely.' Anne made her voice impersonal and calm. 'Is Lyon there?'

'Nope.'

'I have to find him. It's urgent.'

'Well . . .' Neely was yawning. 'If he calls me I'll tell him.'

'Neely, the baby is sick.'

'Call a doctor.'

'I did. He's away for the weekend. She's screaming and has a hundred-and-three fever.'

'Don't panic. Babies always run high fevers, mostly over nothing. Give her half an aspirin.'

'But if Lyon calls you, please tell him.'

'Sure, sure. Now good night. I got a recording session tomorrow. I got to sleep. The twins often ran big fevers – it's nothing.' The receiver clicked.

She believed Neely. Even Neely couldn't be that heartless. God, where *was* Lyon?

*

Neely picked up the phone and left a do-not-disturb order. Where in hell *was* Lyon? Oh yeah, he was at the Victoria Hotel with the arrangers, writing some new lyrics for her theme. He had said he'd be there until two, and then he'd come by. Should she call and tell him about the baby? Aah, it was nothing. Babies always ran temperatures. This was just Anne, using the only hold she had on him. How desperate could a broad get? Well, she wasn't going to fall for it. She'd be asleep when Lyon came by. Then she wouldn't be able to give him the message. Yeah, she'd leave a note on her pillow saying she had taken pills at twelve. Let's see, it was now one-fifteen. If she was bombed out with pills it would be normal to forget about Anne's call when he came in. He'd probably just go to sleep. Or maybe if she was asleep he'd go home and see his stinking wife and baby. Oh, hell. She swallowed three pills and drank a glass of Scotch. Okay, so he could go home one night – she'd have him all the others. Drowsily, she hoped the new theme would be good. Her name was on it as lyricist, a gimmick Lyon had thought up. Every songwriter wanted her to record their songs or sing them on TV. Now she'd demand billing as co-author. Soon she'd have a real good rating at ASCAP. She smiled contentedly as the pills began to work. Finally she slept.

The baby had been rushed to the hospital at two in the morning. The relief doctor had finally checked in with his service. At first they had feared polio, but it was finally diagnosed as pneumonia.

When Lyon found Neely asleep he had wandered home. To his amazement the lights were on, but there was no sign of Anne. The tearful maid mumbled the news. He flew out of the apartment and rushed to the hospital. Anne was sitting, pale and frightened, in the waiting room. She barely acknowledged him.

'What's the matter with her?' he demanded.

'She's in an oxygen tent. Two nurses are with her. They won't let me in the room.'

'I was working with the songwriters on Neely's new theme. We worked late, and when I got home and found you gone . . .'

'I called Neely hours ago,' she said listlessly.

'I wasn't with her,' he said almost righteously. 'Why should you call her?'

'Because I thought she might know where you were. You've been gone for a week – attending to her business, I presume.'

406

He looked at her carefully. 'There's a lot of work that goes into the preparation of a television show. We decided she should have a new theme song, a new identity.'

'Lyon, if you don't mind, I'd rather not talk about Neely's show right now. I'm sick with fear about the baby.'

He reached out and took her hand. It was an unconscious and natural gesture, but it caught her off guard. Had they once been really close? Had this marvelous-looking stranger once belonged to her? He was a stranger now, bound to her by law but belonging to someone else. Yet she loved him. It was a shocking admission. She wanted to hate him. But if possible she desired him even more. She had no pride . . . she'd never let him go. Unless he asked for his release. Oh, God, don't let that happen! And yet how terrible that it took a tragedy to bring him to her side.

It seemed an eternity before the doctor appeared. They held their breath. He was smiling! It was going to be all right. Yes, the fever had broken. Thank God for penicillin – and thank God that babies had fantastic strength.

Lyon came to the hospital each night at seven. Anne had taken a room adjoining the baby's and spent the entire day and night at the hospital. Lyon would peek at the small figure in the crib and make affectionate clucking noises. He insisted on taking Anne down to the restaurant in the hospital for dinner each evening. He would remain at least two hours. At least it was interfering with Neely's evenings, she thought grimly.

Ten days later they took little Jennifer home. Lyon had flowers all over the apartment. They dined at home and he played with the baby. That night he made love to Anne for the first time in weeks and they slept in each other's arms.

It was four o'clock when the phone rang. Anne woke first. She groped for it in the darkness.

It was Neely. Anne could tell by the slurred words that she was loaded with pills. 'Put that sonofabitch on the phone,' she growled.

'He's asleep, Neely.'

'Wake him.'

'I won't.'

'You heard me. Wake him – or I'll come over there and do it myself.'

Lyon opened his eyes. Anne mouthed Neely's name. He took the phone.

'What is it, Neely?' He was lying across Anne to reach the phone. She was able to hear Neely's shrill voice.

'I've been waiting for you all night,' she hollered.

'The baby came home from the hospital tonight.'

'So? She goes to sleep at seven, doesn't she?'

'It was her first night home.'

Anne shut her eyes. He was apologizing for stealing an evening with his wife.

'Well . . . come over now.'

'Neely, it's four in the morning.'

'You'd better come over. I've taken seven pills. I'll take ten more.'

'Neely! You have an interview with *Life* magazine tomorrow!'

'Fuck 'em! I won't be around unless you get your ass over here!'

'All right, Neely. I'll be there.'

Anne watched him get out of bed. I must hang on, she thought. He didn't really want to go there tonight – she's forcing him. If I can hang on, this will be my first victory. She lay back on the bed and kept her eyes closed. He came over to her fully dressed. 'Anne . . . do you understand?'

'I know you don't want to go,' she said.

'Anne – this has been rotten for you. I guess we'll have to do something about it.'

The victory vanished. Could he choose Neely over her and the baby?

'Lyon, things will work out,' she said quickly. 'It's bad to make middle-of-the-night decisions.'

'But we can't go on like this – you, Neely or myself,' he said.

'I can – because I know it can't remain like this. Lyon, you're in a bind.'

'Neely needs me. She's a great talent, Anne, with no discipline. She had to be led by the hand. You're strong.'

Tears came to her eyes. 'No, I'm not strong. The only strong thing about me is my love for you.'

He turned and quickly left the room.

When the new television season began, Anne returned to work. Henry had introduced her to the producer of a new panel show. She found it easy to play the game, and he engaged her immediately. It was a daily show and it kept her busy. It also kept her from noticing how Lyon spent more and more time with Neely.

At the end of September both Lyon and Neely left for the Coast to tape her first show.

Neely's show was a sensation. The ratings placed her in the top ten, and Lyon was credited with masterminding the entire operation. Anne had to marvel at Neely's power – several big stars immediately signed with Lyon and George. *Variety* ran stories about The Three B's, the hottest agency in New York. And it was all spearheaded by Neely O'Hara.

Lyon managed a few brief trips back to New York. During these visits there were times Anne felt there was a chance. The nights he held her close, when she almost forgot he held Neely the same way. But there were always the harassing calls from Neely in California, reminders that Neely came first.

He arrived back in New York a few days after Christmas, loaded with toys for Jennifer and an expensive piece of jewelry for her. She was aware he had split himself again – Christmas with Neely, but back in New York in time to approximate a celebration with her and little Jen.

Three days later Neely called, demanding his instant return. Anne sat in the den, quietly listening in on the extension phone.

'I shall be there soon,' Lyon said with a trace of exasperation.

'Tonight!' Neely shrieked. 'Do you know what day tomorrow is? New Year's Eve!'

'And January first is my daughter's first birthday,' he said firmly.

'Shit! Celebrate it today – the kid won't know the difference.'

'But I will. Now you be a good girl. You're invited to lots of parties, and one of the men from the agency will escort you. I shall be there no later than the fifth. I have to stay here and catch the opening of *Honey Belle.*'

Neely sneered. 'That Margie Parks will come up a big zero.'

'I saw her at the Blue Angel last year,' Lyon said. 'She has a wonderful quality.'

'They'll have to mike her up,' Neely insisted. 'She sings great – listen, I'm the first to admit if someone's good. She uses her voice like an instrument. But I heard the scuttlebutt. They almost replaced her out of town, until they decided to mike her up. She sings in her throat. She'll never last. She's gotta burn out in a few years. I woulda too, if it hadn't been for Zeke Whyte setting me straight.'

'Well, the office wants to sign her,' Lyon said insistently. 'I've got to go to the opening.'

'You mean you'd waste your time servicing her?' Neely's voice was dangerous.

'Of course not. George wouldn't either. She's only nineteen. She'd be handled by Bud Hoff. The women like him, and he'll wet-nurse her.'

'Bud Hoff is a lox,' Neely said. 'He sits around thinking he's God's gift to women. Him and those black suits and black ties. Geez, all the guys in your office look like they wear uniforms. Well, I guess you need guys like that . . .' Neely yawned. 'The damn pills are finally beginning to work. When will you be here?'

'The fifth, at the latest,' he promised.

'Love me?'

'You know I do,' he said quickly.

'How much?'

'Terribly.'

'More than you love Anne and the baby?'

'It would seem so. Now Neely, I must hang up. Anne is home. She could pick up the phone.'

'I hope she has.'

'Do you enjoy hurting people?'

'No, but if she knew, she'd give you up.'

'Perhaps she does know,' Lyon said.

'You've told her?'

'No, but Anne isn't insensitive – or stupid. And the rumors are pretty thick around town.'

'Then why doesn't she let you go?'

Lyon was silent.

'Well, dammit, I'm gonna call and tell her. Then she'll have to let you go. Her pride will make her.'

'Don't do that,' Lyon said.

'I'm gonna—'

'Don't. It won't work, anyway. I've . . . you see, we've already had it out.'

'When? You didn't tell me.'

410

'Just last night.'

Anne hoped she hadn't gasped audibly. They had never been closer than they had been last night.

'What happened?' Neely asked.

'Nothing. She just said she knew all about it, but would shut her eyes. She said she will never give me a divorce.'

'Well, let's make her. We'll neck up a storm in public.'

'You tried that, Neely. Columnists like you. They try to protect you. They don't print all they see.'

'I'll call and give an interview. I'll say you want to marry me and I want you, but you got a wife who wants to sit.'

'And do you know what would happen to your show? There's a morals clause. Your sponsor sells breakfast food. You'd be canceled so quickly—'

'Who cares? We could go to Europe and make another picture.'

'Neely, I have a partner. It would hurt the agency. I cannot think only of myself.'

'Oh, you and that fucking agency. All right, when I make a million bucks, I'll buy you out and we'll tell 'em all to go to hell. I want you with me night and day, every second.'

He laughed. 'See you on the fifth, Neely.'

'Hey, not so fast. Call me at noon, my time, tomorrow.'

'I'll do that.'

'Love me?'

'I adore you.'

Then everyone hung up.

1964

Honey Belle was the musical smash of the season. Anne watched the small, thin little girl with the crooked smile capture the audience. She was nineteen and untrained, but she exuded the excitement that spells 'star.'

'We're lucky,' George whispered. 'Lyon insisted on signing her yesterday. Everybody in town will want her after tonight.'

'This one is strictly your headache,' Lyon whispered as he leaned across Anne.

George smiled. 'Are you kidding? She'll be happy to settle for Bud Hoff or Ken Mitchell or any of the guys in the office who'll service her.'

Anne's thoughts went back to that other evening, so many years ago, when she had sat beside Lyon and watched Neely open on Broadway. She had been a nice kid too, without temperament. Nineteen years ago . . . She had loved Lyon then, and she loved him now. In monitoring Neely's calls she realized she had won – yet somehow the victory was tasteless. Lyon was lying to Neely, pretending he had asked for a divorce. He really didn't want to leave her. He didn't want to be stuck with Neely, now that the cobra in Neely was showing. Tomorrow was the fifth, but Lyon had made no announcement about leaving. In fact, he had spoken about a new opening he wanted to catch on the eighth. But had she really won, or was it a stalemate? Neely was still there – would probably always be there. Did he enjoy Neely's body? Was it the same with Neely as with her? She would never know.

Even the crush backstage was the same. Margie Parks, looking so young, so vulnerable – awed by her brilliant new managers and struck dumb by the famous celebrities who came back to congratulate her.

Anne sat between Lyon and George at the opening-night party later in the evening. At one point, when Lyon had gone to another table to conduct some business, Margie moved over and took his seat. 'I want you to know, Miss Welles, I've always been a fan of yours.'

Anne smiled. 'The panel show? Good Lord, it's nothing.'

'Oh, I love you on the panel show,' Margie insisted. 'But when you were the Gillian Girl – that's when I swooned. I remember, I was ten years old and I stole a dollar from my mother's pocketbook to buy the Gillian lipstick. I wanted to look just like you.'

Anne smiled. Suddenly she understood how Helen Lawson had felt. It was so wonderful to be young, to think you'll always be young. Yet she knew she was a symbol of success to Margie Parks. She was sleek, married to an important man and a small success in her own right. Margie was not pretty – she was wearing a green dress that failed to bring out any of her good points, and her coat was one of those black silk jobs, the kind she had once hunted down at Bloomingdale's. She had noticed Margie's awe at her mink coat. But did Margie know her thick, luxurious hair had to be tinted now? Or that the lines under her eyes had to be carefully hidden with the proper makeup? In a soft light like tonight's she could be striking; in fact, she knew heads turned when she entered a room. She looked well on television, and she could probably go on for another fifteen years with the right makeup and lights. But she would never pretend to be younger than she was. Who would she be fooling? Everyone knew her age.

Margie chatted incessantly. Lyon was openly bored, and they left her in George's care an hour later. That night Lyon looked tired.

There were several messages from Neely. Wearily he called her back. He made no effort to hide the conversation from Anne, but kept it brief and impersonal. Yes, the show had been a hit. Yes, they had signed Margie Parks. Of course she was a small talent. Yes, he'd be out in a few days.

But Margie's success was like brushfire. Her album of the show sold phenomenally well, and the single sides she made hit the top ten. Then in April George signed her for an enormous television deal, to begin a weekly series the following season. The Three B's represented the package.

Lyon continued to shuttle back and forth to California. Neely's shows were doing well, and she was signed up for the following season. The Three B's were opening a California office, and several good agents had left the Johnson Harris office to join them.

Neely was riding the crest of Hollywood's new social wave. She had rented an enormous house and hired a full staff, and her large parties drew all the 'in' people.

She was taping her last show of the season when George summoned Lyon back to New York. The network wanted a rundown of the format Margie Parks would use the following season. 'You're the creative one,' George said. 'I made the sale – now you've got to put the show together.'

Lyon had slipped out of California quietly. He had left Neely a note promising to return in forty-eight hours. He hoped to avoid a scene this way, and he felt fairly safe. Two thirds of the show was already on tape.

Lyon met with the network and sponsors. Everything went well. The director called from the Coast. Neely was furious, but was cooperative so far. Lyon relaxed and decided against rushing back. He took Anne to the theatre . . . he took little Jennifer for her first pony ride in Central Park.

They were in bed watching the Late Show when the news bulletin interrupted: 'Neely O'Hara rushed to hospital, close to death.'

George was on the phone seconds later. He had called California and been told that Neely might make it. She had swallowed half a bottle of pills. Lyon dressed while Anne packed his bags. There was a one-thirty flight to the Coast – he could just about make it. Neely's show wasn't all taped, but Joey Kling would fly out and take over. They'd piece together some kind of a show by airtime.

Neely was weak and hollow-eyed when Lyon came to her hospital room. She had come out of it – she would live. She held out her arms. 'Oh, God, Lyon, when I found out . . . it was the end. I wanted to die!'

'Found out what?' He held her gently and stroked her hair.

'I read it in the trades while I was on the set. It said you were called back to give Margie Parks the star treatment.'

'And that's why you tried . . .' His voice trailed off in amazement.

'Look, Lyon, I'll stand for you giving your wife a hump now and then, and I might even forgive you if you took a flier with another girl – but I'll never stand for you building up another star on my time.'

'But Neely, we're not a one-woman office.'

'I *made* your lousy office – and I can unmake it. Just remember that! If I walk, half your lineup would walk with me. You need me, brother, so when I snap my fingers you be here from now on!'

Lyon rose and walked out of the room. 'Lyon! Come back here!' she shouted.

He continued to walk down the hall.

Lyon went back to New York on the next plane. He called an emergency meeting with George. 'One question,' he said. 'Have you paid back your wife?'

George smiled. 'No, and I don't intend to.'

'I've just written the final check to Anne. I'm in the clear now. From now on, any risks I take I take on my own money. Nothing else is riding—'

'Except my share.' George smiled again.

'Of course. Even so, I've come to the conclusion we have to drop Neely. She's not worth the agony. We don't need her any more.'

'Don't you think it will hurt us?' George asked.

Lyon shook his head. 'Not at all. Margie's show will bring in twice

414

as much revenue – it's a weekly show, don't forget – and we've got Joey Kling going great guns. Neely has to go up in smoke eventually – maybe not next year or even the year after, but she'll go – and we're not going to be a part of it. We resurrected her and got the credit for that. Let's quit her while we're ahead.'

'What makes you think Neely won't go on and on? That funny farm straightened her out pretty well.'

Lyon laughed. 'How long can anyone last when they're on two Demerol shots a day?'

'She said they were vitamin shots,' George said.

'Some vitamins! Look, we're building up some good men in this office. We're a great combination, George. You can sell – there's no one who can touch you there – and I can manage to be fairly creative with talent and the agency people. We can't piddle away half our strength in traveling back and forth across the country as trained nurse and lover to this octopus. God, George, she eats people alive! Heaven knows how Anne has managed to survive. But we've had it with Neely. I know Abe Kingman from the Johnson Harris office flew out there to talk to her – let's release her.'

George grinned. 'Okay, you send the wire personally. I think you deserve that break.'

Neely signed with the Johnson Harris office and made scathing remarks about the inefficiency of her past management. The Three B's were not harmed, and in September the Margie Parks show was launched with great success.

Neely started the new season with good ratings. Three men from the Johnson Harris office were assigned to her around the clock.

'Do you think she'll be all right?' Anne asked.

Lyon nodded. 'For a time. But she's on a self-destructive kick. She's taking on too much – the large house, the servants, too much free booze is flowing. She's a star again, and that nearly killed her before.'

'If she snaps . . .' Anne couldn't help feeling some concern. Neely's destructiveness was so pathetically sick.

'She'll snap one day,' Lyon said. 'She has to.'

'And then what?'

'She'll make a comeback again – and again and again, as long as her body holds out. It's like a civil war, with her emotions against her talent and physical strength. One side has to give. Something has to be destroyed.'

1965

Anne wished she hadn't allowed herself to be talked into giving this New Year's Eve party. She stared at the endless guests – they kept coming and going, crowding into the elevator and standing three deep at the bar. George and Lyon had pressured her into it, but giving a party was not as simple as going to one. You could always leave someone else's party. You were stuck with your own.

Celebrities from the Broadway shows began to arrive. It was past one, and she hadn't seen Lyon since their brief kiss at midnight. It was January first now, Jen's second birthday. She slipped away from everyone and walked down the hall to the nursery. The small night light picked out the dim outline of the sleeping child. 'Happy New Year, angel,' Anne whispered. 'I love you . . . oh, God, how I love you!' She leaned over and kissed the clean little brow, then quietly slipped out of the room. The living room was a wall of noise. The den was packed, too, and the bar was jammed. She went into her bedroom and closed the door. No, this was wrong – the hostess could not duck out. Besides, if she kept the door closed, someone would knock. It was rude. She opened the door and switched off the lights. That was better. If she left the door open and the lights off, no one could see her. She hoped they wouldn't come in. Her head was splitting.

She stretched out on the bed. The shrieks of laughter seemed far away, and the music . . . Somewhere she heard a glass crash . . . bursts of laughter . . . Suddenly she heard footsteps. O Lord, someone was coming. She'd say she just had to lie down. Two silhouettes came into the room. She lay quietly on the bed, hoping they would go.

'Let's close the door,' the girl whispered.

'Nonsense. That would draw attention.'

It was Lyon . . . but she could not distinguish the girl.

'I love you, Lyon.' The voice sounded familiar.

'Oh, come now, you're just a baby.'

416

'I don't care. I love you. My show was better than it's ever been last week because you personally supervised things.'

His kiss silenced her.

'Lyon . . . will you be there every week?'

'I'll try.'

'Not try – *be* there!' The voice was insistent. 'Lyon, I'm one of the office's top properties . . .'

'Margie, are you trying to blackmail my love?' he said lightly.

'Is that what Neely O'Hara did?'

'There was never anything between Neely and me.'

'Ha! Well, anyway, there's going to be plenty between *us*. God, I dig you!'

He kissed her again. 'Now be a good girl. Let's get back to the party before we're missed.'

Anne lay quietly until they were gone. Then she got up and straightened her dress. She went to the bathroom and took a red doll. Strangely enough, she felt no panic. Now it was Margie Parks . . . She found it didn't hurt as much this time. She still loved Lyon, but she loved him less. After Neely had gone he had been more devoted than ever. But there had been no sense of triumph. Something or some part of her had gone with Neely. She knew now there would always be a Neely, or a Margie . . . but each time it would hurt less, and afterward she would love Lyon less, until one day there would be nothing left – no hurt, and no love.

She brushed her hair and freshened her makeup. She looked fine. She had Lyon, the beautiful apartment, the beautiful child, the nice career of her own, New York – everything she had ever wanted. And from now on, she could never be hurt badly. She could always keep busy during the day, and at night – the lonely ones – there were always the beautiful dolls for company. She'd take two of them tonight. Why not? After all, it was New Year's Eve!

VIRAGO MODERN CLASSICS

The first Virago Modern Classic, *Frost in May* by Antonia White, was published in 1978. It launched a list dedicated to the celebration of women writers and to the rediscovery and reprinting of their works. Its aim was, and is, to demonstrate the existence of a female tradition in literature, and to broaden the sometimes narrow definition of a 'classic' which has often led to the neglect of interesting books. Published with new introductions by some of today's best writers, the books are chosen for many reasons: they may be great works of literature; they may be wonderful period pieces; they may reveal particular aspects of women's lives; they may be classics of comedy, storytelling, letter-writing or autobiography.

'Good news for everyone writing and reading today' –
Hilary Mantel

'The Virago Modern Classics list is wonderful. It's quite simply one of the best and most essential things that has happened in publishing in our time. I hate to think where we'd be without it' – *Ali Smith*

'The Virago Modern Classics have reshaped literary history and enriched the reading of us all. No library is complete without them' – *Margaret Drabble*

'The writers are formidable, the production handsome. The whole enterprise is thoroughly grand' – *Louise Erdrich*

'A continuingly magnificent imprint' – *Joanna Trollope*

'The Virago Modern Classics are one of the best things in Britain today' – *Alison Lurie*

'Masterful works' – *Vogue*

virago

To buy any of our books and to find out more
about Virago Press and Virago Modern Classics,
our authors and titles, as well as events and
book club forum, visit our websites

www.virago.co.uk
www.littlebrown.co.uk

and follow us on Twitter

@ViragoBooks

To order any Virago titles p & p free in the UK,
please contact our mail order supplier on:

+ 44 (0)1832 737525

Customers not based in the UK should contact
the same number for appropriate postage
and packing costs.

HEARTBURN

Nora Ephron

Seven months into her pregnancy, Rachel Samstat discovers that her husband Mark is in love with another woman. The fact that the other woman has a 'neck as long as an arm and a nose as long as a thumb and you should see her legs, never mind her feet, which are sort of splayed' is no consolation. Food sometimes is, though, and since Rachel write cookery books for a living, between trying to win Mark back and wishing him dead, she offers us some of her favourite recipes. *Heartburn* is a roller coaster of love, betrayal, loss, and – most satisfyingly – revenge.

Nora Ephron, the screenwriter of *When Harry Met Sally*, *You've Got Mail* and *Sleepless in Seattle*, shows us that the pen is mightier than the sword – for *Heartburn* is her *roman-à-clef*. 'I always thought during the pain of the marriage that one day it would make a funny book,' Ephron once said. And it is!

'Revenge may be sweet but Ephron's writing is sharp, bitter and delicious' *Scotsman*

'I have bought more copies of this book to give to people, in a frenzy of enthusiasm, than any other. *Heartburn* is the perfect, bittersweet, sobbingly funny, all-too-true confessional novel. There is not a wrong word – about food, marriage, life, love, loss – and all rings true and makes you laugh. Who could ask for anything more?' Nigella Lawson

THE GROUP

Mary McCarthy

Introduced by Candace Bushnell

'Absorbing, funny, painful . . . a beautifully managed novel . . .
I consider it a masterpiece' Hilary Mantel

The Group follows eight graduates from exclusive Vassar College as
they find love and heartbreak, and choose careers and husbands
against the backdrop of 1930s New York.

'Focusing on a group of New York friends, its open discussion
of sex and contraception, careers and motherhood was
unprecedented and it can now be seen as the precursor of
the women's novel – without *The Group* there would certainly
be no *Sex and the City*' *Independent*

'She's so funny and bitter and clear-sighted and witty that
it was a real joy to read. I can't recommend it highly enough'
Marian Keyes

'Juicy, shocking, witty, and almost continually brilliant'
Cosmopolitan

'One of my favourite books ever' India Knight

THE DUD AVOCADO

Elaine Dundy

Sally Jay Gorce is a woman with a mission. It's the 1950s, she's twenty-one, she's American and she's in Paris. Having dyed her hair pink and vowed to go native in a way not even the natives can manage, she's busy getting drunk, having affairs and losing money. Charming, sexy, and hilarious, *The Dud Avocado* gained instant cult status when it was first published and it remains a timeless portrait of a woman hellbent on living.

'*The Dud Avocado* made me laugh, scream and guffaw (which, incidentally, is a great name for a law firm)' Groucho Marx

'One of the funniest books I've ever read' Gore Vidal

'Wonderfully touching and funny' Jilly Cooper

'A champagne cocktail . . . One falls for Sally Jay from a great height from the first sentence' *Observer*

JANE AND PRUDENCE

Barbara Pym

Introduced by Jilly Cooper

'I'd sooner read a new Barbara Pym than a new Jane Austen'
Philip Larkin

If Jane Cleveland and Prudence Bates seem an unlikely pair to be walking together at an Oxford reunion, neither of them is aware of it. They couldn't be more different: Jane is an incompetent vicar's wife, who always looks as if she's about to feed the chickens, while Prudence, a pristine hothouse flower, has the most unsuitable affairs. With the move to a rural parish, Jane is determined to find her friend the perfect man. She learns, though, that matchmaking has as many pitfalls as housewifery . . .

'Over the years, as Barbara Pym replaced Nancy Mitford,
Georgette Heyer, even Jane Austen, as my most-loved author,
I devoured all her books, but *Jane and Prudence* remains my
favourite' Jilly Cooper